T0194208

Bill Christian
Private Investigator in:
THE YADKIN RIVER WEREWOLF CASE

LEE KING

iUniverse, Inc.
Bloomington

Bill Christian Private Investigator in:
The Yadkin River Werewolf Case

Copyright © 2011 Lee King

This is a work of fiction. All of the characters, names, incidents,
organizations, and dialogue in this novel are either the products
of the author's imagination or are used fictitiously.

iUniverse books may be ordered through booksellers or by contacting:

iUniverse
1663 Liberty Drive
Bloomington, IN 47403
www.iuniverse.com
1-800-Authors (1-800-288-4677)

Because of the dynamic nature of the Internet, any Web addresses or
links contained in this book may have changed since publication and
may no longer be valid. The views expressed in this work are solely those
of the author and do not necessarily reflect the views of the publisher,
and the publisher hereby disclaims any responsibility for them.

Any people depicted in stock imagery provided by Thinkstock are models,
and such images are being used for illustrative purposes only.

Certain stock imagery © Thinkstock.

ISBN: 978-1-4502-9525-3 (pbk)
ISBN: 978-1-4502-9526-0 (ebk)

Printed in the United States of America

iUniverse rev. date: 2/10/2011

Wolf (Woolf)-n-carnivorous wild animal.

Werewolf (wir'-woolf)-n-human being who, at will, could
take form of wolf while retaining human intelligence.

Lupus est homo homini - man is wolf to
man. I. E. Men prey on one another!

Epilogue

The Missionary man and his companion were walking down the snow covered old wagon road toward the next village of Oskemen after handing out bibles in the village of Semey they had just left somewhere in the eastern mountains of Kazakhstan, Russia and the big moon was high overhead in the sky and shining brightly down on the men walking along the mountain road as it was about 12:00 midnight.

They were strolling along with their hands in their pockets to keep warm in the chilly night air as they left the fields of wheat now vacant in winter and pasture land of cattle and sheep along the deserted mountain road.

They had left the low mountains and entered a towering dark forest of immense trees on both sides of the road in the Altai mountain range that reached to the Mongolian border. Their old Volk's Wagon van had broken down away's back and they were forced to walk the rest of the way on foot. Their constant chatter had stopped as they walked along the spooky road.

The companion kept looking over his shoulder nervously back down the road the way they had come as if they were not alone but saw no one on the road behind them and his mind was full of fear of the unknown in the dark towering woods of the immense Altai mountain range and the dark shadow's that followed them at what now seemed every step of the way.

"I can't wait to get to the Inn in the village and get a cup of hot steaming coffee," said the Missionary man as he looked at his silent companion that he had taken under his wing to help him who was nervously looking in the woods off to the left of him.

"Ye-ye-yes that would be nice right about now and with a shot of Vodka in it," said the companion as he stuttered with fear welling up in his throat as he thought he saw a flash of red eyes off in the woods moving among the trees.

He shook his head in shock as he looked again at the same spot and saw nothing. "My eyes are playing tricks on me, I thought I saw something in the woods to my left," said the companion to the Missionary man who looked at his friend with a smile on his rugged tan bearded face.

"Your not scared of the dark out here tonight," asked the Missionary man who chuckled softly to himself as he adjusted his wide brim hat and scarf around his neck to keep warm?

"I don't know—I've felt uneasy since we have walked into these woods along the mountain road as if something is not right. I've heard the locals talk of strange tall tails of men who turn into beast and run on all fours in these parts of the mountainous region at night," said the companion as he took his hands out of his front pockets and had a handkerchief in one hand as he blew his nose and folded up the handkerchief and wiped the nervous sweat off his brow, sticking the handkerchief back in his front pocket nervously.

"Rubbish just old wise tales," said the Missionary man as they came to a bend in the mountain road with tree limbs that had grown across the top of the road to the other side as the trees grew together from both sides of the road foaming a canopy of tree limbs overhead.

Just as they walked under the tree limbs high overhead they heard a terrible howl from screaming lungs "Wooooooooo, Wooooooooo" above them as both men stopped dead in their tracks and looked up into the tree limbs overhead in rigid fright of the unknown!

"Oh my God," said the Missionary man as he reached out in fear and grabbed his companions coat with his left arm as they both saw two sets of red eyes glaring down at them from the dark big shadowy forms above them. "Heaven help us," said the companion as he looked with terror in his eyes at the Missionary man standing beside him.

"Theirs no Heaven here tonight only a Hellish death," said a growling deep throaty male voice with yellow cat like eyes and then the murderous beasts pounced on the men from above as the two men raising their arms in self defense screamed "Ahhhhhh, Ahhhhhh" together!

The companion felt the huge body smash into his chest knocking the breath out of him as he fell backward to the road with a hard "thud" and he heard the missionary man screaming in mortal terror over to his right as he felt huge jaws bite into his left breast!

The companion screamed in pain "Ahhhhhh—Ahhhhhh" as he was shook violently back and forth in the snow covered road which turned red from his on blood that ran down his coat onto the snow covered road, then he looked into the huge red eyes over top of him, that had got him and his eyes rolled up into his head for a moment from nearly passing out from the frightening fear and pain of the sudden attack. Then he subconsciously saw the white teeth that was drooling with saliva from the huge wolfs mouth that had a death bite on his left breast and then he lost consciousness!

Sometime later the companion awoke from his deep dark sleep and screamed out in fear "Ohhhhh" and every nerve in his body stiffly awoke to a constant dread of fear and he squeezed his fists together in agony and he moved his numb cold legs back and forth trying to awake them. He looked around as his eyes focused on his chest and he saw steam rising from his bloody chest, then he regained his senses to his surroundings.

He looked over to his right and saw the huge wolf setting there watching him from the side of the road as its partner was still tearing up the limp body of the Missionary man just a few feet away.

The werewolf stood up from the Missionary man's corpse and howled over its kill at the big bright moon "AHHH—WHOOOO-O-O-O-O—AHHH—WHOOOO-O-O-O-O" and then it sniffed the body as it moved over beside its mate sitting beside the road watching the companion with red evil eyes!

"What about him," said the raspy female werewolf as its mate eyed the companion laying in the roadway watching them with unbelieving eyes?

"He was the fearful one and that's why I picked him for your changeling bite. Leave him be, he's apart of the pack now," said the male werewolf in a throaty ruff voice to his mate.

The werewolf's looked at the companion and their fierce eyes glowed red as they snarled and barked at the companion!

Then they turned and ran off back into the deep dark foreboding woods and were gone in the pitch black of night.

After some time the companion gathered some courage from deep down within himself that surprised him at first being of little courage before hand and he set up in a sitting position on the snow covered bloody road around him glad to be alive in his heart and mind while he braced himself up with his right arm and his right hand sunk down into the wet blood stained snow behind his back.

He took in several hard pitiful labored breaths and he surveyed his surroundings and he felt all hope was lost in the back of his mind which he couldn't shake off and he wondered why. Then he slowly scrambled up on shaky weak legs whose feet slipped a little bit on the blood covered snow road while he got his footing under him!

He walked over to his friend and bent down looking him over for any sign of life. He saw his friends throat and chest had been tore apart.

The companion got sick too his stomach as his nerves kicked in and got the best of him as he turned away and fell down on one knee— he threw up on the side of the road, retching violently for several minutes! He finely stood back up after wiping his mouth with his right coat sleeve knowing his Missionary friend was beyond help now and in Gods hands.

He kneeled back down and at the same time said a silent prayer over his dear departed missionary friend. He then reached down and grabbed a peace of the cloth on the dead mans coat and ripped it off the body as he pressed it to his left breast bite wound to stop the bleeding after standing back up. He then stumbled off down the snow covered road toward the far village for help.

A Decade or so later in the mid 1990s sometime in the wee morning hours after a Saturday mid-night which had long struck on the old clock over the bar in FOOTHILLS BREWING Pub and Restaurant which looked and feels like the set of "Cheers," at 638 West Fourth Street in Winston-Salem on a cold fall morning where everybody knows your name, the night was pitch dark outside and the drunken man sitting at the table was guzzling down his 12th Pilot Mountain Pale of Ale at his table in the back of the large dining and pub room. You could smell the alcohol and cheap perfume that still lingered in the air from the night's party at the old pub.

The bartender Sally was wiping down the long wooden bar with a wet kitchen towel. The pub was empty and all the customers had left to go home after a fun filled Saturday night and the band had cleared out some time ago. The manager Dale had finished hanging the clean beer mug glasses in the holding racks above the long bar and under the bar top on shelves when he noticed Sam sitting at the table in back.

"Go and see—if you can tell Sam it's time to leave, I'm tired as I'm sure you are Sally after a long night, we need to close up," asked Dale who started wiping down the Beer and Ale taps?

"Sure thing—Dale," replied Sally who emptied her last tip bottle on the pub bar and stuck the money in her white waist apron pocket. Sally walked around the long bar and lifted the counter door up and walked through the bar and shut it behind her.

She walked back to where the older man was sitting at

his table sipping his mug of Ale and Sally put her hand on the older mans shoulder who was startled and looked up at her with large red eyes and a big red nose over his mug of Ale with two day old gray whiskers on his unshaven face.

"Were closing and you have to leave and go home Sam, do you want me to call a cab for you," asked Sally with a concern look on her face?

"Ohhhh—its time tooo—leavvvve," asked Sam the older man who drunkenly slurred his words to Sally the bartender and waitress while squinting his eyes up at her?

"Yes —were closing up, its 2: AM," replied Sally smiling but firmly nodding her tired old head at him.

The older man chugged down the rest of his Ale and handed the mug to Sally who took it from him as the older man got up to leave from his chair which he slid back with a "Screeech" on the floor which made Sally grimace by the look on her sweet face!

The man grabbed up his coat from the back of his chair and slid into it and button up his gray long coat. He put on his hat and wrapped his gray wool scarf around his throat throwing it back over his left shoulder.

Sally watched the older man walk across the hard wood pub floor to the door and he seemed to be holding his own. No need to call the man a taxi thought Sally to herself.

Sally quickly followed after him and locked the door latches when the big oak door shut, flipping the open sign to close in the door window when the man went out the door he had open onto the deserted West Fourth street city sidewalk.

The old cold fall north wind kicked up on the big city street as Sam walked down the deserted sidewalk and he started to stagger back and forth down the empty dark lit street. He bumped into things along the way and the buildings because the cold wind activated the alcohol in his blood more quickly as it hit Sam full in the face and he got even drunker.

He stopped momentarily and flipped up his coat collar for added warmth fore Sam didn't want to catch his death of cold out here this time of night. The drunken man somehow stumbled onto Burke street from somewhere off of Fourth street.

The man walked along a sig sag line down the middle of Burke street and he didn't see the large dark shadows following behind him and off to one side through the dark alleyways on either side of him.

The man stopped at a alleyway that looked familiar to him and he snapped his drunken right fingers "snap" up above his right shoulder!

He was so drunk and high by now the cold fall air rushed the alcohol through his blood to his brain quicker and he could almost hear Heaven in his ringing ears but little did he realized that Hell was following every footstep he took along the dimly lit but dark and deserted city street.

"Eurrrekaaa—That's werrre I parrrked my car," slurred Sam out loud to his drunken self and stumbled down the dark alleyway fore it was a miracle he had even found the right one.

The neighborhood dogs started barking loudly about that time and Sam stopped to listen for a moment which would be his last but he didn't know it and just happen to look up into the night sky. He thought he saw a dark form with flowing hair fly by overhead.

Sam looked up and staggard back drunkenly from shock at the unexpected but didn't see anything that caught his eye.

"Maaan—mmmyyyy eye's are playyyyiiing trrrricks on me," slurred Sam who shook his head to clear his drunkin thoughts.

"Whaaaat in hell has got thoooose dogs stirrrrred uuppp!," shouted Sam with slurred speech who looked around with drunken eyes but didn't see anything but a dark alleyway?

The dark shadows ran across the roof tops dropping down

to the alleyway and along the deserted parked cars in the alleyway!

The street lights glowed dimly in the dark alleyway and Sam stopped at a car that he thought was his. He reached in his left coat pocket and pulled out a set of keys which he fumbled with and dropped in the road.

"Shhhiiiit," said Sam under his drunken breath. Sam reached down to pick up his keys with his right hand and heard a loud metallic thump "Bang"on the car roof above him!

Sam stood back up and his eyes beheld a sight right out of Purgatory while his body jolted back from the shock of what he saw. There sitting before him on top of the car was a very large gray wolf. "Whaaaaat in hell issss thaaaat," asked Sam who was dumb struck and in his drunken mind, he thought his mind was playing tricks on him again?

Sam blinked his drunken eyes several times and squinted his eyes to try to see straight as the dark gray figure sitting on top of the car came in and out of focus.

"This is Hell's kitchen tonight and it's time to dine," replied a deep throaty wicked sounding voice from up on top of the car with wild yellow cat looking eyes. Sam drunkenly not thinking about his dull reaction to that reached up to touch the wolf to see if it was real which growled at him "Grrrrr—Grrrrrr" and then it bit his left hand.   Sam yelled in pain "Ahhhh—OOOuch" and jerked his bitten, bleeding left hand back, shaking it from the pain and looking at his hurt hand and then back at the wolf sitting on top of his parked car with a I don't believe it look on his silly red nose drunk face!

Then fear set in and the wolf saw it in the man's eyes and the wolf smelled the scent of fear coming from its prey.

"I'm not dreaming, that thing is real," screamed Sam who had sobered up quickly and stumbled backward in shock and fell down on the hard pavement with a "thud" which hurt his tail bone and he lost his hat but he held onto his keys with a right hand death grip! He slowly got back up on his feet and looked with a dazed expression back at the wolf who's fierce eyes glowed blood red at him.

He stumbled backward from the car and turned around to run and saw another large wolf standing away up the alleyway looking at him with bright red wild eyes.

Sam stopped dead in his tracks in the middle of the alleyway feeling very overwhelmed by his predicament.

Then he heard the other shadow wolves on his left and right side of him growl at him "Grrr—Grrr!, Grrr—Grrr!" as they came out from between the parked cars and he saw that he was encircled by a pack of real wolfs of some kind!

The woman squatting on the nearby roof top shook her head in vain and new she was too late to intervene and looked on as the pack of wolves had there prey cornered and were about to attack.

Sam turned around to look back incredulous at the wolf on top of his car and it leaped off the roof at him and his body jerked in shock reflex and he screamed "A-A-A-H-H-H-H-H-h-h-h-h-h" with his nearly last breath and threw up his hands in self defense as he was knocked violently to the ground by the big formidable werewolf!

The lead werewolf who was pinning the man down with it's paws, reached down with it's massive head and grabbed the man by the neck with its sharp fangs which pierced the mortal skin through Sam's scarf!

The blood started to flow down the mans neck and soak his scarf while the werewolf spread its legs to brace itself to shake him violently from side to side like a rag doll which it did as blood flew from Sam's poor bitten broken neck from the violent jerking and blood soaked ragged scarf but he was somehow still alive but just barely!

The werewolf howled "AHHHHH—WHOOOO-O-O—AHHHHH—WHOOOO-O-O" at the moon high overhead with blood dripping from its gaping evil looking jaws and then it looked at its pups.

The other werewolf's with bloodlust in their wild red raging eyes and black evil hearts jumped on the man at the nod of their pack leader who was still on top of the pinned down body and they began to tear him apart limb by limb and the spirit of life quickly left poor Sam's torn bleeding body!

The lights started coming on all up and down the street in the West End houses at the terrible fight and noise outside by the back yard neighborhood dogs that howled painfully frightful up and down the street "ooooOOOOHHHH—ooooOOOOHHH", that had awaken the entire West End neighborhood that early Sunday morning!

The tall dark strange woman with long flowing jet black hair flew off the nearby roof top into the night sky with a worried and disgusted look on her face.

The night before which was late Friday night, Bill sat at the Lone Wolf Tavern on Ebert Road on the outskirts of town drinking back a few shots of liquor with his old police pals after a long hectic work week and trying to relax for a fun filled night out at the local police hangout in town.

The jukebox was blaring out shag music from the 1960s and the small dance floor was crowed with people dancing and drinking the night away and the place was jumping with excitement in the air.

Bill was deep in conversation about a cold murder case with one of his old police detective buddies who was working on it when he felt the burning heat from an icy cold stare, that burned into the back of his soul from somewhere across the dark and smoke filled crowed noisy bar.

Bill stopped his conversation and stood straight up at rigid attention on his barstool and set his shot of whisky nervously back on the bar by a strong but trembling hand. He squirmed around and looked for who ever was staring at him from across the packed room while his good old police buddy who was getting very drunk beside him downed another glass of beer that the woman bartender had just sat in front of him.

He saw the everyday people busy at the tables in the middle of the barroom floor busy talking and laughing at small jokes while drinking their glasses of beer or shots of liquor and smoking their cigarettes while having a good time.

Bill looked over at the dark dimly lit booths filled with tall dark strangers having drinks with their companions along the back wall and saw nothing out of the ordinary to draw his attention too.

He scanned the dance floor but everybody was dancing the shag up a storm and having a good time and nobody was eyeballing him from across the dark dance floor that was lit up by the big strobe light ball hanging from overtop spinning from the ceiling. The lights reflected off the walls and mirrors and everybody in the pub. It was hard to see straight in the dim flashing colored lights.

Bill seeing nothing out of the ordinary and shrugged the weird feeling off by hunching his shoulders together and picked up his shot of whisky. He went back to his drinking and talking to his old police buddies who didn't seem to notice what had just taken place with him and he didn't say anything about it either.

He had the same weird feelings from his visit's to other local bars in town over the past few months but for the life of him he couldn't figure out who was watching him or why thought Bill to himself while he ordered another shot of hard whisky from the busy bartender.

Some moments later a tall dark haired woman got up alone from one of the booths along the back wall and made her way through the throng of people on the dance floor and left the bar very discreetly and unnoticed by Bill or anyone else who were all busy having a good time until the bar closed in the wee hours of the late morning.

Later that same weekend Bill had come into work before the crack of dawn to work on some of his current cases and was sitting in his private investigator office off of Healy Drive in

Winston-Salem as he leaned back in his big plush leather high back black chair and heard a "thump!" on his door. Bill worked 24 hours a day and seven days a week and was always on call for a case. Bill got up and went to the front door and opened it knowing his hunch was right and it was the Winston-Salem Sunday newspaper "The journal."

Bill looked out the door and saw the delivery paper boy throwing his newspapers at the other doors down the street as he smiled at himself while he thought of his childhood days with his brother who had his first job as a newspaper delivery boy sitting just before dawn at the old Save- Way food store on Walkertown Road on the front cement porch in front of the drink machines rolling up the newspapers and putting rubber bands on them as dad waited in the car to drive them around the old neighborhood to deliver them by pitching them out the back car windows onto the neighbors driveways—man that brought back memories of the good old days living in Daisy Station thought Bill to himself again.

Bill reached down and picked up the Sunday newspaper and turned around and shut the door behind him. Bill walked back to his chair and sat down pitching the newspaper onto his neat desk.

Bill opened the Krispy Kreme Doughnut box sitting on the corner of his desk he had bought earlier, made fresh that morning on his way to work and pulled out a fresh glazed doughnut. He took a bite and as he chewed the delicious doughnut, he grabbed his coffee mug and took a sip of the Columbian coffee he had just made.

Bill put the doughnut in his mouth as he reached for the paper on the desk and sat his coffee mug down as he slipped off the rubber band and unrolled the newspaper.

On the front page was the headline "Another ghastly Murder." Bill read the article for a few minutes as he switched to the back page, then reading the rest of the story, then he laid the paper down and thought about the new murder on Burke

Street that had happen last night in the West End section of town.

The West End was rich in history and was built in 1890 or 1891 and was planned originally as a resort street car suburb, allowing people who worked downtown to get to and from work easily. It was built for the elite class of citizens of that time many of the original house's remain, leaving the west end a collage of architectural designs ranging from Queen Anne to craftsman, giving the area its nickname of "Winston-Salem's Front Porch."

Bill had been through that section of town many times in the past and had seen "The Millionaire's Row" on North. Spring and West. Fifth street's which was an area of expensive homes for the rich elite. Some of the old houses had been turned into bed and breakfast inns.

The neoclassic design can be seen around the west end with stained glass windows, doors and fanlight in some homes and was popular in the 1900s.

The houses had been characterized by their symmetrical shape, two-story pillars in the front and triangular roof. The houses had been inspired by Classical Greek and Roman buildings which had inspired the builders to build in neoclassic architecture.

Bill new that the old houses aren't the only thing to enjoy in the West End of town.

Through out the area are a variety of restaurants some Italian, mostly privately owned. He new their was pizza shops located there where you could order New York-style pizza and there was also a vibrant nightlife with several bars and pubs spread throughout the area.

Bill leaned back in his chair and thought about what he had read in the newspaper article and then it hit him that the West End was a prime hunting ground at night with many alleyways to hide in for a serial killer on the prowl. Bill quickly looked the article over again for anymore information.

The Journal had read that the man had been a customer at one of the bars and had left when it closed at 2:00 A:M this morning. The neighbors had awoken around 2:30 A:M to all the neighborhood dogs barking and howling at the top of their lungs and they heard someone screaming his head off somewhere down a alleyway and the neighbors called the police to report a disturbance.

The police came in full force and had come upon the mans scattered body in one of the alleyways off Burke Street which they blocked off and taped with crime scene tape.

The Crime Scene Investigators had been called to the crime scene to search for clues in the new murder case and worked till dawn cleaning up body parts.

They had removed the pieces of body parts to the local morgue for an autopsy. A city detective who remained anonymous was interviewed and quoted by a journal reporter and he said "The man had been torn to pieces and it was the worst murder scene he had ever seen in his ten years of law enforcement and the torn right hand of the dead man still had a death grip on his car key's that was forever seared into his memory."

The city detective also said "They had no murder suspects at this time or any motive and no witnesses to the murder after they had interviewed the neighbors who lived close by the crime scene who had saw nothing. They were mystified by these rash of unsolved murders in the city and Triad area which they had detectives working on the cases full time."

Bill thought to himself again that it must be a brutal serial killer and he wasn't working alone either from what he had gathered from the news media over the past few years, he had a hunch he was right as he picked up his case file underneath the newspaper pulling it out and thumped threw it on the cheating rich husband he had been trailing to a local motel 8 to meet his mistress in secret.

The mans wife was a knock out and hired him after she

had become suspicious after smelling some ones else's perfume in his car and a lipstick stain on his shirt collar in the laundry room he had tried to wipe off and hide from his wife which she had found as she picked through the dirty clothes to wash.

Some people have it all and are still not satisfied with what they have thought Bill as he closed the file with the pictures he had took with his Pentax camera with a long range lens from his car in the motel 8 parking lot of the cheating husband and mistress.

It was later around 10:00 o-clock in the morning as he was bending over his file cabinet, that his phone rang "beeep, beeep"! Bill slid the file back in its place somewhat annoyed and walked over to his desk picking up the phone as his answering machine took the call. "Dam" said Bill as he hit the flash button on the remote control phone cutting off the answering machine.

"Hello this is Bill Christian Private Investigator speaking," said Bill very business like as he waited for a response from the caller. "Hello Bill—this is your old pal Dicky Poser chief of police calling, how are you doing to day," asked the chief of police?

Bill was stunned he hadn't heard from his old detective friend from the force in many long years. They had went through the academy together and he had heard he had been promoted to chief some time after he had left the force and retired early.

He wondered to himself if this was bad new's but kept his thoughts to himself.

"Well I'm O.K.— its good to hear your voice again— Dicky, its been along time and how are you doing?" spoke Bill wondering what was up with this important phone call from a higher authority in town on an early Sunday morning.

"I tried to call you at home but got no answer and figured you were at your office. Can you meet me at my office on the third floor of the Metro precinct today at 1:00 o-clock—Bill.

I've got something to talk over with you of an urgent nature and I'm doing as well as can be in this day and time," spoke Dicky with authority in his voice as the phone went quiet on his end?

"Sure I'll see you then—anything for an old friend—and glad to hear it—good-by," replied Bill as he hit the cut off button on the phone. Bill set the phone back in it's charger on the desk as he rubbed his chin with his right hand wondering what this was about.

Bill had a hunch it might be about those new unsolved wild murders in the Journal newspaper that had been happening for some years back thought Bill as he shook the thought off and went back to his case at hand as he picked up the phone to call the nice rich lady about the evidence of her cheating husband.

During that very same Sunday morning at around 8:00 A:M Wilbur had got up and made a quick cereal breakfast in the kitchen.

Clara Bell was on the front porch where she set out a gallon glass jar that was filled to the top with water and eight Lipton ice tea bags floating inside with the metal lid screwed on tight in the bright morning sunlight to make some home brew tea. She went back inside her front porch screen door to go in to her parlor to do some knitting on a Afghan she was working on for church and first but foremost to check on Wilbur's fishing trip.

"Good-by and good luck fishing—Wilbur. This is a nice day to go fishing since the church is closed to day for the church picnic which we've been on everyone from way back and taken the grand kids to a few to have a good time out at Tanglewood Park. Its time for a break from reality and just have a day off to enjoy our selves because God promises today and not tomorrow," said Clara Bell loudly down the hallway who kissed Wilbur on the lips tenderly when she came into the kitchen.

"Thanks—I need all the luck I can get and I'm looking forward to a nice quiet Sunday just relaxing by the river— fishing and I want miss that old picnic and I surely ain't worried about tomorrow until it comes or if it don't come at our age who cares I've lived my life right and I'm ready to go anytime and bust Heaven's gate wide open," replied Wilbur who went out the back kitchen door while Clara Bell shaking her head at Wilbur's optimism headed to her parlor to start her knitting and he stood outside for a moment on the cement steps locking the back kitchen door with his skeleton key. Then he made a fast track out to the barn and grabbed his fishing gear from the storage shed beside the wood kindling shed next to his two car open garage shed beside the big red barn.

He whistled for his small collie dog Sassie who came running up to him from around the big red barn who was his farm work dog who helped with the cattle and cows and she kept the predators away from his live stock during the night because she was always on guard duty which was the way she had been trained since she was a pup by Wilbur himself.

"You want to go fishing with me today girl," asked preacher man Wilbur being a deacon of the old Pentecostal Holiness country faith who stuck his fishing gear in the back bed of the pick-up truck along with a five gallon bucket? Sassie barked "ARF, ARF, ARF" wagging her tail back and forth happily and ran around in small circles to show that she wanted to go for a ride and be with her master.

"O.K.–girl lets go," said Wilbur who walked toward the back of the old pick-up bed truck.

He let down the tail gate and Sassie jumped right into the back of the pick-up bed wagging her tail joyfully. Wilbur shut the tail gate and walked around and open the drivers side door. He hopped in and slammed the old rusty door shut on the old ford pick-up.

He started the old truck up and let it warm up and he

backed out of the old garage shed. He drove down the drive way out onto Payne Road.

He took the short cut to Flat Shoals Road and hit Highway Number 8. That soon led into highway 88 into the town of Danbury.

He soon pulled off to the side of the road before he got to the main town and the Dan River bridge. He parked his old pick-up truck off the main road along side the hilly forest that ran along the vast river down below. He got out of the drivers side door and shut it and locked it up. He grabbed his fishing gear from the back bed.

"Come on Sassie lets go do some fishing in the Dan River," said Wilbur who walked to the edge of the tall pine and oak tree woods and disappeared down a well worn path.

Sassie jumped out of the back of the bed and trotted off at a fast run and followed her master down into the woods on the old worn foot path in hot pursuit.

Wilbur made his way down the steep hill on the curvy path to his favorite fishing hole where he had fished as a young boy on his days off from his father's old farm along a secluded spot on the Dan River. Wilbur came down out of the woods and bushes and walked along the river bank with Sassie who took off running along the river bank barking and smelling new sights and sounds along the edge of the river.

It was a bend in the river and it was about fifty yards across to the opposite river bank with sparkling blue crystal river waters that moved by at a swift pace. It had big tall oak trees on both sides of the river banks and the front big roots from the tree trunks ran off down into the river which was a perfect shady place for fish to gather and hide in plus it was a cool shady spot for them too in the hot sunny day with big tall long branches that hung way out over the river water that gave it peaceful shade during the hottest part of the day. In places it was over your head and deep at the base of the tree roots and up stream it was ankle deep and you could walk across to the other side on the river rocks and sand bars.

"Don't run off girl stay close," shouted Wilbur who set down his fishing gear and five gallon bucket he had brought with him. He open up the small wooden stool and set it near the river's running edge.

He got out his bait can from his tackle box and open the lid while grabbing his rod and reel.

He reached inside the bait can with his finger and got out a dab of moldy corn meal and bunny bread mix that was his old pap's secret fishing bait recipe.

He stuck it onto his fishing hook and firmly mashed it together until he was satisfied with it.

He laid down his rod and reel and grabbed his five gallon bucket and walked to the river's edge and gently stuck in the bucket and filled it about three quarters of the way full with river water.

He set the bucket back onto dry land near him and set down on his wood stool and picked up his fishing rod and cast the hook out into the fast running river current.

He sat there awhile watching the plastic float bobble on the river water. Then he heard a pecking noise and watched his plastic float move in the water back and forth.

"Come on—come on take the bait you dab nab fish," exclaimed Wilbur who watched the plastic float move on the water then it went under and he snapped the rod back setting the hook in the fishes mouth and reeled in his first catch of the day.

He stood up and pulled the two pound big mouth bass out of the river water onto dry land.

"Now that's more like it," said Wilbur who held the rod and reel straight up in the air and the fish swung in front of him and he grabbed it by the mouth with his left hand and laid down his rod on the river bank ground in front of him.

He grabbed the fish hook with his right hand and

unhooked it and held the big fish up in admiration and stuck it in his five gallon bucket which kept it alive and fresh until he got home and cut it up to eat.

Wilbur baited the hook again with the corn meal and bunny bread mix and threw it out into the river again to catch another fish. He looked back over his shoulder and saw Sassie had curled up under a shady bush watching him fish like an obedient dog should and he smiled at her who wagged her tail when she saw him watching her.

Soon he felt his hook line jerk and he reeled in another fish and this time it was a big cat fish. He stood up after reeling it in and grabbed the cat fish behind it's barbed whiskers with his right hand and worked the hook out of its mouth. He tossed the pound of cat fish in his five gallon bucket and went back to baiting his hook.

Wilbur cast out his fish line and set on his stool thinking about how peaceful nature was and the flowing of the river by him was soothing to the mind sight when he got a peck on his fish line and then the plastic float disappeared under the water.

"Man what a whopper," said Wilbur out loud who fought with his rod and reel which bent almost double from the pull on the line which went in a sig sag then in small circle's out in the river water in front of him and he jumped off his stool to put up a good fight. Wilbur fought with his rod and reel and reeled his rod handle hard winding up the fish line by pulling back on his rod and reeling in the slack line until the prey took hold and fought to get loose.

Finely the prey broke the surface of the water and Wilbur was taken by surprise.

"It's a dab blame snapping turtle and its been awhile since I caught one of those," mumbled Wilbur under his breath.

He pulled the turtle which have gave up the good fight to

shore with his rod. He grabbed the fish line and pulled the ten pound snapping turtle up onto dry land.

The turtle just looked at Wilbur dumbfounded and stuck his neck out in dignified manner snapping its mouth up and down while Wilbur dropped his fishing rod on the ground to free up his hands. Sassie came over from her sleeping place barking at the turtle "woof, woof, woof'!

"Now—now Sassie—shush—shush—go back and lay down. I don't need your help," commanded Wilbur who gave the dog a mean look and she quickly obeyed and went back to her sleeping spot on the river bank under the shady bush and laid back down wrapping her tail around herself obediently.

Wilbur reached into his tackle box that was near him and got out a long flat screw driver. He stuck his foot on top of the turtle's back to hold it in place by force who open his hook caught mouth and tried to bite his big foot. Then Wilbur slid in the screw driver before the snapping turtle shut his mouth again which it did but it was now pried open by the screw driver stuck between its jaws.

Wilbur leaned over to his tackle box and got out a long pair of needle nose pliers. He reached into the turtles mouth and unhooked his fish hook quickly and expertly without hurting the poor turtle further.

Wilbur slid out the flat screwdriver and dropped it over into his tackle box along with the needle nose pliers. He took his foot off of the turtle and grabbed the shell behind the head to avoid getting bit on the hand which the snapping turtle retreated into its shell when Wilbur picked it up off the ground.

"Well—I'll just take you down stream and release you unharmed. I love turtle meat but not today just catching fish for me and Clara Bell only because that's what the doctor ordered, its your lucky day," spoke Wilbur who headed off along the beaten path along the river bank headed down stream.

He walked about a hundred feet carrying the turtle until

he came to the rapids. He walked to the river's edge and gently lowered the snapping turtle into the water and released it.

The turtle swam around looking at Wilbur as if to thank him for sparring his life for just a moment and then swam away in the fast river current and into the small rapids and was gone in the blink of an eye.

Wilbur walked back to his fishing spot and baited his hook and set back down on his comfortable little wooden stool and cast it out into the water while he hummed away nonchalantly at being one with nature.

Then Wilbur heard a rustling sound off to his left and he looked intently at the woods back behind him and he saw a six foot long black snake come crawling out onto the river bank not ten feet from him and it flicked its tongue as it went crawling along the rocky ground up to the river's edge.

Then it slithered into the fast water current and was gone in the blink of an eye and Wilbur remembered to a time long gone by in his child hood. It was the early 1940s and his daddy had got him up one Sunday morning bright and early. They had dressed for church, Wilbur in his little two piece black suit and his dad wore his three piece vested black suit with a wide brim yellow straw hat.

They had drove from their dirt road farm in Stokes County and hit highway 52 a dirt and gravel interstate road headed toward Surry County. They had drove for about two hours and had long past Pilot Mountain. Wilbur had looked on with interest out the old model T ford's window at the tall knob of pilot mountain which you could see for miles in any direction and they passed it rather quickly kicking up dust in their wake from the model T's fords wheels. They passed the town of Pilot mountain and soon entered into Surry County. Wilbur's dad turned onto highway 601 headed for the town of Dobson.

They drove through the curving hill's until they reached what is now called the Blue Ridge Parkway. They pulled into a small church parking lot from a road his daddy had turned onto and down at the bottom of a hill. Wilbur looked out his side car window and he saw a one room frame boarded church which stood up on piled up rock pillars underneath the old church that ran from front to back and also served as a one room school house for the area children.

The wood had weathered and had turned black over time. There was a small steeple built on top of the old time church. It begin to rang "ding, dong, ding, dong," calling in the local people for church service.

"I have to use the bathroom—Wilbur come with me," said Horace who open his car door and got out beckoning Wilbur to come with him.

Wilbur followed his father obediently and scooted across the old rumble seat and got out of the car and his father shut the car door quickly.

They walked past the other cars and moved through the throng of women and men talking in front of the church in small groups and children playing in the church yard, dressed in 1940s era style clothing and walked around the side of the old church and came to the back of the church where the out houses were for the men and women and they were marked above the doors in carved black letters and the outhouses were painted white.

Wilbur's father left him at the front of the men's white outhouse while he went inside and done his business. Horace soon came back out quickly and grabbed his sons hand.

"Lets go—Wilbur—the church is about to start its Sunday service," said Horace who grabbed his son's hand and they headed to the front of the old church.

"This is pastor Sam Pickins Primitive Pentecostal Holiness church and this week is the old time revival meeting week for the church and anyone who wants to come," said Horace who grinned at his son while they walked along up the front church steps.

Wilbur could hear the organ music playing "Give Me That

Old Time Religion" hymnal inside the church as they entered inside with the church people who flowed into the church isle and took seats among small pews on both sides of the small one room church. They had the windows up and you could feel the summer August heat in the hot air that floated stuffily inside the church. Wilbur's father led him up to the front second pew and they took seats in the crowed church.

The pastor stood at the front pulpit in the center of the altar stage with a big cross behind him hanging on the wall with a purple robe hanging on the cross and a big framed picture of Jesus and his disciples eating the last supper on the wall behind it and laying in front of it was a big white whicker basket with a big rock on top of it and the little boy in Wilbur wondered what was in it, but he was too shy to ask his father. There were rose's in decorated vases along the back of the Altar and in front too where the preacher's pulpit was at the front of the altar.

They got out the hymn books and they sang old time Christian songs led by pasture Sam Pickins and his two deacons of the church behind him to start the service. After that he open up his bible on the pulpit and began to read from it and he was a fiery hail fire and brimstone style shouting preacher who delivered the word of God to his flock with a raging passion.

"Numbers chapter 21 verse 4—And they journeyed from mount Hor by the way of the red sea, to compass the land of E'-Dom: and the soul of the people was much discouraged because of the way. Aaa—Men," said preacher man Sam who shouted his words and worked himself up into a fiery rage as he read the bible.

"Verse 5—And the people spake against God and against Moses, wherefore have ye brought us up out of Egypt to die in the wilderness? For there is no bread, neither is there any water; and our soul loatheth this light bread. Aaa—Men," said Sam who took in a deep quick breath and comtuined on.

"Verse 6ᵗʰ—And the Lord sent fiery serpents among the people, and they bit the people; and much people of Israel died. Aaa—Men," said Sam who was in a fever pitch that rose and echoed off of the top of the rafters and through out the small church and the flock of people shouted Amen and glory be to God back to the preacher urging him on.

"Verse7—Therefore the people came to Moses, and said, We have sinned, for we have spoken against the Lord, and against thee; pray unto the Lord, that he take away the serpents from us. And Moses prayed for the people. Aaa—Men," said Sam who read on in the bible.

"Verse 8—And the lord said unto Moses, make thee a fiery serpent and set it upon a pole: and it shall come to pass, that everyone that is bitten, when he look upon it, shall live. Aaa—Men," said Sam who raised up his arms in glory to God on high.

"Verse 9—And Moses made a serpent of brass, and put it upon a pole, and it came to pass, that if a serpent had bitten any man, when he beheld the serpent of brass, he lived, Aaa—Men," said Sam who was calling his flock to lift up God and they did by shouting to the rooftops in one Heavenly voice "Hallelujah—Glory be to God."

The pastor flipped his bible pages until he came to the red marked right one and flew back into his shouting command performance.

Mark—chapter 16—This is Jesus talking to his diciples, Aaa—Men," said Sam who gripped the pulpit tightly with his hands and the sweat rolled off his head from the hot August morning which he wiped with his white handkerchief form his left suit pocket with his right hand quickly and stuffed it back in his jacket pocket with out missing a beat.

Verse 15—and he said unto them. Go into all the world and preach the gospel to every creature. Aaa—Men," said Sam who read on in his fever pitch.

Verse 17—And these signs shall follow them that believe;

In my name shall they cast out devils; they shall speak with new tongues. Aaa—Men said Sam who shouted out bless God and give praise too the man above say Amen. The crowd responded and they all shouted "Amen" back to the backwoods preacher man standing before them on the mighty pulpit who read on.

Verse 18—They shall take up serpents; and if they drink any deadly thing; it shall not hurt them; they shall lay hands on the sick, and they shall recover. Aaa—Men," said Sam who walked up and down the altar after that. "Glory be to God on most High," shouted Sam who waved his sweat stained white hanker chief at the church crowed who got up and applauded from the church pews waving fans and bibles praising God and lifting their hands too heaven above.

Then Sam and the two deacons went to the back of the altar to the white whicker basket with a rock on top of it.

Sam removed the big rock and open the whicker basket and reached in. He pulled out a four foot long rattlesnake which he put around his neck. He reached back in the wicker basket and pulled out a three foot long copperhead snake and gave it to one of his deacons who took it and held it up for the church crowd in the pews too see. Then Sam got out a four foot long water mocassin and handed it too his other deacon who lifted the dangerous snake up in his hands over top of his head for all too see who gazed in wide eye wonder at the spectacle before them. Then they walked back to the pulpit together holding the deadly snakes up for everyone too see and believe in the miracle power of God Almighty.

Sam the preacher man began to read from his bible on the pulpit again after thumbing through the Holy Bible.

Acts chapter 1 verse 5— for John truly baptized with water; but ye shall not be baptized with the Holy Ghost not many day hence, Aaa—Men," said Sam who held the deadly rattlesnake that had wrapped itself around his right arm and its tongue darted in and out of its mouth testing the air while it looked with yellow eyes at the captured audience down below it.

"Verse 7—And he said unto them. It is not for you to know the times or the season, which the Father hath put in his own power, Aaa—Men,"said Sam who removed the reptile from his arm and put it around his neck. The other two deacons with their dangerous snakes stayed by his side while they held them in their arms. Seven year old Wilbur stood up on his pew beside his father who was standing up shouting and praising God who looked on spellbound in amazement with his little mind beside the only good father he had ever known until now.

Verse 8—But ye shall receive power, after that the Holy Ghost is come upon you: and ye shall be witness unto me both in Jerusalem and in all Ju-dae-a, and in Sa-ma'-ri-a, and unto the uttermost part of the earth. Aaa—Men," said Sam and the Holy Ghost descended down upon his shoulders also his deacons and he spoke in a arabic foreign tongue to the church congregation while lifting his eyes Heavenly up to his Lord thy God.

The Holy Ghost ran rampant through the adult church crowd who were speaking in foreign tongues and shouting to the rafters to Glorify God on high. The woman spoke in the Holy Ghost and ended their foreign speaking tongue with a shrill whistle by curling up their tongues on end. One man off to the left of Wilbur jumped up in the pew isle as if on fire and danced a jig shouting to the rooftops in a foreign Arabic tongue, then he ran down the center isle and out the church door. Wilbur looked for where the man had run off too and then he looked out the side church window and saw him run by at top speed running around the church. The man did this several times until he was exhausted and came back into the church and he dragged his tired feet back to his church pew and set down with his right hand still up in the air waving at

God and he smile at the young boy who was watching him in awe which was Wilbur who smiled back at him.

The backwoods preacher thumbed through his bible again after the crowd had settled down and the Holy Ghost had run its course among the backwood church crowd.

"John chapter 11 verse 39—Jesus said, take ye away the stone. Martha, the sister of him that was dead, saith unto him. Lord, by this time he stinketh: for he hath been four days. Aaa—Men," said Sam who held the poisonous snake in one hand and the bible in the other hand.

"Verse 40—Jesus saith unto her, said I not unto thee that, if thou wouldest believe, thou shouldest see the glory of God?. Aaa—Men," said Sam who shook the bible in hjs left hand to make his point to the captured audience.

"Verse 41—Then they took away the stone from the place where the dead was laid. And Jesus lifted up his eyes ands said, Father, I thank thee that thou hast heard me. Aaa—Men," said Sam who looked over the pulpit toward every man, woman and child he held hypnotic in the palm of his hand.

"Verse 42—and I knew that thou hearest me always: but because of the people which stand by I said it, that may believe that thou hast sent me. Aaa—Men," said Sam who was near the end of his sermon.

"Verse 43— And when he thus had spoken, he cried with a loud voice, Las'-a-rus, come forth. Aaa—Men," said Sam who read the last verse with divine confidence.

Verse 44—And he that was dead came forth, bound hand and foot with grave clothes: and his face was bound about with a napkin. Jesus said unto them. Loose him, and let him go. Aaa—Men," said Sam who ended his sermon by closing his bible on the pulpit. He motion for his two deacons to follow him back to the white whicker basket and they open the top and put the snakes back into the white basket and preacher Sam closed the basket and he put the big heavy rock back on top and the two deacons set back down in their chairs guarding the basket while Sam closed the revival meeting service. Preacher man Sam nodded to his woman organ player who began playing a slow soulful moody melody note which was "Bringing In The Sheep" on her organ.

"Gods almighty power shut the mouth of these poisonous snakes and we were not bit tonight or harmed in anyway and seeing is believing," said Sam Pickins who smiled at his flock from the pulpit.

"Jesus is the way and the light of the world if you believe in him and want to confess your sins and give your heart and soul to Jesus who will bear any burden and sin who died on the cross for all mankind. Jesus raised Lazarus from death and the grave. He too defeated death by being resurrected after he was crucified on the cross by God. Then if you commit your soul to Jesus, then you will have ever lasting life and you will never die fore God is the Almighty Creator where to him nothing is impossible," said Sam who looked out over his flock with hope in his heart for them.

"Come up to the altar and kneel if you want to confess your sins and be saved," asked Sam who watched a great multitude of people leave their church pews and come forward to be saved in Jesus name? Sam prayed for everyone who came forward to be saved with his two deacons and then the old time revival meeting service was soon over. Horace had said his good-by's to his kin people at the old backwoods church and they left for home. Wilbur was looking out the car window wondering about what he had saw and new he'd never forget it while his daddy drove home in the hot afternoon sun back too their farm in Stokes County along highway 52 filled with the spirit of God in him who sang at the top of his lungs joyfully with Wilbur looking on smiling with a boyish grin on his face.

Wilbur set their thinking about that for awhile and he just shook his head thinking about his days growing up with his old daddy. They don't handle snakes in his church because it was forbidden by their good pastor and old ways gone, but not forgotten. He didn't believe in tempting fate or God and Clara Bell didn't either so he went back to fishing on the river bank thinking about old times in the bible belt with his late dad.

Soon time flew by and before he new it, he had about eight good size fish in his crowded bucket by noon time.

Three big mouth bass and two cat fish and three large wild brim counted Wilbur two himself.

"That's about enough for me and Clara Bell—girl," said Wilbur out loud who stood up and stretched his old tired legs and aching back looking at Sassie who wagged her tail ready to go. He packed up his fishing gear and grabbed the five gallon bucket full of fish and trotted off up the beaten path with Sassie tailing right behind him and he disappeared into the surrounding hilly woods walking up the well worn path.

Later that day Bill parked his Monte-Carlo car at the visitor parking lot at the metro police station on Cherry Street and hopped out locking his car door and walked through the parking lot, then down the steps as he looked over to the memorial to the fallen officers on the left of the red brick building as he went through the doors.

Bill walked to the elevators on the right and some officers were going into the open elevator on the right as they made room for him. Bill squeezed in as the doors closed. "Third floor please" requested Bill as the officers begin pressing buttons for what ever floor they wanted to get off on.

"Aren't you that private investigator Bill Christian who use to work here as a top detective, " asked a curious young police officer?

"Yep—that's me" replied Bill as the other officers looked him over in the crowded elevator as Bill noticed his name plate on his blue uniform which read Mike Darker.

"How did you know it was me" asked Bill with intense curiosity at this bright young police officer?

"I saw your picture in the journal newspaper for saving that young girls life who had been hit by a car walking on highway

52 during rush hour and you stopped and used a tourniquet to stop the bleeding on her leg while you called for a ambulance! You got a commendation from the police department for that one and I never forget a face," said officer Darker.

"Man that's a good memory, that was a very long time ago, you just might make a detective some day," replied Bill smiling as the bell rang for his floor. Officer Darker's face lit up with that comment as the other officers smiled at his memory skills and the encouragement from Bill.

Bill got off on the third floor when the elevator doors opened and walked down the long busy hallway until he came to the chief of police office and opened the door.

Bill shut the door as the young secretary looked up from her desk. "May I help you," asked the pretty young woman with brown hair also dark round beautiful eyes. The secretary had a photogenic face and nice make-up with a small nose over red ruby lips and red blush chicks as she looked Bill over from head to toe?

"I'm Bill Christian and I have a appointment to see the chief of police at 1:00 o-clock today," replied Bill as he stood there waiting for her help and noticed her name plate on the desk which read Pamela Smith.

"Yes— I've heard so much about you, please take a seat and I'll let him know you're here," said the secretary with a flirting wink. "I hope it's all good," replied Bill as he walked over to the office chair and sat down grabbing a magazine off the side table.

"It's all good—just that you're a dam good detective who want let up until you've got your man," replied the brown eyed secretary as she made the call on the office intercom to let the chief know that Bill was here.

"Well you win some and loose some," replied Bill modestly as he thumbed through the magazine.

After awhile Dicky came out of his office with the mayor and Forsyth County Sheriff at large David Holiday.

The mayor who was a little upset had a red face. "I want results and fast —about these cases. It's ruining our downtown night life business," said the mayor!

"You have my assurance that it will be taken cared of" said Dicky as the mayor stomped out of the office with the high Sheriff right behind him looking cool as a cucumber as he tipped his cowboy hat at the cute secretary at her desk.

Bill sat their looking a little shell shocked as he watched the mayor and High Sheriff leave out the door.

"Bill– its good to see you—come on in my office," said Dicky as he adjusted his tie looking a little worried at Bill who got up and shook his out stretched hand.

Dicky ushered Bill into the office and shut the door behind them.

"Take a seat and how about a cigar to smoke while we talk," said Dicky as he reached for the cigar box on his desk while he sat down and leaned back in his big high back leather chair.

"No thanks. To early in the day for me," said Bill as he waited for what was to come.

"I'll get right to it then Bill. No sense beating around the bush old man. I need help and I'm at a wits end on these murder cases. The mayor as you've seen is on my case not to mention the aldermen who are raising hell about the police department not having any suspects or anyone in jail charged with these murders in Winston-Salem and the public is near panic mode as I'm sure you've been reading about it in the local newspaper," spoke Dicky As he leaned back in his chair letting Bill take this all in.

Bill sat in the chair thinking for a few minutes what the police chief was asking of him and it was bad new's like he had thought and probably very dangerous.

"So your beating a mad rabid dog with no luck chasing

down it's tail and catching him," replied Bill very concerned for Dickies grave situation at hand?

"You could say that and you have a lucky nature of being in the right place at the right time and you somehow turn over the right rock's and always catch your man that's hiding under it and you're a great problem solver in getting the job done and never giving up," said Dicky who wiggled just slightly in his chair and gave away his nervousness.

"Well—that might be true but I'm very busy and have clients to take care of Dicky. I just can't drop everything and take your cases besides I might not be of any help if your top people are stumped on these cold cases, their's no guarantee that I can solve them for you either," replied Bill as he leaned forward a little uneasy about his life taking a new direction because he wanted to stay on his old life of working his clients who paid good also when he wanted to take a break he could with no one on his back and their was no pressure to solve the case and going home when he wanted too.

"Bill— I need you and I have no one else to turn too with all of your detective experience and skills. You have a interesting hobby of ghost hunting and the paranormal which my men don't have that might help you. I'll see to it that the city pays you well with a open checkbook and you'll get any rewards that have been offered and a bonus to boot, you will be saving peoples lives if you can catch the murderer or killers, I'll also owe you a favor on this one—a big one if I don't say so my self, " said Dicky fighting to entice Bill to take the cases as he let this sink into Bill's mind. Bill sat their thinking as he asked quietly "how much are the rewards"?

"More then you'll make in quiet a few years and I'll see you get the credit on this one and we are at your disposal and the Forsyth County Sheriffs Office will help too, were all in this together" replied Dicky as he eyed Bill with pleading eyes.

"The families want justice and the killer or killers caught.

We have kept tight lipped about a serial killer on the loose or more then one working the triad which is what we have determined to quite possibly be and my men say it's a phantom ghost that is elusive and can't be caught, we don't want the public to go into a panic because of it" said Dicky as he waited for Bill's answer.

"Well saving lives is what it's all about and the public needs to be protected and I've never put money before people's lives but my knowledge in the paranormal field might help out some but I shelved that hobby a long time ago it was an expensive hobby that lead to a dead end except in one case that I worked on with some old friends from the past but I want talk about that one because you'd say I was a nut case if you heard the wild story and anyway I don't think a ghost is doing the murders at all here because they are from a spiritual realm that just haunts buildings and houses.

They are just wandering lost souls in limbo if you get my drift and never have I found a ghost to be responsible for a murder if you believe in that sort of thing except once like I said before and I couldn't prove it in a court of law anyway but in all my cases in my long detective career it has always led to a human being of some nature who was responsible for the homicides anyway in the first place. That's why I became a policeman in the first place to save lives and protect the public from criminals but it's nice to get rewarded for your hard work and the money will be the last thing on my list and with that said this gun's for hire," said Bill modestly who new bad news was sometimes good business for him on payday and he wanted to help his old police buddy it was the least he could do for him after all the years spent together on the force. Dicky was beaming as he slid forward in his chair.

"You'll take the case then," questioned Dicky with a relieved look on his face?

"Yes— I'll take the case and have the files sent to my office by the end of the day," spoke Bill nonchalantly as he got up to leave and get back to business. Dicky quickly got up from his chair and grabbed a few cigars out of the cigar box and stuck them in Bill's trench coat pocket as he walked around the desk to shake Bill's hand.

Bill shook Dickies outstretched hand then he opened the door and walked out the door without another word spoken. He stopped as he pulled out one of the cigars and stuck it under his nose. "Smells like a Churchill Maduros," said Bill as he winked at the secretary at her desk who smiled her approval at knowing Bill took the case because he had a cigar in hand from the police chief.

Bill strolled across the office floor toward the door. He opened the door and was gone.

Later that day Bill had heard the office door open behind him as he was making coffee at the coffee pot on his file cabinet. Bill turned around and was shocked to see the young officer Mike Darker standing in his doorway.

"Come on in and take a seat and have some coffee," said Bill as he put four scoops of coffee in the lid filter and shut it turning it on. Bill put up the scoop and coffee back in the top drawler of the file cabinet shutting it as he turned around to look at officer Darker who had just taken a seat in one of his chairs in front of the desk.

"How are you doing Mr. Christian and I'll take a cup," replied officer er Darker as he held the boxes of files in his lap while Bill sat down in his chair and scooted forward to his desk?

"I'm fine but I've seen better days and we are in dark days with these killers on the loose here in Winston-Salem," said Bill with a serious look on his face.

"How do you know its more than one killer," questioned officer Darker who was now smiling at Bill?

"Let me take those files off your hands," said Bill as he rose from his seat and officer Darker handed over the files and Bill saw the black tattoo of some kind of dog's head on his right back hand.

That's a very Strange tattoo thought Bill to himself while he held the files in his hands but didn't ask any questions that might arouse suspicion because everyone right now was a suspect in this new case he had taken on.

Bill sat the files on the side of his desk and sat back down leaning back in his chair.

"Let's just say my instinct tells me that with reading the paper and watching the news reports when I have time in my busy schedule to watch the evening news," said Bill as he leaned forward in his chair confidently.

"Well— you are a smart man to have deduced that from just the paper or T.V., you're a smart man and I can see why you made detective in such a short time on the force," replied officer Darker with a exquisite look on his face.

The coffee pot finished brewing as Bill heard the gurgling noise behind him as he looked over his shoulder and saw the steam rising up from under the coffee pot lid as it finished brewing and Bill picked up his mug on the desk and got up to pour himself a cup of joe as he walked over to the file cabinet.

"How do you like your coffee and I made detective from hard earned footwork on the police beat with a few commendations," spoke Bill setting his cup down on the file cabinet as he pulled open a drawer and grabbed a clean cup from the file drawer?

"I like mine black and they still talk about how you caught a rapist and murderer by luring him back to North Carolina and out in the open with a letter mailed to his mother that he had won a clearing house lottery," said officer Darker with admiration in his voice about Bill's smart police work.

Bill grabbed the carafe pouring two full cup's as he reached in the drawer and pulled out some instant creamer in a plastic jar and spoon. Bill unscrewed the creamer and stuck the spoon in and got out some creamer.

Putting it in his coffee stirring it as he laid the spoon down on the place mat the coffee maker was sitting on and walked to his desk handing officer Darker his hot coffee who took it and started sipping it.

"Man that's hot and it's Columbian coffee," said officer Darker as he eyed Bill with a mean look for a second. Bill didn't seem to noticed the look as he said "yeah— that worked out just fine and I got my man— it's all I drink," as he winked at him.

"Well— were are you going to start," asked officer Darker with a interested look on his face?

"I'm going to look through the cold case files first but I don't discuss my cases with anyone but old reliable friends," replied Bill with a stern look on his face as his right hand drummed nervously on his desk at the questions he was being asked.

"Well— I have to go, thanks for the coffee and I know your busy and I have to get back to the police station for a squad meeting," said officer Darker as he got up and sat the empty mug on Bill's desk. Bill was relieved the officer was going but didn't show it as Bill said "thanks for dropping the cold case files off and take it easy and have a nice day,."

Bill watched the officer leave out the door and he was puzzled by the questions the young officer had asked him and it had ran up a red flag. Bill sat there thinking his training told him everybody was a suspect until the fact of truth was found out on who done the murders, their method of operation and the motive of why they did.

it. Bill stayed late at his office studying the crime scene photos and reports that night wanting to get a jump on things.

The first cold case victim in Rural Hall had been killed late at night after he had left his house in the neighborhood down the street for a mid summers cool night walk along the railroad tracks to see the trains.

His wife had reported him missing the next day when he didn't return home. The on scene detectives figured out the estimated time of the murder on that fateful first night walk which was their first guess and by no eyewitnesses to the crime which didn't help them very much in their case and it was a very private place for a murder late at night alone.

The attack took place down by the railroad train depot across from the old Unique furniture manufacturing plant at night because during the day their was plenty of people around working there in the small town.

They would have heard the attack and the killer had some how carried the victim up a big oak tree and left to rot on the big forked tree branch after the mans chest had been torn out. His throat had been slashed which had put the poor man out of his tortured misery.

A few days later a worker from the furniture manufacture had went for a walk along the railroad tracks and stopped for a cigarette break under the tree and noticed a bad smell. The eye witness looked up and discovered the body hanging 20 feet overhead in the tree.

The sheriffs department said it was impossible for the killer alone to have carries a 6ft tall man that weighed two hundred pounds up that big oak tree 20 feet by himself, a ordinary man would have needed a crane or rope pulley system to do it but the pictures didn't lie as Bill looked them over with astonishment.

The killer left no evidence of any kind at the scene the Sheriff detectives had combed the area with a fine tooth comb of examination.

The next cold case was a jogger that had been out late at night running down by the old train tracks along Bethania Station Road in the Old Town section of town during a late summer night in August and had been evidently ambushed before she got to Beck's Church Road. She was dragged into the woods and ripped apart, the poor woman didn't have a chance because she had a small can of mace in her left hand with a death grip on it and the can was empty but from the looks of things at the crime scene, she had put up a terrific fight for her life. Her body had been discovered by some kids playing along the railroad tracks a few days later.

Again no evidence left by the killer and no witnesses but some large paw prints in the mud in the woods around the body which could have been a big bear attracted by the smell of blood at the crime scene, the on scene crime scene investigator officers and police detectives had suspected it was a bear but no proof it was a bear. Bill looked at the big bear paw prints in the photos and he wondered just how they got there if it wasn't a bear attack after all and it mystified him thought Bill.

Bill took a short break from the crime scene photos and lit a cigarette and smoked while he surmised the woman had died a terrible and horrible slow death which she put up some kind of fight as if the killer was playing with her and drawing out every ounce of blood and life in the victim photo which Bill deduced by looking at the crime scene photos again so he would not miss anything from his first look like some rookies would who haven't been trained for a second look until years of law enforcement experience taught them too and he rubbed out his butt in the cigarette tray.

The next cold case file Bill opened from the box was out in Clemmon's behind the shopping center and it had been a home less man and he had been torn apart from limb to limb and the body dumped in the garbage dump'ster behind the Rose's store.

The next day the stock boy had went out to dump some bags of trash and saw the blood on the ground around the dump'ster. The stock boy slid open the trash door and looked inside and discovered the body.

The crime scene was too filthy and it was compromised by

a crowd of people that worked at Rose's department store who climbed in to check the homeless man whose torso was covered up by trash to see if he was a live before calling the Sheriff's and the people didn't realize how much damage the man had to his body underneath the trash until the sheriff's department and paramedics got there on scene while they started pulling pieces of the homeless man's body out of the trash dump'ster looking for clues.

Some of the bystanders watching got sick and threw up which the sheriff's disbursed the crowd and made them leave the crime scene which had been taped off around the dump'ster.

There was no witnesses like the other cases and the detectives suspected the murder happen late at night when no one was around to see anything at the busy shopping center which was deserted by then.

This killer or killers were very clever and didn't leave any clues and covered their tracks except for the bear prints on one murder because it was muddy that day from a rain shower that night of the murder and noted on that report.

Robbery was not a motive for the murders, the victim's had money or jewelry on them that wasn't taken during the attacks noted on the police reports. The autopsy reports read each victim had wounds on them from sharp claws that were typical of a big bear attack and no skin under the victims nails from the attacker or attackers.

The chests had been ripped open and the throats slashed or torn out in most cases. The cause of death for each victim was some kind of animal attack listed on the probable cause of death report from the coroner.

That doesn't make sense thought Bill there has never been a bear attack reported ever in Winston-Salem, Forsyth County history that he new of which this bothered him a lot as he felt a sadness in his heart for these good citizens who had done nothing wrong but being in the wrong place at the wrong time.

Bill would call Dicky in the morning and tell him about maybe having a curfew after dark until these killers were caught if they only struck at night but would he be able to do that in a town of 350,00 thousand people who might not heed the warning and curfew.

It was getting late at night and Bill thought he would call it a day because he was tired and laid the crime scene folders back on the desk.

He put on his coat from where it hung on the back of his big chair and locked up and left heading home for the night as he walked outside to his car in the parking lot.

At supper time that same evening Clara Bell was busy flouring the cat fish and dropping it into her big cast iron skillet that was filled with hot cooking oil to fry the last of the fish on her old cast iron wood cook stove that Wilbur had cut up with his Sharpe filet fish knife and degutted on the killing stump down by the barn that hot afternoon where Wilbur killed the chickens for Sunday dinner and the hogs for winter harvest there too. He sold the hog meat cuts made up of regular bacon also fatback bacon and pork shoulder's also pork ribs for family backyard barbecues during the long hot summer and sausage patties to the local people who bought his pig's meat which he hung up most of the meat preserved in salt down in the cold rock lined cellar underneath the farm house for the long winter. He even sold his butcher hog meat to the local meat markets in town to resale.

Wilbur was eating the big mouth bass she had already cooked for him and he was very quiet while he ate which was usually his manner at the supper table.

He was sitting at the farm table quietly eating his catch of the day and enjoying his meal with homemade cole slaw with fried hush puppies that Clara Bell had made with her own two little hands and fried for him, She had froze the other fish Wilbur had caught in the ice box for a rainy day.

"Nothing like fresh fish to end the day with," said Wilbur between bites of his big mouth bass and hush puppies.

"Yes—your right and I love my cat fish fresh from natures kitchen," replied Clara Bell happily who turned over the frying cat fish in the big hot iron skillet with big silver tong's to cook the other side.

Later Clara Bell had a look of enlightenment on her pug nose wire rim spectacle face as she ate the last of the very tasty fresh cat fish at the supper farm table and drank her homemade sweet tea made fresh on her front porch that sunny day in her quart mason jar filled with lemons for flavor which she had immensely enjoyed drinking and eating while Wilbur finished up his stove perked coffee.

"Honey—I'll do the dishes tonight since you cooked this lovely meal you can go get ready for bed and I'll be right up shortly," said Wilbur who grinned back at her.

"Well—Wilbur I do declare you must be in the mood for some kind of loving tonight," replied Clara Bell who giggled and got up and put her dishes in the kitchen sink. She headed out of the kitchen into the hallway and upstairs to get ready for bed.

It was getting close to 9:00 P:M that Sunday night and the young female clerk was getting ready to lock up at the Old Salem's Taylor Shop in Old Salem and head home for the night. She had finished putting the bolts of fine linen and fabric cloth back in the racks in the center isle tables from today's customers which had been a busy one. She had straighten the sewing patterns for clothes and dresses that were on sale on the front tables beside the big front bay window and swept the small sales floor. The overhead shop lights glowed brightly from the long florescent bulbs and the small shop was lit up like daytime inside.

She was behind the sales counter going over to day's

receipts when she heard fingertips drumming on the sales counter behind her and she jumped in her tracks thinking she was about to get robbed.

The young female clerk turned around quickly half scared to death out of her wits and saw a tall dark haired woman in a blue low cut ball gown watching her intently.

The young female clerk grabbed her chest and took a deep breath from her short lived fright.

"You -you-you—sca–sca—scared me—I didn't no anyone was behind me," said the young female clerk who gathered back her composure quickly at seeing it was just a friendly woman at the counter.

"My name is Lady Victoria Basil and I'm here to pick up my dress order and I get that a lot—now a days and you need a new door bell," replied Lady Victoria who just smiled politely to the young female store clerk.

"Let me check in back at the sewing room and see if your dresses are ready from the Taylor and that door bell must be broke or stuck," replied the young female clerk with relief who had gotten some of her short lived nerve back.

She was gone for a short while and came back with several dresses on metal hangers draped over her arm in clear plastic bags. "Yes—they are all finished and the white wedding dress is beautiful which I think you'll agree with me," with said the young female clerk who hung up the dresses on the overhead rack by the hangers beside the sales counter.

"Yes—they have been made to my expectations and I've already seen them the other night," replied Lady Victoria who checked each one with approval.

"Oh—I was off last night—no wonder I don't remember you I usually work days and I'm filling in for tonight because the regular girl was home sick with the flu," said the young female clerk. "That's going around a lot these days because it's the start of the flu season you know and I've seen you around," replied Lady Victoria who looked on with a sweet face. The young female clerk who was now all business rang up her Bill on the cash register.

"That will be 3500.00 dollars and so many people come in here its hard to keep up with everybody and I hope this flu season I don't get it because I got my flu shot the other day," said the young female clerk who waited patently beside the cash register to be paid.

Lady Victoria pulled out a wad of 100 dollar Bills from her right blue vest pocket and counted out the money on the sales counter for the young female store clerk.

The young female store clerk scooped up the money and counted it putting it in the cash register and handing lady Victoria her sales receipt.

"Who's the lucky guy," asked the young female store clerk trying to be nice ?

"Oh—he don't know it yet but I've already picked him out to be my husband," replied Lady Victoria who picked up her dresses and walked down the isle toward the door without another word spoken.

"Congratulations and I hope you have a nice honeymoon," shouted the young female store clerk who fiddled with her ink pen nervously at the sales counter.

The young store clerk dropped her pen and bent down to retrieve it quickly but by the time she stood back up Lady Victoria was gone.

"Funny I didn't hear the door open and shut," mumbled the young female store clerk to herself who walked through the store and opened the door and the bell rang "ding, ding'.

"Well I'll be a monkey's uncle that bell is working just fine, must have been stuck," mumbled the young female store clerk who shut the door and locked it, she went back toward the sales counter to close up for the night without another gullible thought about the strange woman she had encountered tonight.

The next day which was Monday morning Clara Bell who

was clairvoyant and a psychic of the supernatural realm was showing her 10 year old granddaughter Maggie some magic tricks in the attic from days gone by at her farmhouse on Payne Road in Rural Hall like Clara Bell's grandmother had showed her as a little girl.

Clara Bell made the cards disappear in her right hand as she said "hocus- pocus,"and they reappeared in her left hand when she said "al-a-ca-zam,"!

Maggie jumped with delight as she giggled hysterically with her childish laugh "ha, ha, ha," at her grandmother and clapped and maggie said "yea, yea, yea, do it again Grandma,"!

Runt-Runt Clara Bell's black cat which had been the smallest cat in the litter and been named rightly so with blue eyes and no tail which was a rarity in nature was sitting beside the old broken grandfather clock watching the magic show with intelligent blue gleeful eyes.

Clara Bell puled out a gold 20 dollar coin from her pocket wrapped in a handkerchief and held it in her hand between her thumb and forefinger.

"Now watch this," said Clara Bell as she covered her left hand over the coin hiding it from Maggies smiling face then Grandma Clara Bell said "abrakadavbra," and snapped her right hand thumb and fore finger as her left hand flew straight up and the gold coin was gone!

Maggie screamed with delight "eeeeeeeeehhh." Maggie said "that was real cool grandma," as her smiling face lit up with childish life that only a child could possess! Grandma Clara Bell walked over to the little girl and said "what's that behind your ear dear child" as she reached behind the little girls red hair and pulled out the 20 dollar gold coin showing it to the little girls astonished face who screamed with delight and Maggie said"allll—rrright Grandma that was super,"?

"I have one more trick to show you but it must be our secret," said Grandma Clara Bell as she walked over to the far wall and reached behind the old broken grandfather clock and open the glass door to the pendulum.

"I want tell anybody Grandma Clara Bell because I love you," said Maggie as she played with a lock of red hair on her left shoulder with her left hand as she watched her grandma and Runt Runt the black cat with no tail rubbed up against Clara Bell's leg wanting to be rubbed and petted while it meowed "mee—yow, mee—yow,"!

"Not now dear I'll play with you later," said Clara Bell while she stroked her cats back and pushed him gently away.

Clara Bell pushed a lever behind the pendulum at the bottom of the old timey broke grandfather clock and the back panel clicked opened in half because it was a secret hidden half door behind the pendulum.

Clara Bell reached inside and pulled out a twisted old root cane about 3 feet long and elegantly carved with strange symbols that were X's for evil, crosses (+) for good, a diamond symbol for the lost tribe of juda which some say it's the Cherokee nation and the diamond symbol also represents the bible with O for the symbol for life.

"What's that Grandma," asked Maggie with a astonished curiosity that filled her little mind? "It's a Louisiana twisted swamp root magic cane from the bayou," replied Grandam Clara Bell as she held it in her right hand.

"A old black slave named Latasha cut this cane from a swamp tree at the root base that grew down into the bayou swamp water and in a place she only new and some say that part of the swamp was haunted.

She carved these magic signs in the cane to hold her good spells forever and to defeat the dark satanic forces of evil! Latasha was rumored to be a witch and practice black magic but she was really a good sorceress but new the ways of good white bayou magic and the arts of black magic too.

The art of good white bayou magic was handed down through generations of slaves in her family. Some people feared her as her fame spread for casting spells for people who came to her looking for magic spells of good and also evil voodoo but she only did good spells and the hatred of bad people looking to harm their enemies caused their on bad spells to come back on them for punishment, my own grandma told me all about her when I was a little girl long ago.

My own grandmother Anna summoned her up once from the Alter Realm with a magic spell from this magic cane to introduce me to her and I met her again as a teenager child once at my special school where she was my master teacher," said Grandma Clara Bell with a proud smile on her face remembering her child hood years.

Clara Bell was thirteen years old and sitting in Heaven Gates class of sorcerers and good Witches white magic class at the big Gothic white stone castle Splendor, that was surrounded by the water of life moat in the Alter Realm at Heavens Gates.

That was on a immense white floating asteroid just outside the moon's gravity which was the gateway to Heaven.

It was invisible too the naked eye down below on the earth and naturally hidden from the earths telescopes because it blended in with the moons white landscape, that was it's natural cloak of secrecy.

Clara Bell was playing with her long blonde pig tails and dreaming about meeting the cute little red haired boy sitting in front of her.

She was sitting on her small floating cloud pillow at her floating cloud desk in the center of the courtyard of the centuries old Gothic castle along with the other chosen children brought here by their grandmas to learn the art of white sorcerers magic whom set off to one side at the school doing their knitting until class was over to go home.

The white stone laid court yard was filled with all kinds of strange plants and flowers in earthen pots along the castle white stone walls. Shields of Gods great armies hung on some of the other castle walls with the insignia of the "Coat Of Arms" cross emblazon on the fighting shields of Gods righteous armies. Planted in six ancient Egyptian carved pots around the inner court yard were the tree of sin, tree of goodness, tree of innocense and gullibility, tree of wisdom, tree of death also the tree of life. They all were taught about the knowledge that each of the trees possessed and learned from them by their teacher swamp witch Latasha who taught them well.

Clara Bell had boringly watched overhead the Guardian Angels going and coming from Heaven above down to earth and back to do good deeds or miracles on earth far down below.

She had also watched the Elite Guardian Angels from 7th Heaven bringing new souls down to earth to be born from Heaven above and she saw the dearly departed souls being brought back to Heaven by Elite Guardian Angels who carried their spiritual burden back to the well of souls in 7th Heaven.

She had watched the big black rain clouds go by overhead headed to earth to blend in with the storms down below sent by God to grow things on earth with his special rain growing formula being pushed along by work Angels.

Swamp witch Latasha was giving a demonstration on a magic potion up front at her floating cloud stone podium and she noticed all the other kids in class had her undivided attention except Clara Bell whom she saw was day dreaming at her floating cloud desk.

"Clara Bell—can you tell me the secret main ingredient for the magic potion "Beauty is in the eye of the beholder," asked swamp witch Latasha who patted her foot impatiently waiting for a response on her stone white podium while standing on a floating cloud in the courtyard above everyone else?

Clara Bell snapped to attention embarrassed at being caught off guard and daydreaming and started flipping through her Good Book to the right spot and she quickly read the potion spell.

"It-it-it-it—is the dried heart of a female dragon fly that God sends his love on its wings with a prayer to the four corners of the earth," replied Clara Bell who was scared straight to attention in her pillow seat with her heart beating fast.

She was scared that she was getting into trouble with her teacher and would be punished..

"That's—right—good work Clara Bell—my young apprentice—great comeback—you'll go far. Please pay attention to what the class is doing and quit daydreaming you might need this someday in someway to help somebody or yourself," said swamp witch Latasha who slightly scolded her and continued on with her days lesson for the class.

Clara Bell looked over at her Grandmother for support who was sitting with the other Grandmothers over by the Hall of great Angel Statues in the courtyard knitting who only flashed her a—you better behave and learn smile back at her nicely.

That made her feel some better and she was all eyes and ears for her teacher from then on out.

Moses and Arron the anointed high priest of the Alter Realm at Heavens Gates who were dressed in long flowing white robes had come out onto the top balcony with their staffs in hand which had a big banner with a golden cross on it hanging over the balcony stone railing under one of the four watch tower's that rose high in space above them where Guardian Angel Watch Tower sentries where on duty guarding the castle. They had come out of one of the big main inner chamber room castle wings, that was lit up with a bright yellow light from inside the great chamber, that radiated outward from the massive stone doorway.

"God is pleased with the Good Book knowledge the little blonde haired girl with braided pig tails named Clara Bell has shown to everyone here. She will do well in the Lords service fighting evil where ever it may be," said Moses who looked on at Aaron who nodded his approval.

Moses fearsome eyes watched for awhile taking in the classroom and the Grandma's sitting silently down below knitting and waiting for class to be over for their grandchildren in the massive courtyard who then gave a pleasing smile on his stone cold rugged glowing bearded face at the children hard at work in class who then turned to go back into the inner chamber where God dwelt for matters that only concerned him and he vanished into the bright yellow light behind Aaron who stood watching the class down below from his high balcony with intense interest on his bearded glowing face.

Later when class was over Clara Bell had watched all the other boys and girls fly off on their magic canes with their Grandma's to the far corners of the earth after saying good-by and she climbed onto the magic cane behind her Grandma who slipped her shoulder straps from her knitting bag over her left shoulder tucked under her armpit safely for them to return home.

"Incitatus—take off," commanded Grandma Anna and a white thrusting six foot light shot out of the end of the glowing magic cane back behind Clara Bell that enveloped them from the magic cane shaft in a air tight safety shield light for the ride back to earth that empowered the cane to take flight and they lifted up from the courtyard of the castle and flew off over the castle wall out into outer space.

Afterwards Clara Bell in back was holding on tightly to her Grandma's waist with her small arms and hands holding on for dear life and her Grandma in front was flying through the stratosphere on the magic cane back to earth, then they entered the troposphere that was six miles wide in the sky beginning at the base of the earth that stretches back up to the stratosphere and it is the air that give's life to the planet's inhabitant's that God made with his own two mighty hands and they glided through the large rainbow that was left over from the thunderstorms of clouds from Heavens Gates that had moved off headed North up the long coast to soak the

Northwest land mass with life giving rain water for the crops, farms and lakes.

They soared down to the earth at subsonic speed that seemed to rush up at them at great breath taking speed. Anna turned the magic cane handle left and they turned left in a big long sweeping arc out over the Atlantic ocean coming down out of the low lying clouds and then Anna turned the cane handle straight up with her hands leveling off the flying magic cane at twenty-five hundred feet across the top of the great ocean headed west to the seashores of North Carolina. They soon landed in the backyard of her Grandmother's house in Winston-Salem at no time at all and it was well past mid afternoon and with a hovering gentle soft landing on the backyard grass.

"Ne-plus-ultra —stop," commanded Grandma Anna and the cane's powerful flying light went dim and flamed out in the end of the cane back behind Clara Bell and they both hopped off the magic cane onto the firm ground.

"You had better listen to the teachings up there. You have been chosen as a Centurion keeper of King Solomon's magic seals of sorcery which is a secret society here on earth and you will be a trained sorceress the rest of your good life to fight evil on this earth, when called upon by God who has chosen you," said her Grandmother who leaned on her old craved cane handle for support with her right hand and let her knitting bag slide from her left shoulder down to her left hand that quickly grasped it.

"Yes—I want to learn everything there is about the Good Book and being a sorceress and to serve God," replied Clara Bell who fiddled with her blonde pig tail nervously hoping to get her Grandma's approval.

"Go on and play in the back yard while I go in and fix supper. Don't worry about it—you'll be fine and I'll call you when supper's ready and I love you dear child," said her beaming Grandma Anna who proudly walked across the backyard aided by her cane and unlocked her back kitchen door with her house key from her white apron pocket after she stuck the old cane handle in the crook of her left arm and went inside and shut the door quietly.

Clara Bell skipped off happily like an obedient child who was pleased at what praise she had heard from her Grandma. She hurried with a happy heart to go swing on her swing set in the backyard and play and have adventurous fun like a nice normal kid.

Clara Bell smiled remembering back that very day long ago and she had used that very potion to get her husband Wilbur to fall in love with her and he all ways said she was the beauty of his eye and she smiled silly to herself and went back to telling her granddaughter about the story about the cane.

"The cane was dipped in a big boiling magic pot and blessed with good white spells after which she carved the white magic bayou signs in the cane. It can only do good spells but not evil spells.

It can fight the powers of evil with its magic light spells and hopefully defeat evil with its magic light powers," said Grandma Clara Bell as she held the cane out so Maggie could see it in all its splendid glory. Grandma Clara Bell walked over to a old dresser drawer and pulled it out.

She rummaged around in the drawer and pulled out a old jewelry box and walked back away's as she sat it on the floor in the middle of the attic.

"Now watch," said Grandma Clara Bell as she walked up beside Maggie and turned around facing the jewelry box.

"Unum E Pluribus Unum, Abner father of light come forth," spoke grandma Clara Bell with a strong authority voice as she held the cane in her right hand and pointed the end of the cane at the jewelry box on the floor some distance away from them.

To Maggie's astonished eyes the end of the cane glowed white and a bright beam of white light shot forth striking the jewelry box. Grandma Clara Bell lifted the cane up and the jewelry box was levitated up in the air over their heads by white magic.

Runt Runt the black cat with no tail watched with intelligent eyes as the jewelry box left the floor and his head moved straight up in the air with his bright blue eyes following and watching the jewelry box floating in the air.

Maggie screamed "yeeeaaaah" and danced with delight as she watched in amazement at the powers of the magic light before her very eyes as the attic lit up from the bright beam of light. Grandma Clara Bell spoke again "Hermon—Excelsior" and the jewelry box moved up to the highest peak of the roof as it spun around in the beam of white magic light and the lid popped open.

A little ballerina popped out and started to spin around and dance to the melody of a waltz of the music inside the jewelry box. Then Grandma Clara Bell shouted out " Enchantment, Exodus" and the cane was lowered to the floor as the beam of white light faded and went out as the jewelry box sat back gently down on the floor. The lid snapped closed and all was quiet as Maggie looked in awe at the magic cane that Grandma was now leaning on with her right hand in the dim light of the attic bulb overhead.

"That's enough for one day—dear," said Grandma Clara Bell as she put the magic cane back in it's secret hiding place in the old grandfather clock and shut the half secret door behind the pendulum then shutting the glass door.

"Lets go down the stairs and fix lunch, Wilbur will becoming in for lunch from his fields and your father will be getting off work at the Stoke's County Sheriff's office to come and take you home," said Grandma Clara Bell as she ushered the little red hair granddaughter down the attic stairs followed by Runt Runt the black cat with no tail as she cut the attic light off at the stair wall and they were gone as their steps faded away down the stairs into the farmhouse!

That same Monday morning Bill waited while the phone rang at Dicky's office. "Hello— this is the chief of police office, may I help you?" said Pamela the secretary as she waited to see who was calling this morning.

"This is Private Investigator Bill Christian speaking may I talk to the chief of police about the case I'm own," asked Bill as he waited for a response on the phone?

"Let me check with him, hold on," replied Pam as she put Bill on hold for a moment. Pam buzzed the chief of police from her phone after putting Bill on hold. Dicky was going over some paper work on his desk when the phone started buzzing on his desk from Pam his secretary. He put the papers down and grabbed the phone. "What is it Pam," asked Dicky as leaned back in his chair to stretch a little bit?

"Dicky–the private investigator is on line two," spoke Pam the secretary as she waited for Dicky's reply. "I'll take it," replied Dicky on the phone as he reached across his desk and pushed the line two button on his phone.

"Hello—Bill what have you come up with and how can I help you,?" asked Dicky happy to here that Bill had called him so quickly. "Dicky, what do you think about putting a nighttime curfew on the city and letting the public know we have a serial killer or killers on the loose, for the public's safety," asked Bill wondering in the back of his mind if he would consider doing it?

"No- can- do, that would alarm the public and we can't have citizens carrying guns around like it's the old wild, wild west somebody is sure to get hurt from a scared citizens who pulls a gun and shoots somebody accidently for fear of being attacked by a killer on the loose, we have enough of shooting's going on in this big city now which is normal without escalating a gun war by gun toting vigilantes who think they are the law," spoke Dicky as he waited for Bill to reply.

"Well—I thought I'd asked for the safety of the public," said Bill who was a little disappointed on the phone. "Do you have any ideal where your going to start," asked Dicky as he waited for Bill's reply from his end of the phone?

"Well—I thought I'd check out the local Rural Hall railroad depot's since one of the murders happen there along the train tracks. Its as good as anyplace to start with and I might get lucky and catch a crook who returned to the scene of the crime," replied Bill over the phone.

"Good —keep me posted, good-by Bill," said Dicky who was confident he had the right man now on the case.

"Good-by," replied Bill as he hung up the phone and put it back in his cradle on his desk and started thumbing through the rest of the files in the box on his desk.

Around lunch time Bill organized his desk and put the cold case files back in their box on top of his desk and thought he'd grab lunch at the K&W cafeteria down the street from his office which served breakfast, lunch and dinner.

He grabbed his coat off the chair putting it on quick as he opened the door going out then locked up the office door, he went down the sidewalk to his car unlocking it with his keys and getting in shutting the door.

Bill put the keys in the ignition starting the engine and leaving in his Monte Carlo headed to Healy Drive. It was a bright sunshiny and beautiful warm fall day outside as Bill enjoyed the quick drive to the restaurant. Bill pulled in the crowded parking lot and drove down the parking lanes until he found a empty space and pulled in fast and parked his car.

Bill got out and walked around the red brick building heading to the front past the newspaper machines and went inside through the entrance doors. The cold air-condition hit him in square in the face as he went inside and it felt cold to his body for it was a rather hot day outside.

Bill loved the lobby which was decorated like a lounge with a couch and plush chairs to sit in if your other party had not arrived yet. There was plants in hanging baskets around the room and some trees in pots on the floor and a picture of the founder on the far left wall.

Bill walked past the lobby and got in the partitioned line that was roped off on both sides forming a aisle and you just followed the other people until you came to the service line to get your wrapped silverware napkin and tray where the menu board was on the side wall for what they served that day.

Then stacked high in front of you at the start of the cafeteria line was your silverware and tray and you grabbed a clean tray and silverware and put it on the line. You slid your tray down the line and picked your food out.

First was fresh salad and different dressings you could pick from, then all types of jell-O then a buffet line of any kind of southern style cooked food you could ever want behind the glass serving line. Bill didn't want any salad and moved his tray on down the line.

Bill picked country style steak and gravy his favorite. Then mash potatoes with gravy and some turnip greens which the servers handed him on white plates and small white bowls's from over the glass counter top.

At the end Bill got a biscuit and regular coffee as he slid his tray to the end of the line where the lady sat in her seat at the register and totaled up his bill which she handed him.

Bill picked up his tray and headed out to the cafeteria seating room to pick a two seat table by the parking lot window which had a nice view of the buildings and people down the street.

Bill walked across the dining room filled with mostly retired elderly people whom some spoke to him with a smile and a friendly greeting and he took a seat by a window over looking the parking lot, that suited him just fine.

He emptied his tray of food on the table and took his tray over to the center section that had a place to leave your empty tray which was piled up with empty trays.

It was the refreshment center for fresh pots of coffee and

tea also with packs of sugar with half and half creamers, all you wanted. Bill walked back to his table and sat down unfolding his clean white cloth napkin which he put on his lap and dug into his food with his fork for he was terribly hungry.

When Bill finished his food he went to the refreshment center and poured himself another cup of Arabian coffee and walked back to his table as he glanced around the dining room taking everything in with his detective eyes.

Bill saw things were normal as he sat down and listen to the chatter that was going on all around him by the other patrons. Bill finished his last sip of coffee as he sat his white mug down beside his cleaned plates and grabbed his food bill.

He scooted out of his seat and headed for the cashier counter which was at the front of the building beside the exit double doors. Bill handed the older lady who was named Mabel his ticket and she rang up his bill.

"Are you working on a big case Bill and your bill is eight-fifty," spoke Mabel with a smile on her worn tan face but it was a pretty face with blonde hair?

Bill pulled out his wallet and pulled out a twenty dollar bill and paid his bill.

"You might say that, Mabel," replied Bill as he got a tooth pick from the dispenser on the counter and stuck it in the side of his mouth. "I bet detective work is exciting and pays well," said Mabel as she was smiling at Bill as she handed Bill his change back in his out stretched hand.

"Well it's long hours at night and has it's rewards but sometimes it down right boring and sad for the people who hire you to catch their cheating spouses which usually ends up in divorce court. Digging up dirt on people is not my cup of tea but it pays the bill's. What is rewarding is being hired on a case and finding long lost relatives or children and reuniting them with their families, then you know its all worth while.

I don't miss my years on the force because I can work anytime day or night and set my fee and take off when I want too. Have a good day Mabel," replied Bill as he walked out the exit door before she could reply because he was holding up the line of people behind him who were always in a hurry, putting his billfold back in his right side pants pocket and was gone.

The next evening Bill drove to Rural Hall which was known to be the "Garden Spot of the World"and founded in 1952 and incorporated in 1974. He stopped in at Coronet Seafood Restaurant on highway 65 which was owned by a Greek as he pulled into the parking lot that was beside the old 7-11 gas&convenience store where he use to buy beer and cigarettes when he was a teenager just out for a good time on Saturday night with his girlfriend. He parked his car in a empty space out front of the crowded seafood restaurant that was like a one level french design chateau building with a wooden slanted roof that stopped at the top and then it was really flat on top with a tar and gravel roof.

Bill looked to his right and saw the take out building that jutted out from the side of the building which was busy with takeout customers.

He had ordered take out many times on his cases in the area when he didn't want to sit with the public in the restaurant for fear of being noticed. He picked up take out quiet often from Rose the nicest take out waitress he had ever known and who was the flower of his eye but that was another story thought Bill to himself.

Bill locked up his Monte Carlo and walked across the packed parking lot. Bill looked to his left and took a good look at the new city hall building of Rural Hall that had just been recently built some way's down beside the seafood restaurant but was not open to the public yet.

He walked under the roof extension overhead that was sat on two rock columns for cars to drive under to let out customers who didn't want to get wet if it was raining due to bad weather or the elderly or handicap who got out and went into the front door safely.

Bill proceeded to walk under the overhang roof and opened the front door and went inside the restaurant.

The cool air hit him and it felt good. Bill got in line behind people who were in front of him beside the exotic fish tank beside the inner wall and waited for his turn to be seated.

There were big mounted fish on the walls and fish nets strung up along the walls with seashells and pictures of lighthouses on the painted ocean scene wall around the diningroom. Sometime later the pretty brown hair hostess walked up to Bill when it was his turn to be seated and spoke.

"Dinner for one and will it be smoking or nonsmoking—sir," asked the hostess who waited for Bill's answer?

"Smoking and a private booth," requested Bill who acknowledged the hostess polite charm and manner.

"Yes sir—right this way," said the hostess as she went to the cashier counter and grabbed some menu's and motion Bill to follow her into the dining area. Bill walked to the far back wall and the hostess seated him at his booth and handed him a menu.

"Thank-you, this will be fine," said Bill as he picked up the menu and started looking through it while the hostess nodded her approval and left headed back to her station at the front door. Bill new what he already wanted and it was the fisherman's platter which was the specialty of the house it had fried flounder, popcorn shrimp, deep sea scallops, select oysters and deviled crab in the shell.

This was the best seafood restaurant in the triad as far as he was concern. They had the best tartar sauce he had ever tasted. The waitress came up to Bill a pretty young blonde. Her name tag said Wendy on her shirt. "What will you be having tonight— sir," asked Wendy the waitress with a warm smile on her face?

"I'll have the fisherman's platter with a baked potato and regular coffee," replied Bill who grinned at the young waitress.

"Yes sir that's a very popular choice," said Wendy as she took his order and left with the menu Bill handed her.

Later the waitress brought Bill his coffee and Bill took a sip of the rich dark coffee and new this was going to be a good dinner tonight. Bill was eager for his meal and soon the waitress brought his big platter of seafood to him and sat it down on the table before him.

"Anything else for you," asked Wendy nicely to Bill.

"Just a warm up for some more coffee," requested Bill as he dug into his dinner with his fork after he unwrapped his utensils from the paper napkin which he put on his right knee while the waitress went off to get the coffee pot from her station in the kitchen which was hidden behind the decorated long wall with a painted scene of the ocean as she went through the kitchen doors in the wall and disappeared from sight.

Much later that cloudy night Bill had drove back to Winston-Salem to Krispy Kreme doughnut store on Stratford Road to pick up some stake out coffee and doughnuts and had return later to Rural Hall where he had entered the back parking lot of a business through the open gate and backed his Monte Carlo into the parking lot and loading dock of Unique furniture across from the railroad train depot. Bill was backed up against the loading dock and he cut his car off.

Well—lets see if the murderer returns to the scene of the crime tonight thought Bill to himself as he laid back and settled in for the long stake out night watch in his car.

This furniture company made the best bedroom suites money could buy and some of his kin people had worked here over time thought Bill as he surveyed the parking lot but saw no one else.

Bill reached across his seat and open the bag in the seat when his hungry gear had kicked into overdrive after sitting for what seemed like hour's to him. He pulled out a cup of hot coffee and opened the Krispy Kreme box beside the bag in the front seat and fished out a glazed doughnut from the open box.

Bill took a bite and enjoyed the delicious taste of the doughnut as he chewed! "M-M-M-m-m-m," that taste's great," said Bill to himself who chewed on the doughnut and enjoying the sugar high and licking his fingers. Bill reached into the bag and got out some creamers for his coffee which he pulled the lid off of his large coffee and opened the creamers.

He poured them in and took the stir stick from the bag and stirred in the creamers.

Bill took a sip of his Columbian coffee and sat it down on his console between the seats and took another bite of doughnut. Bill relaxed a bit as he leaned back in his seat.

Man this brings back memories when I was a teenager, me and my dad used to buy box's of these Krispy Kreme doughnuts before sunrise. We'd go around to the gas stations and car lots and sell them to the mechanic who worked there to make money for my dad to pay the bill's when painting houses was slack for dear old dad who sometimes rummaged through the trash cans at the car washes for soda pop bottles that were worth money. He even checked the side ditches where people threw them out their car windows while they rode in their car to places on dads route to sell their doughnuts and he'd stop on the highway and pick them up thought Bill who reminisced about the good old days with his dad.

It also put me through college later in life thought Bill who was still sad of his dad's passing a few years ago. He was as honest of a man as they come thought Bill who smiled to himself on a happier note and took a bite of his doughnut and got back to business at hand.

Bill watched the railroad station across from him for any signs of anything unusual.

The Yadkin Valley railroad which was a short line freight hauler operated from Rural Hall to Mount Airy and North

Wilkesboro with coal runs to the Belews Creek Steam Station In Stokes County.

Bill looked around the parking lot of the now dark and deserted furniture plant and it was a cold and overcast fall night. He spotted a pop bottle laying at the foot of the loading dock.

"Man that pop bottle is worth 15 cents and I can't pass that up," said Bill out loud to himself who got out of his car and walked back to the dock and picked up the pop bottle.

He then walked back to his car and opened his door and stuck it in his backseat floorboard. He got back in the front seat and very easy shut his door so that he wouldn't make too much noise to alert anybody he was in the old furniture parking lot.

The moon was hidden from view and sometime's it broke through the clouds for a moment and then disappeared back behind the clouds.

The cars and trucks parked here were a perfect hiding place for surveillance. His car blended right in and no one would suspect anyone was here at this time of night.

Around 11:00 o-clock Bill had eat his next to last doughnut and finished his coffee but had another one in the bag when he heard the horn blow off in the distance of a train "WOO—WOOOOOO, WOO—WOOOOOO" while coming around the bend and rumbling down the long stretch of track headed his way!

Bill watched the train come chugging down the rail tracks with its big light on shining the way into the train depot through the trees and bushes that ran along side the tracks as the vibration from the locomotive and long train of coal cars vibrated his car slightly in the parking lot from the shear power of it all.

The train pulled to a stop amid the other trains parked in the depot train parking station.

Bill saw the fully loaded coal cars back behind the diesel

engine which had the number 66 painted on its front under the trains light and side of the locomotive engine and deduced it was headed to the Belews Creek Steam Station to drop off the coal on a midnight run from Virginia.

The night train switch watch man came out from his shack with a hurricane lantern that was brightly lit. The hurricane lantern lit up the ground in a big circle around the man as he walked toward the diesel engine along the railroad tracks.

The night watchman climbed up the ladder and went aboard with his clipboard for the engineer to sign.

The moon broke out of the clouds just for a second and Bill was looking at the back of the train when to his amazement he saw a dark shadow appear on top of a boxcar of another train that was parked next to the coal train that had just come in.

Bill watched the shadow run the length of the boxcar and with a running jump the shadow did a impossible leap from the edge of the boxcar to the second coal car in back of the diesel train that had just pulled in which was a good 15 foot jump Bill guessed.

Bill was stunned as the shadow blended into the darkness of the coal car and vanished before his very eyes as the light from the moon retreated back into the clouds.

"Bingo—there he goes I hope it's the murderer I'm looking for—Man this is it. Its game time," said Bill out loud to himself to boost his confidence as he pulled out his snub nose 38 with his right hand and pushed the chamber slide as the chamber clicked out and he checked his bullets.

Then he flipped shut the gun chamber and snapped it back in. He put it back in his holster and snapped the leather strap securing it.

Bill grabbed the small flashlight off his front seat and open his car door. Bill put on his detective Stetson tan hat with a black band around the rim and the flashlight in his left tan trench coat pocket as he exited the car.

Bill quietly locked his door and shut it ever so softly until he heard the latch catch and he took off headed toward the coal train. After John the train conductor had signed his john henry on the clipboard for the night switch watchman who got ready to climb back down the ladder from the trains engine.

"I've got a big load to deliver tonight Ed and I'm five minutes behind schedule will you hurry up," said John the train conductor engineer impatiently.

Ed scooted down the ladder and walked under the engineers window on the train engine that John the conductor was leaning out of watching him walk across the train tracks.

"John your always late and in a hurry, just keep your shirt on, or you might wind up like the dead guy in the tree away's back down the track. You have to keep your cool and check everything out to perfection. They haven't caught his murderer yet—you know," said Ed as he walked over to the track switch box on the side of the tracks in front of the trains!

Ed set his hurricane lantern down on the gravel beside the switch box and set his clipboard on top of the switch box as he produced a set of keys and thumbed through them until he found the right one.

"Well that guy probably stuck his nose in somebody's business where it didn't belong and he paid the price," yelled John out the train window to Ed walking across the train track!

He inserted the key into the lock he had grabbed with his left hand as he unlocked the lock and flipped open the big switch box! Their was several levers inside the box and Ed looked them over until he found the right one. "Ahh— here it is and you might be right about that poor dead guy," said Ed out loud over his shoulder to the train conductor John who was watching from his train engine window impatiently as he leaned out the window and yelled again "Com on— I aint got all night Ed," said John the train conductor who looked on with a smirk on his face out the train window.

Ed reached in and grabbed the third lever and pulled it

back at the same time he squeezed the release lever on the handle. The tracks of the middle rails which the coal train was setting on moved over to the left tracks that headed to the steam station at Belews lake.

Ed locked the switch box and grabbed his clipboard off the top of the box with his left hand. Ed reached down and grabbed the hurricane lantern and started swing it back and forth to signal the go ahead for the coal train.

John the train conductor released his brakes and pushed the throttle forward and the coal loaded locomotive moved forward slowly as the box cars jerked and groaned on the tracks as the couplings engaged from the strain of the pull by the trains engine as it started to pick up speed slowly as the diesel engine roared to life.   Bill walked out from the bushes after climbing the furniture makers parking lot fence and walked down the side of the coal train underneath the tall oak trees looking at the long line of coal cars filled to the brim.

Bill was startled and he jumped in his tracks in the gravel beside the train when the cars jerked from the pull of the coal trains engine and made a big metal "clang" as the trains couplings engaged and started to move the coal cars slowly along the tracks!

Bill hadn't seen hide nor hair of the suspect he saw jump on the coal train as he watched the coal train roll down the train tracks picking up speed.

Bill stood there as the coal train was moving by him at a rapid pace as the coal cars rocked from side to side as they picked up break neck speed fast.

Well its now or never and I hope this isn't a grave mistake because I'm alone with no back up and I can't let the opportunity of this man who might be a killer or hobo get away when I've finely got someone to question as to why he's riding the coal trains late at night and this wasn't no midnight love train riding coast to coast with fun loving descent people on it thought Bill as he made his moment of decision and ran after the train.

He ran fast on his feet and grabbed the ladder at the near to last coal car and climbed up until his feet were on the last rung of the ladder.

He was breathing heavy and his heart was pounding as he was holding on for dear life as his tan trench coat flapped in the breeze from the now fast moving coal train!

The night switch watchman was standing there beside the tracks waiting for the coal train to go buy so he could walk across to his shack when the next to last coal car came buy and Ed had a shocked look on his face as he saw Bill holding on for dear life on the coal car ladder as he passed by him with his trench coat flapping in the breeze!

"Dam hobos or nuts always catching a ride or thrill ride and someday their going to get killed on one of these trains if they fall off and fall under the trains wheels and get cut to pieces," said Ed to himself as he shook his head sadly and walked across the train tracks.

He went in his shack door to call John the conductor that he had a hitcher on the coal train.

Bill climbed up the ladder and climbed over the edge of the coal car as they past over the highway 66 train crossing in the town of Rural Hall and he felt the big coal nuggets as he swung his legs over the side of the coal car looking at the flashing red lights of the train crossing.

He crawled into the coal car and his feet sunk down about a foot into the lumps of coal as he stood wobbly to his feet.

Bill reached into his left pocket and pulled out his flashlight and turned it on as the wind rushed buy him as they left the town.

Bill shined the beam of light up ahead of him as he started his search for the mysterious hobo as he looked around this coal car but didn't see anyone so he started wading through the lumps of coal toward the next coal car.

Bill pain staking moved ahead as he lost his balance and almost slipped and fell several times from the loose coal underneath his feet as he put out his right free hand to catch his fall in the coal car.

Man I'm going to get real dirty and black from this coal tonight thought Bill as he made it to the end of the coal car and shined his flashlight on his dirty black right hand.

Bill then shined the small beam of light over to the next coal car and didn't see anyone but his light only went halfway across the old coal car as he straddled the side of the coal car and strained his eyes to see in the darkness ahead of him looking for a shadow of a man that stood out from the dark of night but he didn't see nothing but pitch darkness past his light.

Bill with some disappointment on his face looked for the ladder on the side of the coal car to climb down on and his beam of light spotted it down below him and to his right. Bill scooted over and put his foot on the top rung.

He started down the ladder very carefully until he came to the end rung with his feet and turned to half face the other ladder on the next coal car which he shined his flashlight light on.

Bill looked down at the dark silver tracks beneath his feet rushing by and the coal cars were rocking back and forth from the speed of the racing coal train and his heart was pounding in his chest!

Bills hands were black from coal dust and then it happened the coal car lunged to one side and Bill lost his grip with his right coal black slippery hand.

Instantly he pushed his left arm through the next ladder rung as he fell down the ladder until his armpit hit and was locked downward on the ladder rung as he bent his forearm back up quickly to wedged it between the ladder and coal car.

He quickly clinched his left fist for strength through his

whole arm to hang on while the flashlight almost squeezed out of his hand.

It hurt like hell as the pain shot through his body and then he dropped his flashlight in shear agony while he fought to hold on to the ladder. It banged "clang, thump, clang" against the side of the coal car and was gone under the train!

He almost fell to his death as he slipped down with his feet dangling off the ladder. Bill grabbed the side of the ladder with his right hand and pulled himself back up painfully cussing every moment of the climb back up the ladder until he was standing back on the ladder by his feet.

Bill took a moment to catch his breath and composure and he breathed hard several times!

He felt the pain shoot underneath his armpit as he doubled over from the pain that shot through his body once again as he winced on the ladder holding on tightly!

"Oooah" moaned Bill as he stood there holding onto the ladder tightly for dear life! Man that's gonna be sore tomorrow thought Bill as he exercised his left arm back and forth to work out the pain and gathered his courage!

He decided to climb across the coupling to the next ladder and coal car no matter what happen or how hard it was or risky. He was on a mission and was not about to give up without a fight.

The engineers phone rang on the coal train at that same time "Beep, Beep."

John startled reached over and picked it up with his left hand and put it to his left ear not expecting a emergency call tonight.

"This is John speaking what's up," asked John as he had his right hand on the throttle looking out the trains engineers window at the track in the diesel locomotives head lights? "This is Ed you have a hitch hiker on your train, he got on at the station," said Ed rather annoyed about it.

"Can't do nothing about it until I get to the steam station

and deliver my load of coal. I'm not about to stop out here in the middle of the woods at this late hour to search the train for a stowaway by my self besides I'm running late tonight, thanks for the warning good buddy, good-by Ed" replied John as he throttled up the train to 70 miles per hour and hung up the phone.

Meanwhile Bill was pondering whether or not to go for the next coal car as he gathered his courage up waiting for the right moment when the coal cars quit rocking back and forth and quieted down for a chance to jump across to the other coal car.

Dam— that was scary, almost bought the farm thought Bill as he tightly hung to the ladder not caring about losing the flashlight and he worried about losing his own bright life.

The train hit a long stretch of track and settled down from rocking back and forth some and it was smooth sailing ahead and Bill saw it was his chance now.

He took a deep breath and stuck his left foot on the rocking, shaking train coupling and balanced his self with his foot as he stretched across between the coal box cars and reached for the next ladder.

Bills hand was almost there and then he let go quickly pushing off from his ladder that he was holding onto with his right hand hurling his body across the dangerous void and grabbed the next ladder on the other coal box car with his left hand pulling his body over to the ladder as his feet leaped onto the bottom rung of the ladder.

"Thank God," said Bill out loud excited as he held on to the ladder of the next coal car for a moment in the chase.

Then he started to climb up the ladder! Dam I needed that flashlight, why didn't I put it in my coat pocket before I tried to climbed across the box cars, I'm blind as a bat now thought Bill as he shook his head in disgust as the wind raced across his face and his hat flapped in the wind which he pulled down tightly on his head.

His trench coat flapped just like a washed sheet hanging out on a clothes line in a cool breeze to dry while he fought against the wind that tugged at his body to fly off the train.

Bill made it to the top in no time at all as his eyes looked over the rim of the coal car and then he spotted the big dark silhouette down at the far end of the coal car standing there looking down toward the train engine with one foot propped up on the coal car as if he owned it.

"Finely—I've found my man, its about time," muttered Bill under his labored breath who was glad the chase was almost over.

Bill climbed over the top of the coal car and into the loose coals once again. Bill stood up in the coal car looking at the dark figure who had its back to him but could not make out any details about this mysterious stranger.

Bill cupped his hands over his mouth and got ready to shout above the trains noise.

"Hey— you— there— I want to talk to you," shouted Bill above the noise of the train as he took off wading through the coal toward the dark stranger?

The dark figure jumped in its tracks with cat like reflex's in the coal car as it turned around quickly to see who was behind him. Bill had made it halfway up the coal car when the moon peaked out from behind the cloud cover for a brief instance.

Bill thought he saw a flash of red eyes far off down the coal car from the dark stranger which made him freeze in his tracks for some unknown reason.

Bill felt the deep sensation of fear well up in his throat and he started to pull his coat back to go for his gun. The moon disappeared behind the clouds again and all was dark again.

Then incredibly the dark stranger took off running through the coal car at break neck speed and was on top of Bill before he could go for his gun!

The dark figure was incredibly fast and grabbed Bills right wrist like a vice with its left hand. Bill saw the man was a white male very big, about 20 something with a rock looking face hidden in the shadow of night as they met eye to eye so to speak and then he was grabbed around the throat by the strangers strong right hand choking him until he could hardly breath.

Bill fought to speak but the man talked to him in a rough voice as he held him effortlessly.

"You've at the end of the line here and your poking your nose into my business and you'd better let sleeping dogs lie, that's not any of your business, if you want to keep on breathing this is your stop," said the dark stranger as he held Bill in his cold hard grip.

Bill reached with his left hand and grabbed the mans front breast pocket and tried to push the man away and felt paper in his hand from the shirt pocket of the dark stranger which instantly he clutched at it with his left hand.

Lightening fast the dark stranger lifted Bill up over his head as if he was light as a feather and threw him back down the coal car!

Bill felt the sensation of flying as what seemed like an eternity as he hit the coals, plowing through them and slid to a stop up against the back of the coal car which banged his head pretty hard!

Bill shook his head trying to stay focus and not loose consciousness from the blow to the back of his head as he looked on at the dark hitcher standing in the middle of the coal car glaring at him with red eyes he thought as he rose groggily to his feet trying to clear his mind from the bump on his head that hurt like hell, man I'm glad he didn't throw me over the side of the coal car thought Bill and then instantly the dark stranger was on him again covering the distance in a flash!

Bill quick thinking stuck the paper he still had in his left hand in his left coat pocket and prepared to fight for his life as he now felt real danger from this man with incredible strength. Bill didn't have time to go for his gun again but swung a round house right at the man as he appeared in front of him in a flash!

"Smack" was the sound as Bill hit the man dead on the face with full force that has knocked many a man down but with little effect this time as he tried to defend his self!

The blow glanced off the dark stranger not even fazing him and then the man hit Bill with a smashing right arm backhand blow across the right side of his body hard and Bill was violently knocked out of his tracks in the coal which flew from his feet in all directions!

Bill sailed through the air from the incredible powerful blow and his body landed partially half over on the left side corner of the coal car with the powerful force of the wind pulling at his body!

Bill then tumbled over the side of the coal car from his own momentum and the wind rushing by him at a terrific force that seemed to latch onto his body! Bill desperately groped and grabbed with his hands for the side of the coal car to save his life as he slipped over to almost certain death beneath the trains steel wheels which would most certainly suck him in and cut him to pieces!

Bill then found himself dangling on the side of the coal car by his left hand that had just barely saved him from certain death as the force of the wind rushed by him pulling at his hanging body to let go and be dragged into the steel wheels beneath his dangling feet by the fast moving rocking train!

Bill with terror filled eyes fought desperately to hold on by a thread while his heart beat like thunder in his chest and he knew it was either life if he grabbed hold with his free hand or certain death if he failed in a matter of seconds as he mustered up the courage and tried grabbing the top of the coal car with his right hand being pushed along by his Guardian Angel unbeknownst to Bill who was hovering just behind his right shoulder which after a superhuman effort that welled up from inside him to live, he did just that!

"Thank-God," cried out Bill in relief who held on for dear life while his coat flapped roughly in the wind behind him kicked up by the fast moving coal train.

The dark stranger suddenly appeared menacing from over the top of the coal car watching him with a evil white smile and Bill new this was it and he had lost the good fight.

Bill looked up at the dark stranger with defiance on his face as he held on to the side of the coal car with a death grip who then lifted his right leg up to smash Bills left hand with his foot.

"Shit," Bill hollered out loud in desperation at seeing his adversary about to do him in with a fatal blow. Bill's quick thinking, new he had not a moment to lose and pulled his feet underneath him and releasing his grip at the same time pushing himself away from the side of the fast coal car with his strong legs so he wouldn't fall and be sucked in by the strong air flow underneath the trains steel wheels.

The dark stranger looked on in shock and disappointment of not finishing the life and death fight to the very end which eluded him while he watched Bill cheat death as Bill fell away from the side of the racing coal train boxcar saving himself and out into thin air.

Bill fell backward into space circling his arms straight out from his body trying to balance and stay straight up on his feet in the air and the sensation of falling made him feel sick to his stomach, but he kept his head hoping he had cleared the train and pulled his feet under him as his feet impacted on the hard gravel and he fell backwards doing a roll over several times on the hard gravel until he fell into the bushes off to the side of the track!

Bill laid there for some time catching his breath as he lifted his aching head and bruised body watching the train go rumbling by until it was gone in the dark of night and he was all alone beside the train tracks except for the crickets who chirped off in the distance in the dark woods beside him.

Well that didn't work out to good and man I didn't see that one coming thought Bill as he untangled himself from the scratchy bushes very slowly as he rose to his feet and checked himself for any broken bones as he felt his legs and moved his arms back and forth and he seemed to be alright.

Bill checked his 38 snub nose and it was still strapped tightly in its holster on his right hip.

Lucky to be alive thought Bill as he reached back into the bushes with his right hand and grabbed his hat out of the bushes where he had fell and started hitting his pants legs with the detective hat madly back and forth knocking the dust and coal dust off his pants legs.

Bill rubbed his sore throat with his right hand and he wondered if he had any welt marks on his neck from the hobo on the train with the red eyes and he thought he was seeing things or his imagination had run frightening wild during the fight over the coal car which he had lost.

Bill stood back up finely as he stretched his back by leaning way back with his hands on his hips and put his detective hat back on his head and bent the brim slightly down on his face and very dignified started walking back down the train tracks toward the Rural Hall train depot.

Bill had been walking for about 45 minutes down the middle of the train tracks in the dark when he saw something shiny up ahead. Bill was stepping across the railroad ties very rapidly now thinking that might be what was left of his flashlight!

After a few minutes Bill got to the shiny object and low and behold it was his flashlight after all laying inside the train track up against the rail.

He bent over and reached down and picked up his flashlight with his right hand.

He looked it over in his hand. It was dented and scratched up a little bit but in one piece and the glass lens wasn't broken to his amazement.

Bill pointed the flash light toward the ground and pushed the on button and the beam shot out onto the ground.

Good it still works what luck thought Bill as he cut the light off and kept on walking down the railroad ties on the train tracks.

A good hour later he saw the outline in the overcast night of the antic stores beside the railroad tracks in Rural Hall and Bill Made a sign of relief "whew" while he walked quietly down the train tracks.

He new he had finely made it back where he had started from and he pulled back his suit and tan trench coat sleeves and looked at his watch and pushed the light button and it was about 3:00 o-clock A:M in the morning accordingly to his watch on his left wrist.

Bill started across the railroad train crossing on the highway 66 road as he felt hard pavement under his feet once again.

He walked across the road and down the side street that ran concurrent with the tracks.

Bill passed by the small shops and the little red caboose hotdog restaurant walking a faster pace because he was sore and tired and wanted to get home. He saw the night switch watchman lighted shack over by the train yard as he crossed the street to Unigue furniture parking lot.

Bill walked through the open furniture parking lot gate and over to his car by the loading dock. Bill fished out his keys and unlocked the car and opened the car door.

He slowly and stiffly got in shutting the door. Bill wiggled down into the leather seat and tried to relax his now sore body and stuck the key in the ignition switch and started the car.

He rolled down his window and sat there quietly letting the car warm up while he checked his coat pockets for his pack of cigarettes.

Bill pulled out the paper from his left pocket with a surprised look on his face knowing in all the ruckus back at the train fight he had forgot about the mysterious paper he had pulled from the front shirt pocket of his dark stranger suspect on the train and quick thinking stuck it in his coat pocket quickly during his altercation with the dark stranger! Bill cut on his dome light and quickly unfolded the paper.

Bill was astonished as he grinned at his luck for it was a brochure of old Bethabara the first German settlement in North Carolina. It was a detailed map of the old settlement and fort with the old cemetery of Gods Acre back up the hill above the settlement.

Bill reasoned this was a brochure for tourist who visited the old settlement and fort. Well he had found his first real clue after all the sacrifices he had made tonight and had almost died for.

Bill laid the brochure map on his front seat and searched his pockets and found his mashed and flatten pack of cigarettes. Bill pulled out one cigarette and it was broken and he pitched it out the window, after finding a couple of more broken cigarettes he finely found one that wasn't broken in the crushed pack, sticking it between his lips and pushed in the car cigarette lighter and waited for it to pop back out. After a minute the cigarette lighter popped out "pop" red hot on the end of the tiny coils!

Bill reached for it and brought the heated coil end of the cigarette lighter up to his mouth to light the cigarette.

He started puffing the cigarette until it lit up, glowing red on the end. Bill took a long deep drag on the cigarette to settled his frayed nerves and blew out the smoke into the car as it drifted lazy out the car window on the nights cool air breeze.

Man I needed that, what a relief as the cigarette dangled in his right fingers while he laid his hand over the steering wheel. I'll have to stake that place out tomorrow night or the next night and maybe that dark stranger will show up again and I'll nab him this time and I'll be ready for him, he want catch me flat footed this time thought Bill sticking the cigarette back in his lips as he reached for the gear shift with his right hand.

Bill put the car in drive and mashed the gas pedal ever so lightly and the car moved forward1 He drove out of the Unigue furniture parking lot and turned left down the neighborhood street onto highway 66 and headed home.

The diesel train pulled slowly down the back of the Belews Creek Steam Station on the rail road tracks beside the huge piles of coal. John the train engineer blew his train whistle "WOOOO— WOOOO," as a signal that he was coming in to the well lighted plant! John looked up at the two massive smoke stacks that towered overhead and the white smoke that billowed out and trailed off into the cool night air!

The clouds had started parting now and the moon was out and very bright. The dark stranger on one of the coal cars howled out at the moon at the same time as John blew his trains whistle "AHHHHHH—WHOOOOO-O-O-O," as the metamorphous began and his howl was covered up by the trains loud whistle!

His feet busted out of his shoes as they grew into big claw feet also his hands grew into big clawed paws.

The hairs came out the pores on all over his skin as his chest grew big and his shirt and pants busted to shreds from the pressure of his body growing big and tall.

The mans face changed as the nose grew into a long wolfs nose with the mans teeth growing into big drooling fangs.

His ears grew into big long pointed ears. The eyes grew red and wild looking and the beast of a werewolf stood on the coal car in all its devilish glory.

It howled at the moon "AHHHHHH—WHOOOOOO," and leaped over the side of the coal car as it landed on its hind legs and it looked down the tracks with red hateful filled eyes and up the tracks for any signs it had been discovered by some unsuspecting person who then would be its next victim and then it climbed the mountain of coal in a flash up over the top past the big conveyor and disappeared into the night searching for it's prey with a fiendish fury.

John had throttled the train down to a stop and pulled back the brake lever locking the train in its tracks.

John checked his twenty-five year railroad pocket watch and saw he was five minutes late it was a little after 3:00 o-clock A:M which he stuck back in his bibbed overhauls side pocket.

He then reached for his flashlight in his tool box on the floor and moved out of the engine room and climbed down the ladder as he flipped the button on the flash light.

The beam shot out into the night air and he walked along the train checking each coal car for any hitch hikers or hobos.

After some time of climbing the ladders on the coal cars one by one and shining his flashlight into the coal cars looking for anybody until the very last one and he saw no sign of anybody.

Well he must have jumped off before he got here thought John to himself as he walked back to the diesel locomotive to unhook the coupling to drop off the coal cars here at the steam sation to be unloaded and make his return to Rural Hall.

John saw the security guard from the gate house walking beside the train toward him to sign his clipboard. I'll call ED after I'm done here and let him know, I didn't find any hitch hikers or hobos on the train thought John as he waved at the security guard who now approached him as he moved in between the diesel engine and the coal car to unhooked the trains coupling.

Sometime after midnight that had come and gone in the early morning hours just before dawn, the man who had been awoken in his bed by his dog barking "ARF, ARF," at something down near the lake next to his boat house where it was chained up at beside its doghouse and he had no earthly ideal that something evil was lurking around his lake house in the darkness of shadowy night.

The man cut on his bedside table lamp light and put on his glasses. "What is it honey," asked his wife beside him as she yawed at this late hour laying in the queen bed on her side?

"Oh—probably nothing sugar but I'd better check, might be a prowler or just a hungry raccoon that old dog is barking his head off at," replied the husband as he stood up from the bed putting on his bed shoes and robe.

The man opened the drawer on the night table and took out a small flashlight. He clicked it off and on making sure it worked and saw it did with a flash of light in his face. He walked across the bedroom loft and headed down the stairs.

The man came out in the living room and turned toward the kitchen headed for the back door but he failed to see the big tall shadow pass by the bay window outside and disappear around the house behind him.

The man went through the kitchen and flipped on the light as the kitchen light came on. He crossed the tile floor of the lake house until he came to the back door.

He moved the curtain back and saw lady their German Shepard dog chained to her dog house by the dock down by the lighted boat house barking her head off at something "ARF, ARF," she had seen on the property at the lake house!

He saw no one on the lighted boat dock and the boat house doors were shut and locked from what he could see out the back kitchen door window pane.

He looked all around the property from the kitchen back door and didn't see anything unusual or out of the ordinary.

He didn't notice the insects had stopped chirping their nightly chorus in the yard and it was deathly quiet outside.

Must be a raccoon thought the man and he turned around and headed back through the kitchen cutting off the light as he went into the living room.

Then he walked past the couch and fireplace to the big

beautiful bay windows which each window with six panes slid up and down for the cool summers breeze on the lake at night which were closed and locked tight. He pulled back the long white curtain and looked out over the wooded side lawn and lake but saw nothing but a few trees and bushes on the property and the shoreline of the lake in the moon light.

"Hummm— must be a racoon again," said the man as he let the curtain go back in place and started to turn around to leave the living room.

He heard glass breaking behind him " SMASH, SMASH," as he jumped from fear in his tracks and looked down and saw two big hairy arms encircle his waist from out of thin air behind him he quickly thought to himself "oh shit" with big fearful eyes on a shocked face! Then he hollered in pain "AHHHHHH,"s as the huge claws from the werewolf's hands dung into his front chest, tearing through the robe and into his white flesh that quickly oozed red blood out from the chest wounds and stained the front of his white robe where the claws had latched on to him with concrete force!

The man dropped his flashlight and grabbed them with his small hands and fought to break free like a bug caught in a praying mantis deadly hands then screamed in fear again after his feeble attempt to break free failed miserably "AHHHHHHH," as he was violently jerked back through the breaking wood and smashing window as he was pulled outside with a supernatural power not of this earth! The werewolf howled with frightening terror from the threshold of Hell in its throat "AHHHHHH—WHOOOOO-O-O-O," as it played with its prey in its arms! Then it growled "ARRRGH,! ARRRGH,!" at the bleeding terrified man in its massive arms who wiggled frightfully to break free with terror filled eyes in a hopeless dazed unbelieving face as the man turned his head looking up into the red dreadful eyes that had no soul at the mighty beast that held him in a death lock.

The man struggled in the werewolf's arms again as the

man fought for his life and the werewolf bit down on the mans jugular vein in his neck as blood gushed out the side of the mans neck and blood ran down his white robe who then went limp from shock at the quick loss of blood from the savage attack!

The werewolf with blood dripping from its massive jaws threw the man down on the ground pinning him with its body weight.

The werewolf howled at the moon standing partially up over the limp form "AHHHHHH—WHOOOOO-O-O-O," with a blood lust from its fiery enraged mind, that had driven it insane long ago!

Then it went for the kill as it dug its sharp claws into the mans chest ripping it open and tearing out the chest bone as the blood flowed thick from the hideous wounds and down the mans stomach and sides.

His ripped white robe was now crimson red with blood amid the tatters of what was once a nice robe. The werewolf opened its massive drooling jaws that were dripping wet with blood and growling ferocious "ARRRGH!, ARRRGH!," and it bit down into the mans bloody and ripped chest who was then violently shook back and forth by the werewolf's massive and powerful jaws which then began to tear out the mans heart in one powerful swift jaw pulling bite as tissue and bone popped and tore apart!

The man gurgled hideously from his throat as he gasped for a last breath "Urrr, Urrr, Urrr," as blood flowed from his mouth and he died instantly into the darkness of death that had come for him!

The werewolf rose its massive head with the mans still beating heart in its massive long drooling snout and chewed the heart up with its gleaming big fanged teeth swallowing every piece until it was bloody gone and then it stood looking with big yellow cat like eyes over the dead murdered body and howled at the moon as blood dripped from its long black quivering lips "AHHHHHH—WHOOOO-O-O-O-O,"!

Then it looked around the yard for anything else to attack and then it saw no threat and ran off on all fours as if Hell was moving across the lake yard in a blur into the woods behind the lake house and was gone in the shadows with its thirst for blood quenched in its evil heart.

The terrified wife in the upstairs bedroom heard her husband scream in terror downstairs in the living room amid the breaking wood and smashing of glass as she was shocked out of her half daze of sleep and startled sat straight up in her bed wide awake listening to all the racket and fighting downstairs.

"David are you alright?," shouted the woman as she waited for her husband to respond from downstairs to her voice up stairs but she heard only fighting going on somewhere outside her lake house.

"David in Gods name answer me?,' screamed the wife but she heard nothing but a terrible howling outside the lake house.

With a trembling hand she new they were in deep trouble from the frightful wolfs howls outside or some unknown prowler that might have attached her husband, she had heard outside and grabbed the phone on her bedside night table and called 911 for help. After what seemed like a eternity listening to the dialing tone of the phone ringing, the young scared woman heard help at last on the phone in her hot sweating hand.

"This is Stokes County 911 what is your emergency," asked the dispatcher? "M-M-M-My husband woke up and heard our da-da-dog bark- bark- barking outside and went to-to-to investigate but all I heard was a lot of noise like glass breaking or something and screa-screa-screaming somewhere outside and my husband did-did-didn't answer me when I shouted for him downstairs to see if everything was alright," said the frighten woman who shook uncontrollable in her bed.

"Listen—if you have a prowler on the property and he's broken into your house and your husband not answering you calls after he went to investigate then you have to protect yourself first and worry about him later. Quickly go lock your bedroom door, the Stokes County Sheriffs deputy's are en route to your home right now and stay on the phone with me until they arrive there," said the sheriffs dispatcher to the young woman on the phone who quickly dropped the phone on the bed.

Then she ran to the bedroom door and shut it locking it and ran back to the bed and jumped in it grabbing the phone off the bed as she talked to the lady at 911 emergency on the phone and she nervously watched the locked door to her bedroom with a frighten face from fear of the unknown demon's that now came screaming back from her childhood past into her frighten mind that just might come and knock her door down and get her too and she trembled on the bed holding on to her life line with a death grip on the phone wishing her dad was here to shoo them away and comfort her that everything would be alright and she could go back to sleep in her warm safe bed.

It was just about sun up when Bill got home and striped down to his underwear and put on his pajamas.

Bill had just crawled into his king size bed and almost fell asleep completely exhausted. Bill had just started to snore when his phone rang on the bedside night table "Beep, Beep."

"Now what is it," said Bill very sleepily as he reached over and cut on his lamp.

Bill picked up the phone, "Hello who is it," asked Bill while he waited for a few moments?

"Its police chief Dicky Poser calling, Bill I hate to wake you this morning but there's been another murder out at Belews lake," said Dicky with concern in his voice.

"Oh—I was just out in that vicinity tonight doing a little detective work that kind of fell to the way side of the tracks— I was just trying to catch a few winks after coming back here in one piece, give me the address and who's on the murder scene," replied Bill as he grabbed the pad and pen off his bedside table?

"The Stokes County Sheriffs department is on the murder scene and here's the address 1445 Pine Hall Road. It's a water front lake house Bill and you can tell me later what didn't pan out for you tonight," replied Chief Dicky a little depressed about the whole situation as he waited on the phone for Bill's response.

"Well— I'll get on my clothes and head right out there, I know those good old boys, I helped them on a case once a long time ago and I'll catch you later," said Bill as he leaned over the bed with his hand rubbing his forehead with worry while he held the phone to his ear in the other then he wrote down the address on the pad which he had laid on the bed then placed it on the bedside table.

"Good— Bill—keep me posted—good-by," said Dicky and he hung up the phone. "Good-by," said Bill as he put the phone back in its cradle on the bedside night table. Bill sat on the bed for a few minutes wondering if the man he chased tonight on the coal train was indeed the murderer he was looking for who just might have committed another murder because he got away and eluded him tonight, but he didn't know at this point in his investigation.

I'll take a quick shave and shower and put on a fresh suit and begone before you know it thought Bill who jumped back into action with renewed energy.

He got up from the bed and headed straight to his big bathroom, because he had more work to do.

After awhile Bill was standing on his bathroom floor drying off his wet body with a towel.

Bill felt squeaky clean from his shave and shower. The

steam still clouded up the bath room medicine cabinet mirror in front of him and distorted Bill's ghostly face as he looked deep into the mirror while he wiped off the fogged up mirror with his right hand and he grinned in the mirror that he was now ready for action and adventure of what ever lay ahead.

Bill pitched the wet towel over the shower curtain rail and walked out of the bathroom humming to himself to his bedroom closet for a fresh clean suit which he quickly pulled from a hanger and threw it on his bed and got clean underwear from his Chest of drawlers and hastily put them on over his naked body.

Bill quickly started to get dressed for the new murder was on his keen mind once again and he was eager to get to the new crime scene.

Sometime later that cold fall morning Bill pulled down the long gravel driveway to the lake house off of Pine Hall Road in Stokes County after showing his I.D. badge to the Stokes County Sheriff's deputy who had the driveway blocked with his patrol car who let him by. Bill drove on down the driveway until he came to the lake house and then drove by the Sheriff's cars parked in front of the lake house and parked beside the rescue squads vehicle which had the back double doors open off to one side of the lake house.

The place was crawling with law enforcement officers checking the grounds for clues and Bill watched the controlled chaos from his car with deep admiration for hard well trained police work. Bill sat in his car and observed the tracking dogs with the Sheriffs dept canine officers unit over beside the house as they tried to pick up a trail of the killer. Bill sat there and watched the dogs growl at the scent "GRRRRR, GRRRRR,", but they refused to follow it.

The Sheriff's officers kept prodding and giving commands to the dogs to follow the tracks but they turned cowardly with their tails between their legs and went back toward there brown Sheriffs canine unit cars whining as they scampered along pulling there masters along as they tried to stop them.

That was strange thought Bill who had seen enough as he got out of his car and walked over to the lake house to get into the thick of things.

The locus delicti which is Latin for "crime scene" was roped off with crime scene tape that was tied around some trees outside a bay looking window that was half tore out and on the ground outside the house thought Bill who gave the scene the once over.

The victim was covered with a white sheet still laying on the ground where he was possibly attacked and killed. The Stokes County sheriffs detectives where going over the scene with a fine tooth comb from what Bill could see and deduce.

The news reporter from The Journal which was Winston-Salem's big city paper was taking pictures of the body under the white sheet and taking notes while he interviewed one of the on scene detectives over to his right.

Bill looked left and down at the boat dock and saw the chained German Shepard dog sitting there in front of its dog house watching them quiet happy in front of the dock. Innocent of what was going on here.

The lead detective came over to Bill who was standing quietly by the crime scene tape beside the tall pine tree taking everything in the side yard.

Captain Jack Stanley stuck out his hand in greeting. "Hey–Bill its good to see you again its been a long time since we last met on our first and last case together," said Captain Jack Stanley as Bill grabbed his out stretched hand shaking it firmly.

"That was on the case of Payne Road,' replied Bill remembering his old friend. "Yeah— funny how those murders stopped after you were hired to investigate those serial murders out there," said Captain Jack Stanley with a puzzled look on his face as his mind drifted back to that place in time.

"Well— those murders stopped and that's what mattered," spoke Bill with a big grin on his face of self satisfaction and confidence about his old case while he proudly stuck his hands in his trouser pockets and kinda stood straight up on his shoe tips in the air for a gleeful moment, but kept his wise mouth shut about supernatural matters of the night that no one believed in—these days anyway.

"Some say those killers have returned here to this part of the country and I hear you have been hired to investigate these new case's too," replied Captain Jack Stanley as a matter of fact.

"Well—I don't know about that, but yes I'm on the city's payroll now and checking things out in my way," said Bill with a frown look on his face about the remark by the Captain and then the confident look about him returned.

"Good—we need all the help from the very best people retired or active from law enforcement, anyway I can help let me know," said Jack with a grin on his face.

"I just need to snoop around the place and see what I can find out," replied Bill with his hands still in his trouser pockets, that made him feel at ease.

"Your free to look about all you want and my Crime Scene Investigator detective has checked out the crime scene throughly," replied Jack as he waved Bill to come past the crime scene tape.

Bill ducked under the tape and walked over to the victim and lifted the white sheet.

The mans heart had been tore out of his chest and he had died a violent death and it looked like a wild animal attack from the way he was tore up around his neck by huge bite marks and Bill saw the big paw prints around the mans body Bill quickly surmised as he covered the man back up with the white sheet and looked away for a moment to steady his cold nerves.

Bill had seen dead people before and he was hard core

to seeing death in any form so it didn't bother him like some people who threw up at the first sight of blood, he was use to it.

Bill walked over to the window and looked around to see anything out of the ordinary. Bill saw the half torn white curtain laying on the ground beside the victim.

"The man was knocked through the window from the inside some how. We didn't fine any entry point for an intruder on the inside or where a bear might have broken in and attacked the man from inside the house and knocking him through the window and killing him out here in a forced violent interior exit. We found big paw prints in front of the bay window and around the deceased on the ground. We took plaster casts of the big paw prints and no fingerprints on the bay window it was wiped clean as a fresh washed table by the owner's a week ago doing routine house maintenance and yard work which didn't help us out today," said Jack informing Bill of what they had deduced from the crime scene.

"Well— that sounds like good police work reasoning," said Bill politely as Jack was called by one of his lead detectives to come over where they were standing talking among themselves. They were talking up away's from the crime scene at the front porch.

"I'll see you later Bill," said Jack as he left to see what his men wanted.

"See ya—later," replied Bill absent minded as he went to work automatically looking for clues of any kind that might help his case.   Bill reached into his right coat pocket and pulled out a big magnifying glass. Bill looked through it at the window casing as he walked along the side of the house. Bill was looking about half way up the window when he saw the long hairs sticking in one of the broken bloody glass panes.

"Aha," said Bill as he muttered to himself quiet intrigued at finding something out of the ordinary. Bill looked at the hairs closer and deduced they may not be human but of some type of animal after all like Captain Jack had theorized from the crime scene facts.

Bill pulled out a small plastic bag from his left side coat pocket and at the same time stuck his magnifying glass back in the same pocket.

Bill opened the bag and then reached into his right trouser pocket. He pulled out his grandpa's yellow banana Schrade pocket knife and open the long Sharpe blade.

Bill carefully scraped the hairs into the bag off the broken window glass into the bag and Bill sealed it shut.

Maybe Jack's detectives were right after all, maybe it was some kind of bear attack, it was the most reasonable explanation thought Bill as he stuck the bag in his left coat pocket and folded up his knife and stuck it back in his right trouser pocket too.

Bill pulled out the magnifying glass again and continued to study the window frame, but didn't find anything else, but fingerprint dust from the crime scene people who had gone over the window thoroughly before him.

Bill didn't know if they had found the hairs or missed them on the broken bay window and the Crime Scene Investigator must have thought the hairs belonged to the owner's pet dog, but kept what he found to himself and he didn't take anything for granted that might help him solve his case.

Bill pondered for a minute about his dark suspect he had chased on the coal train last night who was headed this way because the coal plant wasn't to far away from here where the coal train was headed and he had a hunch his dark suspect hobo on the train was somehow involved, but it was all he had to go on right now, but he'd keep it to himself for right now and he had no proof of who or why of anything at this point in his investigation while he headed to the front of the lake house.

Bill saw the woman with the detectives on the front porch

of the lake house and left the bay window to go talk to her if he could in her time of mourning thought Bill.

"Jack—can I talk to her for a second," asked Bill who new the live witness was important to his ongoing investigation?

"Sure— you can, her kin people are here to take her to their house for a few days, she doesn't feel safe here alone anymore after what happen here last night," said Jack very sadly at the woman's loss.

Bill walked to the front porch were the woman was being comforted by her family, a man and a woman of middle age for she was very young and Bill thought theses people were her parents.

"My name is Bill Christian and I'm a Private Investigator hired by the city police department of Winston-Salem," said Bill to the crying young woman and her parents who just looked at him as if they had enough of questions from the detectives which seemed to make the situation worse for the young woman's broken heart.

'I hate to bother you, but what did you see or here last night," asked Bill as he watched the crying woman in her mothers arms?

The woman looked at Bill for a second as she wiped her red teary eyes with a tissue in her hand.

"I heard the dog barking after David my husband got out of bed to go see what Lady which is our German Shepard dog's name was barking at in the early morning hours. I stayed in the bed upstairs and heard a horrible howling noise from a coyote or dog outside and then breaking glass downstairs," said the crying upset woman who wiped her red nose with her tissue and then she continued on with her story for Bill after a brief moment who waited sympathetically.

"Then a fight like a pack of wild dogs or something going on outside the house. Then I called 911 for I was afraid something bad had happen here with David when he didn't answer my calls for him.

Sometime later and very quickly I might add the Stokes County Sheriff's deputies was knocking on my front door and I answered it after they got here and the emergency dispatcher on the phone said it was them and safe to come out from my bedroom," said the woman as she begin to cry again.

"Thank-you Mam you have been very helpful. I'm sorry for your loss here today," replied Bill very respectful who's heart went out to the young woman's loss.

Bill watched the parents walk the crying woman off the front porch and out to the waiting car.

They all got in the vehicle and left driving up the lake road and were gone into the bright sunshine of another day. Bill watched the paramedics remove the body and put it in the ambulance and they left also for their job was done here.

Bill walked across the front porch checking everything in site out and saw the front porch rocking chairs and side tables were in place and not knocked around or turned over. He looked at the front door and he checked the lock which was sound and not broken.

The door jam for the latch was sound too and not broken also, he walked into the house and looked at the living room and the broken bay window.

Bill checked the kitchen and saw it was spotlessly clean and the kitchen door was in one piece and no forced entry from that point by a bear who would have broken into the refrigerator for the food that it smelled from outside the lake house.

Bill could only figure that the bay window had been knocked outside some how and for the life of him he was puzzled by the weird crime scene as if the man had ran across the living room and jumped right through the bay window willingly into the open arms of death thought Bill with a shrug of his tired shoulders. Bill returned to the living room and took a last look around.

There was some broken glass on the floor and wood from

the broken window panes and the curtain had been torn, but that was it and most of it was outside and not inside.

No sign of forced entry, but only a forced exit like Captain Jack had said which seemed impossible thought Bill and it spooked him who had seen enough, turned and walked back out of the lake house while the detectives locked it up.

Bill noticed a maintenance truck parked beside the house now and some carpenter man was starting to board up the bay window with plywood while he came around the side of the house headed to his car for he was done as he waved to Captain Jack Stanley who was talking to the carpenter.

"Take it easy Bill and I'll send you the case report," said Captain Jack and who waved back at Bill.

"Good enough Jack and I don't need the case report. I have more than I care to need or look at by now, you take care until we meet again," said Bill who fumbled in his pocket for his car keys.

"Well—if that's the way you want it, then I want worry about sending it, I guess you've seen enough today and got what you wanted here at this crime scene," replied Captain Jack who watched Bill head to his car.

Bill got in his Monte Carlo and started the engine up and backed around in the driveway very carefully to not bump into the Sheriff's cars.

Bill put the gear shift in drive and gunned the gas pedal and took off down the lake front property driveway heading back to his office in Winston-Salem, but first stopping off at the Winston- Salem police precinct CSI department to see if they could help his case with what little clue he had come up with at the murder scene who drove hard and fast to get there over the open highways as fast as he could with little sleep to go on.

After dropping off the hairs in the plastic bag to the crime scene unit at the Winston-Salem city police department building at the back of the building, at the big roll up door for testing and analysis which the young redhead CSI woman in a white CSI coat opened the smaller side door and took them glad fully off of Bill's hands after he rang the back door buzzer and she shut the door with a polite thank-you smile to Bill who very tiredly headed for his car.

Some time later Bill unlocked his office door and put the (Do Not Disturb) sign on the outside door knob from his inside door knob as he walked into his office off Healy Drive.

He took off his coat jacket and laid it over his high back leather chair and headed for the couch to catch some much needed Z's.

Bill felt very tired and very sleepy while he stretched out on his couch and kicked his shoes off.

He pulled the afghan blanket over him which was laying folded up on the top of the couch while he stretched his hands and arms straight out over his head and stretched his feet straight out over the arm of the couch as he stretched his tired and sore stiff body and he yawned sleepily to himself after a while he soon fell fast asleep.

The phone beeped on Bill's desk "Beep, Beep, Beep" which awoke him out of a deep sleep as he sat up to a sitting position on the couch with the afghan between his legs and now on the floor too and it was now late afternoon!

Bill quickly stood up and walked quickly to his desk and grabbed the phone before the answering machine came on.

"This is Private Investigator Bill Christian speaking, can I help you" said Bill as he waited for a reply on the phone?

"Hi—Bill— this is Roxanne from the Crime scene unit here at the police department. I have your test results on the hairs in the plastic bag you dropped off this morning," spoke Roxanne who thought the private investigator was kinda cute looking for his age.

"Well—are they human or animal," asked Bill with a quick guess of sleepy logic in his mind?

"Bill— they are not human and not a bear but a canine dog of some type that we don't have a match for in our data base library," replied Roxanne who felt bum fuddled for her first time in twenty years of investigated police work about the hairs in the plastic bag from the new murder crime scene which Bill had given her this morning at the back door of the police department lab unit.

"What was it close to in a match," asked Bill who waited patiently for a few moments on the phone?

"Hold on and I'll check the file," replied Roxanne who put Bill on hold for a while.

A few minutes later Roxanne picked up the phone on her desk and pushed the phone button.

"Bill—your not going to believe this but the closes match we have is to the Wolf family," spoke Roxanne with a puzzled look on her face.

"There's no Wolfs around here and especially not down by Belews Lake," replied Bill while his mind came fully awake and raced with reasoning about this new mysteries clue.

"We have Wolfs in the eastern and western mountains in North Carolina but they have never been sighted this far inland, only coyotes that have been let lose here to restart there species here in Forsyth county, North Carolina after being hunted to extinction here a long time ago by hunters and they are now a federal protected species here," spoke Roxanne smiling to herself for her knowledge and love of animals.

"Well —thanks for the help maybe it will be useful after some more research later," replied Bill wondering how in the world, wolf hairs got in the window after all.

"I don't think it was a stray wolf down here this far, they are very territorial creatures after all and stay in the mountains where they are born and your guess is as good as mine about how those hairs got there at that crime scene unless it was a one in a Million animal attack after all," replied Roxanne over the phone with a confident smile of her knowledge of her home state background on her sweet face.

"Well—the odds don't add up if you ask me. Thanks any way and have a good day. Good-by," said Bill who hung up the phone perplexed about the animal hairs.

"If you need us you know where were at," said Roxanne as she heard Bill hang up wondering if he even heard her.

She put the phone back in its receiver and grabbed some papers on her desk and went out the door of her office headed to the lab down the hall to go back to work in the lab.

Bill made some Columbian coffee in his coffee pot and had a few cups while he pondered the new clue he had found while sitting at his desk which didn't make sense to him at all, but he'd figure it out sooner or later.

Bill thought he'd head down to the catholic church on fourth street for a little praying which wouldn't hurt and his momma always said God listen to every bodies heartfelt problems that was sent to Heaven on a wing and a prayer which she had drilled into him as a boy in church every Sunday until he got grown up and quit going because he had enough religion, but he still went every once in a while when things where not going his way and felt he needed to ask forgiveness of his sins to set him on the right path again.

Bill shut off the coffee pot and folded up the afghan blanket putting it back on top of the couch for next time.

Bill cut off his office lights and put on his coat and straighten his black tie with his right hand. Bill put on his trench coat and detective hat and headed out the front door.

Bill turned and locked the door with his key and very briskly walked to his car. The strong caffeine coffee had woke him up and he was up wired wide open.

He opened the car door and hopped in starting the car right up. Bill sat there while his car warmed up wondering if he was doing the right thing.

Bill made his decision and put the car in reverse and backed out of his private parking space.

Bill pulled the gear shift down in drive and mashed down on the gas pedal with his right foot and the Monte Carlo took off through the parking lot out into the street and he was long gone in the dust that the car kicked up down the road.

One hour later Bill pulled up in front of the huge gold dome catholic church on forth street with the last rays of sunshine vanishing over the tree tops like molasses in the sky and pass the tall buildings all around him and it was cold again.

Bill now felt something wickedly had come here to this town on a dark path it had followed here to this part of the country and he had a hunch the murder cases were somehow all tied together but he couldn't put his finger on who, what and why?

He new deep down inside of him that he was now walking along that same crooked path since Chief Dicky had hired him for the job and it chilled him to his bones just thinking about it. He was alone as he always was as a private detective without backup and he missed the force where he had plenty of trained officers with hired guns ready for action and all he had to do was call on his police radio and they were their instantly and it would be nice for a little backup help.

He missed the brotherhood of police but he saw his old buddies at the local pub on nights he went for a quick drink to wash away his days work of catching sinners at their worst. He thought somehow that what ever it was, it was rooted deep in this big town and was blended in among the unsuspecting public at large and that bothered him a lot fore whom could he trust. He shrugged the thought off and looked for a parking space.

Bill parked along the side of the road in a metered parking space. Bill got out and locked his car door.

Bill walked around the side of the car to the meter and

put in two shiny quarters for a hour as he turned the meter switch button with his right hand each time he pushed a coin through the slot.

Bill headed down the sidewalk and up the tall steps to the church Bill went in through the big oak doors and walked through the lobby into the chapel past the confession booths down to his right. The place was dark and quiet with some people down front praying with rosemary beads in their hands by themselves in the churched wooded oak pews.

The young father was lighting the prayer candles on the sides of the alter for his church members.

Bill quietly walked down to the front pew and took a seat behind it and bent his head to pray.

After some time Bill felt a hand on his shoulder and looked up at the smiling young priest who was standing in the isle beside him.

"Son do you wish to go to confession," asked the young priest inquisitively?

"Well—I don't know. You look a little too young for me to confess too and it's been a long time sense I've confessed to anything," said Bill looking up at the young priest, then he eyed him up and down with a mischievous smile on his face.

Just then Bill felt a cold deathly draft of wind come from somewhere behind him and he looked down toward the alter and saw the candle lights flicker as the rush of air suddenly vanished into thin air and was gone which Bill quickly looked over his shoulder to see if anyone had open the church doors and came in down the isle from behind him letting in the fresh air, but there was no one walking down the isle and the church doors were closed behind him.

"I'm Bill Christian," said Bill who stood up and introduced himself and shook the young priest right hand while his soul felt chilled to the bone from the cold rush of air and Bill glanced up at the huge gold dome over his head as if to see some sign from above but only fear of the unknown registered in his mind at this 6ft tall mid 30s looking young stranger with dark brown eyes and hair with a strong looking medium build and handsome pug nose face as Bill took all this in with his years of police training to observe suspects with a quick glance.

"I'm Father Marion," replied the young priest as Bill looked down and noticed a dogs black head tattoo with fangs on father Marion's right back hand while he shook his hand just almost like on officer Darker's hand which Bill quickly realized.

Bill thought that was very strange that two people he now had just met had almost the same type of strange tattoo's but didn't say anything about it to the young priest who quickly let go of his hand and he just briefly saw the tattoo and didn't get that good a look at it, but he didn't want to raise any suspicious inquires to anybody by asking question's.

"I'm just here for a little heavenly guidance, and your new here because I'm in and out of here all the time and I've never seen you here before," spoke Bill as he sat back down in the church pew.

"Well—we can certainly send you on your way and I've been here for a quiet a few years and there's quiet a few priest here at the church, we move around a lot in God's service all over the country," replied Father Marion with a gleam of meanness in his eyes just for a second then the smiling happy face returned as Bill looked up at him.

"Thanks— but I'm just fine and I'll just sit here and pray for awhile," said Bill as he thought about the fathers remark which he thought was very odd and he new they had quiet a few priest here at this church and thought the young father had come here at about the same time that the murders had started from a few years ago from what the young father had just told him and Bill pondered about that and it raised a eyebrow up on his hard rock quizzical look on his face.

"Have a blessed good day Mr. Christian and our doors

are always open to the people and of different faiths too," said Father Marion and the young priest moved off back down the isle and back to where he was lighting the candles beside the alter.

Bill noticed the young priest hadn't spoken to the other people praying in the church unless he had before he had come into the church, but he didn't think it mattered much anyway.

Bill had never seen a priest with a tattoo on his body but this was the new modern age and all the young kids had them thought Bill as he bent his head in silent prayer still thinking about that dog tattoo and hoped God would answer his heart felt prayer of deliverance of a murder suspect to solve his case.

Bill thought that was some how a bad sign and he got up and left the church rather quickly for to him everybody was now a suspect. He had better head home for a night cap and a nice warm bed to rest his tired and weary bruised body from last night's detective hunt.

Later that same night Clara Bell had gone to sleep up stairs in her bedroom farmhouse on Payne Road. Her and Wilbur had always went to bed at sundown for nearly forty years and he was a part of her soul and heart.

Wilbur had his night cap and pajamas on like always and had fell fast asleep like usual, but tonight Clara Bell had a hard time falling asleep and she was nervous as if something terrible was about to happen to a member of her inner circle of people who she considered family and friends. She had a very troubled mind as she drifted in and out of a fitful sleep.

Then when night had finely settled over Clara Bell's fitful sleep and the darkness had cast it's deep magic spell of sleep over her. Clara Bell drifter in her dream void for sometime and who was now mystified at finding herself in the middle of a lonesome fog covered road and she saw the lights of the old classic ten foot tall 1920s era candle carriage lamps of old

Bethabara which were now lighted with electric light bulbs as her sixth senses took in her surroundings.

The fog was swirling around her as she stood in the center of the one lane brick road and looked up at the big new moon covered in clouds through the massive oak tree limbs high in the sky over her head.

When I went to bed tonight the moon wasn't out in full view only a half moon when I looked through the curtain's of my bedroom window just before bed..

The new moon isn't suppose to be out in full view until tomorrow night according to the new farmers almanac calender, that she had looked at today and recorded today's events on like her grandmother had taught her as a little child, the older folks in the old days always kept a record of what happen on that day by writing it on their day calendars as a record and keeping them for looking back at what happen in past days, strange thought Clara Bell to herself standing in the middle of the old settlement all alone while she listen for the insect's chirping around her but heard only silence.

The old restored log house was beside her on her left and the corner of the fort was on the other right side of her. Clara Bell saw the old oak tree at the corner of the fort and in front of the oak tree was the Gremeinhaus 18th century Moravian Church where the two lane road stopped at a gate and stop sign and turned into a one lane brick road for only car traffic to come through slowly and not heavy trucks so that the vibrations were kept at a minimum for the old settlement.

Clara Bell felt the urge to look down the road as she strained her eyes through her glass rimed spectacles to see through the dim fog down the road past the old church. Then she saw the young woman jogger come running down the two lane road toward her out of the flowing fog and into the lights.

Then she heard a terrible howl "AHHHHHH—WHOOOOO-O-O-O," from off to her right from behind the tree which stopped the young woman jogger in her tracks on the road in front of her down the road just beside the 1788 Gemeinhaus Moravian church as the young jogger looked around for the thing that made the terrible howling noise.

Then Clara Bell saw the red eyes come out from behind the oak tree and she saw the massive outline of an animal standing not less the ten feet from her which she quickly recognized as a werewolf in this day and age and Clara Bell was stunned at the frightening sight before her very eyes.

Clara Bell spoke under her breath "Kyrie eleison" in Latin which means Lord have mercy.

Then Clara Bell tried to scream "RUN" to warn the young woman jogger to run away but she didn't hear Clara Bells scream of danger but the young woman jogger also now saw the werewolf at the oak tree as her eyes spotted the beast of the dark night but was now scared and frighten as if frozen to her very spot from shaking fear on the two lane road and she let out a blood curdling hysterical scream for help "Y-E-E-E-E-E-E-EK—H—E-L-P,"!

The werewolf now down on all fours now ran across the two lane road toward its helpless victim and stood up on its back legs towering over the woman as it reached out with a massive clawed hand and grabbed the young woman jogger around the throat and lifted her up in the air like a rag doll in a child's hand.

The woman quit screaming while she tried to breath in the massive grip of the werewolf as she struggled and scratched with both hands on the werewolf's massive forearm trying to fight for her life.

Then Clara Bell heard a familiar voice behind her that shocked her wits to attention as she turned around and looked in stunned disbelief.

"Let go of her— you devil bastard," said Bill Christian as he pointed his 38 nickel plated snub nose pistol and fired at the werewolf's back "BAM, BAM, BAM,"!

Clara Bell flinched as the bullet's passed "Zip, Zip, Zip," through her body and slammed into the back of the werewolf's back "thunk, thunk, thunk," while she looked down at her chest and seeing no bullet holes and then at her old friend Bill Christian the Private Investigator standing now right in front of her who looked dripping wet from head to toe which she hadn't seen in some years.

"Bill—it's me, your old friend Clara Bell Parker," spoke Clara Bell, but Bill just looked right through her as if she wasn't there at the werewolf standing down by the church. Then it hit Clara Bell like a ton of bricks that she was in a dream vision of future things yet to come and only her spirit was here.

She saw the time ripple's effect before her very eye's that reflected off of her spectacles here in the third dream dimension between light and darkness which was told to her long ago by her grandmother that it was between heaven and hell and mortal earth but now she new that her mortal body was not here in this third dream dimension. She reached out and touched the time ripples with her left hand in front of her while she looked over her glass eye spectacles as they spread out in a ripple wave before her into infinity!

"Its DE-JA-VU'," exclaimed Clara Bell who instantly recognized she had been here before from somewhere in time.

The werewolf behind her lifted its massive head up and glanced back over its shoulder with menacing red eyes at Bill the new threat standing in front of the old log cabin on the single brick street pointing his gun ready to shoot again then it lifted its drooling snout toward the big moon and howled up at the night sky "AHHHHHH—WOOOOO-O-O-O,"! The bullet holes leaked out blood down the werewolf's back and then miraculously the bullets came back out the holes one by one and fell to the street with a metal pinging noise "ding,

ding, ding," and then the holes healed up, leaving no trace of any wounds!

The werewolf pitched its unconscious victim over to the side of the road and turned around to face Bill who saw his gun had no effect on the hellish force of a being standing before him down the very road he stood on.

"Run— Bill—run—your gun is no good against that Hellish creature of the knight, that's in Satan's service, it's your only chance," shouted Clara Bell at Bill who reached in his pocket and pulled out his grandpas yellow banana schrade pocket knife and opened the long blade as a last resort after seeing that his gun had no effect on the creature of the night, that was now facing him but had let go of it's intended victim that he was here to save at all cost.

Clara Bell new he didn't see or hear her now. Clara Bell watched Bill make his final stand as the werewolf behind her charged at Bill down the two lane crossing road unto the single brick road at a lightening fast dead run who threw his gun at the charging werewolf, hitting it square in the chest and it bounced off falling on the brick road wayside with a "clatter,"!

The werewolf ran right through Clara Bell's spirit and then leaped up into the air in front of her and she felt her soul on fire from Hell's fury as it's evil life force burned hotly within the reaches of her inner soul as it passed through her life force standing on the road. Clara Bell heard Bill holler out a rebel fighting yell "WHAAAA—WHOOOO," as she saw Bill bravely meet the charge of the werewolf in full stride and stabbed the werewolf in the chest with his pocket knife which was in his natural right hand as it descended down with certain death from its awesome leap of attack from the air above on it's new victim with its deadly razor sharp claws which were about to strike and engulf its new victim in its big long strong arms which it did and then she watched the death bite on Bill's left side neck with long gleaming razor Sharpe werewolf fangs that sank deep into the very flesh and Clara Bell heard the sickening crunch of bone's in Bill's neck. Then she woke up in a dripping hot sweat panic from her nightmarish dream.

Sitting straight up in bed and throwing off her wedding band quilt and sheet covers over unto Wilbur who quit snoring "zzzzzz—ZZZ" and woke up! Wilbur rubbed his eyes with his hands and looked sleepily at his wife siting up in bed beside him.

Clara Bell was breathing hard as she placed her right hand to her aching hot chest.

"It's 4:00 o-clock in the morning for Pete's sake what's wrong," asked Wilbur looking at the old wind up clock sitting on his bedside night table?

"It's Bill sake," replied Clara Bell as she laid back down on the bed with her head sinking back in her feather pillow. "What are you talking about," asked Wilbur while he looked questioningly at his wife up on one elbow in bed?

"It's just a bad dream and I'll tell you about it in the morning, go back to sleep," replied Clara Bell who had caught her breath back now and felt much better while her beating heart in her chest returned to normal and her feeble heat beat felt strong once again and now her hot sweaty body had cooled back down to normal temperature.

"Yeah— sounds like it—good—good-night," said Wilbur as he laid back down and turned over on his side and fluffed up his pillow with his right hand and pushed his feather pillow under his head.

He snuggled back under the warm quilt and covers. Clara Bell heard her husband start snoring again on his side of the bed and after awhile she pulled the quilt back over her and was fast asleep in her warm safe old antic spring bed on a feather soft mattress.

After dusk that same time of night that Clara went to dream sleep in her warm bed, the twelve strange multi colored lights appeared in her backyard in front of her grand children's swing set.

They were hovering over the grass and dancing around on thin air when poof the little tiny fairies from the Alter Realm appeared in the floating lights which were white, red, green, blue, yellow, orange, pink, purple, gold, silver, violet and brown.

They had on little tights that resembled each color of the lights that they floated in and their bodies and hair and wings were the same color as their lights too.

The mother fairy in white flew to the center of the circle of bright fairy lights and with her little magic wand she brought forth a small magic caldron pot out of thin air by snapping her wand in front of her.

"Tonight we begin the moonbeam fairy dance to cast our seasonal spells," said Mother white fairy to her children who giggled with a mischievous laughter all around her.

Mother fairy nodded at violet fairy and the brown fairy who flew up to the magic pot and each grabbed the handles on both sides of the magic caldron pot to hold it for their magic spells.

Mother fairy who glowed white in her bright light lit the pixie dust in the magic pot with her tiny magic wand and flew back to her place in the floating circle.

Mother white fairy started to sing and they all joined in and sang in chorus. "Merrily, Merrily, here we go dancing around the magic pixie pot casting our spells one by one of goodness too and fro, chanted the fairies in unison.

On her command "start the fairy enchanted dance," said Mother white fairy looking up at the moonbeam light that shined down on them from the half moon above high overhead and they begin to float around the pot and cast their magic spells with their tiny magic wands and the pixie dust spewed out with every hit of their magic wands and a multi color of rainbow of sparks floated down to the grass while they all were hovering over the grass in front of the child's swing set in Clara Bell's backyard dancing on tip-toe in the dark of moonlit night going round and round singing their magic chant while they moved over the backyard back and forth in little circles flying on their little wings in the moon's beam's light till the break of dawn and then they just winked out of existence.

That next morning Bill arrived at his office rather early again to get a jump on things. Bill parked his car in his private parking space, throwing the car in park and turned off the engine switch and pulling out the key.

Bill was about to get out of the car when he noticed the brochure for old Bethabara laying on his front seat.

Bill picked it up and open his car door and got out. Bill pushed down the latch, locking his car door after pushing the door shut.

He walked to the side walk from the car rather quickly and scurried up his steps to his office and fumbled for his keys while picking up the morning newspaper on the step.

Then he found the right key which he slide into the key hole of the dead bolt lock. Bill twisted the key and the latch slid back and he opened the door and went inside his office. Bill dropped his newspaper on the desk with the brochure.

Bill took off his coat and hung it on the back of his high back black leather chair. Bill went over to his file cabinet and opened the top drawer.

He got out a coffee filter and opened the brewing lid and stuck it in. Bill filled up the twelve cup coffee pot in the small sink in the bathroom and poured the carafe of water into the back of the coffee pot.

Bill grabbed the jar of coffee and spooned in the right amount for twelve cups, then he shut the brewing lid. Bill flipped the switch and took a seat while he waited for his coffee to brew while he checked his messages on his answering machine.

Bill soon heard the gurgling noise behind him and new the

coffee pot had finished brewing as he put down the morning newspaper.

Just then Bill felt his ears burning and new someone was talking about him somewhere. He rubbed his ears with both his hands and thought about the old wives tale his momma had always told him about burning ears meant people were talking about you when he was a small boy and he smiled to himself because she always swore by it to be true.

He shrugged it off and then got up to get himself a cup of coffee and sat back down at his desk to read the morning news about the latest mystery murder in the triad. Bill turned on his desk radio and listen to his favorite 80s radio station to pass the morning.

Just then "private eye's" by Hall&Oates came on the radio station while Bill smiled to himself thinking about the video with them dressed up in tan trench coats wearing tan detective hats with wide black brim hats while dancing to their own music and it was his favorite video of the 80's as he listen to one of his favorite songs of the 80s too!

Bill picked up his coffee cup from his desk and took a sip while he opened the morning newspaper and began reading on the front page about the latest new murder and he leaned back in his high back black leather chair and he just new this was going to be a great day.

That same morning Clara Bell was telling Wilbur about her nightmarish dream.

"You are sure, you saw the future last night, in your dream," asked Wilbur with raised eyebrows while he studied his wife's sincere face at the breakfast table in the farmhouse kitchen who was across from him at the table while he sipped his coffee?

"Yes— and Bill Christian is in danger of a horrible death at the hands of a werewolf and I now believe a pack of them has been doing these murders around here for the last couple of years from seeing this vison from the third dream dimension between light and darkness," replied Clara Bell with a stern look on her face.

"Where do you come up with these unbelievable wild tales," asked Wilbur as he shook his head in disbelief?

"Wilbur how can you say that after all these years together as husband and wife. You know I don't make up wild stories, that dream was a warning of a bad omen to come. I'm as sane as you and it's a blessing from God for a call to arms," replied Clara Bell looking over her glass rimmed spectacles with a mean, but calm look on her pug nose face while she sipped her morning coffee.

"Werewolf's in today's modern time's, -aaahhh- come on honey, lets be reasonable here, that's old wives tales's, this is not the middle ages and nobody goes on a witch hunt anymore because the 18th Century was yesterday," spoke Wilbur who kept thinking about the supernaturally weird and wild things he has seen and done in his years with his wife Clara Bell by his side who just might be right again which he some how suspected deep down in his own minds thinking because she was nobodies fool in the mystic world.

"If I'm right and we don't act to save lives, then people will die tonight, do you want that on your soul standing before God," asked Clara Bell with a I told you so look on her grandma face?

"Look— I'll give you that your telling the truth and your 99 percent right most of the time, why don't you call Bill Christian and tell him what you know and warn him, even if it's been years since we've seen him," spoke Wilbur with a concern look on his face?

"He want believe me and seeing is believing, we must get involved and help him tonight for Gods sake. Its his only chance at survival with our help," said Clara Bell with heartfelt eagerness.

"Your sure this attack in your dream happens tonight during the new moon at old Bethabara and Bill and some woman jogger is in mortal danger," asked Wilbur with a now concern look on his elderly face?

"Yes—I'm sure as I'm standing here—and we can change the future by being there and getting involved and stopping this evil supernatural creature of the night from killing that poor jogger woman and Bill," said Clara Bell with good intentions at the thought of saving her old private eye friend.

"O.K.—I'm in on this one because God don't make men like Bill everyday. Bill's a good decent honest man and I'll do it for his sake and I'm a believer in you and your good white magic faith which you have dazzled me with as your mate over some near forty years, tell me about your plan of action and you can deal me in?" asked Wilbur with renewed eagerness on his sun tan rugged face while he sat his coffee cup on the table and put up his elbows on the kitchen table who was now all ears looking at his wife while Clara Bell who had a radiant smile on her face adjusted her wire rim spectacles on her face and new she had won the argument as she got up to cook Wilbur's breakfast on the old antic wood stove in the farm house kitchen.

At sundown Wilbur and Clara Bell Parker parked their car in the gravel parking lot which was beside the old 1782 potters house in the old Bethabara German settlement and across from the 1788 Gremeinhaus Moravian church.

Wilbur opened his car door and stepped his rugged old farm body out of the car onto the gravel parking lot as his farm boots crunched on the gravel underneath his boots.

He adjusted his bib overhaul strap over his white short sleeved tee shirt which was loose on the front right small buckle with one muscular hairy left arm and hand while he stood looking around the deserted settlement with a red bandana hanging out of his right side back pocket and got out his pitch fork from the back seat while he adjusted his yellow straw cowboy hat nervously with his right hand making sure it was down tight on his big head and shut the door.

Wilbur walked around the back of the car until he came to Clara Bell's car door which he opened for his wife and she stuck her cane and feet out onto the gravel parking lot from the car and got out with her twisted swamp root cane.

Clara Bell leaned on her cane and walked around the car while Wilbur shut and locked her car door.

"Hurry up— Wilbur the night is falling and evil is a foot here, we must make haste before we are discovered," said Clara Bell who was now standing at the two lane street across from the old church and was now agitated at Wilbur's slowness.

Wilbur came up beside her quickly from hearing her stern voice. "There's no one here. The curator, tourist guides and maintenance people have locked up and left for the night," replied Wilbur who looked up and down the two lane road which was deserted except for a lone car that was coming down the one lane brick road up ahead that was built in the middle of the old settlement street to slow down traffic on the two lane road at either end of the one lane road and coming toward them at the stop crossing for tourist where they now stood.

"We have to make haste," spoke Clara as she looked at the lighted antic carriage style 1920s era lamp posts that were spaced out down the old street of the old Bethabara settlement toward the Tourist Pavilion center and darkness has fallen completely on them.

When the car passed them by Clara Bell took her twisted swamp root cane and walked across the street as the cane made a taping noise "tap, tap, tap" while she walked followed by her husband who fiddled with his yellow straw hat nervously at what they were about to do here this very night.

Clara Bell walked past the first small doorway to the church chapel and then on over to the next church step doorway that led into the inner hallway where the bell rope was which she remembered from her memory of touring the centuries old church long ago and she was looking around for any people that she might have missed, seeing nobody and making sure the coast was clear stepped up on the stoup step in front of the tall old oak door that was below the four window panes overhead in the church doorway.

Clara Bell hooked her cane over her left forearm and reached into her apron right pocket with her right hand which had a old mason jar stuck in it and fiddled around in the pocket for her special skeleton key she had brought with her just for this occasion.

"AHH—here it is," said Clara Bell as she pulled out a small handkerchief and unwrapped it in her right hand.

"Some people would call this felony breaking and entering," said a worried Wilbur who looked on at his wife.

"Shush—Wilbur get a grip on things, were doing the right thing, just keep a look out for the cops who park here down the road a piece below the fort to sometimes to do their nightly reports," replied Clara Bell who then stuck the old skeleton key into the old brass lock in the old oak door of the Moravian church and tried to turn it to unlock the door.

After some moments with Wilbur sweating anxiously behind her who took his red bandana handkerchief out of his side pocket and took his hat off to wipe his sweating face and head and he watched her as she pulled it back out of the skeleton key hole after it wouldn't unlock the old door.

"I have to make a adjustment on the key," spoke Clara Bell back over her shoulder to Wilbur behind her.

"I told you that old skeleton key wouldn't work in that old brass lock," replied Wilbur with a look of fright at being caught on his face while he looked up the street and saw headlights coming there way and quickly put his hat back on his bald head and stuck the red bandana back in his right back pocket.

"Chancelor—keeper of the king's seal—thread the eye of the needle," commanded Clara Bell very enchantly. Clara Bell rubbed her left forefinger up and down the length of the old skeleton key and it started to glow with magic life as the key cuts on the end of the old skeleton key started to move back and forth and reposition them selves for a different lock.

The old skeleton key's light faded and was dark again in her small hand. "Hurry up a car is coming down the street," spoke Wilbur with urgency in his voice who now put a hand on Clara bell's shoulder as if to help her. "I'm hurrying as fast as I can go—you can't rush delicate work," replied Clara Bell who quickly stuck the old skeleton key back in the brass key hole lock and turned it, and to Wilbur's surprise the brass slide lock clicked open.

Clara Bell turned the unlocked door knob to the right and heard the catch slide from its latch in the door jam.

She opened the door and they scurried inside the old Moravian church just in time and shut the door as the car came down the single brick street toward the old church.

Clara Bell and Wilbur leaned against the old oak church door afraid to look out the windows at fear of being caught and she wrapped the old magic key back up in her handkerchief and stuck it back in her right front pocket for safe keeping.

The car's headlights reflected and shined into the church's window's and went on down the two lane black top road.

"Good— they didn't see us," spoke a relieved Wilbur who looked at his wife with shock at breaking the law for what they had done and leaned on his pitchfork for support.

"I told you it would be alright," replied Clara Bell as she looked around the dark hallway and pulled out a small flashlight and went to work.

At about the same evening Bill had closed up shop early that day and went home after stopping at the one hour dry cleaners to pick up his fresh cleaned and pressed suit's.

Bill had taken a quick shower and changed into a fresh suit of clothes and strapped his 38 pistol in a black police holster on his belt eager for tonight' stake out.

Bill walked out of his bedroom and flipped off the light

and headed down the hallway when he stopped for some unknown reason.

Bill felt a strong urge of premonition within his keen mind of something bad was going to happen tonight and he had better be prepared at all cost to outwit his phantom assailant which flashed in his mind for a second and that bothered him to no end.

He felt like he had forgotten something and he turned around and walked back down the hallway to his bedroom. Bill flipped the light switch back on and looked around the room with puzzled eyes. Bill walked over to his dresser and fiddled with his jewelry box and lo and behold his eyes fell on the silver cross his father had given him before he passed away in the open jewelry box.

Bill picked it up with his left hand and looked at the silver necklace while he held the cross in his right hand doing a balancing act with it by gently flipping it up and down on his palm nervously while pondering in his mind just what he was looking for.

I think I'll wear it to tonight for good luck since the only luck I have is getting knocked on my can thought Bill as he took both hands and put the silver cross chain around his neck.

Bill stood thinking for a minute about what compelled him to come back and get the silver cross.

He shrugged it off and strolled out of the bedroom and flipped off the light switch again, walking back down the hallway toward his coat closet beside the front door in the living room.

Bill opened the living room closet and got out his cleaned trench coat he had got back from the cleaners today. He tore off the plastic wrap and put it on over his fresh cleaned and pressed wool blue suit from the cleaners.

Bill grabbed his tan detective hat with a black band off the hat rack on his wall and stuck it on his head then he cut on his stereo system in the living room to scare away any would be thieves by making them think somebody was home.

Bill button up his tan trench coat and buckled his waste belt pulling it tight around his waist and opened the front door and after cutting on his home security lights was gone out into the evening night air.

Later that gloomy and overcast foggy night, Bill drove down Old Town Drive and pulled into the Bethabara Park par course and playground entrance gate and cruised down the black top road toward the playground.

This small park and playground was built away's up from Bethabara's God's Acker cemetery where the original settlers were buried with their families which was chosen long ago up on a hill top by the Moravians from the old Bethabara settlement down below it.

He backed his Monte Carlo into a parking space in front of the deserted playground and exercise par course.

Bill opened the hot coffee he had picked up at the drive through at Macdonald's on Reynolda Road and peeled back a creamer and poured it in stirring it into the coffee with the stir stick.

He took a sip of the steaming hot coffee and relaxed for the long night ahead on stake out at the park.

Bill laid his seat back and disappeared inside his car. His car now looked empty from anyone coming by at this hour of the night but he could sit up slightly and see over the car door and dash.

The fog was a heavy swirling mist now as it rolled in across his hood and the night was overcast and the moon's light was partially hidden from view in the overcast night sky.

Near midnight Bill saw head lights coming down the park road, that flashed in his windshield and he watched the car stop and back in the parking space across the parking lot from him and to Bill's relief it was a young couple who had parked to make out and Bill saw them when the young boy cut on the dome light to find something.

Probably a joint for them to smoke and get high together thought Bill who chuckled to himself about his young romance days too. After some time staying hidden from the young lovers Bill had thought the clue about the Bethabara park brochure was no good and another dead end when he heard a car's engine coming down the park road and out of the darkness and fog appeared a dark car. It came down the park road with it's headlights off.

The car passed by Bill while he watched from over his dashboard from his hiding place in the laid back seat and parked at the gates to the old God's Acker cemetery just down below him. A sinister looking dark form got out of the car and walked around the locked gate into the woods.

Bill thought this might be his man and opened his car door and got out knowing this was the right place he had chosen for a criminal to hide his getaway car and commit a crime down at the old settlement undetected and Bill patted himself on the back for staking it out. He shut it to the surprise of the young lovers who quit kissing each other and looked own in surprise at the noise of the car door closing "Slam"!

"Crap—didn't mean to do that must be in too big of a hurry to catch a crook," muttered Bill under his breath while he looked over at the young lovers.

The young lovers were in shock at seeing Bill get out of what they thought was a empty car as they looked at each other and they had thought that they were all alone at the park and watched him take off down the park road after his new suspect.

Bill quickly made it to the suspect's car and pulled out a small pad and pen from his inside left coat pocket. He made a note of the car which was a old blue 1987 Buick La Sabre and wrote down the license plate number which was WBK 6970 and stuck the pad with pen back in his left coat pocket.

Bill walked around the car and approached the chain locked cemetery gates and scurried around them stepping into the woods for a second, then back out on the black top road. Bill walked away's and stopped as he listen to any distant sounds off in the distance.

Bill heard the mans heavy foot steps off in the distance way up ahead of him and Bill quickly took off headed in that direction toward the old cemetery following the sounds of the foot steps way down in front of him now, that had entered the parking lot at the front of the old cemetery.

The woods on both sides of the road were dark and foreboding with foggy shadows everywhere coming toward him from all sides. Bravely Bill quicken his pace to ketch up to the new suspect and when Bill came out of the dark woods into the parking lot, he saw the suspect's upper half dark form through the fog about seventy-five feet in front of him walk under the arch way into the cemetery.

Good the man didn't know he was being followed thought Bill as he walked on the tar parking lot by the small mausoleum off to his right and saw the archway loom up ahead of him.

Bill noticed the black top parking lot off to his left and it was deserted with no other cars in site because it was locked by the gate keeper after sundown every night and closed on weekends.

This was a very private place for a murder thought Bill to himself who kept walking a fast pace to try and keep up with his new suspect. Bill saw the old fashion rail fence that went from the left side of the red brick archway running down the front of the cemetery to the access black top road into the old cemetery to his left beside the woods and on the right side of the red brick archway was another old fashion rail fence that ran the length of the front of the cemetery going to the woods in that direction too and then turned left down the length of the woods to the back.

Bill looked up at the archway and could just make out

the letters in the dark and fog as he went under it through the wrought iron gates that were open into the grave yard. It read "Bethabara God's Acker."

Bill looked back over his shoulder and saw the writing on the other side of the archway and it read "Till The Dawn Break" and I hope I live to see it if things go bad for me tonight thought Bill and he walked on into the old cemetery with the caution of an ambush on his mind.

Bill saw the white flat grave stones and started to walk through them and he was in a hurry to catch up to the suspect and he new there was no out let here because he had been here many times in the past with his family years ago when he was a small child to tour the old settlement park.

Bill was nearing the back right side of the grave yard as the ground started to slant down hill.

Bill looked everywhere in the dark at the back of the old cemetery for his suspect and the fog drifted on the midnight air over the old cemetery flat grave markers and he was nowhere in site. He couldn't have disappeared into thin air thought Bill to himself.

Bill stopped among the grave markers and listen with his keen hearing and then he heard rustling through the woods off to his right.

Bill picked up on the sound standing in the dark and foggy graveyard and heard the leaves rustling in the woods in front of him and he new his suspect was walking through the woods towards the lower par course trail.

Bill quickly walked to the end of the graveyard and looked the old rail fence over and spotted a break in the fence just a few yards from him.

With a beating heart Bill thought it's now or never and walked over to the broken fence rail and stepped over it into the pitch black forest and vanished into the floating fog. Bill was moving as fast as he could through the thick woods pushing small saplings out of his face and way with his hands while he dodged the trees!

He ran into a maze of spider webs that were strung between some small saplings trees he didn't see and he walked through them, but that quickly scared him to stiff attention and the webs clung to his hat and coat!

"Shit—why do I always feel like I'm in the middle of the twilight zone out here in these dark old woods—blind as a bat on these stupid odd detective murder cases—I take on for hire because I need the money to pay my bills," cussed Bill somewhat disgusted with outstretched arms and fists clenched by his sides at his new predicament that tore at his nerves as he stopped where he was at in the middle of the dark and foggy forest and picked off the spider webs from his face and hat which he took off and pulled the spider webs off as the big writing spider fell to the ground from his hat and ran off into the leaves beside his feet while Bill knocked the spider webs off the front of his coat!

"Ooooh—Ooooh—Ooooooooohhh" Bill stood at shocked attention and stopped what he was doing and listen to the long soulful howl off in the distance.

"Oh—crap that sounds like wild coyote's somewhere out in the dark forest down below me in the valley at the Old Bethabara fort," said Bill who was now somewhat worried about the sudden intrusion of another bad problem to deal with out in the dark woods.

Since those coyote's have been released back into the wild here in North Carolina they have attacked farmers cows in the pastures late at night and killed them and just eating their guts only and that's how the game warden's new it was coyote's and not another big wild animal. I'll have to be on the lookout for the pack but to date they haven't killed any human beings yet—just people's cats and dogs and they have grown in large numbers here in the state and their's talk about hunting them down to thin out the population problem thought Bill intrigued to himself who quickly got the rest of the spider webs off his trench coat..

Bill moved on after putting on his hat in the dark woods and begin swatting the spider webs out of his way with a stick he picked up to feel his way through the woods to avoid anymore spider webs and tear them down out of his path.

He new the lower par course trail led down the hill to a curvy trail that intersected it and led to the bottom of the hill and the back of the settlement thought Bill to himself while he walked through the dark and foggy woods very cautiously looking for his suspect in the dark swirling fog ahead of him in the woods while he stopped and listen from time to time to get his bearings on his suspect and ready to defend himself if his suspect saw him tailing him and thought to attacked him.

Finely Bill broke out of the woods unto the lower par course trail with a heart felt thanks to the good lord above who he hoped watched over him tonight thought Bill who whistled a sigh of relief and he turned left going down the steep hilly trial and tossed his safety stick into the woods, the lower par course trail wound around and then down the hill which he knew from past visit's here.

After some time following the trail Bill realized he had missed the trial to the old settlement and cussed himself under his breath as he back tracked back up the hill quickly while he tried to visualize where the trail was from memory and guessed it was about seventy-five feet back up the trail and with a little blind luck he finely found it in the dark when he saw the break in the woods and bushes off the lower par course trail.

Bill quickly entered the trail toward the old fort and settlement and he new he was not out of the woods yet.

Man how could I have missed that and I've lost my suspect and he could be anywhere by now thought Bill to himself as he picked up his pace into a trot down the hilly trail.

The sky over head was starting to clear up and the moons light was trying to break out over the drifting fog that covered the small valley where the old Bethabara settlement lay and Bill was walking at a down hill trot until he came out of the path from the woods into the old settlement grounds.

Bill had some short lived relief, that he was now safely in the small clearing field beside the woods he had came out of and heard the running water of the stream up ahead as he approached the foggy stream bank through some scattered trees left for shade during the summer for tourist to sit under and have picnics.

He turned left along the stream bank walking along it looking for the old wooden foot bridge to cross over to the old fort and settlement which was in the other big clearing field across Monarcas creek.

Bill walked away's along the creek bank until he saw the dark out line of the old wooden foot bridge coming out of the darkness of the fog that sat on the bank's of Monarcas creek up ahead of him.

Bill approached it quiet gladly hoping he was on the right path to find his suspect who was out here somewhere in this vicinity, he was sure of this in his mind as he stepped out on the old foot bridge that creaked under his weight.

Bill walked halfway across the wooden foot bridge and heard the only sounds around him which was his shoes "clunk, clunk, clunk, clunk" and the rushing water of the creek passing under him and the fog rolled across the wooden bridge from the light breeze off of the creek and it was as thick as pea soup.

Bill couldn't see a foot in front of him hardly and then he saw the flash of red eyes in the dark fog in front of him that sent a shock wave through his body and caught him off guard.

Then from out of the fog a dark figure flashed in front of him blocking his way and Bill stopped instantly in his tracks on the foot bridge caught completely by surprise.

Bill heard the low throaty voice come from the dark towering figure in front of him.

"Go back to what ever rock you crawled out from under before you get smashed like a bug," said the dark figure before Bill could react who new in an instant he had been ambushed.

Bill saw the dark hands shoot out of the fog and he felt the force of a sledge hammer hit his chest.

Bill cried out "OOOOFFF" from the shock of being hit so hard in his chest. Bill was knocked backward's from the powerful blow and lost his balance as he stumbled backward off his feet.

Bill tried to regain his footing as his left foot reached out to feel for the old foot bridge under him but it only dangled in the air as he felt around with his left foot for a firm foot hold on the bridge.

Bill fell on his butt hard on the side of the old wooden foot bridge with his left leg dangling off the bridge and the momentum from the blow and his weight carried his body over the side of the bridge, with his right leg dragging roughly across the wooden bridge edge scraping his right leg painfully.

He fell backward into the air for a long awkward and frightening moment. Then Bill's body went into shock from hitting the cold creek water from the surprise fall and he had a hard look of grimace on his face when he "splashed" into the creek water!

Bill heard running foot steps across the bridge "clunk, clunk, clunk, clunk" as he sat up in the cold creek water that came up to his chest and snorted the water out of his nose "Swooosh, Swooosh" and throat "hack, hack", that choked him "cough, cough " while he regained his sense's!

Then the full harvest moon came out from behind the clouds in the southern sky as the wind blew them away and shined it's light down on the valley for a brief moment and Bill sitting up foolishly in the creek bed water.

The big full moon was calling the man's inner demon's whom Bill was chasing as his suspect and he started to quickly transform from man to wolf of the ominous dark night and his clothes and shoes started to shred and rip apart on his mongrel hairy body beside the old church and in a manner of running seconds there stood a towering mammoth of a werewolf beside the oak tree trunk back behind the 1788 Moravian church next to the old wooden palisade fort.

Bill suddenly heard a deathly howl "AHHHHHH—WHOOOOO-O-O-O," somewhere up the hilly creek bank from him while he sat stunned in the knee deep water beside the old wooden foot bridge. Bill caught his breath and quickly got up on his feet. He heard the clinking of loose change falling "clink, clink, clink" from his wet pants pockets into the cold water "plunk, plunk, plunk' around his knees while he was standing there in the middle of Monarcas Creek soaking wet from head to toe shriveling from the cold creek water and unbuckled his tan trench coat belt, then unbutton his coat and checked his gun on his side which was still there in it's holster alongside his ammo belt and wallet in his right back pocket.

Bill quickly felt for his car keys and knife in his right pants pocket which to his relief were still there also.

Good—I didn't loose my gun or ammo belt and wallet or my knife and keys just some loose change I had in my front pocket. I ought to make a wishing well wish thought Bill trying to see the good side of his predicament while he slightly chuckled very sarcastical mean full to himself "ha, ha, ha" under his cold frosty vapor breath at his situation in the chilly creek bottom water.

I guess the tricks on me and I'm glad this part of the creek has a small soft sandbar bottom instead of a rocky bottom because I'd broke my tail bone on hard creek rocks instead and that smart ass suspect is going to get it when I get my hands on him thought Bill who stopped for a moment in the creek thinking about what he just saw on the foot bridge and reached down with his right hand and rubbed his right bruised leg to ease the pain he felt quickly and the cold numbing water helped ease the scrap pain too.

Then he stood back up and it hit him, it was the same red eyes the other night from the coal car chase and it must be the same suspect thought Bill with a vengeful look on his rugged tan wet face who now madly waded through the creek bottom water toward the foot bridge.

He grabbed hold of the wooden planks edge above him and jumped out of the water doing a half waist hand stand on the bridge and throwing his right foot over the side of the bridge and pulling himself back up onto the bridge and he stood up dripping wet on the foot bridge while checking out his surroundings!

At that moment Clara Bell was standing by the church window inside the small chapel watching the street and Wilbur was at the old oak church door, in the hallway ready to open it and rush out with his pitch fork. "Did you hear that—Clara Bell—sounded like a wolf howling outside," said Wilbur with eagerness and fright in his voice?

The young woman jogger came out of the darkness and fog and screamed at the top of her lungs from fright for help at seeing the werewolf while Clara Bell watched from the church window.

"I see her— go and get her Wilbur the time is now to intervene and save them and I'm right behind you don't step on the holy sea salt on the door's threshold," shouted Clara Bell from the church's chapel who rushed into action.

Wilbur open the church door and stepped over the threshold and rushed out onto the front step without a moment to loose.

He quickly looked down the church side walk toward the old fort and saw the beast standing there beside the big old oak tree with glowing red then yellow eyes looking back at him with evil intentions of a murderous nature of awful things to come for those who crossed its path.

With a tight grip on his pitch fork Wilbur ran across the street to the stricken woman jogger.

The woman screamed in fear at seeing Wilbur "E-E-E-E-EEK" who approached her and she sunk to her knees!

"I'm here to help you— get up—your life's in mortal danger," yelled Wilbur with haste who looked back over his shoulder in defiance at the werewolf standing by the old oak tree beside the old fort not fifty feet from them, that was glaring at this unexpected intrusion in front of him and then he reached down with his right hand and grabbed the young female jogger's right arm to help her to her feet.

"Get up—right now—we are here to save you, move your ass–right now and run with me to the church for shelter," commanded Clara Bell who came up beside Wilbur walking fast for her old age on her cane.

The woman jogger took one look at Clara Bell and seeing a old grandma in front of her made her feel safe and trust them and she came to her senses quickly.

She got up on her feet with Wilbur pulling her up fast with his right hand.

The werewolf got down on all fours as it prepared to charge them and Wilbur facing the werewolf brought his pitch fork around for a last stand from his left hand letting go of the young female jogger only after Clara Bell had taken hold of the young woman around her shoulders.

"Take her—Clara Bell and I'll hold him off until ya'll get inside the church," said Wilbur who was now fighting mad at the murderous werewolf within his sight and it was now or never he bravely thought to himself.

Clara Bell took the young woman jogger and they ran for the safety of the church door with Wilbur running beside them to protect and shield them from any assault.

The werewolf ran straight for them and leaped up in the

air for a downward attack and Wilbur braced himself for the charge spreading his feet in a forward fighting stance and stuck the pitch fork sharp prong's deep into the werewolf's chest when it came down out of the air on top of him and it screamed in pain "AHHHHH!" and he flipped it over his head while turning his body around and pushed the pitch fork forward throwing the werewolf back across the street to the far side of the road.

The werewolf rolled head over heel's on the two lane road and jumped up on it's hind legs while standing in front of the old potter's house on Bethabara Road with respect at it's new adversary standing across the road watching him with a grim determination while holding the bloody pitch fork in a fighting defense stance with strong arms and hands from years of hard work in his fields on his farm on Payne Road.

The four stab wound holes made by the pitchfork in the werewolf's chest healed up and were gone in the blink of an eye and the werewolf glared at Wilbur with a bloodlust in it's evil eye's.

Meanwhile Clara Bell pushed the young woman jogger through the church door to safety and she kicked the holy sea salt across the floor as her frighten stiff feet dragged across the threshold of the old oak door.

Clara Bell saw the skid marks across the door threshold but had no time to fix it for fear of her husband being killed by the werewolf but she new they had to retreat inside the church or all was lost. "Come on—Wilbur we must seek shelter and safety inside the church, the battle has been won on our side," spoke Clara Bell who stood on the church steps holding onto her cane watching the standoff between her husband and the werewolf in the street.

The werewolf prepared to charge Wilbur again who was ready for the attack again with his pitch fork.

The young female jogger was walking backward inside the hallway of the church from fear, that wanted her to run and hide and she bumped into the church steeple bell rope behind her which scared her and she tripped over her own feet and grabbed it to keep from falling and for support and she rode the rope to the floor.

The bell rang "Dong, Dong, Dong, Dong" across the old fort settlement waking the neighbors up in their beds up and down the street that still lived there in their house's! Wilbur backed across the street toward the old church door and looked up at the bell steeple on the roof top that rang out a loud and clear warning that someone was here at the old Moravian church in the middle of the night.

"What about Bill," asked Wilbur from where he stood in the street just a few yards away who looked quickly at his wife and then back at the werewolf across the street?

"The future has been changed and Bill can take care of himself and his fate rest in God's ever loving hands— now— and we don't want to tempt fate," said Clara Bell with apprehension in her voice. "I hope your right," replied Wilbur back over his shoulder to his wife in the church doorway.

Wilbur kept the pitch fork out in front of him and started walking backward toward the open church door and keeping a eye on the werewolf standing across the road.

The werewolf growled a low throaty roar from it's huge long snout" GRRRRR!—GRRRRR!" and got down on all fours and prepared to charge Wilbur again who had now backed up to the church step in front of the door! "He's going to charge again," shouted Clara Bell who reached out from the door and grabbed Wilbur by the back of his bib overhauls and pulled him back toward the safety of the church door.

The werewolf moved like lightening and was on Wilbur in a matter of seconds before he could react and this time it grabbed for the pitch fork and jerked it out of Wilbur's hands and Wilbur fell backward inside the church door.

Clara Bell dragged her husband across the threshold of the old church door. Wilbur crawled to the side of the door and tried to kick the door shut with his left foot. Clara Bell backed up down the hallway watching the werewolf in the doorway with rigid eye's.

The werewolf growled menacingly at the church door "GRRRRRR,!—GRRRRRR,!" and broke the pitch fork handle with it's massive clawed paws and threw the broken pieces down at its sharp clawed feet!

It stuck a massive muscular right leg and clawed foot into the church hallway while it grabbed the inside of the door with a right razor clawed paw which "banged" the door against the wall behind it and then it grabbed the door jam with it's razor sharp left claw paw!

The werewolf hunkered down and stuck in its massive head through the doorway and roared "ARRRGHH!—ARRRGHH!"!

The werewolf came into the church hallway standing over Wilbur who laid on the wooden floor beside the front church doorway looking up in plain sight of the beast within the church petrified.

"Satan get behind thee," cried Wilbur the Preacher man who remember the old Jesus bible verse when Satan had tempted Jesus in the desert mountain top in the bible, that he had been taught years ago by his Holiness Sunday school teacher when he was a little boy while he tried to muster up the strength to move away from the hellish sight before him as he kicked at anything to get out of the way.

"Behold—before your very eyes stands Tartarus in the church doorway which was the very lowest level of Hell a person could be banished to for punishment with pits of dense darkness to lock away their souls and Satan casting them out as werewolves on his nightmarish time of earth after darkness has come past daylight.

They are the Fallen dark angels from Hell with a wrath that can only be filled by a hungry maniac full moon with a bloodlust at night on earth and by daytime a ordinary human being blending in with humanity who have been granted by Satan to live forever and do his evilness by night," exclaimed Clara Bell who firmly looked at the young scared female jogger back over her left shoulder very quickly whom she was protecting from certain death.

Then Clara Bell wasting no more time lifted her twisted cane up and pointed it at the werewolf as a last resort with her right hand.

"Unum E plurisbus Unum, Abner father of spiritual light come forth," commanded Clara Bell while she heard the young woman jogger whose nerves got the best of her and who went haywire again from freight as she screamed in fear "E-E-E-E-E-E-E" back behind her somewhere in the dark church hallway at seeing the werewolf again standing in the church doorway.

The cane glowed white on the end and a brilliant white light shot out and engulfed the werewolf standing in front of the old oak door before it could attack Wilbur on the floor and it went rigid in the bright white light unable to break free, that lit up the whole church hallway in a bright white light.

The young woman jogger stood looking at a site to behold over Clara Bell's left shoulder as she forgot about her fear and watched in wonderment at this Heavenly site before her very eye's which must be sent from God on high she now thought of her protectors.

"Hermon—Excelsior" commanded Clara Bell with authority in her voice and she walked forward and the werewolf was lifted off it's massive feet up into the air and it was trapped solid in the bright beam of magic white light.

She pushed the werewolf's massive hulk out the old oak church doorway very roughly and forceful with the bright magic white light from her magic twisted swamp root cane as it's massive body was squeezed through the small opening of the old church door way like a cork in a bottle "POP" and it floated out onto the street outside bathed in the white magic light!

"On my command shut the door and lock it," shouted Clara Bell to Wilbur who stood up from the floor where he had fell beside the church doorway. Clara Bell had walked almost up to the old oak church doorway and the werewolf was outside the old church door levitated up in the air over the two lane road while the bright beam of light flowed through the doorway and out onto the street.

"Now Wilbur—Enchantment—Exodus," commanded Clara Bell and the white light faded from her magic twisted swamp root cane and Clara Bell watched the werewolf fall onto the street outside with a "Thud"!

Then Wilbur slammed the old oak church door shut"SLAM"! He pushed down the slide latch and locked the old skeleton key brass door knob in the darken hallway.

Clara Bell hooked her cane over her left arm and pulled out the small flashlight from her apron pocket and flipped it on.

Then she quickly walked over to the church door and pulled out a mason jar from her left apron pocket and quickly unscrewed the lid and pulled the holy sea salt along the doorway of the old front door sill to fill up the slid marks from the woman jogger who broke the salt sill. Then she screwed the lid back on the old mason jar and stuck it back in her apron pocket.

"Now—we're safe, it can't cross that line of sea salt unless something human breaks the seal and that's not going to happen on my watch until the coast is clear and safe for us to leave here tonight in one piece together," said Clara Bel shining the small flashlight at the ceiling so that everyone could see and feel safer in the light.

Clara Bell looked at the woman jogger, they had saved tonight from the werewolf attack, standing a few feet away from her in the center of the hallway who had an open mouth and wide eyed expression on her glowing face from the small flashlight beam who looked back at her, then Wilbur with unbelieving eyes at what she had just witnessed. Wilbur just winked a right eye at her and smiled a big sheepish grin back at the astonished woman jogger.

"Clara Bell-honey-I'm sorry, I had my doubts about the werewolf, you were right-honey," said Wilbur who just shook his head sorrowful side to side at his wife with a still sheepish grin on his weathered face.

"That's alright Wilbur—seeing is believing," replied Clara Bell who just smiled back at her husband with a I told you so look on her tired old grandma wrinkled pug nose face behind her wire rimmed spectacle's.

Meanwhile some frantic minutes earlier Bill had ran across the old wooden foot bridge with wet feet in his shoes that went "squish, squish, squish, squish" and up the hill and started to followed the path that ran along the side of the old fort and then he thought he heard a woman scream!

Bill looked skyward and saw the full moon which was big and bright shining in the partly overcast sky overhead.

The fog was still hard to see through and then Bill heard the church steeple bell's slow, solemn tolling of the church bell ringing "Dong, Dong, Dong, Dong" as he stopped in his tracks beside the old fort and looked up at the church steeple for a few moments wondering what was going on in the old Moravian church off to his right!

Maybe my suspect broke into the old church looking for antic's to steal or some valuables thought Bill standing there beside the old fort in the fog trying to see with his strained tired old eyes through the whipping and swirling fog blown by the wind.

Bill full of wonderment looked at the church windows in back of the old church and saw a bright light of immense power radiating out of the windows beside the back door to the chapel for a brief second and then it was gone and he then shook his head to clear his groggy senses and thought he was seeing things in his numb mind.

Bill felt tired and wet and he felt chilled to the bone by the old October cold north wind. Bill felt a little confused at losing his suspect and being knocked off the bridge into the icy creek water and slowly his strength was being zapped by the heavy weight of his soggy cold clothes while his bodies life force system kicked in to high gear to try and warm itself back up.

With a monumental second effort he took off running as best he could in his soggy shoes and wet clothing toward the street and stumbled on a small hole or depression in the old path nearly falling in the dark and Bill reached down and caught himself with his right hand on the foggy path next to the old fort and kept going at full steam.

Bill saw the street lights up ahead and he ran past the old oak tree to his right and the corner of the old fort to his left.

He stumbled out onto the single red brick road at a very fast drunken angle across the road and when he tried to stop his feet, the momentum from his run in his wet loafers made him slide across the red brick laid road and he nearly fell again in front of the old log cabin beside the road while he fell backward and caught himself with his hands behind him, that scraped some of his skin off the palms of his hands on the hard brick single road.

"Ooouch," cried Bill who stood up quickly rubbing the palms of his hands back and forth to ease the pain of red scrapped palm hands that burned him terribly! Bill heard a low growl "GRRR!—GRRR!" off in the distance from behind him and he spun around quickly from fear of the unknown!

"OOOOH–Lord what now," pleaded Bill to himself subconsciously out loud with a heavy alarmed heart and his eyes darted around and checked the area out before him and the lazy forbidding fog rolled in and surrounded him and it was glowing white from the glow of the old style antic streetlights on his left and from the full moon high overhead in front of him that was shining down on the small valley settlement?

He looked to the left beside the old log cabin and saw the field and parking lot with one car parked there through the swirling fog and saw nothing else in the ancient settlement on that side of the old use to be wagon plank road that now was a modern paved street.

Then he looked quickly to the surrounding area to his right and saw the side of the church with the old plank fence in back of it and no one standing there.

Then some sixth sense from within his tired mind told him to check the road in front of him which he quickly focused his eyes on through the foggy dimly lit dark road in front of him and then he spotted it through the murky fog what looked like a big wolf or maybe a coyote sitting down in front of the old ancient Moravian church in the middle of the street.

The werewolf looked back at Bill with red fierce eyes that jumped out at Bill through the fog.

"Oh—Shit!", Man—I've got a bad feeling about this and that animal is to big to be a coyote or it must be a wolf instead," exclaimed Bill with surprise and awe in his voice and then it hit him square in the face, that this might not be no small wolf from the eastern mountains that had wondered down here looking for food either.

Bill's years of law enforcement training taught him in tight situation's to act quickly on instinct and fearing a deadly threat he then pulled his wet trench coat back and pulled out his snub nose 38 pistol with his right hand and decided to cut loose with his gun in self defence.

The werewolf stood up on all fours and prepared to charge it's new prey with a terrible frightening howl AHHHHHH—WHOOOOO-O-O-O,"! Bill aimed his 38 pistol at the werewolf's chest and fired three quick shots "BAM, BAM, BAM," that hit it square in the chest "thunk, thunk, thunk," and the red blood spewed out in spurts on impact from the bullets!

The werewolf howled in a mad rage"ARRRRGH!—ARRRG!—ARRRG!" at being shot!

The bullets were quickly pushed back out of the wounds and fell to the street with a pinging noise "ding, ding, ding" and the wounds healed up miraculously by some unseen supernatural force not of this earth.

The werewolf took off with brazing fast speed and covered the distance between Bill and where it had been sitting at in front of the church in no time at all. Bill quickly saw his gun had no effect and threw his gun at the head of the charging beast which was now within ten feet of him and it bounced off the werewolf's massive head with a "thud" and fell in the street with a metallic clatter "clang, clang, clang' as it slid to a stop in the road with little affect!

Bill's coat flowed and flapped behind him blown by the cold October night wind that kicked up by a howling rage down below him as his arm reaction was lightening fast as he started to reach into his right pant's pocket for his old pocket knife while he stood his ground bravely like a tall stone statue of strength in the face of approaching death but the werewolf slammed into his chest with it's massive paws "SMACK" before he had time to pull his knife out!

Bill was knocked back off his feet backward once again into the midnight air!

"OOOFFF" cried Bill as the wind was knocked out of him from the sudden impact and he sailed backward through the air!

His hat flew off his head and his trench coat flapped through the air and then he hit hard on his back with a "THUD" in the middle of the single brick road and Bill's silver chain and cross flew past the left side of his head!

The werewolf growled and howled "GRRR!—GRRR!" "AHHHHHH—WHOOOOO-O-O-O!,"at the moon standing on top of its prey with its massive clawed paws and the tips from it's claw's dug into Bill's flesh through his clothes for a firm hold on it's prey before it made it's kill and that gave Bill enough time to gather his wind and stength back quickly under the ton of animal on top of him.

Bill had felt the claws tips dig into his flesh through his clothes and he had to bite his tongue to keep from crying out in pain.

He could smell the awful rotten breath on his face that came out of the werewolf's jaw's.

He heard the lungs that breathed in and blew out the wolf's nostril's with each breath of Hell's legion's of fury intake and out— of steamy Hellish breath "PUFF, PUFF" full on his face!

It was almost unbearable with the smell and stench of death that dripped from the werewolf's drooling saliva and hot breath unto his chest.

With a last ditch effort at survival his life force kicked into high gear once again and he pulled back his hands flat beside his head to assault the wolf on top of him. He pushed up with all his force and his silver chain was instantly pushed over by his Guardian Angel which got entangled in his left fingers that lay draped over his left shoulder!

Bill pushed up with both hands and the silver chain slipped between his fingers pulling the silver cross into the palm of his left hand and the werewolf plunged's it's massive head down to bite and tear out Bill's exposed jugular vein in his neck and throat at the same instant.

Bill grabbed the werewolf by its massive head with both hands and not realizing the cross was in his left palm and pushed with all his might fore his will to live was great within his life force which gave him great strength from deep within his spiritual soul and the silver cross burned deep inside the right side of the werewolf's massive head.

The werewolf froze in mid strike and it's red flaming eyes

was now void of rage and went to yellow then turned a ice cold blue and it howled in pain "oooooOOOOHHH,"!

Bill smelled burning hair and skin above him and the werewolf's black heart felt the icy cold fingers of death caress it as the silver cross started to burned deep into its skull.

The werewolf's body shook on top of Bill as if struck by a bolt of lightening.

The werewolf fearing for it's life, for the first time in a life time of giving pain and death to other's that had consumed it's mortal soul, jerked its massive head out of Bill's hands and rolled off the top of Bill and stood up a few feet away scratching the right smoldering side of it's head with it's right paw as if it was on fire. The werewolf's eyes turned back to burning crimson red with fury from it's prey getting the upper hand and it growled and snapped "GRRRRR!—GRRRRR!— ARRRRRFF!— ARRRRRFF,!" at Bill laying in the road who sat up stunned on his elbow's that he was still alive!

"Ooouch," said Bill who tossed the hot silver cross onto his chest, that was hot to the touch and Bill heard a "Sisssssss" from the wet clothing touching the silver cross on his chest!

The werewolf watching him shook it's massive head in front of Bill as if to clear it's evil mind and thought it had better retreat in fear of it's own life after looking at the silver cross on Bill's chest which it didn't want to tangle with again.

It took off across the road with it's tail between it's legs and jumped the side ditch of the road and ran past the waist high rock water fountain for tourist inside the old broken section of the old fort and disappeared into the swirling fog past the old covered hand dug thirty feet down rock lined well that had been dug by hand long ago by the first German settlers here on it's right.

It dodged and jumped among the old excavated deep hand dug ruins of the old flat rock lined cellars of the long vanished log houses by the old settlers of yesteryear and came out of the back side of the old fort broken section and it ran across the field onto the small tar road for the park workers access golf carts past the first restored log cabin built here at Old Bethabara and past the flower and herb garden built in front of it off to it's right which had also been restored too!

Bill laid back down in the middle of the road of the single paved road catching his breath and every bone in his body seemed to ached in pain.

Bill heard the church door open and "slam" shut down below him at the old Moravian church and then some people talking out in the street, somewhere down below him!

Bill raised his tired head and looked down the road and to his amazement he heard the tapping of a cane coming his way up the road"tap, tap, tap" and big footsteps "clunk, clunk"!

Then out of the fog and into the light came two women and a man walking down the street toward him.

"What are you people doing out here this time of night. This place is closed," asked Bill with a painful curious face who thought he was alone in the deserted settlement?

"Bill it's good to see your alive and still kicking," spoke Clara Bell very joyfully who hobbled up to Bill's body lying in the middle of the street and stopped at his feet and touched his right wingtip shoe with her cane.

Bill who was nebulously amazed couldn't believe his very eyes and he watched Wilbur her husband come up with a young woman standing beside them. Then he was dumb struck and bedazzled at the same time wondering what his good old friends from years past where doing out here this time of night.

Just at that moment a truck was coming down the hill of Old Town Drive and the werewolf came running out of the golf cart black top access road from the old fort and jumped over the top of the chain that was strung across the access road to keep vehicles out of and ran toward the road.

"What in the hell is that," asked Josh who saw what looked like a big dog enter the road who then hit his brakes and slowed the old truck down to keep from hitting the big dog he thought?

The werewolf was caught dead in the old Mitsubishi truck's headlight's in the middle of the road.

"Don't stop Josh that's no dog but a big wolf, keep on going," shouted Shannon his girlfriend who screamed in fear real quick of the wolf and Josh stopping the old truck to investigate which they had seen and grabbed Josh by his right arm and tugged on it with a death grip to leave!

Without stopping the werewolf ran across to the other side of the road and disappeared down the old trail that led to the old Moravian flour mill ruins and was gone in the darkness.

"That's the biggest Gaw darn wolf I ever saw," spoke Josh looking out his truck window peering into the dark foggy woods to his left and at the small empty parking lot beside the old Mill trail.

Josh floored the gas pedal with his girlfriend beside him urging him on to get the Hell out of dodge and the old truck picked up speed and took off down the road toward the curve.

It tore around the sharp right curve and then they came to the stop sign beside the old herb and flower garden of Old Bethabara settlement.

Josh saw the people standing in the street light's amidst the fog on the old single black top road away's down in the old settlement in front of him and instead of going through the main road he decided to turn left onto Bethania Station Road for a fast getaway from the area for his girlfriend's frighten sake who was shaking with fear from their brief encounter with the wolf.

Sometime earlier that night the old blue buick La Sabra car stopped along the fence on Reynolda Road. That was adjacent to Reynolda House Museum of American Art and Gardens.

The young dark headed woman got out of the passenger

side of the car and stepped up on the sidewalk while cars passed by in the night time air.

The dome light was on in the top of the old car and cast a faint light on the man driving the car in the drivers seat.

"Good hunting," said the man who waved good-by to the woman who shut the car door.

"The same to you," replied the young dark headed woman who ran to the fence and looked around quickly to see if anybody was watching her and saw no one and she climbed over the wire fence into Reynolda Gardens as the car pulled off into traffic and disappeared down the streetlight lit dark foggy road.

Much later that night James Clayton who was out for a little evening exercise and also headed for a late night dinner at a fine restaurant in Reynolda Village that use to be part of the tobacco baron R. J. Reynolds big estate that was built in 1912 to 1917.

The former support buildings at Reynolda Village of the old 1,067 acre estate was now converted to restaurants and specialty shops, the village once housed state of the art dairy barns, a school, central power plant, laundry, ice house, carriage sheds, blacksmith shop, smoker house and cottages for the staff and caretaker families of the old estate. He was walking along the lighted joggers path at Grayland Mansion where he lived back behind in the old neighborhood and had passed through the big wrought iron open gates where a Wake Forest college conference was going on at that time of night and the old mansion was all lit up with lights and cars were lined up in the big long driveway.

He had crossed Reynolda Road and walked up to the chained wrought iron gates of Reynolda House, that had been closed at sundown.

He reached through the gate and pulled up the slide latch release gate handle that anchored the big gates to the pavement and pulled open the gates as far as the locked chain would allow it to swing open.

He squeezed his skinny body through the small opening and onto the dark and deserted grounds. He pulled the big wrought iron gates back until they closed up meeting together and slid the gate latch release handle back down until the metal rod went back into the concrete opening in the pavement securing the gates across the blacktop paved driveway into the old mansion.

He had been doing this since he was a small boy and had came to play along the front open grounds of the big tobacco mansion where people flew kites which he also did as a young boy too in March and people played frisbee together and young college lovers laid on blankets during the hot summer time, drinking sodas and eating snacks that they had brought with them in small coolers and had a good time listening to the top 40 radio stations in the triad until closing at dusk.

He followed the paved driveway until he came up to the big mansion house which was silently dark and foreboding in the floating fog across the estate grounds. He left the paved circle driveway and went around the side of the big mansion and onto the back of the house. He walked past the long greenhouse looking for the old joggers path that led to Reynolda Village.

He found it in the moonlight that broke out from the overhead clouds after standing in the fog of darkness in the backyard trying to guess where it was from memory for what seemed like an eternity.

"A-ha—there it is," said James who took off walking at a fast pace and went down the old joggers path deep into the foggy woods back behind the old tobacco mansion.

He had been walking for a while happily along the old joggers path when he heard a deathly howl "OOOOOOOOOHHHH," off in the woods to his right.

James stopped cold in his tracks and surveyed the woods

with his scared darting eyes off to his right but didn't hear anything else or see what ever that was in the dark woods.

"Holy-cow what was that," asked James to himself who now stopped and turned around and stared at the woods behind him? He nervously ran his right hand fingers through his shirt crewcut hair but couldn't make out anything in the dark moonlit woods.

"Must be those wild pesky coyote's that run lose around here in the woods and are hunting food," said James under his nervous breath who turned away from the woods and started walking again on the joggers path toward the old Reynolda village and he would have felt braver if is wife had joined him on his walk tonight, but he was alone out here thought James and he felt foolish as an adult at being scared of the dark like a child.

He had walked this jogger's path many a time over the years, but had never felt fear until tonight and something was not quiet right out here tonight but he couldn't quiet put his finger on it thought James to himself who kept on quietly walking on pins and needles down the dark path.

He was glad his wife was safe at home tonight watching t.v. and he hadn't brought his cell phone leaving it on his dresser thinking he wouldn't be needing it on this short trip who now thought to himself, he wished, he had stayed home in the safety of his house tonight and watched t.v. with his wife too, but how could he had foreseen this ominous event tonight and he wanted a evening meal so bad and a little break from the monotony of a boring married life thought James who kept looking back over his shoulder ever so often to make sure nothing was following behind him on the joggers path.

O-well maybe it's just my nerves getting the best of me tonight in this gloomy dark place all alone thought James a little scared to admit it to himself who shrugged his shoulders and tried to make the best of it and it was too late now to turn back, he was almost there and he kept moving on down the joggers path trying to shake off his weird paranoid feeling of impending doom.

He now walked at a faster pace to make it to Reynolda Village which was his final destination for a midnight meal in the The Village Tavern Restaurant and then back home on the sidewalk by the road traffic which was safer he thought to himself.

Then he heard a lonesome old hoot owl "hoot, hoot," off in the distance of the woods off to his left which startled him further for a second and his body was getting ready to kick into high survival gear.

He kept looking over his shoulder wondering if something in the dark woods was following him and he felt fear well up in his dry nervous throat and he kept imagining in the back of his mind that something uncanny was hot on his trail and he tried to shake off the second scary paranoid feeling he was having in his frantic mind.

He heard limbs breaking in the woods off in the distance to his right where he had heard the howl earlier and his heart skipped a beat in all the excitement and he new something big was coming his way for sure by the rustling of the leaves in the dark woods behind him maybe it was a wild deer on the prowl he thought uneasy to himself.

Fear of the unknown kicked in his frighten mind again and he started to pick up his pace and on second thought he started to run fast fearing a mugger was about to rob him out here on this desert path or worse yet attacked by a lone bear that had wondered down here from the mountains looking for food and finely his survival gear kicked in high panic mode.

How stupid he felt for getting himself into this dangerous situation tonight on this dark path out here all alone in the foggy dense woods and he wished now he had walked on the sidewalk instead under the street lights with Reynolds Road traffic passing him by where he could flag some one down if he needed help. He quickly thought in his near panic mode stricken mind.

Then he heard another hideous howl closer and behind him "AHHHHHH,—WHOOOOO-O-O-O," and he looked back panic stricken over his right shoulder with big fearing eyes while running at top speed along the path with his heart thumping in his throat and saw a big dark body jump out from the woods into the air over the tall bushes beside him in the dark moonlight.

He was startled near to death and his body went rigid waiting for the impact and he screamed "AAAHHHH," in fright that he was being attacked by someone or something. The female beast landed on his back knocking him to the ground on his stomach instantly and he was pinned down by Sharpe clawed paws that dug into his skin on his back and he hollered in excruciating pain.

"OOOUCH—that hurts like fire," screamed out James in fear to his assailant behind him.

"Get off me—let me go," begged James who tried to roll away and throw his attacker off his back, but the female werewolf was too heavy and powerful who briefly jumped up on her hind legs and landed back down on his back without letting go of her prey so he was forcefully pinned to the ground again.

"OOOF," cried James gasping for air who looked back over his right shoulder in the dark and saw red evil menacing eyes that glared back at him with big pointed ears and a long snout with big razor Sharpe canine drooling teeth and its fur stood up on end around the face madly looking at him. He new it wasn't no mugger that had him but some type of wolf he quickly deduced in his fearful pitiful mind.

A big right clawed paw smacked him silly on the right side of his head "SMACK," and blood trickled down his forehead unto the ground from his head wound and claw cuts. His head hurt awful while he laid still on the ground and rolled his head and face around in the dirt on the joggers path half unconscious.

The female werewolf stood up over him and howled at the glowing moon "AHHHHHH,—WHOOOOO-O-O-O,"and with blood hungry red eyes reached down with its big clawed paws and grabbed James's ankles in each of its paws and he awoke back to reality fast in fear of his own life as it dragged him screaming at the top of his lungs "AAAAHHHHH—SOOOME BOODY HELLLP MEEEeeeee, " off the joggers path where he scratched the dirt with his finger nails trying to hold onto the dirt path with a fingernail grip and into the bushes he was forcefully pulled which he then grabbed the bushes with his hands to pull himself to freedom, but they were yanked from out of his hands and deep down into the woods he was violently pulled where she could do its dirty work alone and undisturbed by anyone and the foggy woods consumed both the attacker and prey in mere seconds and only the sound of echo's remained behind on the jogger's path which not a soul heard through the dark lonely woods.

Meanwhile back at the Old Bethabara Settlement the trio were looking at each other in shocked togetherness that they were once again in the right place at the right time.

"Well—Clara Bell and Wilbur Parker your surely a sight for sore eyes, it's been years sense I've seen y'all," replied Bill who had gained some of his composure back with a sheepish grin on his tired southern face while lying in the middle of the street.

"It's been a long time—Bill," replied Clara Bell who stood beside her husband confidently that the night was won for them.

"I thought I was hot on the trail of a suspected serial killer out here tonight, but I've been a rocking and rolling out here on this road with some kind of lone timber wolf that wondered down here from the mountain's—or—from somewhere looking for food and that's my only guess," spoke

Bill who was breathing hard from all the excitement and was now sitting up right in the brick street.

"After it attacked me and was scared off by y'all I presume and while I was laying here thinking about it for a few minutes—it's the only thing that fits because my suspect has disappeared into thin air or was scared off by y'all too and I think it's the same suspect I chased from the other night who got away. What in Gods name is going on out here tonight. What are y'all doing here tonight," asked Bill who sat up watching them with a starry eyed questionable foolish face?

"Looks' like you've been rolling and rocking all over this road and got the bad end of it, but you can't keep a good man down for long," replied Wilbur laughing who extended his hand down to help Bill up off the brick top road.

"Yeah—it hurt's worse than it looks," replied Bill who started to reach up and grabbed Wilbur's hand and he winced in pain from his sore back and rubbed the back of his aching neck instead for a moment with his red scrapped palmed right hand.

Clara Bell bit her lip and then spoke her peace to Bill lying on the street.

"Bill are you off your rocker—I'm mightily afraid your suspect might have turned into a werewolf out here this very moonlit night. That was no ordinary murderous man of this earth, but a supernatural werewolf not of this good earth either, but from the dark underworld, its what we country people call a skin shed-er and the underworld term is a Lycan, and if you ran into him the other night count your self lucky to have survived that night too with Guardian Angels who must have been looking out for you," replied Clara Bell with a serious look on her old grandma face looking down through her wire rim spectacles that seemed to slide down to the end of her nose?

Bill was taken aback at that and after satisfying his painful neck with a soothing hand rub he grabbed the out stretched hand and Wilbur harden his stance and braced his body and pulled.

Bill was lifted up on his feet by a strong arm and back from Wilbur who shook Bill's hand and let go.

"A werewolf—I thought that was only a myth or an old legend ghost tale to scare you late at night around a campfire with fellow campers from church and I was lucky the other night that I didn't fall to my death from a train chase which I saved myself from certain death, but I didn't have time to look over my shoulder to see if a Guardian Angel had my back," spoke Bill looking at Clara Bell bemused and skeptical about the run in with the wolf and Clara Bells Christian beliefs while he exercised his sore back by moving his hips back and forth in a swaying circle motion from side to side to work out the kinks in his lower back.

"When the sun goes down the dark side of humanity come's out at night that no one wants to face or talk about. Most people don't believe in mysticism these days anyhow," replied Clara Bell who watched Bill intently with a cold poker face who new better than to show all her cards out here tonight in front of strangers.

"Sows running with the old devil if you asked me," said a bible totten Wilbur out right smartly to Bill who grinned back foolishly at Wilbur's religious quote from the bible.

"I thought I was off my game tonight after being knocked off that footbridge by my suspect I was chasing and taking a spill in the small creek behind the old fort tonight where I lost sight of him and then he got away and then I got kicked twice again on my butt again out here where that lone wolf that attacked me in the middle of the street and I hope there's not a third time tonight because the third time's the charm and it's all over but the crying," spoke Bill who was very disgusted with himself in front of everybody, but was feeling a little bit better after exercising his sore back.

"Look on the bright side of it—Bill. I'd say your game was

right on tonight because your still alive and kicking out here tonight and your living on a prayer because I prayed hard for the good lord to spare your life tonight and that third charm is not going to happen again if I can help it," replied Clara Bell who leaned on her cane firmly in the dimly lit foggy shrouded street looking at Bill with concern for his safety on her dear old grandmother face.

"And your ahead of the game as usual and I guess by you being here tonight in the middle of my murder case proves it and thanks for saying a prayer for me. I guess it helped me out here tonight after all because I was fighting on a wing and a prayer with that old wolf and thank the good lord for that," responded Bill honestly without a shadow of a doubt in his mind about the old elderly woman's credibility he thought to himself and Bill just shrugged his shoulders at those remark's and looked at Wilbur who was smiling at his wet dirty suit.

"Bill—don't be so ignorant—listen to what the woman has to say because she's been right on out here tonight and she saved your butt. There's no rest for the weary—Bill—and that's you and us, I'd say who got involved on this wild goose chase of yours looking for murder suspects in the middle of the night," replied Wilbur who gave Bill the once over to make sure he was alright and he found out soon enough.

"I should have recognized those size 16 dirt clod knocker boots coming down the street you old farmers always wear out in the tobacco fields and I think its time for a bucking up with each other as they say down on the farm when two bulls go head to head in the pasture," said Bill smiling sheepishly pissed off toward Wilbur who was startled at what Bill had said to him and smiled back at him again standing in the middle of the old settlement street watching him with an amused face at his predicament.

"The source of all your problems is because you ain't living right if you asked me," replied Wilbur who eyed Bill cooly standing in the street wondering if he could save his lost soul for the lord.

"Who asked you in the first place," shouted Bill angrily back at Wilbur who felt his feathers had been ruffled a bit!

"What in the hell has got into you," snapped Wilbur back in self defense of his own person?

"I've had a rough week and the way I run my life is none of your business—preacher man," uttered Bill sarcastically mean with irony in his voice.

"Alright Bill you asked for it and your going to get it right now because of those smart remarks and what you need is a swift kick in the ass. You young whippersnapper," replied Wilbur who's temper flared up and stood his ground on the old fort settlement street.

Bill watched as Wilbur reached into his right side tool pocket down beside his right thigh on his bib overhauls and pulled out a small round plastic snuff can that was labeled "Big Horn" moist snuff long cut wintergreen. Wilbur open the round plastic lid and with a now steady hand got a good pinch of moist snuff between his right thumb and forefinger.

Wilbur shook off the loose snuff by tapping it over the can which fell back into the small round plastic snuff can and he closed the lid.

Wilbur pulled open his bottom right side lip with his left hand while holding the snuff can and inserted the pinch of snuff in between his cheek and gum quickly.

"M-M-M-M-mmmm," that's good snuff and I feel relaxed with a good taste of nicotine snuff in my mouth. I was born in the red dirt fields of North Carolina riding on my daddy's tractor by my momma who gave birth right there on Gods good green earth and I've been a natural farmer ever since birth and my grand pap held my hand on the steering wheel as a baby while we plowed the fields on his old green john deer tractor. My daddy could bring life to frozen ground and he taught me the same way about growing thing's.

Makes me feel right at home out here this time of night but I'm a corn and tobacco farmer by day now and back in the day a real urban cowboy at night on the mechanical bull at the old Country Corral in King.

I also rode the Brama bulls on the rodeo circuit in my younger days and won a few trophies and ribbons,"said Wilbur laughing "HA-HA-HA-HA," who winked a right eye at Bill under neath his yellow cowboy style straw hat and after a few moments spit out the nicotine into the side ditch over by the old log cabin by tuning his body around and putting his two first right hand fingers on his lips like he was making a small peace sign over his lips which he spitted through "Piissss—splat," on the ground and then he slid the can of snuff back in his right side bib overhaul tool pocket down beside his right leg thigh.

"I'm a spittin and a grinnin' and not falling down on the job like you," said Wilbur who laughed whole heartily out loud "Ha-Ha-Ha," again with his hands holding on to his bib coveralls front straps pulled out away's from his chest standing there on the brick road right proudly of himself at Bill's expense.

"I was born in the hospital with a badge pinned to my diaper when I was just a wee baby and I come from a long line of top cops in my family. I'm a real cowboy of a lawman too with the time, I've put in on the force before I retired years ago as a big dick city detective, but I just smoke big Churchill Maduro cigars and drink hard whiskey while listening to my favorite 80s music.

I don't dip snuff and I'm a street tough city slicker and not an old country boy sod buster farmer like you and I hate country music and Pabst Blue Ribbon beer which is for red necks anyway—where I come from and anyway—you do what ever it takes to catch a crook even if you get all wet behind the ears," replied Bill with a sarcastic face who looked slightly annoyed at Wilbur and the snuff that was spit on the ground not far from him and Bill laughed sarcastically "heh-heh-heh" under his breath at Wilbur's country upbringing.

Clara Bell with a mean face started to clear her throat at the two men who had briefly forgot about her during their big city country style bucking up to each other like they had in the past down on the farm to get their attention which she always had to step in and break up their foolish argument game with each other.

"UH-UH-M-M-M!, UH-UH—M-M-M!" came the sound from Clara Bell who cleared her throat rather loudly at the two men.

"Stop that bucking up and bickering among your selves like two old tired and stubborn Missouri farm mule's hitched to a plow that want move out in the corn field after a hard day's work in the sun.

The only thing you ever won in your younger rodeo days was me—Wilbur—and Bill—I'm surprised at you, you were raised better than that and should no better than to pick a fuss with an old codger like Wilbur out here tonight after what just happen here in this deserted place with a lone Lycan wolf on the prowl if that be the case because they sometimes hunt in pairs or packs usually and I'd bet my mason jar of jellybeans that another one is close by," spoke Clara Bell right madly with a smirk look on her dear old round pug nosed face with her wire rim spectacles still at the edge of her nose.

She pushed them back up quickly on her face with an agitated finger on her cane hand and the two old friends quit bickering playfully like two old school boys with one raised in the city and the other raised on a country farm trying to best each other like they always do with each other and both looked at her with an undivided attention!

"ALLL—right now—that's better—your all wet Bill and you'll catch your death of cold if you don't get out of those wet clothes and I see you wore your fathers silver cross tonight," said Clara Bell smiling at being a old, but polite sentimental grandma who didn't give a hoot about their foolish bickering with each other.

She walked over to Bill and picked up his cross that dangled in front of his torn and ripped shirt looking at it with admiration in her heart.

"Bill—there's some partially singed hair stuck to your cross which helped saved you tonight and I'll bet its from that werewolf you just tangled with who got more than he bargained for out here tonight," said Clara Bell very smartly with her all seeing eyes who let go of the silver cross that dangled on Bill's chest.

Bill picked up the silver cross from his chest and looked at it for a surprised moment in shock disbelief.

"Say—your right and I'll have to bag it for evidence," replied Bill who reached into his left side coat pocket and pulled out a small wet plastic zip bag. Bill got out his knife from his right pants pocket and flicked opened the long blade. He preceded to scrape the hairs off the silver cross into the plastic bag and he sealed it shut and stuck it back in his left coat pocket. He shut the knife and stuck it back in his right pants pocket and thought about his fight with Wilbur and new they were only trying to help him. He was having feeling's of a guilty conscious.

"I'm sorry Clara Bell for picking a fight with Wilbur and taking it out on him, but I've had a rough time out here tonight and when I started to leave the house tonight something made me go back and get it and wear it for good luck tonight," said a grateful and apologetic Bill who thought about his dear old departed father.

"Apology excepted—no problem among old friends," said Wilbur who patted Bill on his wet back good naturally with a friendly weathered old left hand.

"Well—the good lord was watching out for you with Divine intervention tonight and your father as well. It's funny how parents can give their children things to protect them through life long after they are gone.

I had a bad omen dream the other night from my second sight. This young jogger woman was attacked by a werewolf and you tried to save her and both of you were killed here this very night," spoke Clara Bell with a wise look about her over her eyeglasses on her old wrinkled face.

"That's why you and Wilbur were here tonight, to intervene and save us," replied Bill with a heartfelt look of gratitude on his face after deducing what had happen here tonight was not out of the ordinary with his quick witted mind.

"Yes— that about sums it all up, by our presence here we altered the time line of event's to come," replied Clara Bell leaning on her cane that had started to glow with a illumination of spiritual light.

"That some how explains all of what has transpired here tonight with you good folks being here in the nick of time to save us if what you say is true, even if I started to believe it was a real werewolf that attacked me here tonight and it still blows my mind away because its hard for me to believe it, I deal only in facts not fantasy," replied Bill the sometimes paranormal skeptic who then noticed her cane in her hand.

"Uhhh—your cane is glowing," spoke Bill with a look of astonishment on his face.

"Oh—it's just recharging in the light—dear," replied Clara Bell who tapped the end of the cane real quick twice "tap, tap" and the light faded out.

"I didn't get to thank-you both for saving my life tonight," spoke the young woman jogger to Clara Bell and Wilbur who had been taking this all in.

"You can thank him too. He ran that hellish creature of the night off from here with his lucky silver cross," replied Wilbur while he gestured toward Bill standing off to his rightside on the road.

"Thank-you mister, I want for get it, not ever and these

two good people here with you too, but who'd believe my story about tonight's events?," asked the young woman jogger who looked at Bill with deep blue eyes.

"I'm just doing my job and mum's the word about what happen out here tonight unless you want to end up in the looney bin," spoke Bill modestly to the young woman jogger to keep her mouth shut.

"Oh— you're a policeman—then," asked the young woman jogger who waited for Bill's reply?

"Well—sort of, I'm a private investigator and retired detective from the Winston-Salem police department whose now at your service and like I said before I'd keep what happen here tonight to myself young lady and people want think your off your rocker," replied Bill who stood up on the balls of his feet with pride in his heart at being a honest ex cop and private eye for hire who hopped to convince her into silence.

"That answer's my question completely and I'll take that advise to heart and not say another word about it," replied the young female jogger who shuffled her feet nervously standing among the strange group of people she had just met by a twist of fate on her nightly jog through the park.

"What kind of wolf was that—again," asked Bill who saw he had convinced the young jogger who turning his attention back at Clara Bell with a school boy's admiration in class on the first day of school for his new teacher?

"I swani—Bill—don't be as dumb as a box of rocks. That was a werewolf Bill and a pack of them have taken up territorial root here in Winston- Salem and that's what's been doing these grisly murders around here and I'm sure of it—now. They come out after dark on a moonlit night even Jesus told his disciples that they must take shelter for the night cometh fore evil things come out at night and lurk about in the dark which no man can stand against alone in their dark wicked underworld, " spoke Clara Bell the master teacher looking over her wire rim spectacle's at Bill with a look of I'm always right on her face.

"After seeing that thing tonight and tangling with it. It dam near killed me and I almost winked out of existence laying on that lighted fog covered brick road with it on top of me about to tear me apart and I guess it wasn't my time to go tonight—lucky me," said Bill who thought about it some more for a moment and spoke again quickly to Finnish up what he had to say before anyone else got a word in edgewise.

"I some how believe you now after thinking about it because from the first time I laid eyes on that weird wolf it just didn't look natural to me, but it all happen so quick its hard to tell if the wolf was real that had wondered down here from the mountains or your version was real about it being a werewolf and besides the games a foot on my new case that I have been working on.

I couldn't just stay at home tonight and miss out on chasing down my clues I've found in the course of certain events to try and solve my murder case and I can't let the killer or killers escape justice that I'm after," replied Bill who had arched his eyebrows up in awe at what Clara Bell had said with a good deal of respect for this old clairvoyant grandma, but he still wasn't convinced in his dim witted unbelieving mind just yet about the werewolf that had attacked him just now in the old settlement.

"Your messing with supernatural power's of the dark underworld realm and only pure silver can kill a werewolf and they have immense power from the gates of hell, that flows through their Lycan bodies when the moon is full at night. The gates of hell are thrown wide open to send demonic life force into their evil blood lusting minds and they have powers that rival a ordinary man such as you—Bill," spoke Clara Bell with a smiling face of spiritual awareness from deep within herself.

"Well—I need all the help I can get and I'm glad you and Wilbur showed up to night with your knowledge of the dark underworld to save us. I guess it was my lucky night to wear my silver cross. I'm alive and still ticking because of it and I lived to tell the tale—again," replied Bill with a beaming foolish face who had started to except his fate that he was almost killed by a real werewolf after going over it in his mind from front to back with quick photogenic reasoning and finely deduced it must have been the real thing like she said it was, but he still had his doubt's.

"I'd say you do. We will team up again together and fight the forces of underworld darkness and evil again, just like we did out on Payne Road In Rural Hall a few year's back and we will make sure that swift justice is served southern style," spoke Clara Bell who winked at Wilbur and Bill with a brave smile.

"That sounds like a winner to me and takes a load off my shoulders. I need some back up on this murder case who-dun'it which is out of my league and over my head—if what you say it true because y'all are the experts in that supernatural field," replied Bill modestly with knowing that this old grandma was nobody's fool and was supernaturally smart and he shook his head back and forth with awe as 'The Ghost of Payne Road Case" came flooding back to his memory now which had made him a believer at one time of the supernatural world which his factual law enforcement mind had always conflicted with and over time he had moved on and forgotten about it by putting it behind him long ago after that case had been closed for good.

"Then it's a done deal and we need to go before anymore come out of the woodwork and attack us because werewolf's are a powerful force to be reckon with in this day and time. I'll bet my prize cow that there's murder on the roadside tonight and we can't be everywhere at once to outsmart them or stop them like here tonight," replied Clara Bell who winked at Bill with a air of confidence about her old country self.

"I guess your right Clara Bell," replied Bill concerned for everybody's safety and he looked quickly around the old dark and dimly lit settlement but saw nothing lurking in the lighted road or dark shadows to be alarmed about around the old fort.

"Well— it's getting late and we are going to run this nice lady home Bill, do you want a ride," asked Wilbur who was ready for a hard snort of liquor and a nice warm bed after tonight and he thought to himself that he was too old to cut the mustard anyhow?

"Sure—let me find my gun which I'm sure is down the road a peace where I threw it trying to hit that wolf and I'll take you up on that offer," said Bill who looked around and spotted his detective hat laying in the side ditch not a few feet from where he was standing.

Bill's keen mind was thinking about his suspect's car parked at the top of the hill at the old Bethabara par course and playground. He hoped it was still there intact while he walked over and bent down and retrieved his hat with his right hand.

Bill stood straight up and arched his back to stretched his aching back with his left hand for support on his left hip and put his hat back on his head after that and ran his fingers across the brim of the detective hat to slightly bend the brim downward over his face just like he liked it. Bill soon felt better standing there in the lighted foggy street back in one piece so it seemed to himself and in good company with old reliable friends.

"Lets go," said Wilbur who ushered them all down the street and off they went all together down the red brick road. They all walked back down the brick lined street toward the potters house.

"Is that your gun Bill, in the street by the side ditch, underneath the big oak tree," asked Clara Bel who spotted it and pointed at it with her twisted swamp root cane at the same time before anyone else did while they walked down the single brick road?

"Yep—that's it," replied Bill who left the group and walked over by the big oak tree on the side of the road and picked it up. Bill quickly unloaded his gun and put the three spent shells in his coat pocket and loaded three more rounds in the chamber from his spare bullet's in his small ammo belt that held twelve bullet's clipped on his backside belt beside his holster and clicked the barrel shut and put his gun back in his right hip holster.

"Lets go," said Wilbur who walked down to the old Moravian church front door away's down the street and picked up his broken pitch fork lying in the street with his party of people behind him and then he crossed the road to his car in the potter's house parking lot and unlocked his car trunk with the keys.

Wilbur put the broken pieces of his pitch fork in the trunk and slammed the lid shut. Wilbur walked around the side of the car and unlocked the driver's door. He opened the car door and slid into the front seat and stuck his car key in the ignition and started the engine while unlocking the passenger door for Clara Bell. He grabbed his old blue plastic spit cup from the floor console and spit nicotine into and tucked it in between his legs for the long ride home.

The young female jogger got into the back seat while Clara Bell held the front seat that she had pushed forward for Bill and the young woman jogger to get into the backseat of the car.

When Bill slid into the back seat Clara Bell pushed the front seat back in a upright position and sat down onto the front seat and slid her feet into the car shutting the car door.

"You can drop me off at the par course and playground up the hill on Old Town Drive. I have a suspects vehicle to check out if it's still there and that's where my car's parked on stake-out," spoke Bill with a little luck in his voice and determination of a old city cop on the beat.

"Sounds good to me," replied Wilbur who put the car

in reverse and backed around in the gravel parking lot of the potter's house and turned on the car's headlight's.

"Where do you live," asked Clara Bell who looked back over the front seat at the young female jogger woman reply while Wilbur pulled the car's stick shift in drive and took off out of the parking lot onto Bethabara Road? Wilbur drove slowly down the single brick road past the old fort.

"Crystal Lake apartments is where I live up on Reynolda Road," replied the young female jogger who eyed Clara Bell then looked at Bill with a interested quick eye. Clara Bell smiled at that look, but Bill didn't notice it because he had his mind on his case at hand in far off thought's.

"That's not far up the road and it's on the way," spoke Wilbur who slowed the car down to stop at the stop sign at Bethania Station Road intersection. Wilbur hit the gas when he saw no cars coming his way at the other stop signs. He drove past the Herb Garden on his left and made the sharp 90 degree bad curve left turn on Old Town drive as Clara Bell turned back around in her seat.

They drove up the hill and in a few minutes Wilbur turned onto the par course and playground road. He drove down the access road and through the gates.

"Yes—it's still there," shouted Bill with excitement in his voice from the back seat after he saw the suspect's vehicle still parked at the cemetery gates down the road from his parked car at the Bethabara par course and playground parking lot.

"There's my old Monte Carlo you can let me out there," suggested Bill with eagerness in his voice.

"O. K.," Replied Wilbur who pulled the car up in front of Bill's car parked in the playground parking lot space.

"Call me Bill, we have some more talking to do about this case and plan what we need to do about our dark adversaries," spoke Clara Bell as she open the car door and scooted forward and pulled the front seat forward with her to let Bill out.

"I'll call you sometime tomorrow if I have time," replied

Bill as he squeezed out of the back seat and stepped out onto the parking lot.

Clara Bell shut the door and Wilbur turned around in the parking lot and was gone down the access road and disappeared into the darkness of night by the car's fading headlight's that was all Bill could see down the dark road and then it was gone.

Bill fished out his car keys and walked to his car and unlocked the door. Bill reached in and pulled out his cell phone from his front seat and dialed 911 while sitting down in the front seat watching the suspect's car and he noticed the young lover's car had long gone from their little romantic spot.

Bill pulled out his 38 snub nose revolver with his right hand just in case he needed it and he sure didn't want to get caught off guard again while on the phone as he dangled the gun between his legs sitting partly on the front seat of his car with his feet in the parking lot. "This is 911 what's the emergency," asked the young female police officer over the phone?

"This is Private Investigator Bill Christian calling. I'm working on a case for your police department and I have a suspect's car to be checked out by our crime scene unit," replied Bill with some stress in his voice who waited a moment for a response. "Oh"—hi—Bill this is Patty, where are you and I'll dispatch them to your location," asked Patty who was all business?

"I'm on scene at the Bethabara Park par course and playground on Oldtown Drive and send a unit with them. I might need some help because the suspect might return here and he's a handful. By the way how's your dad doing, last I heard, he had retired from the force," replied Bill without giving out further information that he new they wouldn't believe after tonight's little run in with a deadly wolf. Even he was in doubt about himself believing in his old friends wild werewolf ghost story, but he couldn't rule anything out just yet, until he new all the facts which don't lie in his murder case.

"I'll do that Bill and dispatch them to your location and they will be there in ten minutes, just hold on till they get there and dad and mom moved to Pilot Mountain and bought a cabin with a little land on it, you know how he likes to hunt game," replied Patty with concern for Bill in her voice who had recognized the daughter of one of his old police buddies from the force by the moment he had talk to her on the phone which brought back memories of police brotherhood and backyard cookouts.

"Thanks—that's a big 10-4 and after this case I'm on is over I'll have to get up with your dad and do a little hunting with him at his retirement cabin in the mountains, see ya later," replied Bill and he hung up the cell phone while his eyes darted around the dark parking lot looking for anything out of the wood work that might be a threat while he waited for his people to show up.

About ten minutes later Bill looked up from his front car seat and saw the headlights of vehicles headed his way down the access road and heard cars fast approaching his position, then the police cruiser entered the parking lot of Bethabara Park par course and playground and pulled up in front of his parked Montle Carlo followed by the crime scene unit van.

Bill slid out of his front seat and holstered his snub nose 38 and walked around the police cruiser and introduced himself.

The young rookie police officer rolled down his driver's side window and smiled politely at Bill.

"I'm Bill Christian Private Investigator and I'm working on a case for your department," spoke Bill as he watched the rookie officer sitting in his patrol car which reminded him of memories how he started with the Winston-Salem police department some twenty years ago as a shift patrolman police officer until he got promoted up through the ranks to first class detective.

"Yes—sir all shifts have been briefed about you and I'm here to assist you in any way I can," replied rookie officer Decker with polite respect for an old police veteran of the force.

"I need that old blue car checked out parked down there at the gates to the cemetery and run this licence plate to see who owns it and if it's stolen," asked Bill handing the young rookie officer his pad through the window of the police cruiser? The rookie police officer noticed that Bill was wringing wet from head to toe but didn't say anything.

The young officer got on the radio as more units pulled into the parking lot to assist Bill who watched the calvary come rolling in.

The young CIS technician got out of his van behind the police cruiser and walked quickly up to Bill who was standing in the parking lot still talking to the rookie police officer and he also noticed Bill was wringing wet from head to toe then Bill noticed him watching him with eagerness to start work.

"That old blue 1987 Buick La Sabre car down at the gate is our suspect vehicle that you need to check out tonight," ordered Bill who took charge of the crime scene situation.

"I'm William Walters from the CSI unit and it's nice to meet such a distinguished officer and man," said William who stuck out his hand toward Bill smiling at the wet duck in front of him, but no way was he about to ask what happen to Bill and embarrass him.

Bill grabbed the mans hand smiling and shook it firmly and he noticed William's grip was also firm and he had been taught by his father that a firm handshake meant he was an honest man and a loose handshake meant you couldn't trust him.

"Nice to meet you," replied Bill while he shook the lawman's hand. "I'll pull my van down there beside the car and start checking it out from top to bottom and I will take control of the crime scene as of now," said William with enthusiasm in his voice and he turned to go back to his CSI van and Bill noticed the big white CSI letters on the back of the man's jacket, that distinguished him from regular police.

Bill was glad help from his old force had arrived as he stood in the middled of the Bethabara par course and playground thinking about tonight's events looking at all the cop cars in the parking lot. Sometime later the suspect's car which had been unlocked had been dusted for fingerprints and the CSI investigator had found a right thumb print on the rear view mirror which every good CSI knows to look there first because everybody in a new car always adjust the rear view mirror first before driving the new car and a left hand palm print on the driver's side window.

"This car's door has been jimmied," said William standing there in the shadow of his portable lights he had sat up to shine on the suspect's car with his fingerprint brush in his left gloved hand after he had dusted the open door.

"See the grove marks on top of the door between the glass and the door's silver chrome. It even scraped off the paint some while the suspect worked the jimmy tool to unlock the door and then he pulled out the ignition wires from under the dash to start the car," said CSI William while Bill looked on with interest.

"I suspected the car had been stolen from the first time I saw it. I guess you can call it a hunch," replied Bill with confidence in his manner.

"Well—I'd say were both right," said CSI William who pulled out fingerprint and palm tape from his technician tool box to transfer the prints to clear tape for analysis at the lab back at the Winston-Salem CSI police department.

Bill waited until the CSI technician transferred the prints to clear plastic tape from outside and inside the car. Bill then looked inside the car and noticed some red mud on the driver's floorboard that was lit up by the cars interior floorboard lights.

"Get a sample of that red mud there and send it to the lab, it may tell us where the suspect has been or lives," said Bill as the CSI investigator guickly got out a clear plastic bag from his CSI tool box and tweezers and went to work on getting a good sample for his pals back at the lab.

"Good eye," said CSI William while he reached in to get a sample of mud off the floorboard. While Bill watched the CSI investigator scraping the mud into the bag, the young rookie officer came up to him at the suspect's car.

"The car was stolen from Clemmons a few days ago and it came up on my police information criminal database system lap-top," said rookie officer Decker.

"Yeah—I thought it was stolen and now were getting somewhere," replied Bill with a now relaxed expression on his face.

The CSI put the bag of mud in his evidence bag and reached inside the car and popped the trunk release latch. Bill heard the trunk pop open in back of the car as he tuned back his attention the the CSI investigator behind him looking with a questionable face at him.

"Let's check and make sure those not a body in the trunk," said CSI William standing up watching Bill with a very bright look on his face. "That's a great ideal but I hope it's empty," replied Bill eagerly as they walked around the suspect's car to the trunk.

The CSI took out a small flashlight from his front shirt pocket and clicked it on and he pushed up the trunk lid and shined the beam in the trunk which they all looked eagerly in at but it was empty, all they saw was a spare tire while CSI William searched through the trunk for any evidence.

Bill and the rookie police officer Decker smiled at each other relieved that there wasn't a dead body in the trunk. "Thank-God no dead body in the trunk tonight and its clean, must be our lucky night," said CSI William who smiled at Bill and the rookie cop.

"You can say that again and that would have been a bummer after tonight," said Bill who looked down at the ground and nervously shuffled his feet.

"What are you talking about," asked CSI William looking at Bill with a dead in the face look of wondering what happen here tonight, I don't know about smirk of surprise?

"Never mind," replied Bill who didn't want to look foolish in front of these professional police officers. Bill knew they would never believe his wild story about what happen to him tonight at old Bethabara park.

"Well we can't do any more here tonight, I'll have the suspect's car towed to the police impound lot," said CSI William to Bill who was impressed with the man's professionalism while CSI William made the call for a tow truck and didn't stick his nose any further in Bill's business because he had been taught well by his father who was a retired police officer not to not question a fellow cop's motives either active or on the force or retired in business for himself.

They were all out for the same thing apprehend the suspect and justice for the courts and families of the victims thought CSI William to himself listening to his cell phone and then someone answered the phone.

"This is Johnny's towing and recovery, Johnny speaking," said Johnny who waited to hear who was calling at this late hour and CSI William began speaking on his cell phone to order the tow truck.

"That's fine—I saw you go over this car with a fine tooth comb and didn't miss anything tonight—I hope, call me if anything comes up," replied Bill with a confident smile on his face. William beamed at Bill in the glare of lights from his portable lights at the praise but couldn't reply just yet because he hadn't finished his phone call for a tow truck yet.

"Make sure Roxanne gets this plastic bag filled with some

hair's in it for examination," said Bill who pulled the bag out of his coat pocket and handed to the CSI William.

"I'll certainly do just that," said CSI William who took the bag and quickly labeled it with the black permanent marker he carried in his shirt pocket and stuck it in his CSI tool box.

"I'm heading home for some much needed sleep William, we can do no more here tonight and its almost morning, thank-you for coming out here at this late hour," replied Bill who walked off toward his car.

"Thank-you and no problem and you'll be the first to hear anything," said CSI William who had finished his call and was listening to Bill talk to him while Bill walked past him and he flipped his cell phone shut, sliding it in his right front pocket and grabbed up his crime scene tool box and headed for his van with his evidence bags in hand.

"Have a good rest of the night—sir," said rookie officer Decker who watched Bill wave at him as he got in his car and start it up and pulled off past the parked police cruiser's in the parking lot. Then rookie officer Decker turned around and walked off to help CSI William load up his portable lights while they waited on the tow truck to come and get the suspect's car for police impound.

"That guy looked like he'd been through a rain storm and rode hard and put up wet," said rookie officer Decker with a laugh "ha, ha, ha," to CSI William as he grabbed a potable light in his hands to put in the CSI van.

"What ever he got into tonight, something is watching over him and he sure as Hell lived to tell the tale about his personal business here tonight. I'd be careful what you say about that man whose a highly decorated and ex legendary lawman of the Winston-Salem police detective force, he has friends in high places—you know," replied a wise CSI William who walked past him with a mad attitude at the joke officer Decker had made about Bill and picked up the last portable light to put in his van and saw the tow truck pull into the parking lot back behind him.

Rookie officer Decker's face turned white at hearing that from CSI William as he quickly looked around the parking lot and saw some of the older cops watching him intently.

Meanwhile that same night Wilbur had gone into the kitchen for a snort of his white liquor moonshine that he made at his still back down in his hidden secret cellar behind his house that was cleverly hidden from them old rascal federal revenues who always busted his friends rivalry stills up in Forsyth County but they some how never bothered his still around here because country people around these parts in Stokes County kept their mouth's shut.

Wilbur walked over to the kitchen cabinets beside the kitchen sink and open the cabinet door and got out a old quart mason glass jar that he liked to drink from which he saved them for drinking glasses after eating the dill pickles out of them that Clara Bell made from the summer garden until she used them to can her pickles again and Wilbur also bought the can pickles jars from the country store down the road which he liked from time to time.

He walked to the kitchen sink and pulled the curtain back that hid the old plumbing and Clara Bells cleaning supplies also her special cast iron cooking pots. He grabbed the top of his gallon moonshine pickle jar and lifted it out and up onto the kitchen counter top.

Wilbur sat down his glass and unscrewed the metal lid and set it on the kitchen counter top and gabbed the gallon moonshine old pickle jar and poured himself a good strong drink about halfway up in the old mason glass jar.

Wilbur smelled the 90 proof strong clear liquor and it took his breath away for a moment.

"Whew—that's strong stuff and it will knock your socks off and grow hair on you chest," said Wilbur to himself who chuckled heartily out loud to himself and then he took a big swig.

The strong liquor burned his throat all the way down and warmed up his stomach innards.

"Man that was some good sour mash whisky moonshine I made from my families secret southern recipe that has been handed down from generation to generation over the years and named "Blue Moon" so rightly so," said Wilbur smiling with a air of connoisseur knowledge about himself and then he rubbed his mouth with the back of his left hand and then he finished the rest of his glass and set it in the kitchen sink.

He always sold what he made at his moonshine still to all of his friends in Rural Hall with no trouble for he was always sold out on payday Friday for the local people who came from near and far to buy his home made brew whisky down on his farm.

He had hid his still under the floor in his barn and ran the smokestack from the boiler through the walls tied into his wood stove flue in the tack room and out the top of the roof that blended in with the barn and those darn revenue men who worked for the federal government could never find it because he ran it at night instead of the daytime when they were around on the prowl to bust it up if they ever found it, but that would be the day they had outsmarted him which would be when Hell froze over thought Wilbur who chuckled to himself proudly whole heartedly "ha, ha, ha," under his moonshine breath.

He picked up the metal lid and screwed the metal lid back on the gallon glass jar of moonshine and set it back under the kitchen sink and closed the sink curtain back to hide it from prying eyes.

He walked across the kitchen floor and his farm work boots made a clumping sound "clump, clump" while he walked over to the light switch on the wall and he flipped it off and made his way down the hall to the stairs to go up to his bedroom and join Clara Bell who had long took her heart medicine and went to bed as soon as they had walked in the front door.

His old foot steps disappeared up the flight of carpeted stairs while the old oak hand rail on the side of the old stairs balanced his big tall body.

He grabbed it each time as he moved up the tall stairs with his right tanned strong farm hand and his footsteps softly echoed down the long patted carpeted hallway overhead and he was gone in the shadows of the old farm house.

Bill saw the sunrise in the east over the fall treetops when he pulled into his driveway and parked his Monte Carlo car. He cut his car's engine off and open the car door and pushed down the door latch with the keys in his hand to lock it.

Then he got out and shut the car door and walked across his driveway to his concrete walkway and strolled up to his front door and unlocked his front door with his house key on his key ring.

He then went inside his house shutting and locking his front door after turning off his night security house lights.

Bill felt very tired while he walked down the hallway to his laundry room and took off his cross also he pulled out his keys, wallet, gun holster, cell phone, pad & pen and spare change laying them on his laundry table with his hat. Then he took off his shoes and stripped down to bear skin.

He dried his hair with a towel and then his body that he had grabbed off the dryer that had been folded up among clean linen by his house keeper as he ran his hands through his hair, checking it to make sure it was dry.

It didn't matter anyway he'd take a shower today anyway after waking up and dry his hair with a dryer thought Bill who tossed the wet towel in the laundry basket after he was done. He just didn't want to wake up sick from a cold and anyway the heat was on in the house and it felt warm to his naked body thought Bill so he felt he was O.K..

Bill piled his suit of wet clothes in his laundry basket for his part time house keeper to wash or dry clean and he didn't care fore he was too exhausted to think about it anymore and he headed for his bedroom back down the hall.

He cut on his bedroom light and was very exhausted walking into his bedroom butt naked. He strode over to his dresser and pulled open a top drawer and got out some fresh underwear and fresh pajamas.

Bill put them on quickly almost falling on the hard floor when he lost his balance stepping into his pajamas pants.

"Gee—whizz," cried out Bill while he struggled into his pajama pants who then fell onto the bed with some relief that the long night was finely over.

Bill pulled the sheets and quilt down from underneath the pillows from the headboard and crawled under them.

He pushed his pillow under his head and soon fell fast asleep and was dead to the world with his bedroom light left on.

That morning officer Darker waited while his phone rang at the post command headquarters second floor section at the Winston-Salem police department.

"This is officer Julie Sanders of the post command speaking my I help you," asked Julie who waited for a reply on the phone?

"Hi—Julie this is officer Darker and I'm calling in sick. I have a migraine head ache and I want be in for a few days," replied officer Darker who waited on his end of the phone for a response.

"Hold on for a second, while I talk to the shift commander," replied officer Julie. Officer Darker sat on his couch for a tense moment hoping he didn't have to report for duty today.

"The shift commander says your excused as long as you bring in a doctor's excuse with you when you return to work and I hope you get to feeling better," said officer Julie Sanders cheerfully over the phone.

"Thanks—I hope so too—see ya later,' replied officer

Darker who hung up the phone and put a hot water bottle up to his right side of his head and he leaned back somewhat relaxed on his couch.

That same morning the Bethabara park maintenance worker was picking up trash around the old 1756 palisade fort beside the old 1788 Gemeinhaus Moravian church.

"Man—these homeless people or those crazy wild boys and teenager girls smoking dope just tear up their clothes and toss them on the ground. Must have been some wild party here last night," said the old gray haired park maintenance man who just scratched his head under his cap and picked up the man size shredded and tore up blue shoes. He stuffed them into his garbage bag while he cleaned up the strewn ripped blue shirt with a blue tie still attached to it and blue pants that were ripped to shreds laying around the old worn path in between the old fort and church without another thought as he went about his daily job at the park never realizing beyond his wildest imagination what had happen there last night.

Bill woke up with a jolt off the bed sitting up to a raised position scared out of his wits, that something was after him.

Bill quickly looked around the bedroom and to his relief he saw in was in his own bedroom and fell back in bed with a yawn, that he covered briefly with his right hand. Bill laid there for a few minutes collecting his thoughts and got up off the bed.

Bill crossed the bedroom quickly to his bathroom and grabbed a quick shower. He snatched his white bathrobe off its hook on the wall behind the bathroom door and quickly jumped into it. Bill looked at his clock on his night side table beside the bed and saw it was 5:30 P:M.

Bill headed out his bedroom door and down the hallway to the kitchen to make coffee. While the coffee was making Bill put toast in the toaster while he scrambled a egg in butter in the nonstick flying pan on his kitchen stove.

Bill made his toasted egg sandwich with mayonnaise on

the toast, just the way he liked it. Bill poured a hot cup of Columbian coffee and sat down with his finished egg sandwich and coffee.

He began to eat at the kitchen table in silence which sometimes does the heart good to be alone.

Later Bill finished up and put his dishes in the kitchen sink. Bill headed out of the kitchen to his bedroom to get dressed and stopped at his laundry room and grabbed up his silver cross off the table and hurried down the hallway to his bedroom.

Bill walked into his bedroom and walked over to his dresser and laid the silver cross back in his jewelry box for safe keeping. He walked over to his closet and thumbed through his suits.

Bill picked out a new gray blue suit from his closet which he put on and tied his red tie in the dresser mirror.

Bill reached down and got his silver cross from his jewelry box on his dresser and put it around his neck.

Saved my life last time and I think I'll wear it tonight and from now on for divine protection thought Bill.

Bill got out a clean detective hat from the top shelf in his closet put it on and adjusted the brim in the dresser mirror slightly bent down over his forehead and eyes.

Bill walked out of his bedroom, cutting off his light and down the hallway to his laundry room.

He got his personal items that he had left on the laundry table and his gun holster which he strapped to his belt.

Bill made a double check to make sure he had everything and new he was good to go.

Bill walked back down the hallway passed his bedroom and into the living room.

Bill flipped the switch on the wall beside his front door for his security lights and stereo system to come on in the living room and outside flood lights which lit up the front and backyard.

Bill open the front door and locked the door knob latch at the same time.

Bill walked out and shut the door behind him, confident that his house was safe from any would be thieves.

Later the sun was setting in the west when Bill pulled up in his parking place at his office.

Bill thought it was a cold looking sky with a beautiful fall sunset between the colors of the trees while he admired God's natural handy work. Bill got out of his car and locked it and headed to his front door of his office.

Bill bent down and picked up his daily newspaper which he tucked under his left armpit and had it delivered to his office where he was always at instead of his home.

Bill found the right key and stuck it in his lock and heard the tumblers click as he turned the deadbolt and the door popped open. Bill walked in and flipped on his bankers lamp on his desk which cast a gloomy light and shadow over his desk.

The small light cast shadows around his office. Bill pulled out his chair and unbutton his coat and set down. He laid his hat on his desk with his newspaper.

Then his nose started itching real bad and he ran his right forefinger back and forth under his nose to satisfy the scratchy and fiery itchy nose. It got worse and he got up and grabbed a tissue from his box on the file cabinet and he set back down in his chair while blowing his nose into the tissue and rubbing it back and forth under his nose and then he cleaned out both sides of his nose with the tail end of the tissue.

"Man—somebody must be coming to see me," said Bill out loud to himself and he thought about the old wives tale if your nose itched you could expect company from someone soon his mom use to say thought Bill who remembered back in his early childhood days about his southern mama and he chuckled under his breath "he, he, he" who thought it was nonsense to believe in old wives tales these days.

He later felt better and his itchy nose spell had passed and he read his newspaper, then rummaged through his cold case files and time flew by, later there was a small knock on his office door.

Strange who could that be at this time of night thought Bill who got up from his desk and slid his coat back over his right hip behind his gun holster in case he needed to draw his gun quickly and walked over to the front door of his office and opened it slightly peering out into the darkness to see who it was.

Bill saw the dark silhouette of a woman standing there on his door stoup.

"May I help you," asked Bill wondering if the woman's car had broken down, down the street away's sense he didn't hear one pull up outside his door with his keen hearing?

"I have urgent information on the case you are handling—may I come in Mister Christian," asked the tall dark haired woman with gold looking blue eyes that were the windows of her soul which charmed Bill at first sight who was dressed in a dark flowing Victorian vested style dress with a black waist length Shawl on over her shoulders to keep warm?

Bill felt uneasy about this unexpected intrusion after dark, but his instinct's told him to let the woman in if she had information on his case at hand which might bust it wide open. He had solved more than one case from a tipster, but watch her very carefully thought Bill to himself.

Bill open the door wide open and he gestured for her to come in with a sweep of his arm.

"Come on in and take a seat in front of the desk," spoke Bill charmingly who held onto the door and watched the woman come into his office and take a seat in front of his desk.

The whole time Bill's instinct's kept this person of interest in front of him and didn't turn his back at all on the woman.

After the tall dark haired gorgeous woman sat down Bill

pushed the door shut with his hand and walked from where he had been standing and sat down in his chair and slid it up to his desk, but kept his right hand in his lap just in case he needed to draw his gun fast even a woman can kill you now a days thought Bill to himself, but didn't say anything while he looked on with interest in his eyes.

The woman smiled at Bill sitting in front of him at his desk just with her face partially hidden in the light and the rest of her body in shadow from his bankers lamp light that dimly lit up his office.

Bill noticed the woman's beautiful big breasts that filled her long flowing vested dress up front and he was taken aback by her charms.

"Good—you didn't turn your back on me. You are a smart and well trained lawman and sharp as a tack," spoke the mysterious woman to Bill who watched her intently and felt somehow this woman didn't fit right in his scheme of things and he wondered why.

"Yes–I'm well trained and I don't miss much in my profession. Did your car break down on the road, do you need assistance, you know my name but I don't know yours" asked Bill wondering if this might be his lucky night after all and his good fortune to meet this knockout of a woman who some how looked familiar to him?

"You silly man—I don't need a car to get around with and I certainly don't need assistance at all," replied the tall dark haired naughty woman who edged closer to Bill's desk and leaned forward showing off her wonderful assets which Bill could not help, but look at. Her big boobs seemed to be straining from within her vested low blouse top of her dark Victorian style dress to unleash themselves at him.

Man—what a drop dead gorgeous woman thought Bill to himself and he wiggled fitfully and nerve racking in his office chair by this imposing woman and he now thought his mom's wives tales might just be true in the first place because unexpected company was sitting right in front of him.

Bill's face blushed red when he saw the woman staring at him knowing he was enticed by her bosom and that she made him feel very nervous. He felt his heart start to sweat and beat in double time. His body started to shake slightly from his blood pressure rising rapidly, but there's no doubt—in his mind he was in deep lust for this woman. These feelings hadn't happen too him in a long time and it took him quiet by surprise.

"What is your name again for the second time and what information do you have for me," asked Bill watching the difficult woman with suspicious eyes, but didn't reply to what the woman had already said to him twice and he tried hard to keep his composure?

"My name is Lady Victoria Basil and my people emigrated from Russia to America during the Revolutionary War and we lived in Virginia until we moved down here years ago," replied Lady Victoria with a solemn voice.

"What is your information that you have for me," asked Bill with a questionable look in his eye, but just only heard what he wanted to hear and some how missed that she was alive during the Revolutionary War by her radiate beauty that seemed to charm him into a slight trance which was very unusual for him to miss anything?

"You must stop working on this case at all cost because your mortal life is in danger and your good friends too because you all have been marked for death by the same evil ones you all are searching for on your new murder case because there's more that one killer and they are blended into society among you and you can't trust anyone," replied Lady Victoria who arched her right eyebrow up with a smug I know look on her pretty face.

"Who has threaten my life and my friends and I don't trust anyone no way, I'm not that gullible and everybody's a suspect to me until they are cleared by me to be innocent of the crime," spoke Bill who had changed his soft voice to a deep ruff warning tone in his voice, that said don't mess with me or my friends no matter what, even if you are a beautiful stranger in distress with a sinful looking smile on Bill's blushed embarrassed face ?

"There are darkening forces that you don't begin to understand, that are coming together to strike against you and I want to avoid that at all cost because it would cause a lot of grief for all of us and I wold be forced to intervene or leave my old home," replied Lady Victoria with a stern look on her face.

"I have been shot at and threaten many times in my long law enforcement career and the line for enemies forms around the block and most of my friends can take care of them selves and with a little help from my old friends maybe I can solve this murder case I'm on sooner than later," spoke Bill who made a thumb ups gesture toward his door who then eased back in his seat looking the woman dead in her eyes which seemed to Bill's guess where quiet fearless looking and she had the most beautiful bedroom blue eye's he had ever seen and he thought she was trying to pull the wool over his eyes at the same time so to speak.

Lady Victoria Basil eyed the silver cross hanging around Bill's neck and leaned forward in her chair.

"I'll knock you into next week you hardheaded man because I'm trying to help, can't you understand that through your thick skull. If you don't open your ears and listen to me, there's going to be Hell to pay for you and your old friends," replied Lady Victoria who was about to lose her cool trying to communicate which as of now was a failure with this lawman she thought to herself.

"You don't have to crawl down my throat," replied Bill arguably pleading with this pissed off woman in front of him to cool off he thought.

"I don't think were own the same page and I can't fathom what your trying to tell me about my dangerous murder case that I don't already know," said Bill perplexed over this striking intrusion of a woman sitting in front of him.

"I don't never kill unless I have too and my victims are criminal killers that prey on society and want be missed, but you just don't know who or what your messing with and it's well over your head and out of your league. Non est vivere sed valere vita est—that's Latin for "life is not just to be alive, but to be well," spoke Lady Victoria with a look of death about her white masked face that appeared out of no where and her gold blue eyes turned to red to Bill's astonished eye's.

Bill watched fangs grow down in the woman's mouth from her beautiful perfect front white teeth and he blinked his eyes several times in stunned bugged eyed disbelief!

"Do you get my meaning," asked lady Victoria Basil who looked hypnotic into Bill's eye's? Bill shook his head as if he was in a trance and all most agreed with the devil of a woman and snapped out of it quickly.

"I'm a lot tougher than I look and I don't dare back down from a fight," responded Bill who felt his temper flare up in him sitting in his seat across from this dark charming woman of the night who he thought was blowing wind his way and sticking her nose where it don't belong on his case which he had heard this kind of talk before from cornered suspects who said he had the wrong man thought Bill to himself on edge in his chair who was looking for a way out of this unexpected argument, that was making his day a bad day already.

Bill felt mad and horrified, but hot under the collar at the same time at what he saw and heard in front of him from this nosy good looking woman and he felt a bad migraine headache coming on from her nagging mouth about his case and she should mind her own business he thought, but he didn't say anything else. He now felt threaten and started to reach for his gun and the tall dark gorgeous vampire woman unexpectedly stood up.

Then Bill spotted the old colt 45 revolver in the vampire's wide belt that buckled around her tiny waste partially hidden by her dark vest she was wearing sitting in his seat and his eyes grew wide with alarm and he hesitated going for his gun because she could have killed him the minute she entered his office thought Bill to himself sitting rigid in his office chair.

Then Bill eye's shot up to the ceiling and back down to the beautiful woman quickly thinking "oh crap" how could he have missed the gun, but now new he had been charmed by the woman the minute he had laid eyes on her and if it had been a snake it would have coiled up and bit him because he missed it. He was now hanging on the edge of his seat with anticipation of what was to come next.

"Do—do—do you have a permit for that gun your carrying on your person," asked Bill looking up at the cool looking woman in front of him with some authority gathered in his low nervous voice and yet he felt admiration for her?

'Yes—I do—its called the second amendment of the constitution. The right to bear arms," replied Lady Victoria rather angry who had lost her temper on Bill who seemed taken aback on that sharp witted quick answer to him sitting across the desk and he new he had been put in his place.

Lady Victoria stood in front of the desk and towered over Bill who was sitting shocked silly in his boots by now and madly spoke her mind.

"You want need that gun because it want do you any good tonight, but that silver cross is another thing and your lucky—you are wearing it tonight or on second thought, I might just settle this permanently tonight if I give into my cravings since I can't convince you otherwise unless my charms entice your manhood tonight and your feeling frisky.

I'll make you my first and only love slave in my nest which I never started like the other vampires before me because I wanted to be different from them and just have a mate only and not a horde to do my bidding fore I'm a good person still at will. I've been watching you from afar for quiet some time around town at the night spots and bars you go to for relaxation and fun with your old police pals.

Maybe I've been love struck on you for some time and want to help save you on your dangerous case you've undertaken and now's the time for my introduction.

Your just not getting the message mister Bill Christian, you had better wake up and smell the coffee—you dim witted man.

You have been forewarned Mister Bill Christian about interfering with business that doesn't concern you, you had better quit while the getting is good and not bad that comes your way, I'm giving you a chance to save your life tonight and your friends too because I have a heavenly conscious within my evil soul and I want to exist too within this frail mortal world in peace and not worry about a witch hunt around town for people like myself by you and your friends, I want to help and I guess I'll have to get involved now for your sake and mine and help you find the right man your after and not a cornered innocent man," spoke Lady Victoria Basil who ran to the front door in a blur and opened it faster than Bill could react and disappeared into the dark night air.

Bill watched the incredible gorgeous vixen vampire leave his office at incredible speed and he sat there horrified and his own madness turned into stunned disbelief at this little unexpected romantic vivacious encounter and he breathed deeply with a hot sign of sultry relief and his lust he had felt was almost sinful "OOOH—BOY—women never cease to amaze me and she must have a rude dislike for men and she read my mind of all things, how could she know that I was thinking about old cornered suspects who pleaded I had the wrong man," signed Bill with a look of a old hound dog in heat on his tanned rugged face and what a night to remember after all this hoopla thought Bill to himself and he new now he was a whipped dog at first sight of that dark and mysterious woman in black.

He sat in his chair, thinking about what had just happen here tonight in his office for awhile. Then he got up from his desk and went and shut his office door after he got himself back in a good frame of mind.

Bill sat back down at his desk and was in deep thought for a long time again trying to figure out what that woman was up too and he ran his hand nervously through his hair rubbing his sore aching head and ears.

He opened his right hand top desk drawer and got out a bottle of aspirin. He popped the child proof lid and poured two aspirin out into his left hand and threw them into his open mouth. He swallowed hard, but didn't have the spit to wash it down with from being stressed out by tonight's encounter with this lovely lady of the night's mad spell and so he turned around in his chair and grabbed a water bottle from the six pack off his file cabinet that was next to his coffee pot to chase the aspirin with. He dropped the empty bottle in his side desk trash can which had quenched his dry thirsty mouth.

After awhile the aspirin's had taken effect and he felt better like his old self and he put the aspirin bottle back in the right hand desk drawer, ready for the next headache to come into his office unannounced and lay it on him which happen a lot in his line of work of being a private eye.

"Man—I should have got her phone number before she madly left and Hell knows no fury like a woman's scorn and after thinking about it now, she still looks awful familiar and I'd bet my life on it that I've seen her at the local bars in town late at night and never suspected a thing, funny how people can watch you out in public places and you never know it" said Bill relieved out loud and he laughed to himself "Ha, Ha, Ha" to ease the tension and disbelief he felt from his first very strange encounter with what appeared to be a female vampire of all things.

Bill thought about his old friends whose supernatural knowledge had saved him the other night and the girl jogger.

I'd better call the experts on this thought Bill and he grabbed his Rolodex off his desk and thumbed through it until he found the phone number he was looking for.

Bill picked up his desk phone and dialed the number and he listen to the dialing ring tone while he waited for someone to pick-up. Wilbur heard the phone ring in the kitchen and went to answer it from the parlor where he had been sitting in his favorite lazy boy chair reading the days newspaper with Clara Bell who was sitting on the old red antic sofa couch across from him doing needle work on a hoop for a wedding band quilt.

Wilbur grabbed the phone off the kitchen wall and put it to the side of his face to talk. "Hello—this is Wilbur speaking," spoke Wilbur into the old style wall phone.

"Hi—Wilbur this is Bill Christian calling may I speak to Clara Bell," asked Bill rather nonchalantly hoping that Wilbur was in a good mood and didn't notice he was still upset about his little agitated argument with a lovely strange woman he had just met?

"Sure you can, Ohhh—Bill by the way how are you doing, did you recover from the other night," asked Wilbur smiling at his old friend on the phone?

"I got a good night's rest and ready to hit the road again," replied Bill with some enthusiasm. Wilbur laughed out loud into the phone "Ha, Ha, Ha—well—good to hear it Bill—I'll go and get Clara Bell, just hold on," said Wilbur who laid the phone down on the kitchen counter and went off down the hallway to get Clara Bell who looked up seriously when he came into the parlor and she new the phone call was for her!

It was around midnight and Lady Victoria Basil sat on the rooftop of a house off of 23third street behind a tall chimney and smoke rolled out of it into the nigh time air and you could smell the burning wood in the air which was the scene for a well known crime area in Winston-Salem.

She watched the drug deal down below between some men go down on the street corner across from her hiding place. Leon stood on the street corner and watched the two men drive up and park their dark blue 1976 Chevrolet Impala car with the big chrome wheels and skinny tires across the street.

"Hey—Leon do you have the kilo of smack," asked Marvin who had gotten out of the car and leaned over the top of the car looking him over while the other man got out of the car into the street and slammed his car door shut?

"Yeah—I got it right here in my back pack, let me see the cash," replied Leon with a friendly grin on his face. Marvin and Donald walked across the street and stopped at the curb corner a safe distance away from him.

Donald opened the pillow case bag he was carrying and Leon saw the pile of money in the bag under the street light. Leon smiled at seeing the money and lust filled his cold hard eyes. "Twenty thousand dollars just like we agreed on," asked Leon smiling devilishly with a wide eye look about his face? "Yep—its all there," replied Marvin who was a little nervous Leon hadn't walked over to them and seen for him self.

Leon took a last quick look around the street corner and saw they were the only one's on the deserted street. "There's been a change in plans," said Leon who had moved his right arm behind his back which they hadn't noticed in the dim street light.

The drug dealer pulled out a 357 magnum gun from behind his back and pointed the barrel at the cocaine buyers.

"Give me the bag of money," barked Leon who's face turned dead eye serious and walked off the curb toward Donald?

"Can't we-we- we talk about this," stuttered Marvin who was now shaking in his boots with the fear of death hovering over him. "Here take the money, but spare our lives," begged

Donald who handed over the pillow case of money which Leon jerked out of his hand and stepped back up onto the curb.

Lady Victoria Basil could sense the men's fear that welled up in their mortal minds from knowing that each now faced an unexpected death unless they could talk their way out of it. This she saw with intense hungry jet black eye's from her roof top hiding place and the breeze picked up blowing her long jet black hair off her back and around her face.

"Time for talk is over—you owed me a debt when you and your friends ganged bang my cousin at that crack house party awhile back on 16th street— say your prayers," replied Leon who cocked the trigger back on the large pistol.

"Hey—man we were just partying your cousin agreed to it after we all got high on smack," pleaded Marvin who held out his hands in a pleading gesture toward Leon.

He then shot Marvin through the heart "BAM" that left a big hole in his chest and blood shot out everywhere and ran down his shirt while Marvin fell back in the street dead!

Donald stepped back a few feet and had a frantic shocked look on his face and he started to turn and run for it! Leon aimed the gun at his target which was the man's head and fired "BAM" instantly blowing half his head off his shoulders with the big gun and Donald was dead on his feet as he fell back into the street!

Leon took off running down the street and turned off into an side alleyway with the pillow case of money and his kilo of cocaine still in his backpack while the female vampire huntress watched it all well hidden on the nearby house rooftop.

Lady Victoria Basil listen to the killer's fast heat beat down the street and excited breath and the distant running footsteps, that echoed from down the street. She leaped off the roof top and flew through the air over the tree tops and over the rooftops past fireplace chimney's while dodging the dimly lit street light poles and her dress flapped in the wind.

The man's natural scent led her way right to him until she

came upon the drug dealer on the street who was now a serial want a be killer in the back alleyway of town going over his loot.

The man looked up from where he was squatting behind the garbage cans and heard a flapping noise above and down below him.

Then he quickly scanned the night sky and spotted a dark form coming at him down the back alleyway in mid-air among the dimly lit light pole on the corner that cast a Erie light upon the alleyway street. The wild fiery flash of red eye's jumped out at him from above him in the night sky and the killer's fast beating heart froze in fear of the terror before him. The drug dealer was surprised at this floating phantom before him and his reflex kicked in and he took a deep breath of air "GASP" in shock!

The drug dealer felt fear well up in his throat and he pulled out his 357 magnum pistol and fired at the floating dark form "BAM, BAM, BAM," that rushed down at him in the alleyway!

The drug dealer screamed "AHHHHHH" when he saw his gun had no effect on this flying dark form as he stood up in the alley behind the garbage cans in fear, that gripped his feet to that very spot! He saw the red eyes of a Demon coming for him and he tried to turn and run as a mighty small hand "smacked" the big gun out of his hand!

The female vampire grabbed her victim in a death embrace and they fell to the pavement struggling and the female vampire sank her fangs deep into the drug dealers neck.

The blood flowed down the drug dealers neck while the female vampire drank thirstily as her victim struggled in her grip pitifully and soon died in her arms. When her victim had been drained of all his blood, she let go of him and sat up wiping her mouth with her handkerchief that she had pulled from under her dress sleeve.

The female vampire sat there on the back alleyway street

looking at her victim lying dead on the pavement beside her and new the man's just end had been served and tucked her handkerchief back in her left dress sleeve and her red eyes turned back normal to a golden blue once again.

The female vampire heard siren's off in the distance coming fast toward the crime scene that had been called in by scared neighbors who had awaken to gunshots up the street at the shooting where two men lay dead done in by greed.

The female vampire stood up and grabbed her dead victim up in her arms from where he laid on the alleyway street as if she had picked up a child's rag doll and she ignored the pillow case bag of money that lay scattered on the alleyway street and gun.

She flew up into the night sky with her burden and was gone without a trace of any crime left behind.

Much later that same night the crickets sensed that something dark and foreboding was coming there way on the night air as they went silent in the back yard of the old farmhouse house on Waughtown Street and the nesting black birds scattered for safety at a safe distance away across the street.

The wind quit blowing and died down among the tree tops and the tree branches quit shaking from the wind as if waiting for some unseen force to arrive.

Quiet suddenly the dark form appeared in the darken night sky over the tree tops and glided down into the backyard, effortlessly and dropped it's human burden down on the ground.

The female vampire Lady Victoria Basil looked around and saw the child's swing set in front of her and saw no one in sight. The female vampire took in her surroundings and looked at the houses on both sides and the backyards which all was quiet and dark. She saw no threat to herself in the backyard.

She looked at the almost dark house in front of her and saw the glow of a night light on in the children's room too her left through the window because she heard there small hearts beating there and the rush of blood through their veins from head to toe while they slept safely in their home and her senses told her so, she then smiled because her human side loved innocent children and she new they were snuggled in their nice warm beds.

Off to the right side of the old farmhouse was the parents room and she also heard mom and dad's big hearts beating and the rush of blood through their bodies too which she could smell them and hear them all at rest and at peace in deep dark sleep with her supernatural senses unaware of the dark foreboding knight in the backyard. The lady vampire walked over to the sewer lid and lifted it away from its place in the ground over the sewer tank exposing it's square hole opening.

The lady vampire walked back away's and picked up her victim in her arm's like it was light as a feather and walked over to the sewer hole and dropped him in, feet first into the dark smelly black waters that engulfed the body and then it was gone in a matter of seconds.

The dirty deed was done and the lady vampire rubbed her hands together as if she was cleaning them of any guilt because that murderous man wouldn't hurt no one ever again and the law could do little to stop him for there hands where tied unless they caught him in the act which hadn't happen in a dozen or so homicides on the city streets thought Lady Victoria who was street savvy about the criminals that roamed her city streets.

She reached down and grabbed the sewer lid and placed it back over the top of the opening to the back yard sewer.

She stood up for a second admiring her handy work and then she reached for the night sky and flew off riding the wind over the top of the old farm house and was gone.

Earlier that same night Clara Bell picked the phone off the counter top in the farmhouse kitchen after Wilbur had come and got her for her phone call.

"Hello—Bill what's up," asked Clara Bell while she waited a moment for Bill's reply?

"Hi—Clara Bell I hate to bother you this late evening, but your not going to believe this, but I had an unexpected office visit by what appeared to be a beautiful female vampire tonight who was rude and to the point. It looks like werewolf's are not the only thing we have to worry about right now. She told me to drop the case because me and my friends were in danger. I don't know of anyone who'd believe me, but you and Wilbur, everybody else would think I'm going off the deep end and need to see a head shrink," spoke Bill who nervously laughed over the phone "ha, ha, ha," and waited for a response from Clara Bell on her end of the phone.

Clara Bell let this sink deep in her mind while she gave it a moments thought. "Bill—I've always believed in vampires and run into a few in my time, but on the other hand they are not to be taken lightly because they are murderous by nature in their bloodlust to survive and are the walking dead at night, This adds another hand to the card table and it could be good or bad I just don't know, but by my guess your being alive and that's a good sign and danger is our business and I'm not scared off by an idle threat and neither is Wilbur when people's lives are at stake in these parts," replied Clara Bell with a serious tone in her sweet old grandma voice.

"Yeah—I'm still here in one piece and she didn't attack me when she had me—shall we say transfixed," replied Bill a little sheepishly.

"Well—maybe she has a crush on you and has good intentions for all of us with the warning she gave you and after all you're a right handsome fellow and maybe you got bit by the love bug instead of a vampires bite which can happen only once in a blue moon to some very lonely people," said Clara Bell who grinned on the other end of the phone at Bill.

"Maybe so," replied Bill who fiddled with his Rolodex on his desk nervously.

"Bill—just remember every rose has it's thorn and you have to be very careful in life at what comes your way because you can get hurt or rewarded, it just depend's on how you handle the situation," said Clara Bell very motherly to Bill.

"I—guess your right about that," replied Bill who took her advise to heart.

"My hillbilly momma who was born and raised in West Virginia use to have an old country folks saying "if I live I'll do it"! We need to get together and do some hunting for those werewolf's lair, we will worry about the lady vampire later if we live, who knows we might just run into her out in the woods somewhere," spoke Clara Bell with an amused smile on her pretty wrinkled nosed face who silently shook her face back and forth at Bill with a inside laugh to herself.

She looked over her wire rimed spectacle's at Bill through the phone which thinking to herself quietly, she knew obviously he was taken by the woman's obvious deadly, but beautiful charms.

"I'll call you and let you know when we can meet to plan a course of action. I hope that woman vampire has good intentions by our little visit at my office tonight and I'd like to run into her again," replied Bill with some excitement in his voice that showed that he was still charmed by her vision of loveliness.

"Sounds good Bill—until then good-by," spoke Clara Bell who hung the phone back up on the kitchen wall and walked out of the kitchen down her hallway toward the parlor to see what Wilbur was doing and to tell him about Bill's encounter with a female vampire tonight that had some how impressed her with some hope from the supernatural world and she wondered if it was just a woman's intuition.

Clara Bell shrugged her shoulder's and thought better about it while she stopped and looked at her grandfather clock in the hallway. Father time wake up your five minutes late, its after eight spoke Clara Bell to the clock that seem to come alive and look at her with eyes from the wind up key holes in the face of the old grandfather clock.

"Yes—yes—I was dozing and Wilbur forgot to wind me today, you know I'm a 31 day clock," replied the grandfather clock to Clara Bell who grabbed the key off the hook on the wall beside the clock and inserted the key through the key hole and started winding the grandfather clock up who was now fussing about his slow time.

"A stitch in time saves nine," spoke the grandfather clock who was now wound up fully by Clara Bell who looked at the old clock face over her wire rim spectacles and read the Latin on it at the top of the face of the old clock which was written on a old gold globe world atlas earth which read Tempus Fugit which translated into English-means(time flies).

"Well—I'm not sewing today. I'm quilting on my hoop and I have better things to do then to take up Wilbur's chores, or wind a silly old worn out Ansonian brass clock. You can go back to sleep now and rest your tired old solid brass insides that probably need a good oiling after several hundred years of ticking every day," spoke Clara Bell who hung up the clock key back on the wall and walked into her parlor room to check on Wilbur her husband.

She saw he had fell fast asleep reading his paper in his easy chair. Clara Bell walked over to the side table and pulled out a tie off lap quilt. She unfolded it while pulling the newspaper out of his lap and laying it on the side table.

Then she laid the lap quilt over her dear husband to keep him warm while he slept in the easy chair beside the fireplace.

Clara Bell walked across the parlor floor to her old red antic sofa and picked up her hoop and sat back down to Finnish her quilting for tonight.

Bill had just hung up the phone when it rang to his surprise. "I hope that's good news," spoke Bill out loud and picked up the receiver to his ear.

"This is private investigator Bill Christians office Bill speaking," said Bill who waited for a response on the phone.

"Hey—Bill this in Crime Scene Investigator William Walters speaking and I've got the lab results from your stolen car here at CSI headquarters at the Winston-Salem police department and the hairs in your plastic bag," spoke CSI William over the phone to Bill who listen intently from his chair at his office.

"Go–ahead and tell me what you found out," replied Bill who fidgeted in his chair in eagerness?

"We ran the left finger prints and palm print also the right thumb print in the state's criminal data base and no hits on the prints. We ran them through the FBI's nationwide criminal data base in Raleigh but know hits there either, your suspect is unknown at this time," spoke CSI Willam as a matter of factly.

"Well—that sucks is there anything else," asked Bill wondering if he had hit a dead end on his suspect the other night?

"I was saving the best for last. Your mud was tested against out water treatment sewer plants water intake sample's and dirt samples from our city's database of North Carolina water and soil conservation sample's of North Carolina. We intake water from the Yadkin River and also discharge treated water into it too and we also take water from Salem lake. We have all of this on record in our CSI computers here at the lab and we had a match.

The water extracted from the mud comes from the Yadkin River and the dirt sample matched the dirt taken from samples a long time ago along the banks of the Yadkin River some where along the river corridor in Clemmon's and Roxanne checked out your hairs and they are basically the same type of hairs you found at the other murder scene in stokes county. They are of a type of wolf's hair unknown in this region," replied CSI William Walters who felt pride at his hard work, but was puzzled about the wolf hairs in Bill's evidence bag.

"Well—that's good to know and it looks like I now have a solid place to start searching for clues in my investigation after I found out the other night the car was stolen in Clemmon's which seems to point me in the right place. That's good hard police work, that's a job well done. Thanks a lot for the information—good-by," replied Bill who's mind was racing with plans as he hung up the phone.

"Your welcome Bill—if there's anything else we can do for you let us know," replied CSI Willam who just heard a dial tone on his phone which he hung up and rubbed his chin wondering if Mr. Christian heard his last part of the conversation.

Clara Bell had went into the kitchen before bedtime and had poured herself a glass of buttermilk when the phone rang on the kitchen wall. Clara Bell put the gallon jar of buttermilk back in the ice box.

Her and Wilbur made there own buttermilk from there prized cow Mabel on the farm and they always had fresh milk to drink also.

Wilbur had a secret recipe to make the milk taste sweet just like store bought and some said it was better than what they bought at the store too after tasting Wilbur's old fashion home spun milk. Clara Bell wiped her hands on her apron and walked over to the kitchen counter and answered the phone.

"Hello," said Clara Bell when she put the receiver to her face and listen for who was on the other end of the line.

"I hate to bother you again Clara Bell, but something has come up tonight and it's important," spoke Bill with urgency into the phone. "Oh—Bill its you what's up," replied Clara Bell wondering why Bill was calling back again tonight?

"The test results came back from the CSI police lab in Winston-Salem and it confirms my thinking that we should be looking for our killer or killers out in Clemmons because the mud in the stolen car was from the Yadkin River along the river banks somewhere in Clemmons from the test done on the soil and water sample the CSI found in the car.

The car was also stolen from a residence in Clemmons too and one murder happen out in Clemmons and it just can't all be a coincidence and the wolf's hairs you found on my silver cross turned out to be from a real wolf," spoke Bill with amazement that the stolen car and hairs was a diamond in the ruff after all.

"The killers are werewolf's Bill and those wolf hairs prove my story. How can you talk like a human did the murders. Didn't you learn anything the other night at old Bethabara when that werewolf pounced on you, if it hadn't been for me and Wilbur intervening you just might be dead by now and case closed with the murderers still at large killing as they please among the public," replied Clara Bell with a sincere knowledge of things in the dark world but she had to set him right and she hated getting onto him.

"Yes—your right as usual Clara Bell and that brings me back to the edge of reality, where these creatures exist between out world and their's and sometime's it hard for me to believe in these things after all I'm still a human being and I make mistakes like everybody else but I'm a firm believer now after the tests prove it was a werewolf I tangled with on the street of Old Bethabara the other night because the crime scene facts don't lie," spoke Bill who was feeling a bit scolded by his old friend but he new deep down it was for his on good.

"Wilbur has a Cherokee Indian canoe out in the barn with a trolling motor on it he had rigged up for fishing with a two gallon tank and two rowing paddles if we need them and you need to come over to our farm in a couple of days for our wolf hunting trip, But beware of the new moon tonight and the next fool moon is in a few days and I hope too God were ready by then. I'll get him to load it up on his old beat up ford pick-up. We will pick a starting point on the Yadkin River and cruise up the Yadkin River and look for their lair along the way and there's a lot of old caves up that way to hide in which I remember going fishing with my dad when I was a little girl in those parts and seeing them along the river," replied Clara Bell very smartly and precisely about old times not forgotten in her childhood.

"There is a picnic area on the Yadkin River on the Forsyth County line that is across from the Yadkin County line. You just follow Reynolda road that runs into 67 that goes to East Bend in Yadkin County and stop at the old concrete bridge down past the old country store of the Forsyth County line where the picnic area is. The picnic area has a river access on it too. The park is always busy in the summer time with families on picnics and canoe enthusiastic's who stop there at the end of their trips down the Yadkin from Clemmons where they have left their cars for the preplanned trip. It would be a good starting point," spoke Bill who paused for a moment on the phone.

"Sounds like the adventure of a life time and we will be ready to go in a day or two before the next full moon," replied Clara Bell with sleep in her voice because it was getting close to her bedtime and she picked up her buttermilk glass off the kitchen counter to take it with her upstairs to her bedroom where Wilbur was already getting ready for bed.

"O. K.—see ya then," said Bill and he hung up the phone. Bill looked at his wrist watch and saw it was getting near 10:00 o-clock and he closed up his office for the night.

Bill headed out his office door towards his car in the parking lot and then the fall rain storm hit just as he got into his car.

Later Bill pulled into his driveway and the rain had poured down like out of a giant bucket and finely stopped but the wind had picked up from the storm fronts that were starting to roll into the triad area one after another in a series of storm events.

Bill got out of his car and looked up at the dark night sky and saw the full moon up in the western sky that shone brightly and he saw the eastern star high above the horizon, that shone brightly like a beacon to his left.

The clouds had receded over the tree tops in the western sky down below the big full moon. Man this fall thunderstorm might carry some tornadoes thought Bill to himself and he hurried inside to the safety of his house.

Bill got ready for bed but strangely enough he wore his silver cross to bed over top of his shirt pajamas and Bill laid his loaded 38 snub nose pistol on his bedside table within easy reach and he felt safer wearing his silver cross close to his heart.

Bill reached over and flipped on his weather radio which was on his bedside table for any tornado alerts and settled down into his warm bed for the night.

He soon fell fast asleep under his warm covers and started dreaming about a beautiful long black haired woman who was wearing a long flowing black dress with ruby red lips.

At around midnight Bill woke up to the sound of rolling thunder "KA—BOOM, KA—BOOM," and his weather alert radio going off on his bedside table. "Beep—beep—beep, "this is the national weather alert system and a tornado warning alert has been issued for the following counties—Davidson, Forsyth and Stokes counties until 3:00 A:M by the national weather alert system," said the announcer over the weather radio.

"Man the big fall thunderstorm must have hit us," said Bill who cut on the lamp light on the bedside table and yawned sleepily while sitting up in bed.

"Better check every thing out and batten down the hatches," said Bill to himself who then noticed and listen to the high wind rumbling across his roof top in bed overhead and the rain pelting his roof top shingles overhead like small drums. He heard the wind and rain blowing hard outside and pelting his bedroom windows with a glass rattling sound.

Bill open his drawer on his night time bedside table and got out a long black police style flashlight. Bill jumped out of bed and grabbed his robe and put it on over his pajamas and tied the belt.

Bill grabbed the weather alert battery operated radio under his arm and walked out of the bedroom and down the hallway to his living room.

Bill looked out the livingroom window to check his car in the driveway which was alright and Bill turned around and headed down the hallway checking everything to make sure it was off until he got to his basement door.

Bill open the door and flipped on the basement lights and walked down the steps into the basement.

Bill hopped off the basement steps and walked over to his old couch and he set the weather radio on the old desk and sat on the couch safely listening to the raging storm outside his house.

Then the lights flickered on and off and dimmed in the basement and Bill clutched his flashlight tightly in his lap ready to turn it on if need be in the dark.

At about the same time Clara Bell had been trying to wake Wilbur up out of a sound sleep in his straw mattress farm bed for a few minutes.

"Wake–up—Wilbur—Rise and Shine," said Clara Bell who shook her husbands shoulder gently to wake him up out of a dead sleep.

"What is it Clara Bell," asked Wilbur who sat up on one elbow in bed looking sleepy at her sitting on the side of the bed rubbing his eyes with his other hand?

"Tornado's are coming this way the battery operated weather radio went off a few minutes ago and I've been trying to wake you up for a spell now—get up and get dressed quickly time's a wasting," replied Clara Bell who got up and started to get out of her full length night gown and put on her day clothes.

Wilbur heard the howling wind outside the window in the bedroom and he heard the hard rain beating down on the old tin roof above him with a terrible drum racket of immanent warning of approaching danger outside that was different tonight from a calm rainy night which he could tell right away that something wasn't quiet right outside with the weather.

With that said Wilbur turned and grabbed his bib overhaul's off the cane bottom chair next to his bedside table on his side of the bed and preceded to slide them on over his now cold feet on the cold farm house floor.

Wilbur and Clara Bell fully clothed stepped quickly down the old stairs with her magic twisted root swamp walking cane helping her ascend the steps quickly one at a time and they walked hastily down the hallway into the farmhouse kitchen.

Wilbur walked over to the kitchen counter and grabbed his red flashlight off the top of the old ice box beside it and they headed for the back kitchen door.

The wind and rain was blowing terrible as Wilbur shut the kitchen door behind them and down the cement steps they moved hastily.

Wilbur turned on the flashlight shining the way toward the buried storm cellar in the backyard that he had dug and built fifty years ago when they had first bought the small farm. Clara Bell hobbled on her cane while Wilbur held her left arm and the full fury of the storm hit them in the middle of the backyard and the backyard farm was lit up with lightening that cracked and thundered overhead with the stinging sideways rain hitting them hard in their faces. The down burst wind's blew and howled terribly all around them and tore at their clothes and bodies. They both struggled and fought against the strong wind and rain that seemed to hold them in their tracks in the middle of the backyard while they moved forward step by step against the sheer force of the raging storm by their stout hardworking farm strong willed bodies.

Clara Bell held on to her bottom skirt with her free hand to keep it from blowing up around her waist in the wind and embarrassing her by showing her pink cotton bloomers out here this time of night in front of Wilbur and only God knows who else might be watching this time of night thought Clara Bell frantically in the mist of the raging storm.

The swing set was blowing and making a terrible racket with the swing chains hitting the side poles that were anchored in the ground a good foot by cement that held it in place against the ferocious wind blowing it over and out into the pasture behind it. "Come on were almost there." cried Wilbur who let go of Clara Bell to open the buried storm cellar door that was off to one side of the swing set.

Wilbur who had got a strong grip on the left door handle pulled it partially open against the strong wind and then had the door jerked out of his hand by the strong winds and it flipped open to his left with a loud crashing "Bam" and without thinking he went on inside and down the cement steps to safety thinking Clara Bell was right behind him.

Clara Bell had stopped behind Wilbur and turned against the ferocious wind and pelting rain who stood her ground. She searched the thunderstorm filled sky with her defiant eyes that was lit up by lightening thunder bolts that cracked with a deafening roar high overhead "KA—BOOM, KA—BOOM," and then cascaded down to the ground in electrifying steaks all around them in all directions while the hard rain soaked her clothes and bonnet she was wearing over her head to protect her hair and face.

Then quarter size hail started to fall from the stormy skies and started to cover the ground all around her in a white spectacle.

She saw the swirling violent thunderstorm clouds heading their way and she saw the funnel cloud start to form and drop down right in the farm's path way across the road by a big lightening flash that lit up the sky overhead for miles and small wooded hills in front of the farm heading their way.

She new she had no time to lose and Clara Bell decided to act swiftly to try and save the farm also her neighbors farms and houses from certain destruction by the will of god and his saving grace from these devilish high winds kicking up by a twister event before her very eyes and headed their way for certain destruction only if he would permit it she thought in the blink of an eye.

"Unum—E—plurisbus—Unum, Abner father of spiritual light come forth," commanded Clara Bell who lifted her cane high in the air and aimed the shaft at the rotating funnel cloud in front of her in the sky off in the distance.

The bright light glowed and formed on the end of the cane and then shot out the end of the shaft over top of the old farmhouse toward the descending funnel cloud engulfing it with a bright circle of light into the cloud and the rotation stopped in mid-air.

"Hermon—Excelsior—back up," commanded Clara Bell who felts God's presence all around her and moved the light back up into the thunderstorm cloud majestically stopping the funnel clouds rotation downward and it disappeared back up inside the thunderstorm cloud and was gone from sight inside the glowing cloud.

"Enchantment—Exodus," commanded Clara Bell and the light on her cane dimmed and went out in the rainstorm.

Meanwhile Wilbur had quickly found the hurricane lantern and lit a match to light the wick and he adjusted the flame and set the glass back down on it by the lever and set it on the small table in the middle of the small underground room. Then he looked around and saw his wife was no where to be seen.

"Oh—dear God—no—not now," said Wilbur who rambled back to the stairs with his heart jumping a leap frog in his chest and he bent over for a moment from the intense pain in his chest.

Wilbur felt his heart pain go up in his throat with worry and his strong mind gathered inner strength deep down inside his good soul and he quickly and confidently regained his strength. He climbed back up the cement stairs hastily to look for his wife who he feared had fallen down outside and then he saw her through the doorway standing in the wind and rain just outside looking up at the sky and he sensed she was in one of her mad stubborn fighting moods.

"Land sakes honey—you can't fight this storm—that's mother nature your messing with—get on in here," exclaimed Wilbur who stepped up back outside and grabbed his wife and started to pull her down into the storm cellar to safety.

Then he saw the glowing white light fading in the bottom of the thunderstorm up top and it was now located overhead. He watched in dumb founded awe at what he must have thought she did with her old cane to save the farm from any wind damage.

"I've done my duty—Wilbur—because this old cane and me still has a few divine tricks up our sleeve for nonbelievers by God willing, with his helping hand," replied Clara Bell who looked very humbled at her husband and moved by him on down into the storm cellar by the steps to safety while he reached and shut the storm cellar door latching it securely from inside by the big slide latch bolt.

"I'm not going to even ask what you even did up there because I don't want to know and I wouldn't believe it anyway unless I saw it with my own two eyes and my Christianity beliefs only go so far as the bible says which Jesus and the twelve apostles were given power from God only," replied Wilbur who sat down on the small bench frightened of the power his wife had yielded and he hoped it would never consume them someday like it had almost did her grandmother years ago before she had past away.

"I have true faith from God—Wilbur and that's all it takes to follow in the footsteps of Jesus and the apostles who always helped needy people by using the Holy Ghost which is divine power from God and with a little teaching of white magic from the Alter realm where I was taught as a little school girl at heavens gates by my master teacher swamp witch Latasha and also my good hearted grandmother, doesn't hurt either. You should know better than to doubt me or my moral's—I can handle it and I helped out my unsuspecting neighbors farms tonight and quiet possibly saved our beloved farm tonight from wind destruction out here this time of night too," replied Clara Bell who stubbornly took her seat by her husband with an air of blessings about her radiate glowing wet face.

He sat on the small wooded bench beside his wife quietly praying humbly for forgiveness of any and all of their sins and trespasses while they road out the bad thunderstorm in the small damp underground tornado cellar soaking wet.

Bill who had been dozing off and on woke up and looked at his watched and saw it was almost 3:00 A:M and new the tornado warning watch was over so he grabbed the weather radio off the old desk and climbed the basement stairs very tiredly.

He cut the light off to the basement door and shut it and walked to his bedroom down the hallway. Bill sat the weather radio on his night stand and flashlight within easy reach if he needed it and got back under the warm covers of his bed and with light's out was soon fast asleep.

Just then Wilbur had got out of his wet clothes and got back into his nightgown and cap. He crawled under the quilt covers and the bed warmed him right up. Clara Bell had taken the wet clothes and put them in the hamper beside the dresser. She had put her nightgown back on and she too crawled back in bed and the springs under the straw mattress moaned squeakily.

"Well—I'm glad the storm has past safely without any

bad damage to the farm," mumbled Wilbur who rolled over and tucked his straw pillow underneath his bald head without giving his wife any praise for what she had done fore it scared the life out of him.

"Yes—me too and its time for a good night's rest or what's left of it," replied Clara Bell who had a air of enlightenment about her good heart and soul for what she had been allowed to do by saving her home and her neighbors homes from utter destruction by that devil of a storm event that had passed on by outside with the wind knocked out of it who settled down into her nice warm bed for the night without a care in the world for the first time in many years.

Back at Bill's house around 4:00 o-clock in the morning the neighborhood dogs started barking and making a terrible racket " Arf!, Arf!, Arf!, Arf!, Bow—Wow, Bow—Wow," and then the dogs went strangely quiet as if something Ominous was interring their marked territory and something was tearing through the underbrush in the woods behind the neighborhood houses.

Lady Victoria Basil was setting up in the top of a tall whispering pine tree not far from Bill's backyard on a big long and crooked pine tree limb and she was on her own little vigilantly stakeout.

Her beautiful long black jet black hair flowed in the wind behind her and she held onto her long skirt so it wouldn't flap in the breeze and give her hiding place away.

She smelled the sent on the night's air of a big wolf coming her way down below her in the woods and she watched with devilish eyes for any sign of a lone hunter wolf far down below her.

Then the biggest werewolf you ever could imagine from the depths of Hell busted out of the underbrush and tree line behind Bill's back yard and stopped at the edge of the tree line and it scanned the entire back yard with yellow cat eyes in night vision mode for any sign of a threat.

It was all of 7ft tall and must have weighed three hundred pounds of solid rock hard hairy muscle.

The werewolf's yellow cat eye's turned and glowed red hot with immense evil that turned even the smallest creatures of the night into stone afraid to move for fear of being attacked from it's drooling salvia of razor sharp teeth in its black lips of a snout that seemed to quiver back and forth as if it was mad at something.

Just then a hoot owl hooted off in the trees beside the garden swing in Bill's backyard "Hoot, Hoo, Hoo, Hoot, "and the werewolf looked at the owl up in the tree to his right and saw no threat and it took a massive clawed foot step forward into its new domain.

The werewolf scanned the entire backyard with it's supernatural yellow eye's as it moved on all four's cautiously looking for any sign of danger to it's self and saw none.

Lady Victoria Basil watched the werewolf cross Bill's backyard and she got ready to spring her trap.

The werewolf was looking for anything, that might sound the alarm of it's lurking presence which was vital to it's surprise attack. The werewolf covered the half Acker back yard in no time.

The werewolf stood back up and stepped up on Bill's wet puddled patio from the early thunderstorm and silently moved past the barbecued grill and wrought iron furniture toward Bill's french doors that led to his kitchen.

The werewolf drew back its clawed fist to punch a hole through the french door glass so that it could reach in and unlock the door. "No—no—no, its not polite to come in unannounced," said Lady Victoria Basil who floated in the air back behind the werewolf and she was floating about ten feet off the ground.

The werewolf jumped in it's tracks for the first time in it's long miserable life and turned around and looked up at the female vampire floating in the air before it in shock!

"You can't stop me your not allowed to interfere with human history—by your master," replied a low throaty voice that rumbled from the werewolf standing in front of the french doors on the patio.

"My master is in Pennsylvania and I left him and went out on my own because I didn't agree to cold blooded murder of anyone who is innocent in life. I hunt the murderer's in this life who escape human justice or never get caught and I do the human race a favor by getting rid of those who prey on them and I'm not about to stop now," replied lady Victoria Basil with a cold icy look of blue steel from her beautiful golden blue eyes.

The werewolf's yellow hairy eyeballs flashed furiously red and took a step forward toward the beautiful vampire woman and clinched it's fist together in a in a mad fit of rage.

"You can't stop me from killing Bill Christian the private investigator, he's a threat to us all and his friends too, I'm to bite him and make him a changeling or kill him at my discretion on orders from my pack leader," replied the werewolf who now challenged it's new threat.

"Want—aaaah—bet! You had better leave and I mean right now, if you want your pitiful self to continue to exist, and it will be over my dead body," said Lady Victoria Basil who now floated down to the patio and stood toe to toe with the beast from hell and her eyes flashed crimson red in vampire anger.

Lady Victoria Basil pulled out her old colt 45 revolver with her lovely right hand out of her waist belt and she cocked the hammer back "click"!

"No—I've never failed my pack leader's orders and I'll kill anyone who get's in my way—death to you all," said the werewolf who became more enraged at being stopped on his threshold of revenge while it's fur stood up around it's neck ready to attack. The werewolf jumped toward her at incredible speed and charged straight at her.

She brought up the old colt 45 revolver lightening fast and aimed it at the werewolf's chest and fired "BAM"!

The werewolf was knocked backward by the force of the shot in mid leap and it hit the werewolf square in the chest and dark red blood spurted out from the gunshot wound.

The werewolf was slammed backward through the air head first onto the concrete patio by the force of the shot's high velocity impact with a sickening "THUD," and it slid up against the wet wrought iron patio furniture, knocking it over!

Bill was awoke by the gunshot outside and sat straight up in bed listening for anything outside.

"What the hell was that and what's going on outside," spoke Bill Christian who quickly deduced he had prowlers outside his house? He got up and quickly grabbed his 38 snub nose gun off his night table and raced to his window.

He pulled the curtain back and looked outside, but didn't see anything and then hastily put on his white cotton robe that laid on the bottom of his bed. He then left his bedroom to go investigate. Bill went down the hallway to his kitchen from where the shot seemed to come from.

On entering the kitchen, he cut on his kitchen light. He proceeded across his kitchen floor past his round oak table and he pulled back the curtain from his french door and peered through the glass pane looking outside and at the same time he flipped on his outdoor floodlight.

To his amazement he saw a huge body laying in front of his door and his wrought iron furniture had been knocked over to one side of his wet and puddled patio beside his barbecue grill he saw a woman standing there holding a gun in the light. Bill opened the french door and cautiously stepped out onto his back patio.

"What in God's name is going on out here," asked Bill in gazed wonderment at the dead animal body and then back at the woman with the gun?

"Its me Lady Victoria. I came here tonight to save you from a fate worse than death. This werewolf was going to attack you and quiet possibly make you a changeling or worse yet kill you in your own bed in your house and I had a hunch tonight that you would be attacked by one of them," replied Lady Victoria Basil who Bill now recognized from her office visit earlier tonight.

Bill looked back stunned and didn't say anything quiet yet. "Look— the metamorphous is starting," said Lady Victoria who pointed at the dead beast at her feet.

The werewolf's snout and eye's started to change back into a man's face and the claws receded back into fingernails and hands so did the feet from clawed paws into human feet.

The hair all over the body was pulled back inside the body and soon the body of a dead man lay at Bill's feet.

Bill walked around to get a front view of the dead man face and he saw the bullet wound in the man's chest that had penetrated his heart and killed him. Blood was oozing out of the big hole and running down the dead mans chest and onto his patio in a pool of blood.

Bill was stunned to the very end of his core when he kneeled down and looked at the dead man's face. Bill dangled his 38 snub nose gun across his bent right leg with his right hand ready if need be for action.

He recognized the mans face very quickly, it was officer Darker and he had a look of utter disappointment on his face.

"Huh—he's a police office on the Winston-Salem police force," said Bill in awe at what he saw and he looked at Lady Victoria Basil with sad eye's.

"That can't be," said Bill in utter disbelief and then he quickly looked back down at the dead officer face and then he noticed the cross burn on the right side of officer Darker's head.

"Why not—Bill Christian, evil in it's on time comes to

everybody if it get's a chance," replied Lady Victoria Basil who put her gun back in her waist belt and folded her arms while nervously tapping her left foot on the concrete patio.

"Aren't you evil too after being turned into a vampire," asked Bill watching the vampire vixen with wondering eyes?

"God's light shines on the dark side of the moon too and a person's soul is never completely turned evil if the heavenly soul and heart was good from the beginning which inhabits it in the first place when they are born from the well of soul's in heaven and some are born with a wicked heart too from the well of shadow's on the dark side of heaven where lucifer reign until his fall from grace, but those place's in heaven still exist even today and I've seen them. Only people who have a evil heart are turned completely to the dark side and corrupted by evil in the first place," replied Lady Victoria Basil who smiled very wickedly at Bill with golden blue eyes.

This is the creature that attacked me at old Bethabara the other night thought Bill, but he kept it to himself while he shook his head in disbelief at what the vampire woman had said to him.

"Well—lets just say I believe you have a good side too," replied Bill who now had good intentions toward this beautiful woman who impressed him very much with her bravery and the situation he was caught up in had changed course dramatically.

"What kind of bullet kills a werewolf," asked Bill looking the body all over from head to toe, but saw only the chest wound?

"Silver bullet's are the only thing that can be fired from a safe distance and I have more if I need them," replied Lady Victoria Basil with a confident look about her pretty face.

Bill stood back up and looked at the lady vampire with renewed confidence and pride and Bill slipped his 38 snub nose gun into his right robe pocket and he felt very safe for some unknown reason.

"Thanks for saving my life tonight. I owe you one and I remember my dear friend Clara Bell told me the same thing the other night about that silver bullet and I guess she was right after all and it looks like your over your mad spell from the other night in my office because you showed up on watch for me," said Bill who stretched out his hand in friendship toward the lady vampire. Lady Victoria Basil walked forward and grabbed Bill's hand.

"Lets just say I'm willing to give you a chance at redeeming yourself as a man in my good grace because I hate most men that I've met over the years, they just use you up and toss you in the side ditch when their done getting what they want and I've got your back Bill Christian," replied Lady Victoria who stood toe to toe with Bill on the patio.

"I'm not like most men and I have manners around a beautiful woman and I treat them with respect and thank-you," replied Bill honesty who looked down at the ground shyly for a second and then gazed back at Lady Victoria caught up in the moment.

Bill could smell the seductive perfume she was wearing and it smelled out of this world to him while he fought to control his new turned on emotions which were running in high gear for this lovely lady of the night and he couldn't understand why he felt this way after all she was just a woman and he had dated and run with many beautiful woman in his lifetime.

"The needs of the many out way the needs of the few or the one and they need you because your all they have and I mean the public at large and that's why I came here tonight to save you for them and will see," replied Lady Victoria Basil who shook Bills hand cooly but said nothing more about his last comment to her.

Bill noticed the grip was firm and her hand as cold as

ice, but he kept it to himself while he shook her hand in gratitude.

"I have to leave now, but we will meet again you can be sure of that and I hope to change your mind about me someday and maybe get a piece of your heart too," said Lady Victoria Basil who leaned over and quickly kissed Bill with ice cold ruby red lips dead on his lips and released his hand.

Bill felt shocked like a lightening bolt out of the sky had hit him when she pulled her lips from his and he was tingling all over. He felt his face go red from embarrassment at being caught off guard by the scented lure of a woman.

Then she reached up for the black night sky and she flew up silently into the air and disappeared over Bill's roof top before he could react with his stunned body and mind.

Bill quickly gathered his wits about him and turned around to look over his roof top and then spoke out loud on impulse.

"Maybe so and I hope that wasn't a fatal kiss of death, but a kiss of stimulating life between us," said Bill hopefully under his breath softly to himself and he looked up quickly to catch another glimpse of her.

Bill's heart was beating fast and the lure of passion and seduction had almost got the best of him as he stood there searching the star lit nighttime sky where the woman of his dreams had vanished without a trace.

Then he looked at the body again and that brought him back to reality and he walked back to his french doors to go inside and call the precinct.

Bill was wondering how he was going to explain a dead naked body which was one of Winston-Salem finest laying on his back patio.

"Man I need a snort of liquor and the whole world is going to hell in a hand basket," said Bill in disgust and disappointment at the dead officer who was a brother in arms and he was still a police officer at heart while he bowed his head for a moment at his french door and he prayed a silent prayer for the fallen officer Darker, then he looked back over his left shoulder and up at the full high moon over head standing there on his back patio and he felt real small in this big wide world and he had been warned about the full moon tonight by Clara Bell, but a man's got to sleep sometime.

Bill shuddered to think what the outcome would have been tonight if the werewolf had broke in and murdered him in his own bed tonight thought Bill to himself in heart felt thankfulness to his new found female vampire protector.

Bill cussed himself for not thinking of checking the law enforcement finger and hand prints on file of every officer in Forsyth County at the Winston-Salem police department personnel data base to the right thumb print and left hand palm print they had gotten off the stolen car at Old Bethabara Park and Par Course parking lot the other night and the Crime Scene Investigator William Walters had missed it too—and he new they would have a perfect match to Officer Darker's left hand palm and right thumb print, but who would have even thought of a lawman involved in the killings—well you can't win them all thought Bill standing in his kitchen doorway with a serious look on his face and he felt somewhat chilled at the thought standing in the cold night air on his back patio.

Bill walked on into the kitchen and shut his back kitchen french door and locked the latch then he headed for the phone on the far wall and on second thought he had better make a pot of coffee it was going to be a long morning and then he'd hit his liquor cabinet in the living room.

In the dusk of twilight Lady Victoria Basil flew among the trees over God's Acker on Cemetery Street. She flew down to the Basil family mausoleum ever so gracefully and landed ever so softly on tip toes.

She looked around at the deserted old graveyard that was adjacent to Old Salem and smiled at seeing such old friends buried around her from her past and she felt at home here.

The man she had saved tonight was handsome and she hoped again for a chance at love and life once again, it was always in her dreams when she slept at rest thought Lady Victoria Basil who stood in the crypt doorway for a lingering moment thinking about her night's encounter.

Lady Victoria Basil produced an old skeleton key from her vest pocket and she unlocked the vault door to the Basil family mausoleum.

The vault door creaked open when she pushed it inside "Crrreeeeeeaaak," from rusty old hinges and the cobwebs scattered from around the vault door!

She took a last look around and entered herself into her only realm of solitude she new and she was gone into the shadows when the vault door slowly closed shut as if by itself "Crrreeeeeeaaak—"thud,"!

You could here the ghostly door slide latch lock the massive door from inside "click" and then deathly silence while she put her soul to sleep.

Later at daybreak Bill was talking to the crime scene investigators on his back patio still in his pajamas and robe while they took pictures of the body on the patio.

The Winston-Salem police force had swarmed in force to his house. His driveway was packed with police cruisers and CSI vans and cars.

The neighborhood had awaken to a police presence and his neighbors had gathered on their lawns to watch and talk about what was going on at Bill's house on the block which his driveway was taped off with crime scene tape, guarded by two police officers. "You was awaken by a shot outside your house," asked CSI William Walters with concern on his young face?

"Yes—that's about it," replied Bill who shuffled his feet nervously.

" And you got up from your bed and went to see what had happen outside," asked CSI William Walters?

"Yes—sir that's when I found officer Darker dead on my

patio," replied Bill who was a little on edge about the whole thing.

"You didn't see anyone else and you didn't discharge your weapon," asked CSI William Walters?

"No—there was only one shot, but I had my gun just in case," responded Bill with wondering where this was going and he missed the first question very cleverly.

"Yes—your neighbors confirmed they heard only one shot from your house. Let me see your weapon," asked CSI William Walters and Bill pulled the 38 snub nose from his right robe pocket and handed it over?

CSI William Walters checked Bill's gun and pushed the barrel release and the cylinder popped out and it was fully loaded with no spent shells.

He flipped the cylinder shut then he smelled the barrel and made a happy face.

"This gun hasn't been fired," spoke CSI William Walters who handed the gun back to Bill who put it back in his right robe pocket.

"Please hold out your hands for a gunpowder residue check," requested CSI William Walters. Bill obediently stuck out his hands and waited while CSI William Walters got a Que tip packet from his CSI tool box and chemical spray gun while the other police officers watched with interest.

CSI Willam Walters broke the packet and got out the Que tip and rubbed Bill's back hands with the tip.

CSI William Walters sprayed the Que tip with the chemical spray and the Que tip remained clear.

"Well—it didn't turn bright blue for gun powder residue. Your definitely clear—you didn't fire a weapon hear tonight," spoke CSI William Walters who seemed relieved by the test.

"Do you know why officer Darker came here last night," asked CSI William Walters?

"I don't know why he came here or what he wanted unless he had information on the case that were all working on together and he was killed for it outside my house," replied Bill with a sternly look to remind the CSI that he was a retired distinguished officer from the force too.

"Yes– I suppose that could have been the case," replied CSI William Walters who nodded his head in approval, that he got the message real quick.

Just then Police Chief Dicky Poser showed up on Bill's backyard patio with his inner circle of top cops and took in the scene quickly.

"If your all through with your pictures and the crime scene. You men can get that body moved out of here now," ordered Police Chief Dicky Poser as his men took off the white sheet and got ready to move the body into a body bag and to a paramedic stretcher that they had already on standby at the patio.

"Bill lets talk for a moment alone while they remove the body," said Police Chief Dicky Poser and he walked inside with Bill to his kitchen.

They stood in the kitchen for a awkward moment and Dicky broke the silence.

"Bill I don't know what transpired here last night except what my on scene detectives told me, but I'm going to cover for you and I trust you will do the right thing, I believe this all ties in somehow to the murder cases your own and I'm going to let you do your job you were hired for, this might look bad for us, but believe me when I say that—I've got you covered on this one and I will keep the news media at bay and in the dark on what transpired here last night until your case is solved with word of a drunken hobo that died on your patio from hypothermia. You fired a shot to scare him off and then you saw he was dead and called us which is partly true, but with a white lie mixed in to protect the public at large and us. You didn't see who shot him did you?" asked Police chief Dicky Poser who patted Bill on the back good naturally in his kitchen.

"I'm doing the best I can with what I've got to work with. I'll stake my life on it and "NO" I didn't see the altercation out back I was in bed like I said and got up to see what had happen in my back yard on hearing the shot that was fired and found the body," said Bill knowing the chief would never believe his wild story about last night, but didn't outright lie to him.

He would have lost it too except for his new female guardian angel friend who had saved him and he didn't want to spend a week in the psychiatric ward either for telling it.

"That's my man always on the case. If you need me call me and try to stay out of the lime light if you get my drift," said Police Chief Dicky Poser who winked at Bill and he left with his entourage.

Bill thought he'd just spend a quiet day at home after all the excitement had died down and the police had left him in peace and besides he could take off from work when he wanted too because he was the boss.

His mother had taught him cooking was healthy for the soul and his love sick heart. He new his heart was growing fonder by the minute of being enticed by a beautiful woman.

Bill couldn't help, but think of that dark lovely vision that had come to his rescue last night.

He spent a quiet day in solitude playing his beloved 80s music in his kitchen and cooking his favorite food "spaghetti sauce with hamburger and noodle's" all afternoon and he had it for supper that night with some good red wine, but alas alone.

Bill made extra spaghetti sauce which he froze in his freezer. And soon the day turned into night and Bill sat outside looking up at the stars on his patio after supper in his Adirondack chair smoking a big Churchill cigar and drinking Columbian coffee until bedtime.

At the crack of dawn that same day Clara Bell had cooked Wilbur a big country breakfast of scrambled eggs with country ham and grits with a side of bacon and he was out doing chores around the farm and cleaning up any wind damage left by the storm last night.

She had gone back again to the wood shed beside the big red barn that morning and got up another mess of oak and pine kindling in her big galvanized farm pail and walked back to her kitchen in the old tin roof farmhouse.

After going up the cement steps and going inside her kitchen and shutting her screen door to keep the flies out. She walked over to her cook stove in the warm kitchen and set her wood chip pail down within easy reach on the stove top side board. She lifted the cast iron stove eye with her small eye tong handle and shoved it off to the side on the old wood cook stove. Clara Bell stuck in the mess of wood kindling through the stove eye to keep the fire burning hot from her pail of wood chips.

Then she got some small green wood pieces from the wood pile beside the back door and last, but not least stuck it overtop of her kindling chips.

She put the eight inch cast iron stove eye back on the wood stove with eye tong handle and hug it by its leather strap onto the side of the wood stove down by the water boiler that was built into the side of it to heat water for cooking or a hot bath fore it had a water spigot on the bottom of the hot water tank to drain out the hot water for those purposes.

She sat the empty pail back in the corner by the flue for the old wood cook stove in her spotless and clean kitchen.

Clara Bell walked over to her kitchen sink and grabbed the cast iron pot of pinto beans that she had looked through and got out the bad beans or rocks and washed that morning from her sink.

She filled the iron pot up to just about the top rim with water and she put the lid back on top. She carried the heavy iron pot over to the wood stove and set it on the big eye burner.

Then she carried a big tea kettle full of water from her

kitchen sink and set it on the opposite eye to refill the pinto bean cast iron pot back up with hot water when the water boiled out from the steam while cooking her pinto beans on a slow boil.

She walked across her kitchen to the pantry door and open her old style glass medicine cabinet door that was hanging on the wall beside the door.

She reached in and got out one of her spice jars and popped out the cork and poured out four beef bouillon cubes wrapped in red wrappers into her left hand.

She popped the old cork back in the spice bottle and set it back inside on the top rack with the rest of her spices, shutting the glass door.

She walked back to her cast iron wood stove and she open the iron lid on her pot of pinto beans and laid it off to one side. She unwrapped the beef cubes one by one and dropped them into the water inside the cast iron cooking pot to make a great tasting thick beefy season broth for the pinto beans.

Then she walked over to her ice box and got out a fresh open box of baking soda with a plastic spoon in side it while throwing the red wrappers in her waste basket beside the ice box.

She walked back to her cook stove and picked up the spoon and carefully got out a half teaspoon of baking soda from the box and dropped it into the pot also to soften the hard water and cut down on the gas.

She went back to her old fashion ice box and opening the door, put the baking soda back in and she grabbed a bottle of canola oil and she shut the door and walked back to her wood cook stove and twisted the lid off and poured in about two tablespoons of canola oil too season the pinto beans.

"They ought to be ready and slowly cooked through for Wilbur in about three hours with the green wood on top of the fire inside the firebox to make the fire burn more slowly and that will be about one o-clock in the afternoon just after lunch and I'll salt my beans the last hour at lunch time which makes the pintos taste better than an old piece of fatback that cooks the whole time in the beans which I learned from my dear old grandmothers secret southern pinto bean recipe. That was handed down to my family through generations ago and had been changed some over the years by my grandmother who always had stayed up to date on things," said Clara Bell out loud to herself who was very pleased with her cooking self standing over a hot stove.

She wiped the sweat from her brow with her apron bottom in her left hand and turned around and walked quickly over to her old kitchen hutch. She grabbed a spoon of lard from the lard bucket and proceeded to grease her big cast iron skillet on the inside with her right hand from the lard on the spoon.

When Clara Bell was done she stuck the spoon of lard back in the lard bucket. She went to the sink and washed her greasy hands and then dried them on her white apron which she was always wearing with her dress and she wouldn't be caught dead without it either.

She went back to the old kitchen hutch and started mixing the big two cups of cornbread that was in a big white plastic bowel with a big wooden spoon that she had already measured out before hand and poured in her big white mixing bowel.

She stopped and walked across the kitchen and open her ice box door and got out a half gallon of butter milk and a basket of fresh eggs from her hen house from the old ice box.

Clara Bell walked back to her hutch and set them off to one side and then she measured out two cups of buttermilk into her measuring jar and she cracked two large eggs and dropped them into the bowel and dropped the egg shells into her scrap bowel for her garden.

She then poured the buttermilk into the bowel and grabbed the old wooden spoon and started mixing again with a vengeance.

Then she poured in her half cup of melted lard that she had

set on the hot stove top a while ago in a small metal cup and also blended that into the cornbread batter too, vigorously.

She then poured the cornbread batter into her large greased iron skillet and scraped out the last of the batter into the old skillet with the big wooden spoon. She walked over to her kitchen sink and dropped the white mixing bowel into her sink along with the small metal cup.

She then went back to her old hutch and picked up the skillet with both hands and shook it back and forth to even out the batter on top of the big skillet. She still wasn't satisfied so she walked over to her kitchen counter and banged it up and done softly on her hard kitchen counter top until the batter was smoother on top of the old skillet.

"There—that ought to do the trick—rather nicely," said Clara Bell to herself happily who put on her oven mitten's and carried it to the old iron cook stove which she set it on top.

Then she bent down and opened the hot oven door with her left mitten hand and at about the same time she grabbed the iron skillet handle with her right mitten hand while holding open the oven door and slid the skillet with the cornbread batter into the hot oven for baking while turning the skillet handle to the left side of the oven out of the way and within easy reach when it was time to slide it back out of the oven after it had fully cooked.

She shut the oven door ever so softly and slightly pleased with herself in her kitchen cooking duties.

Clara Bell stood back up and slid off her mittens and turned around quickly and pitched them onto her farm table behind her. She turned back to her wood cook stove and reached up for the wind up timer on top of the pie shelf part of the old wood cook stove.

She turned the timer to forty-five minutes and set it back on top of the pie shelf while it started ticking down to ring at zero when her cornbread was done.

Clara Bell walked back to her old hutch and grabbed the

buttermilk and eggs and stuck them back in her old ice box. Then she went back and wiped down the old hutch enamel counter top with her wet dish rag and then she threw it back in the sink while she walked by.

Well that about does it and I can read my home and garden magazine at the farm table now to pass the time while my kitchen work is done for now until Wilbur comes in for lunch at one 0 clock thought Clara Bell who pulled at her wooden back chair and sat down at her place at the farm table and grabbed her favorite magazine.

She commenced to thumbing through it until she found the page she wanted and then she started reading about rose's in the flower garden while she watched her food cook away behind her with a blind third eye and she was glad most of her day was about over with because they would have beans and cornbread for supper too and they didn't waste anything down on the farm and the day passed quickly for Clara Bell and Wilbur who were hardworking honest country folk who went about their daily appointed rounds contentedly and the day soon passed into night.

The next morning Bill pulled his Monte Carlo into the parking lot of "The Walk In Closet Thrift Store" off of Bethania Station Road.

Bill got out and locked his car door and headed across the parking lot and through the double door's of the store.

"Can I help you," asked the tall blonde haired good looking young woman with a fair complexion who wore her blonde hair in a pony tail since she was a little school girl when Bill came through the big double door into the store?

"Hi—I just need a few Sunday go to meeting suit's because I wore out a few over the last week and may I find them on my own if you don't mind," replied Bill politely who wanted to shop alone.

"Suit your self if you need any help just—holler," said Sherry who recognized Bill quickly as a regular customer who shopped there quiet often and she went back to being busy behind the sales counter and wondering what happen to his old suit's, but didn't ask because she had been taught not to get into peoples personal business by her great parents who had raised her right.

Bill looked around the store as he browsed through the racks. This store has everything a person needs for their home thought Bill who saw clothes, dishes, coffee pots, silverware, t.v's and small appliances and sofas. They even had children's clothes and toys and a good selection of the latest C. D's and VHS movies.

Bill made his way to the mens suits and started going through the racks and soon had picked out two very nice wool second hand suit's that looked like brand new. Bill threw them over his right arm and walked back up front to the sales counter to pay for them. Sherry smiled at Bill who laid the suit's on the sales counter.

"Did—you find everything you needed —Bill," asked Sherry who eyed Bill with polite eyes?

'Oh—you remembered my name and of course—yes I did," replied Bill who was somewhat surprised at the smart business woman and a little embarrassed at being caught off guard by first personal names.

"I never forget a good customer," said Sherry who rung up Bills merchandise who looked somewhat relieved in his face by her friendly manner.

"Let me see—I never forget a pretty face and if my memory serves me right—your name is Sherry the owner," spoke Bill right out proudly of himself.

"That's right—land sakes you hit the nail on the head," replied Sherry with a slight southern female accent who was slightly amused at Bill's intuitiveness.

"That will be one hundred and twenty-five dollars with tax and that's a good price for these almost new three hundred dollar suit's at almost sixty dollars a piece," said Sherry who put Bill's suit's into a big carry bag with a handle.

"That's a good bargain and that's why I shop here," replied Bill who felt like he had got the best deal in town today.

"Thanks for shopping with us today and y'all come back now," said Sherry while Bill grabbed the carry bag handle.

"Thanks-you and have a nice day," replied Bill who tipped his Stetson hat at Sherry behind the sales counter as he left the store and was gone through the big double doors in a flash.

The next day Bill had arrived at the Parker's old farm house out on Payne Road with a tin roof in his nice new second hand wool suit and knocked on the front door"knock,—knock,"!

Clara Bell and Wilbur had gotten up at the crack of dawn to do the farm chores before Bill showed up that morning so they would be ready for him that day and not have to worry about the farm animals being fed on time that day.

Clara Bell answered the door and was glad to see it was Bill through her screen porch front door who had come calling on her rocking chair front porch where Wilbur would set for hour's in the evening after farming all day and play his banjo and drink his homemade moonshine till nightfall.

"Come on in Bill and have some percolated coffee made on a old cast iron wood stove and some fresh homemade butter milk biscuits made from scratch in the old wood stove oven there on the kitchen table in the bun warmer wrapped in a kitchen towel to keep them warm. I've just made them in the kitchen this morning and Wilbur is out back loading up his old ford pick-up truck with our Indian canoe. That's a nice wool suit your wearing and you look swell in it," said Clara Bell who held the door open for him.

"Thanks—Clara Bell don't mind if I do and I just bought this suit yesterday to replace the wet and ruined one from the other night," replied Bill who walked into the old farm house and down the hallway followed by Clara Bell.

"New clothes makes you feel worth while and like a new

man," replied Clara Bell who walked down the hallway and into the kitchen.

Bill was admiring the old grandfather clock in the hallway when he could have swore it winked at him as he noticed the time of 8:30 A:M when it chimed "dong," on the half hour.

Bill did a double take, but saw just a regular clock face and he shook his head in disbelief.

That can't have happen thought Bill to himself while he rolled his eye's up at the farmhouse ceiling.

"What's wrong Bill did you get out of the wrong side of the bed this morning," asked Clara Bell smiling at Bill while she teased him whom seemed unsure of himself in the hallway?

"No—no—no, for a second I thought your grandfather clock winked at me," replied Bill modestly watching Clara Bell with anxious eyes who stood in the kitchen doorway.

"Who knows what your eyes may see when they play tricks on you so early in the morning," replied Clara Bell who winked at the old grandfather clock behind Bill's back and it smiled and winked back at her while she laughed playfully "he-he-he" at her old confused friend under her breath mild mannerly.

Bill quickly looked back at the old clock again and the clock face looked normal to him.

Bill shrugged his shoulders and walked on into the kitchen and took a seat at the old farm table.

He thought for a moment Clara Bell was pulling his leg, but he didn't say nothing about it and he somehow felt silly inside like a school boy being teased by his classmates, but that was a long time ago or so he thought.

Bill started looking around the place and at the tall ceilings in the kitchen overhead and then he saw the antic china cabinet filled with white porcelain painted china and thought to himself it must be worth a small fortune.

Clara Bell had some pictures of a rooster and hen done in multicolor beans on her far wall which was white like her outside farm house which looked very nice and country.

He hadn't seen them since he was a little boy at his grandmas house years long ago before she passed which took him back in time for a while to a happier time when he was a young foolish gullible school boy. There was an old antic farmer's almanac tin with a small thermometer hung on the wall beside the wall phone with paper and pencil in the box which you could grab and write a phone message down on the kitchen counter for somebody.

Bill just loved the old antic wood burning cook stove beside the kitchen sink and the aroma of burning oak and hickory wood drifted to his nostrils which smelled down home and good to him for a change from his electric world which he new it cooked the best food you could ever taste in your mouth and old time's from yesterday country past when this great country was still young stood still in this mystical place in his mind from what he saw with his own eyes.

Bill looked at the old timer bread box holder with a small roll up door built into it setting on the kitchen counter, that had bread painted in big white letters on it across the small roll up door and a set of porcelain canisters hand painted with daisy flowers beside it.

There was an old white painted with red trim big antic roll top desk hutch that was built into it with a pull out white porcelain red trim shelf for people to sit at and eat when the kitchen was full of good neighbors or for a old style tupperware party with family and friends in the big old farm house style kitchen where everyone gathered to meet after church on Sunday.

It had small cabinet doors overtop for pots and pans with a built in flour holder on the bottom left side shelf for baking on the hutch counter top if you wanted to mix pies or biscuits there and he'd bet his bottom dollar that Clara Bell made these biscuits right there that morning which were made fresh from scratch.

He pulled the green bun warmer over to him from across

the farm table to get at the warm biscuits. He noticed the air vent on top that you could open by hand or close it and it was a cut flower type design and it looked late 1960s or early 1970s by his first guess on when the green bun warmer was made which intrigued him to no end. He turned his curious attention back to the old hutch after lifting the bun lid to satisfy his eye for fine old antics. The bottom had a big door with right hand side small drawers for utensils all the way down to the floor legs which Bill had never seen on one before and then he looked inside the bun warmer.

Bill carefully unfolded the warm kitchen towel and grabbed him a fresh buttermilk biscuit and folded the towel back up and politely replaced the lid.

He continued looking the old style kitchen over while he ate his biscuit and noticed the open door on the other side of the old hutch.

Beside it was a big walk in pantry food closet with the door open and Bill could see inside the open doorway and he saw the wooden white painted shelves were full from top to bottom with quart mason jars filled with fresh canned corn, tomatoes, green beans, peas also canned pickles from Clara Bell's and Wilbur's summer garden on the farm. He was impressed at their ingenuity and it was enough to feed a small army or at least last all winter and saved them plenty of money at the grocery store which produce in today's modern time was expensive with rising gas prices in summer and fall of the year he thought.

Beside the pantry door hanging on the wall was an old style glass medicine cabinet with old time remedy and portion glass bottle's filled with all kinds of herbs, spices and medicines for aliments and cures with rubber cork's stuck in the top of the glass bottles to seal them up to stay fresh for Bill's guess which was forever and he was intrigued, but he didn't ask for fear of a long lecture which was too early in the morning for him anyhow.

There was a big old shell service station clock on the wall which he new was rare indeed and he was amazed that this place actually existed in modern times with him use to being a city slicker who bought food at the supermarket and ate most of his meals at restaurants around town.

Clara Bell had old antic hand painted Avon china dish plates hung on the wall under her kitchen cabinets and woven hand basket decorated another wall beside the back door and Bill somehow felt right at home and at peace with himself in the old warm farmhouse kitchen. Clara Bell came up smiling at him and placed a white porcelain rose painted cup down in front of him on a rose painted saucer and poured him a steaming cup of hot perked coffee. She went and put the coffee back on the old iron stove eye to keep it hot. She then grabbed a small creamer and sugar bowel tray from her kitchen counter and set it down beside him with a small spoon in it for his coffee, that was painted with roses on it too and she went back to her kitchen duties humming cheerfully as a busy bee.

Sometime later Bill was drinking his cup of coffee and eating another buttermilk biscuit when Wilbur came in the back door and hung his straw cowboy hat on an old rusty 16 penny nail beside the back door.

"All the farm animals have been fed and the chores are done. The truck's all ready Clara Bell and Bill you look wide awake after some strong perked coffee which wake's America up every morning. Did you get up late after a rough night," asked Wilbur who sat down across from Bill watching him eat with a grin on his face down at the end of the kitchen table?

"I know that old saying from the coffee commercial's on t.v. that I've seen as a young boy growing up in Winston-Salem back in my day and It's been a rough few day's for me,' replied Bill in between bite's of his third buttermilk biscuit which seemed to melt in his hungry mouth and he fidgeted nervously in his seat at Wilbur's presence because he was in no mood for a good or bad argument today.

Clara Bell nodded her approval from the kitchen sink where she was washing the morning breakfast dishes and gave Wilbur her stern dirty look not to bother Bill which he understood rather quickly and he shut up at the table. Clara Bell grabbed a cup from her corner cupboard after drying her hands on her apron and poured Wilbur a steaming cup of perked coffee from the old wood stove who reached for a buttermilk biscuit in the old bun warmer on the kitchen table and grabbed one and proceeded to chow down.

Wilbur then picked up this months farmer almanac laying on the old style farm kitchen table at his place which was head of the table and proceeded to thumbed through it. He found his old place and read about the weather to come and planting seasons to keep his mind busy.

"An idle mind is the devil's work shop," said Wilbur to Bill who looked at him back across the farm house table somewhat slightly amused at his old religious friend.

"Roger that," said Bill politely and he took another bite of his buttermilk biscuit and he sipped his hot caffeine perked coffee in silence thinking about what he had gotten himself and his friends into and hoped for the best for today.

"You boys Finnish your coffee and buttermilk biscuits up. We have to go and check out what's up the Yadkin River before night set's in when no man can work," said Clara Bell itching to get going on her day trip.

Bill had briefly told Clara Bell and Wilbur what had happen at his house last night.

They both were smiling at Bill the whole time, but he left out the part about the kiss from the female vampire.

"Sounds like you have a Guardian Angel of a devil watching over you," said Wilbur who just grinned like a farm boy who had just won a blue ribbon at the county fair with his best calf.

"Yes—sir— re, she must really like your style," said Clara Bell who winked at Wilbur who rubbed his bald head and looked the other way to keep from laughing at what might be true love at last.

"I hate it about your officer friend's death the other night, but life goes on and anyway at least his suffering is over here on earth and your lady friend was justifiable in her actions. He got what he deserved and your old department saved themselves from public embarrassment by covering it up through no fault of their own to keep the public's trust fore they are most certainly honorable lawmen like you Bill," said Clara Bell and Wilbur who agreed whole heartily with her.

"Yep—that's right," said Wilbur who got up from the farm table and pitched his farmers almanac back on the table. He walked across the kitchen floor and put his dirty cup in the kitchen sink.

"I'll warm up the truck. Y'all come on when your ready," said Wilbur and with that Wilbur walked across the floor and grabbed his straw cowboy hat off the rusty 16 penny nail sticking in the back door top side molding and left out the kitchen back door without another word spoken.

Bill stirred his spoon in his coffee and sat there at the old country table and was deep in thought about what had been said and Clara Bell left him alone and finished up her kitchen chores quickly before they left the farm on their diligent search for a wolf's lair.

Later just before noon they had parked the old ford pickup truck at the river bridge access and picnic park just across the river from Yadkin County on highway 67.

Bill looked out the truck window at the old country store just up the road a ways and saw the customers cars parked in the parking lot doing normal things.

He guessed they were buying gas and supplies. Bill opened the truck door and stepped down out of the cab and quickly stretched his legs a bit.

He turned around and helped Clara Bell down the side rail and unto the gravel parking lot.

Clara Bell stood looking at Bill while she held on to her twisted swamp root cane.

"Did you pack my old Indian bald eagle design queen size patchwork quilt like I told you," asked Clara Bell to Wilbur who had got out of the truck and walked around to the back and started to untie the Indian canoe?

"Yes—it's inside the canoe with your other stuff," replied Wilbur while he untied the rope on the canoe.

"What quilt. It's not cold enough today and besides were coming back before sunset. I hope," asked Bill who spoked looking very puzzled?

"It's my magic Indian quilt," replied Clara Bell who tapped her twisted swamp root cane on the canoe where it was stored away at the bow of the Indian canoe.

Bill made a funny face at that one and looked the other way to keep from laughing.

"Oh—come on. There ain't no such thing as a magic quilt," replied Bill with a silly smirk on his face.

"Bill—you had better be quiet while your ahead before you get fussed at," said a wise Wilbur who had untied the canoe and was rolling up the rope on his left arm in a loop with his right hand which he stored away in the back of the pick-up front seat when he was done and locked the door.

Bill shook his head in solemn agreement knowing this old wise woman had a few tricks up her sleeve from her long time on this earth and he had better respect that.

He could only begin to wonder if it was maybe a magic quilt after all he had seen from being involved with these good people for many years who after all lived on a haunted road out in the country.   Bill and Wilbur carried the big Indian canoe down to the water's edge and sat it in the river bow first while Wilbur held the stern section.

Clara Bell hopped into the front of the Indian canoe and rested her twisted swamp root cane across her folded legs while Bill held her hand and then he climbed in too behind her.

Wilbur pushed the canoe off the shore and jumped in the back quickly to keep from getting his feet wet in the water.

Wilbur quickly dropped the trolling motor in the river water at the back of the canoe and pulled the starting cord and it fired and sputtered to life.

They were off as Wilbur turned the canoe in the river by the rear handle on the trolling motor that controlled the trolling fin in the river water in back of the canoe towards the concrete bridge and up the mighty Yadkin River they sped at a slow pace leaving a small wake behind them.

Under the bridge they sailed for sights unknown and what ever adventure that laid before them. In a matter of seconds they had passed under the old concrete bridge and were gone up around the bend and disappeared from sight.

The cold landscape river was a place of nature 's beauty to behold and the scenery was beautiful along the river banks in fall leave colors of Autumn. They saw some deer drinking water along the river banks with eyes and ears perked up as they approached them in their natural habitat.

They lifted their heads up at the first sign of danger and galloped off into the safety of the underbrush and back into the woods.

Everybody in the canoe laughed and smiled at each other at seeing nature at its best in the wild and they sailed on and Wilbur steered the Indian canoe around the big long sandbars that came up toward them in the river every once in awhile while they sailed up the Yadkin River.

Bill kept looking for sign's of fish swimming in the water and sometimes he thought he saw the ripples in the water that were made by a bass fish or channel catfish which were swimming by as they proceeded up the river and he smiled at himself when he saw a fish break the surface of the water off to his left while they sailed down the river because he loved to fish and this was a good hot day for it and they might be hungry for a worm or cricket on a hook thought Bill with wishful thinking.

They followed the Yadkin River as it snaked it's way up through Forsyth County and on into the little town of Clemmon's and the sun was hot and bright as the day wore on tiring out the band of thrill seekers in the canoe.

"We've seen no place along the river so far that could be a den of operation by your werewolf's theory, and there lair could be anywhere around these parts and the caves we've seen along the river have been empty and deserted with no signs of life, all we've seen is the wide open river and wild life along the banks and woods. I'm getting tired and hungry also thirsty," said Bill who wiggled in the canoe to stretch his aching crossed legs and it was near 3:00 P:M by his wrist watched that he glanced at and he was getting very impatient as the long day wore on.

"Just wait a bit longer if we don't see anything or run across anything we will turn back because it's a dead end and here is some water to drink in this milk jug that I brought along to quench our thirst and here's some nabs I brought along in case we got hungry that I had Wilbur put up in the front of the canoe with my quilt," replied Clara Bell who wasn't ready to turn around and give up just yet and she passed the water milk jug and nabs back to Bill who took it and drank thirstily and open the nabs and popped one in his mouth and he began to eat.

"Smart thinking of bringing water and food on this little trip Clara Bell," replied Bill with renewed enthusiasm while he filled his hunger and thirst. "I always am prepared and didn't you hear what I said a moment ago," replied Clara Bell who looked down at her crossed feet in the canoe?

"Yes—I did—Well for what's at stake which is people's lives I hope so for their sake," replied Bill with a mouth full of nabs who thought this river trail led to nowhere and wiped his mouth off with the back of his coat sleeve and passed the water milk jug back to Wilbur who took a swig also from the water milk jug.

"Clara Bell— honey—we have almost reached the end of the line. The gas tank is almost empty for the trolling motor. We have maybe a couple of cups left of gasoline before we run out," said Wilbur who rolled the gas tank back and forth as he listen to the gas swishing back and forth.

"Well—we will go onward until we run out of gas and if we don't find the den of thieves, so to speak by then, we will turn the canoe around and let the river current carry us back to where we started from and we will try another day," replied Clara Bell who was in supreme command of her little war party and was not about to give up when she felt they were so close.

"Yeah—I don't want to come back and do this again. Its been a long ride and a hot day for canoeing on the river," said Bill who wanting to arrive at their final destination before sundown.

No one else spoke as they sailed up the Yadkin river each one keeping their eyes peeled for anything out of the ordinary along the river banks and the vast stretches of bottom farm land and the dark forbidding river woods on both sides of the canoe and them.   Sometime later they came around a long bend in the river and they all saw the big long dam loom straight up ahead across the river on the vast edge of the horizon and they heard the rush of white breakwater way up ahead, that flowed over the old dam gates into the river.

"There's your answer Bill way up the river—that's it. The wolf's lair I can feel it in my bones," said a happy Clara Bell who now looked relieved at finding what she hoped was a needle in the haystack. Bill looked back at Wilbur who smiled and winked at him with a my wife's always right look and he pointed at the old dam up ahead and began to speak.

"That's the Old Idols Hydroelectric Dam it was built in 1897 by inventors Thomas Edison and Frank Sprague my grand pap used to work there back in the roaring 1920's I had for gotten about this place," said Wilbur who thought back to yesteryear when he was a small boy and his grandparents were still alive.

"Yes—I remember it too from when I was a small girl growing up in these parts," replied Clara Bell who put her hand over her face so she could see the old dam with the ruins of the power station on top of it because the sun was setting in her eyes.

"I've never heard of it and the river mud clue from the stolen car back at old Bethabara seems to have paid off in my investigation with help from the Winston-Salem police department Crime Scene Investigator William Walters who worked very hard to identify that river mud clue—if your right—it looks like a deserted and perfect place to run a den of evil out of in the middle of the night out here on the Yadkin River which runs right by the major towns in this area," said Bill incredulously looking down the wide stretch of river that lay ahead in front of their canoe.

"Most people don't know about this old relic from the past it's a forgotten part of yesteryear," said Wilbur with a thinking face of child hood memory's that came flooding back to his old mind of past days gone by.

"My grand pap said people would hop on their riding horse's and hitch up their buggies and ride out to the Yadkin River to watch the Idols Hydroelectric Plant being built in the summer of 1897 which was one of the engineering marvels of their time, fries Manufacturing and Power Company built the dam and hydroelectric station which I believed he said it open in 1898 from what my grand pap had told me from his stories when we were siting on his rocking chair front porch when I was a small boy.

He also said the plant was used for small-scale operations for the day of, providing power to textile and fertilizer mills, wood and metal workshops, electric street lighting and an electric railway system in Winston-Salem to power the rail cars in town and also power to the houses of the surrounding area.

The plant had six generators in a shed behind the dam that was later run by Duke Power which bought the dam and power plant property in 1914 and updated all the equipment at that time. It put Winston- Salem at the forefront of the 20th century and a leader in the state.

I believe that's correct about the history if my memory serves me correctly from what my grand pap told me long ago," said Wilbur with a happy proud heart from recalling his grand pap's past. Just at that point in time the trolling motor coughed and sputtered and went silent.

"Well everybody guess what—we just ran out of gas," said Wilbur who looked for a place along the river bank to land the old Indian canoe.

"Not a moment to soon—for lucks with us today," replied Clara Bell who looked at her tired old men sitting back behind her in the canoe.

"There's a old deer trail past that sandbar," said Wilbur who turned the rudder handle and turned the canoe at a slight slant across the river and guided the forward momentum of the canoe to the river bank shore before the current pushed them back down river.

The canoe's forward motion was enough for them to land safely on the far river bank with soft jolt.

Bill quickly jumped out and "splashed" knee deep in the river water and waded to shore!

He held onto the end of the canoe to keep it from being pushed back down the fast river current.

"Come on—Clara Bell and hop on out," said Bill who grabbed Clara Bell's hand and helped her out of the front of the canoe onto dry land.

Wilbur got up and raised the trolling motor up out of the river water and stowed it in the bow of the canoe.

The canoe wobbled in the water while Wilbur hopped forward and jumped onto dry land.

"Why am I always the one getting wet all the time," asked a sorrowful Bill who looked down at his wet knees and shoes?

"It's because your always in the thick of things feet first," replied Clara Bell and she and Wilbur laughed together "Ha—Ha—Ha—Ha" at their funny old wet pal.

"Lets move on quickly the sun is setting and y'all need to hide the canoe in the bushes over there," said Clara Bell with haste in her voice and pointed back behind her toward the top of the river bank with her twisted swamp root cane.

Bill looked up over the river bank and saw the last light of the setting sun through the tall whispering pines.

"Your right lets do it," said Wilbur and Bill and he grabbed the Indian canoe and hauled it out of the river water and up the river bank they scrambled kicking rocks and dirt along the way.

"Don't forget my quilt," spoke Clara Bell to them as they struggled by with their heavy burden.

"I'll get it—don't worry," replied Wilbur who was huffing and puffing up the river bank with Bill.

After they hid the Indian canoe behind the bushes Wilbur got some old tree limbs that had fell down in the trees and marked the spot with an X on the ground with them.

"X—marks the spot where we left our transportation out of here," said Wilbur who carried Clara Bell's quilt under his arm happy at his old Indian trick.

They followed the old worn deer path, that wound along the river bank toward the old Idol's Dam.

Just as they got to the end of the deer trail where it passed by the dam they stopped fore they had run into a old dirt and gravel service road and they looked amazed out across the top of the dam toward the old iron rusted gatehouse and they saw the big "No Trespassing, Violators will be prosecuted" sign on the metal stake in the ground at the front of the dam, just a few feet from them.

"Go—look and see what you can find—me and Wilbur will wait here and be on guard for anyone coming by— besides you're the one with the gun," spoke Clara Bell honestly.

"Well—your right about that and I know how to use it too," replied Bill who stood looking transfixed at the beckoning old spooky looking dam.

Listen to me real good— Bill—put your best foot forward and Cave Canem which is latin meaning (beware of the dog),' said Clara Bell who looked over her wire rim spectacle's at Bill who came to attention fast and new it was show time for him the reluctant antihero.

"All right—ya'll stay here and keep watch and I'll go see what I can check-out and find," replied Bill who took off walking across the top of the dam with the ruins of the old power station underneath his feet while looking at the white spillway water that rushed underneath his feet through the dam gates just below him and at the spectra of a ghostly old iron gate house that was rapidly approaching him on the dark side of the dam as he walked across the top of the dam.

Bill hurried walking across the dam and turned back briefly and his companions waved at him bravely encouraging him on in the red glow of the fading sun light behind them that winked out behind them in the tall woods.

Dusk had now settled and the place came alive with the night sounds of black birds "ARK, ARK" that swooped across the old dam and flew into the trees along the river bank to land on a limb somewhere behind him who were hungry for nighttime food.

Bill flinched at the low flying birds that came out of nowhere while he walked the long dam and crickets chirping their loudly nightly chorus "CHIRP, CHIRP" all around him were these wicked sounding noises of the night that made Bill have a cold shiver up and down his spine when a cold north wind kicked up and his trench coat flapped in the cold breeze behind him who then pulled out his 38 snub nose gun when he got to the gate house iron door.

"At last," said Bill under his nervous breath who was glad when he had finely made it in one piece across the old dam.

He kept his trigger finger straight out across the side of the trigger guard so he wouldn't have a accidental missfire like he was taught in police shooting training and could quickly stick his finger in the trigger guard and fire if he wanted too.

Bill pulled out his pocket pen flash light form his inside left shirt pocket and clicked it on.

Bill pushed the old iron door open and it creaked slowly open "creeeeek" and Bill shined his light through the door and saw the dirty cement floor that was covered with leaves and sticks.

Bill shined his light around the gatehouse room and saw a big huge old wooden spool that had once held big electrical power cable's that had been turned over to make a table.

Bill saw the old rusty metal buckets around the table used for chairs and he thought it was abandon and empty so he went inside to investigate further. Bill's stopped just inside the old iron gatehouse door and his light swept the room.

He saw the control handles and turning wheels for the flood gates across the room on the far side long wall and also other types of electric boxes and wheel controls that he didn't know what they were for and at that moment he didn't care fore caution was his main driving force and no time to examine how this old stuff from the past worked here at the old hydroelectric plant which tugged at his inventive mind.

Bill walked across the cement floor and his footsteps echoed off the walls around him which gave him the jitters in this Erie place. Bill was astonished to see plastic bags on top of the old rusty metal buckets and he took a step backward in unforeseen surprise.

Bill picked up one and shined his light on it and saw it was a dry clean towel and wash cloth with soap in the bag which was on top of a bigger plastic bag.

Bill shined his light on that and saw it held a woman's clean dress in it with shoes and under garments Bill was astonished at what he had found.

Bill walked quickly around the table and counted four women's clothes and eight men's clothes and the last one looked like a priest black suit and white chest collar.

Bill gasped when he thought about father Marion at the church last week he has visited for a brief time. Then he noticed the head of a black dog painted on top of the spool beside the kerosene hurricane glass lamp with fangs in the middle of the table and he shined his pen light on it for a better look at it and he realized he had seen the same tattoo on two recent people he had just met and he wondered about that for a moment if it was connected to his case which a wild hunch in the back of his mind told him yes and Bill moved overjoyed on around the table pondering his racing mind, but he had to believe in his clues that led him here which were starting to fall in place all at once.

Who ever the artist was they were very good at drawing thought Bill and he had found enough and new they were on the right trail from all the clues that had led them here to their wolf's lair.

Bill was sure of it now this Erie place fit the hub of the Triad to a tee and they had a base to launch their attacks on the good citizens of his proud city on many highways and trains that ran along the Yadkin river.

Bill had seen enough and was alarmed they might show up at any time and catch him here so he made his way back to the old iron gate house door and left it just like it was shut.

Bill did a fast track across the dam and raced back to his companions who were ever vigilant at the old deer path at the front of the dam.

Bill slid to a stop and bent over double to catch his breath and then stood back up and holstered his gun on his right side after getting his second wind.

"This is the place and no one would have never expected this here at this abandon dam no one probably never comes here at all because this place is so spooky and off limits to people by the property owners and most people don't know about this place like ya'll all have said because it's been forgotten in history," said a aspirated Bill who took a deep breath and kept on talking.

"They have a round table sat up with twelve chairs and fresh clothes in plastic bags and soap to clean up with after their night's battle of killing their victims to wash away their bloody body sins in the river and fresh clothes to wear back to their place's in society without anyone having the slightest ideal about who the real killers are or what they have all been up too at night. The round table has a black dog with fangs painted on it and I've seen that same likeness on two people in a tattoo on the back of their hands," said Bill who was all wound up from his little adventure into the unknown.

"I new it the minute I laid eyes on this place it was the perfect place for a hide-out and their's twelve wolfs on the prowl, but wait your newfound lady friend the seductive female vampire killed one outside your residence the other night," said Clara Bell and then they heard the cars engine off in the distance coming down the road toward them and the car's lights that flashed through the woods?

"Yes—I think so and she did kill one while protecting me the other night for reasons I can't quiet fathom who bore the same black fang dog head tattoo on his right hand," replied Bill who looked off down the dirt and gravel service road to the old dam to see what was coming their way.

"Well—it's good to know what were up against and maybe she's love struck on you," replied Clara Bell who stood in deep thought on that very spot of ground and shook her head at the shock that hit her from being love struck once herself with her husband Wilbur when she and him was young once upon a time.

"We must hide quickly back down the deer trail before we are discovered," said Wilbur and they took off running, but Clara Bell cleared up her thoughts quickly and stopped them in their tracks.

"Hold up—give me that quilt—Wilbur," barked Clara Bell who obediently came back and handed over the quilt to Clara Bell with Bill coming up at the rear.

"What's up with the quilt–they will be here any second and catch us out in the open and the game will be up for us," asked Bill wondering what the old grandma was up too?

"You'll see–just hold your horses," said Clara Bell who quickly spread it out on the ground.

"Lay down," commanded Clara Bell who herself got onto the quilt with her twisted swamp root cane in her hand while she grabbed the corner of the old Indian eagle queen size patchwork quilt with her free hand.

Bill looked at Wilbur with wondering eye's on his tired old face.

"Don't ask, but do as she says—it will be all right," said Wilbur who also got on the middle of the quilt and pulled Bill down beside him on the end.

"ALLAH—BABBRA—RISE UP," commanded Clara Bell and to Bill's amazement the quilt stiffen underneath them and rose straight up in the air. They were levitated off the ground and he looked over the side of the Indian quilt and way down at the dam that looked smaller to him now. They were a good twenty feet off the dam and water rushed by them down below.

"It is a magic quilt," shouted Bill in amazement and Wilbur "shooshed" him with his finger over his lips.

"They can still hear us on the ground," said Wilbur who whispered to Bill to be quiet.

They heard the car park and some people get out and walk

onto the dam. Bill looked over the quilt as the rest of them did too, but it was very dark now and they saw four tall figures walking along the dam toward the old gate house iron door and one appeared to be a woman in a dress.

The people went inside and then they saw the light come on in the old gate house windows and the door closed.

"How long can we stay afloat and why didn't they see us," whispered Bill earnestly?

"The white magic that blessed this quilt will last forever and underneath—it is invisible in the air to anyone who looks up at it because the white magic makes it transparent—now stop asking questions and just take it easy—while we wait for them to leave," replied Clara Bell in a sternly whisper.

"I can do that," whispered Bill who rolled over and put his hands behind his head and watched the stars for a little while. Wilbur got tired after awhile and he too rolled over on his back and soon fell asleep and he began to snore "zzzzzZZZ"!

Clara Bell nudged her sleeping husband and woke him up. "Wilbur you snore when you sleep you'll give us away," said Clara Bell who whispered ever so softly to her husband.

"Oh—sorry honey I got sleepy," replied Wilbur who rolled over on his side and sat up on his elbow to stay awake.

The four people took their appointed seats around the table after the oil lamp was lit.

"we must take a vote tonight about the private investigator and his two meddlesome old friends. The vote will be death for my vote and it must be unanimous with the pack," said the tall dark hair man with a mustache and he gestured a thumbs down to his friends sitting at the round table while the old oil lamp cast a Erie light amid the flickering shadows off the old rusting walls of the gatehouse.

"I second that vote—its better them then us," said the young brunette woman with a satin looking slim hand which she balled into a fist and gave the thumbs down sign for death.

The man wearing the white collar moved from his shadow partially into the light where he was sitting.

"Our top trained assassin brother Darker with law enforcement training must have failed the other night in killing Mr. Christian on my orders and we presumed he was somehow killed by that meddlesome Private Investigator Bill Christian instead because he never returned here to tell us the dirty deed was done and no one knows about his whereabouts at his precinct.

From what I could make out on the neighborhood gossip where the private dick lives something did happen at his home the other night and some poor drunken hobo was found there in the backyard deader than a door nail.

The police was called there after shots were fired, but the public was kept away and in the dark about it and that private dick still lives and that was all I could find out. We must not make any more mistakes about them because they are very dangerous people who can do us great harm and they know about us now and we may not get a second chance for survival of our beloved pack—if we fail," spoke the angry man wearing the white collar who gave a thumbs down sign as did the last man sitting across from him did.

"Good—its settled then and the hit woman should be arriving shortly and we will indeed hire her and pay her price. Now on to other business," spoke the tall dark haired man with the mustache who folded his arms across his chest satisfied with tonight's meeting of pack leaders.

At midnight Lady Victoria had left her fortress of solitude in the graveyard and flew over the old tin coffee pot that was the gateway to Old Salem and then over the town watching the cars riding on the cities street's below that she passed over from above and over top of the lighted neighborhoods on the outskirts of the great city.

Soon she passed above the Oldtown section of town headed

north out of Winston-Salem flying like a bird, but faster than a nighthawk out on the prowl.

Soon she was flying along the banks of the Yadkin River that ran by highway 67 toward the town of Eastbend, Lady Victoria Basil flew low on the river and she dipped her right hand in the water and she screamed "weeeee" out loud as a spray stream of water shot out in a graceful long white arc behind her while she flew low over the river and then she flew back up into the dark night sky!

She heard the night calls of the birds and insect that lived along the river banks and from the woods which she sensed were there and she saw the black birds and hawks hunting along the Yadkin River with her red vampire night vision on full alert.

At time's she even heard the heat beats of the black birds when they flew close to her to check her out, then they flew off scared by the dark force from within her that radiated outward as a warning to all who came near her lethal attack range.

Tonight she wasn't hunting humans for prey, but she was intervening in dark forces that only she could reckon with in due time because she had the edge of playing both sides.

She soon crossed the river bridge that went into the town of Clemmon's and she followed the crooked running Yadkin River that ran parallel outside the town.

She soon saw the dam up ahead that crossed the river banks and when she flew over the dam to check it out her eyes beheld a sight that intrigued her heavenly side conscious.

She smiled wickedly fore above the roaring river and dam was a quilt with the would be heroes laying on top of it suspended in mid-air not twenty feet over top of the dam that she was trying to protect, but it was good to know where they were as if they needed help.

She was amazed by the magic quilt she had seen the likely cast of heroes laying on it as it floated above the dam and water which hid them from prying eyes far down below and she new those old country folks Bill was with had the right stuff and she wondered how those good people had the knowledge of white magic spells from seeing the flying magic quilt down below her.

She thought they might be trained sorcerers of the Alter Realm which she had run into in other parts of the country, but she had to attend to dangerous business at hand and worry about that later. If need be for her own safety and their safety was what mattered right now thought Lady Victoria who flew on by.

Then Lady Victoria Basil who was the princess of darkness flew off to the right side so she wouldn't be spotted by the trio on the quilt and raise an alarm and she landed ever so softly behind the old iron gate house.

She walked over to the old iron gate house back door and she cocked her 45 pistol that was in her waist belt in case she needed to draw and shoot quickly like a old gun slinger in the old wild west. Then Lady Victoria Basil pushed open the old creaking iron gate house back door and stepped inside through the dim light that came beckoning out the door.

She pulled the door shut with her left hand behind her and she walked toward the old wooden spool which four people sat at around with a old glass hurricane lantern that glowed brightly on the wooden table and cast dark shadows on the gate house walls and some sat in the shadows hidden by the darkness of the room and the light flickered from the old hurricane lantern from time to time and the room dimmed ominously in and out of the light.

"I see you followed my directions carefully to find the old dam and you must be Lady Victoria the hit woman for hire that was recommended by shall we say good charming people," spoke the tall dark hair man with a mustache.

"That will be me," replied Lady Victoria Basil with a smug look on her face and her golden blue keen eyes darted around the gate house taking everything in while she stayed in the shadows too.

"Please take a seat and make yourself comfortable," spoke the young brunette woman with ruby red lips.

"I'd rather stand my ground and do business right here," replied Lady Victoria Basil cautiously and she had a gunslinger's angle of attack on them which they didn't seem to notice.

"Well—let's get right to it then. We want you to kill these three people here in these pictures and dispose of the bodies down some mine shaft or shallow grave out in the woods with extreme prejudiced," said the tall dark haired man who threw the photos of Bill Christian and Clara Bell and Wilbur Parker on the table.

Lady Victoria Basil looked at the photos and for a micro second her red eyes flamed up in anger from golden blue, then back to golden blue again in the dark dim light, but it was too quick for anyone to notice, even them.

"No—problem consider it done, but I must have payment up front like we talked about," replied lady Victoria Basil with a business like attitude.

The young brunette woman opened her purse and took out a small brown manila envelope and tossed it on the table toward Lady Victoria Basil.

"Those are the high quality carat diamonds you bargained for and if you do the job right there's a lot more where they came from and we could use you again if need be," said the young brunette woman who snapped her purse shut. Lady Victoria Basil who had a look of enjoyment on her lovely card bluffing poker playing face and being all business like with all her cards on the table walked over and picked the diamonds off the table nonchalantly and backed away with caution in her eyes with an ace still up her sleeve to play later.

"Well—diamonds are a girls best friend," replied Lady Victoria Basil who smiled with her own ruby red lips seductively at them seated at the round table and who checked the diamonds in the manila envelope to make sure they were the real McCoy. Then stuck the pack of diamonds inside her vest while she looked at the black dog with fangs painted on the old wooden spool.

Then she spotted the white collar of the man hidden in dark shadow across the table in back and for a moment he looked like a man of the cloth to her, but it was hard to see in the dimly lit light flickering in the darkness of the room which she saw the red glow of heat from his body and the others with her hidden vampire eyes, that looked human and she new if she used her red vampire eyes to see in the dark and check him out, then they would no in an instant she was a vampire and not a frail human being so she shrugged it off and finished her business at hand.

"Nice drawing of your pet mascot and until we meet again," said Lady Victoria Basil rather cooly who backed out from the table and left watching back over her shoulder while she left.

After closing the old iron gate house door lady Victoria Basil walked across the end of the dam and down deep into the woods along the other access road. When she was safe from prying eyes, she took to the night skies and was gone.

Sometime later after midnight the lights went out in the old gatehouse and the old iron gate house door creaked open and the four people came out through the door and shut it behind them.

They all walked across the dam as if they were on a evening stroll through the park overtop of the power station ruins and they could here them talking when they walked by.

"Are you sure we have to get rid of them because it could cause serious trouble by law enforcement looking into their disappearance for all of us," asked the pretty female voice?

"Yes—that Private Detective and his old elderly friends have to be rubbed out of existence before they do us in and before the next full moon. We have no choice in the matter and after tonight our worries will be over and the night will be ours once again and our hired hit woman will do the dirty job for us, but there was something peculiar about that gorgeous black haired woman, that I can't quiet put my wicked finger on" replied a husky male voice.

The people passed on underneath them and soon the voices faded and they heard the car doors shut. The car started up and it turned around and was gone in the night down the old dirt and gravel road and the headlights faded from view. "One of those voice's sounded very familiar to me, but I can't quiet place it," said Bill to Wilbur who looked at him with questioning eyes.

"Your guess is as good as mine it could be anybody and besides we didn't see their faces because it was too dark out here," replied Wilbur who shrugged his shoulders at that comment laying on the magic quilt beside Bill who shook his head in bitter disappointment. "Pro—Sterno," commanded Clara Bell in latin which meant (to throw down to the ground) and the magic quilt flew down to the ground and landed softly beside the dam from whence they had come from.

"Man that's far out. I have to get me on of those,' said Bill who looked at the magic Indian quilt with childish playful eyes.

"Your not approved for flying yet Bill—see me after this case your on is solved and I'll give you a few flying quilt lessons," said Clara Bell with a heavenly eye on Bill and she laughed "hee, hee, hee," while she folded up the quilt and handed it to Wilbur who took it putting it under his arm.

"Well—they said they have hired a hit woman on us and we had better be on alert from here on out until we formulate a plan of attack," said Bill who watched his companion's faces for a response.

"Well let's hit the road—we have to get home and do some planning to eradicate this wolf's lair and we will worry about that hit woman if and when she shows up and we will be ready for her if need be," replied Clara Bell who walked off down the deer trail toward the hidden canoe without another word said.

Bill and Wilbur looked at each other in mock surprise at the calmness of Clara Bell's odd courage and fell in behind her as she walked with her twisted swamp root cane down the old deer trail toward the canoe.

Later Bill and Wilbur had gotten the Indian canoe out from it's hiding place and put it back in the river water at the banks edge after helping Clara Bell in the front with Bill in the middle.

Wilbur pushed it off from the river bank with his right foot and sat down in the backseat snugly. They broke out the rowing paddles secured in the side of the canoe and Bill and Wilbur started paddling away to head down stream. They where swept away by the fast river current and were swallowed up in a matter of second's by the fast flowing river and darkness of night.

Sometime after the stroke of twelve Wilbur guided the old Indian canoe into the access ramp past the bridge on highway 76 that went toward Eastbend.

"Man that was a fast trip back down the Yadkin River," said Bill who hopped out onto dry land and pulled the Indian canoe up further so the current wouldn't drag it off with the fast downstream river current.

"The return trip is away's faster than going on a trip," replied a wise Clara Bell who was helped out of the canoe by Bill. Wilbur jumped out onto dry ground and stumped his feet to shake the sleep out of them.

"Whew"—glad to be back where we started on dry land," said Wilbur who took off his straw hat and wiped his nearly bald head with a handkerchief bandana that had been wet with sweat.

Bill and Wilbur hauled the canoe out of the river water

and carried it back to the old ford pick-up truck and loaded it on and tied it down.

With a last check on the ropes Wilbur said "lets head out for home" and he open the truck door and got in to start the engine. Later riding toward Payne Road Clara Bell began to speak about her newly devised plan for the upcoming ambush at the old dam she had in mind.

"Bill you need to take some 99 percent pure silver to the gunsmith and have him make you some silver bullets, this very day before the next full moon and you'll have a razors edge to fight and kill them with" said Clara Bell who looked at Bill who was in deep thought about his vampire vixen and he wondered if he'd ever see her again.

"Bill did you not hear me," asked Clara Bell who nudged Bill in his ribs with her right elbow?

"Oh—yes—yes— silver bullets. I'll have some made right away because I know you said I needed them to kill a werewolf with," replied Bill who was startled back to reality.

"Yes dear—you will need twelve of them for your gun and if you don't have enough silver maybe Wilbur can loan you some from his stash and that should do the trick," said Clara Bell who looked up at the dark night sky through the truck windshield.

"Yeah — that ought to do the trick right," said Wilbur who turned onto Payne Road from highway 66 out of Rural Hall and headed toward their farmhouse down the old dusty dirt and gravel old tobacco road.

Later when Bill had gotten home and laid the small silver ingot down that Wilbur had given him on his bedside table and Bill got ready for bed who was give out from his river trip.

Bill disrobed and put on his pajamas and he put his gun on his night table within easy reach. He kept his silver cross around his neck for safety sake.

Bill soon drifted off to sleep and was soon awaken by a nock on his bedroom window"pang, pang,"!

Bill sat up rubbing the sleep out of his eyes and he stared at his bedroom window and then he made out the outline of a female figure standing in the window from her waste up by the outside flood light which cast her shadow against the window.

Now—who could that be at this time of night thought Bill who kicked off his bed sheets and walked over to the window and pulled the window curtains back.

"Hi," said a seductive voice through the window pane and to Bill's surprise face he recognized it was Lady Victoria Basil ghostly dark shadow he was looking at through his bedroom window.

"What do you want at this time of the night and I have a big day planned for tomorrow, but I'm glad to see you again," said Bill who rubbed the sleep from his eyes with both hands and yawned and then he stretched his body by reaching for the ceiling on tip toes?

"I have to talk to you about some information on your current case, it want take long," replied Lady Victoria Basil who stood looking quit lovely in Bill's flood light when she stepped back into the light.

"Well—I'm not talking here—come to my kitchen back door," said Bill who shut the curtain and grabbed his robe off his bed. Then he grabbed his gun which he stuck in his right robe pocket and walked out of his bedroom toward his kitchen down the hallway.

Bill entered his kitchen and cut on his pot rack light while he walked across the floor to his kitchen door and opened it looking out at the starlit night sky.

Lady Victoria Basil gently floated down in front of his wide open eyes out of the night sky and landed at his kitchen doorstep.

"Is this a Midnight Rendezvous, that's been dying to

happen between us," asked Bill who winked at the lovely lady standing on his back kitchen door stoup with a beaming smile of friendship in her appearance and the feeling of a teenagers first love starting in his heart after so many years had come and gone by?

"Yes—it may be—may I come in," asked Lady Victoria Basil who smiled friendly at Bill who was taken a back by her honest looking face and lovely golden blue eyes?

"Yes—you may come in," said Bill who motioned her inside and shut the door.

"That is a lovely blue Victorian ball gown, your wearing and you look gorgeous in it," said Bill who complemented her appearance as he looked her up and down and was taken a back by the young woman's shear radiate beauty.

"Thank-you and your not so bad looking either," replied Lady Victoria Basil who giggled at Bill in his robe and pajamas.

"Come and take a seat here at my kitchen table and would you like a glass of something to drink," asked Bill who was showing polite manners to his nighttime guest who had quiet possibly had saved his life the other night from an awful death?

"Yes—some cold red wine would be nice," replied Lady Victoria Basil who sat down in the chair Bill pulled out from his kitchen table.

Bill walked to his kitchen cabinet and open the door. He got out two tall wine glasses and shut the cabinet door.

Bill walked over to his refrigerator and open it and looked for a open bottle of red wine that he had the other day with his spaghetti dinner.

"Ah-ha," said Bill who pulled out the bottle of wine from inside the condiment door section and shut the refrigerator door.

He walked back to his kitchen table and sat down across

from Lady Victoria Basil who eyed him deeply with polite concern on her face.

Bill popped the long cork from the wine bottle and pulled both glasses full that he had set down on the table in front of him.

Bill passed the red wine glass to Lady Victoria Basil who touched his hand and they felt each other's passion for one another as they looked into each other's love struck eye's and it was electrifying for the love struck couple for just a moment and then Lady Victoria Basil took the wine glass in her hand and then she brought the glass up to her ruby red lips and tasted the red wine.

"That's a delicious red wine," said Lady Victoria Basil who set her wine glass on the table in front of her and looked at Bill with far away dreamy eyes.

"Yes—that was a very good year I'd say about 1966 and several hundred dollars for a bottle of Napa ValleyVineyards finest Merlot," replied Bill who swished his wine around in his wine glass and looked deep inside it as if searching his inner soul about the beauty in front of him.

Bill took another sip of wine from his glass and he swished it around in his mouth and tasted it, then he swallowed it while looking at this vision of loveliness in front of him who still had him spellbound in his heart.

"What information on my case do you have," asked Bill who eyed the woman's enticing chest of charms that turned him on from the very moment they had met?

"Well—lets say I just found out a about a hit person that was hired to rub you and your friends out, but I've already taken care of it by outfoxing them without blowing my cover," replied lady Victoria Basil who winked at Bill and she took another drink of her red wine glass.

Bill "choked" on his sip of red wine at that one, but managed to swallow it without embarrassing himself in front of this gorgeous female vampire who had him hypnotize from the moment he laid eyes on her the other night at his office.

"Tha–tha–that's good to know and after the way you took care of that werewolf the other night I feel safe in your lovely hands tonight and also my dear friends do too, but how did you read my mind the other night at my office which blew my mind" said Bill very humbled who was nervously trying to finish his wine glass and he poured himself another one with heart felt admiration in mind at this fine woman of the night sitting in front of him at the table who made him very hot under the collar?

Lady Victoria Basil quietly finished her glass and set it back on the table and patted the old colt 45 in her belt.

"Well—you can say that again pardner and I can always read what's on a man's mind being a poker playing vixen with years of experience that connects one's mind together," replied Lady Victoria Basil with a flirting gunslinger smirk on her lovely white cosmetic powdered face with ruby red lips underneath red eyes that seemed to beckon to Bill's inner mind.

"Ha, ha, ha," laughed Bill good naturally at the old wild west sarcastic joke, but he new she'd pull and shoot her gun in a heart beat to defend herself against any and all foes which she had proven one time already for him and he didn't want to make her mad again.

Bill leaned over the table and filled her glass with another round of red wine.

"I know there are two sides to every coin and I want to hear your story—how did you become a vampire," asked Bill who arched his eyebrows up on that one and he watched her reaction intently?

Lady Victoria Basil lovely face turned to stone while she thought back to that period in time.

"Well—it's a long story, but to make it short during

the Revolutionary War of 1812 at the battle of Guilford Courthouse.

I worked as a field nurse for the American army commanded by Nathaniel Greene and it happen on my way back home that is now called Old Salem.

I was walking home alone after the battle had been fought and was over and done with the American side winning the battle. My service as a field nurse was finished with the good doctor who I had been assigned with who left with the American army and the wounded we had fought so hard to save and then I had made a bad choice to leave without a escort, but the American army needed all available men and I had to get back home to my ailing father.

I was attacked and bitten at midnight while I was heading west toward Salem which was my home and I was walking along the old wagon road from Guildford Courthouse to Salem and attacked by my master vampire Lord Williams who was fighting for the English and saw me tending to the wounded on the battle field after sunset.

He stalked after me wanting me for his nest and he turned me into a vampire by making me drink his blood that very night back in his tent that was pitched near the battle field for which he had kidnaped me and brought me there for that very deed whom I later escaped from some years later and that broke up his nest in Pennsylvania where he had brought me and settled after the Revolutionary War of 1812 with his people because I would not kill in cold blood and feed on innocent people and I led a mutiny with his other slave vampires to break free of his evil dominate will so I sought to escaped for my freedom from pure satanic evil and that is why I have a bad distrust of men for what happen to me on that fate full night," said Lady Victoria Basil who now relived the past horror of shame she had felt again through her eyes.

Bill felt his heart go out to this woman who had come from out of the darkness of night into his bright daytime life and he could see the pain in her sweet bedroom blue eyes and he new they had been to many lonely old nights and days for both of them.

"Time heals all wounds," said Bill softly who saw his chance for human touch when she bowed her head in sorrow at the table.

Bill felt sorry for her and he got up and walked around the kitchen table and laid his hand on her shoulder to comfort her who then stood up and kissed him quickly with cold passionate ruby red lips that he had been longing fore in his dreams of her at night after meeting her and that caught him quietly by surprise and they tasted like wild strawberries to him and took his breath away.

"Heaven and Hell are united in our universal loving souls this very romantic evening and the desire is burning in my heart," said Lady Victoria who had drew back from the kiss and gazed deep into Bill's brown eyes to see his reaction.

"You can say that again," said Bill and then it quickly dawned on him that he might get lucky tonight and he grew excited deep in his desiring mind.

Bill couldn't resist her and the temptation of delicious sin and he kissed her back lustfully wanting her and her wanting him. Then he swept her off her feet into his strong arms and still kissing her passionately, he quickly carried her down the hallway to his bedroom and he knew in an instant, he was spellbound too her and had been love sick for her all along.

They fell on the bed and quickly disrobed and tossed their clothes to the side of the bed and where in each other's loving arms under the sheets of linen with Bill who was now a red hot blooded lover who's cheeks were flamed red with passion as he french kissed her ruby red lips madly and fondled her cold body and she was only a cold blooded vampire who lusted to be human again.

"Darling hold me forever and never leave me alone in this life time or the next," whispered Lady Victoria into Bill's ear that she nibbled on playfully with her lips and teeth lying between the satin sheets in the soft bed enveloped in each others hot arms.

"Never in a million years and what's happening between us tonight is called "A Total Eclipse of the Heart" where the night moon meets the day sun and that's us in the very lives we both have lead on different paths, one in daylight and one in the darkness which led us to this very fateful moment in the sands of time—and that's enough of the small talk for me and let's get back to romance at hand," replied Bill with attraction in his heart who pulled her closer to him and ran his hot wet tongue into her lovely cold ear which excited her passionate mind further and beyond her wildest heartfelt fantasy and then he found her ruby red lips again.

Lady Victoria had only an intense emotional heart from the memory of her human past in her hot seductive mind which now yearned to be set free and it was as she french kissed Bill hotly back madly enjoying the touch of his hot wet moist tongue with her icy cold tongue within her ruby red mouth as they playfully enjoyed rubbing tongues together in a steamy rage of passionate kissing and their lips mashed firmly to each other holding on for all it was worth while they fondled each other's body. She felt his man hood which sent a thrill to the very core of her being, but their inner intense passion for human love and touch warmed them both up as one human being during intense love making heart to heart in the nice warm bed and the night passed quickly.

"Sweet dreams in paradise my love because I've had an obsession to possess your soul in my Garden of Eden," whispered Lady Victoria softly into Bill's ear who was snuggled up next to her in the nice warm bed. She laid her head back on her pillow with her arm behind her head confidently thinking about the night's events and she was so happy with the way things had worked out for both of them here tonight in each other's loving arm's.

Bill soon fell fast asleep exhausted with Lady Victoria Basil laying beside him under the sheets watching him with a pleasing smile on her face.

She had a intense love for this self made honest lawman and she'd never turn him to the dark side of vampire hell or anyone else for that matter because she loathed what she had become through no fault of her on and she always had hope for a way out of this mess she was entangled in thought Lady Victoria to her self lying on the bed watching Bill sleep peacefully in the bed beside her. Then she silently slipped out of bed and walked over to Bill's bathroom and disappeared inside the bathroom. She half closed the door and soon the sound of running water drifted out from behind the bathroom door while Bill snored loudly in bed like an innocent baby.

Lady Victoria poured in the bubble bath she had found in Bill's towel closet underneath the flowing hot facet and she stirred the nice hot water with her silky hand testing the water and making more bubbles.

She quickly wrapped her long jet black hair in a bath towel around her head and flipped it back behind her head to protect her beautiful clean hair from the bath water because it didn't need washing.

"The water is just right," said Lady Victoria to herself who stepped down into the bathtub and slipped her naked body down underneath all the white foamy bubbles and into the nice hot bubbly bathtub.

She stretched out her silky smooth legs and her red painted toe nails stuck out of the hot water amidst the soap bubbles underneath the big facet on the other end of the tub which she had just leaned forward and cut off.

She leaned back against the end of the bath tub and laid her arms around the edge of the tub and relaxed in the hot bathtub and let the soaking water do its trick on her cold body while the soaking warmth of the water eased her mind and her tantalizing big boobs floated on the bubbly water in front of her for quite a spell.

It's been awhile since I needed a bath thought Lady Victoria who grabbed the wash cloth from the side of the bathtub where she had laid it and grabbed a new bar of ivory soap from the soap dish in the corner of the bathtub where several fresh bars laid.

Bill's got good taste in soap thought Lady Victoria who lathered up the wash cloth and began to wash the sex smell off of her body, starting with her long sensual legs which she lifted up one after the other up out of the water covered in bubbles as she washed away.

After a time Lady Victoria heard the gurgling water behind her as the last of it went down the bath tub drain while she dried off her wet soapy boobs and body with a clean towel.

She unwrapped the towel from her jet black hair after a few minutes and fluffed her hair up with her hands and hug it over the curtain wrack over the tub.

She picked up the wet towel off of the floor that she had dried her body with and hung it also over the curtain wrack. She tip toed over to the medicine cabinet mirror and grabbed one of Bill's big combs off the vanity sink and she quickly combed out her hair.

She smiled into the empty mirror and pretended playfully to check her white teeth with her pinky finger and she saw no reflection looking back at her in bitter disappointment.

She left rather smartly after that tossing the comb madly onto the sink and cut off the bathroom light because time was running out for her naked gorgeous vixen body.

She got dressed swiftly and left before dawn's early rays broke over the east horizon and then the alarm awoke him up at 9:00 A:M that sunny morning.

Bill set up in bed and rubbed the sleep out of his eyes with his fists and took in his surroundings quickly. He saw Lady Victoria was long gone and not a trace showed she had ever been at his home or in his bed.

He smiled at the wild night of love making and he wished she could have stayed just a little bit longer, but he new it was impossible for her right now in the deadly sunlight and he yearned for the night to return in his heart and they would be together once again he hoped in his satisfied mind.

He got up and put on his white bath robe and went off with a satisfied happy heart to make breakfast in his kitchen which was sugar cornflakes and milk also some good old Columbian coffee.

Bill had taken a fast shower that morning and put on a fresh suit of clothes and was busy brushing his teeth in his bedroom bathroom after finishing up breakfast.

He had deduced his new found love had taken a quick bath this early morning by the wet towel's hanging over his shower curtain he had found this morning before she had vacated his house thought Bill who seemed rather happy today and it had been a long time since he had gotten laid so very well he thought to himself cheerfully humming while he got ready for a long hard days work in the field.

Bill put up his tooth brush in his holder bedside the vanity medicine cabinet and rinsed out his mouth with a crazy gargling noise and spit out the water into his bathroom sink.

Bill wiped his face on his hand tile and leaned over the sink and grinned in the mirror to check his teeth which looked alright.

Bill strolled out and walked over to his hidden safe on his bedroom wall behind a seashore scene picture. Bill pulled the picture which was on hinges out and started to open his safe.

Bill rubbed his chin. "Lets see—it was start at 0 then 24 left then 11to the right and then back all the way around left to 7," spoke Bill under his breath who soon had the little safe door open.

He got out another small ingot of pure silver and he stuck it in his right coat pocket.

Bill shut the safe door and closed the picture back in place until the latch caught it and all was well thought Bill who quickly strolled across his bedroom and grabbed Wilbur's small silver ingot off his bedside table and also put it in his pocket too.

Bill did a quick double check of himself to make sure he had everything on him and in its place, his gun which he had gotten out of his bathrobe pocket, key's, wallet, money clip and other item's and then he left his bedroom headed for the Salem gunsmith shop in town with no time to lose.

In the early morning hours of dawn breaking over the eastern treetops Clara Bell had got out her small iron cast iron cauldron pot with four small legs on it from behind her kitchen sink curtain where it was hidden from view.

She walked over to her stove and set it on the old cast iron wood cook stove's small six inch eye. She stood there for a few minutes while the pot warmed up.

"Must have the Good Book for the spell," said Clara Bell who walked out of the kitchen and down the hallway into her parlor. She walked over to the big oak mantle above her fireplace and opened a big glass book case sitting in the middle of the mantle and got out a big heavy book. It was an old leather bound 12x9 book with a gold embroidered big cross that covered the front of it with a big round King Solomon seal in the top of the cross. The title of the book was engraved into the great gold seal of King Solomon.

That read as follows:

" The Good Book Guide To White Magic Remedy and Potion Spells and The Art of Sorcery."

Clara Bell walked out of the parlor with the good book

carefully under her right arm. It had been in her family for generations handed down to the next of kin who inherited it only after being trained in the ways of white magic from childhood to adult hood in the Alter Realm of Heavens Gates.

Clara Bell walked back into the kitchen and laid the book down on her kitchen table and she opened it thumbing through the pages until she found the right page.

"Ahhhh—here it is. The ACHILLES POTION," said Clara Bell who read the instructions and incantations with a kind heart of knowledge.

She walked over to her glass medicine cabinet and open the glass door and she rummaged around until she found a big vial of holy water and a bag of sassafras tea in a small herbal tea container. She walked over to her kitchen counter and got out a measuring cup and she pulled out the big cork and poured out four ounces of holy water into the glass measuring cup.

She put the cork back in the big vial and crossed her kitchen floor quickly and put it back in the glass medicine cabinet.

Clara Bell walked back over and grabbed the measuring cup and walked over to the stove and poured in the holy water into the hot small kettle pot on the iron cook stove and dropped in the sassafras tea bag according to the instructions from the good book while it heated up and the tea bag flavored the concoction.

She went back to the good book and read the rest of the ingredients. Hoof of a white bob tail deer, hair of the black panther, claw of the hawk, and the key ingredient a four leaf clover laced with pixie dust for good luck that empowered the magic enchanted potion.

Clara Bell grabbed a small glass bowel from off her kitchen counter on her way over to her glass medicine cabinet and she got out each of the four dried ingredients her spell called for from her witches ingredient bottles that were labeled specifically on each bottle what it was inside it and she popped the cork on each bottle and got out one dried ingredient each at a time and stuffed the cork back in the bottles and put them one at a time in the small glass bowel in her left hand until she was finished.

She scooted over to the old hutch beside the old glass medicine cabinet and reached up and got down her white mortar mixing bowel and pestle smasher.

She walked back to the table and set them down with her ingredients in the glass bowel. She put the dried ingredients into the white mortar bowel except the four leaf clover and started mashing them up with her pestle smasher.

She worked hard on it for several minutes until she had a ground up fine powder but the panther hair was just intertwined in the grayish and dark powder.

She got her cutting scissors form her knitting bag on the floor beside the table and picked out the panther hair and she cut it up into fine pieces into the mortar bowel.

She grabbed her pestle masher and started mashing it again until the cut up hair was blended in with the fine grayish dark powder.

"Well—that ought to do the trick," said Clara Bell who wiped back a loose curl of her white hair that had slipped out of the black pin in the back side of her head with her right hand and she adjusted her round white bun in back of her dear old head to make sure it was still pinned up properly for her old ways.

She then went over to the black kettle cauldron pot and dumped the ingredients into the slow boiling pot. she went back to the kitchen table and reached down into her knitting bag and pulled out a two foot long old crooked hickory wand switch that half stuck out of the knitting bag.

She picked up the book from the table along with the four leaf clover laced with pixie dust and she walked over to her black kettle cauldron pot. She held the book in her left hand and started to read the incarnation mystical chant from the Good Book while she waved the old crooked hickory wand switch over the slow boiling black kettle cauldron pot.

"Inposse—Inposse—Achilles—Achilles—great warrior of Greece and Troy—rise up —rise up your spirit—rise up from the ashes of eternal Adinfinitum of Hades and let your spirit soar across the river Stixxs to my white magic iron black kettle cauldron brewing pot. Coram—Coram—Perfecto—Presto," chanted Clara Bell out loud while she waved the old crooked hickory wand switch back and forth above the smoldering pot casting her spell.

Then a crack of blinding white light appeared for a second from the end of her old hickory wand switch and "POOF" a small white cloud appeared above the black cauldron pot from the end of the old hickory wand switch with the blonde hair warrior's face floating in the hovering cloud.

Clara Bell quickly read the last of the instructions in the good book quickly and stuck her crooked wand underneath her left armpit and threw in the four leaf clover laced with pixie dust into the black cauldron pot with her free right hand.

She heard a fast popping noise "pop, pop, pop, pop" and crackling sounds and she saw an explosion of white, blue, green and red also yellow sparks came out of the pot in a rainbow of colors that flew out in all directions over the old iron wood cook stove that enveloped the cloud with the blonde warriors face in it. Then it dissolved back down into the fast bubbling pot that boiled almost over at the top of the pot with a rainbow of colors and then faded slowly out down into the old kettle cauldron iron pot.

Clara Bell turned and walked to her kitchen table and laid her Good Book and her white witches old crooked hickory wand switch down on the table.

She ran to her kitchen sink and grabbed a pot holder and

quickly ran to the old iron wood cook stove and grabbed the old black cauldron kettle handle and removed it from her stove to a hot plate on her kitchen counter to cool off.

"Well the Good Book spell is done and we need all the extra help we can get in our Holy war against wickedness that is a plague on our town," said Clara Bell to herself who put her white witches old crooked hickory wand switch back in her knitting bag along with her scissors.

She picked up the Good Book off her table with both hands hugging it to her chest lovingly and carried it back to her parlor and stuck it back in her glass book case proudly on the mantle for safe keeping until the next time she needed it.

Later when the magic potion had cooled for thirty minutes like the instructions from the good book had read. Clara Bell had spooned out the tea bag and poured the magic potion into the four ounce potion bottle and popped in the cork to seal it and she slipped it into her front right apron pocket for safe keeping until it was ready to be used.

Clara Bell stuck the old kettle cauldron pot in her kitchen sink and started washing it up with dishwashing detergent until she needed it next time for another magic spell.

Minutes later she had wiped down the clean pot with a clean kitchen towel she had got out from her hutch drawer and stuck it back behind the curtain underneath her kitchen sink hidden away from prying eyes.

She went back to her regular duties around the house and she needed to prepare Wilbur's lunch because he'd be coming in from the barn hot, tired and thirsty from doing his Dailey chores.

Around noon Bill stood at the counter in the Salem gunsmith store while he waited for the gun clerk who had left to go in back to check on his order of bullets.

Bill looked at the wall to wall guns in the gun racks and the display counter in front of him had all kinds of pistols in the display case for sale with a approved gun permit by the buying customer. The other gun clerk was busy with a customer at the cash register who was buying hunting stuff.

Bill looked at the racks of gun clothes hanging in racks in the isles and picked through them momentarily to pass the time.

Bill walked back over to the counter and leaned on his elbow's looking through the glass display case at the pistol's while he wondered what was taking so long to get up his order he had left this morning.

About ten minutes later the clerk appeared through the swinging doors from the warehouse in back.

"Sorry—it took so long, but the gunsmith had just finished the last bullet and I had to wait, the box contains twenty-five silver bullets" said Joey the gun clerk who handed Bill the box of twenty-five rimfire 180 grain cartridges.

Bill took the box of bullets from him and stuck them in his right trench coat pocket.

"Thanks—what do I owe you," asked Bill who fumbled for his money clip in his right trouser pocket?

"What are you hunting around here with silver bullet's like the lone ranger uses on bad guys or are you hunting some kind of wolfman" asked Joey the gun clerk with amusement on his face?

"It's better you don't know and none of your business," replied Bill with a mean scow on his face at the smart aleck joke made by the sales clerk.

"Well—now—that will be one hundred and twenty dollars with tax for the melt down and molding of the bullets and pressing them into the live shells," replied Joey the gun clerk who checked Bill's ticket to make sure he was right and his smile was gone now at Bill's mean tone and back to all business and was sorry he had asked in the first place from Bill's mad look at him.

Bill took out two one hundred dollar bills from his money clip and handed them to the gun clerk.

"I'll need a receipt for that," asked Bill who smiled at Joey the young gun clerk while he followed him over to the now vacant cash register?

"No—problem detective," replied Joey respectfully who rung up the sale and handed Bill his change and receipt.

"Thanks—it's a pleasure doing business with you," said Bill right smartly and he left the stunned gun clerk scratching his head before he could reply back and headed for the front door past the customers shopping in the crowded store isles.

At the same moment in time Clara Bell was out at the big red barn behind her house. Clara Bell walked by Wilbur's wood working room and she open the door and peered inside the dimly lit room to see what Wilbur had been doing lately, the scent of fresh cut pine wood and new paint drifted to her nostrils at the doorway entrance.

She saw the ten white small birds houses with a copper tin roof on them, that were freshly painted and drying in the faint light of the window across the wood working room that shined a sun beam down on Wilbur's work bench in the middle of the room among his power wood cutting tools.

Wilbur loved to make them and sale them at King hardware in the town of King. They always sold everyone he made for them and the manager always ordered more from her husband who was a master carpenter and Wilbur built all kinds.

He painted yellow and red and blue ones for people who wanted a birdhouse of a different color or he made bird houses with a single slanted roof to nail up on a fence post or the side of a barn and he made also made them with a two sided shingle slanted roof on them too. Their farm had them up hanging in the trees out back of the farm house tied to a branch by a strong wire and nailed to the top fence post's that ran along their pasture land and apartment style bird houses up on tall poles around their garden.

Clara Bell smiled at Wilbur's sweat and hard work ingenuity nature and she closed the door and shut the latch to lock the door. She moved on down past specials work and storage rooms in the big red barn and soon came to the tack room door.

She open the tack room door and went inside the almost darken room with her twisted swamp root cane tapping the way across the old wooden floor "tap, tap, tap,"!

It glowed with a weird illumination of green light in the back of the tack room with a brilliant green light coming from the shelves on the far wall that faced the barn window which she always had open at night for the moons beam to shine in and charge her lightening bugs she had collected in mason jars from her backyard over the long hot summer.

Clara Bell walked across the room filled with all kinds of tools on the walls and past the work station old Wilbur her husband had and among the saddles and mule harness on barrel stands.

She looked in wide wonder at her super charged lightening bugs flying overtop the wax seals in the six old quart size mason jars filled with cotton balls dipped in turpentine in the bottom of the jars.

"Are y'all ready for a little night trip," asked Clara Bell and as if on cue the lightening bugs glowed brightly green that lit up her face with illumination while she picked one after another off the shelf and stuck them in her milk crate and finely she covered them up with a wool blanket to keep the sun from draining their moon beam power?

Well—those wild dogs will get a taste of my homemade turpentine remedy tonight and it will burn the fur right off their bodies, that's inside this milk crate thought Clara Bell who had a sly smile to herself.

Clara Bell picked up her small burden and held the old milk crate under her left arm and crossed the tack room floor with her cane tapping ever so softly "tap, tap, tap," as if she didn't want to wake up her burden inside the milk crate and left shutting the tack room door behind her as she went back to her farm house to give Wilbur the precious crate to be loaded on the back of the truck with the rest of their stuff.

Later that afternoon Bill was out at Clara Bell's and Wilbur's farmhouse out on Payne Road.

"We must make ready for our surprise attack at the old Idol's Dam tonight, during the start of the full moon," said Clara Bell who handed Bill a cup of steaming hot perked joe.

Bill took the coffee cup and took a sip and it was good to the last drop.

"Here are the twenty-five silver bullets," said Bill who pulled the silver bullets box out from his trench coat pocket and laid them on the white farmhouse table.

"That should do the trick," said Wilbur who winked at Bill and Clara Bell who rubbed her wet hands on her apron dress.

"Well at least we have a fighting chance now," replied Clara Bell who sat down at the farmhouse table and watched Bill load his gun with watch full eyes.

Bill took out his 38 snub nose pistol and clicked open the slide latch on the side of the gun and the barrel fell out. Bill emptied out the live standard rounds into the palm of his hand by pushing the bullet release mechanism pin that was built into the gun barrel for quick cartage release and stuck them in his left trench coat pocket.

Bill open the side of the silver bullet box and slid out the box of rimfire cartridges and started loading his gun with six live silver shells. He snapped it shut and put it back in his right side holster ready for action.

Bill put the box of silver shells back in his right trench coat pocket and kept the other rimfire shells separated in his left trench coat pocket so there would be no mix up when he needed more silver ammo and patted his loaded pistol that made him an equal among man or beast.

"I'm as ready as I'll ever be," replied Bill who looked ready for anything that came his way or crawled out of the wood work.

"I'd say you are and its now or never," replied Wilbur who smiled and winked at Bill his old friend.

"Wilbur—do you have the old ford truck ready like I told you to do and a full tank of gas. You know how I hate riding on empty like you always do—its like riding on pin's and needle's," asked Clara Bell who looked over her wire rim glasses at her dear husband of near forty years or so?

"Yes—I loaded it up like I was told to do with your milk crate in the back covered up by a blanket and the white paint and chalk.

I stopped yesterday at the gas station and filled it up for ya," replied Wilbur who looked somewhat amused at his nagging wife.

"Well—lets go times a wasting and we ain't got all night," said Clara Bell who got up and grabbed her twisted swamp root cane from where she had leaned it against the farm table.

Much later at around 4:00P:M Clara Bell in the middle and Wilbur who was driving the old beat up ford pick up truck with Bill riding shotgun pulled down the old dirt and gravel access road to Idol's Dam.

"We must make quick work of this before sundown," said Clara Bell who held her red dot tie-off lap top quilt in her lap.

"Is that another magic quilt," asked Bill who had it on his mind every since he got in the old beat up farm truck?

"Yes—it is enchanted by white magic spells on my dear departed grandmother's side and has been handed down for generations in my family and it goes to my granddaughter next after we depart this hard life," replied Clara Bell who gave Bill a smile who looked as if all his question's had been answered on his lean rock hard smiling tan face and he quickly looked away and rolled his eyes up at the sky with a I should have known anyhow look on his face after all they had been through over the years and he let out a soft chuckle to himself and cleared his throat knowing he had the right people for the right job.

Wilbur navigated the old ford pick up truck through the grown up weeds and down the winding access road dodging rocks and small ravines in the road that had formed from water run off on their way to Idol's Dam.

They saw the clearing up ahead after ten minutes of bumpy riding on the old river road.

"You had better park it in the trees over their and cover it with cut bushes," spoke Bill who pointed between two trees that was off to the side of the river road and was a good hiding spot.

"Sounds good to me," replied Wilbur who maneuvered the truck on up in front of the two trees.

Wilbur pulled up at that very spot and backed the old ford pick-up into the trees for a fast getaway if they needed it.

Wilbur cut off the old truck and reached down into his right lower tool pocket and pulled out a plug of brown mule tobacco. He opened the plastic wrap and leaned back to get at his pants pocket. He reached into his right bib overhaul pocket and got out his old yellow banana knife and flicked open the long blade knife with his right thumb. He sliced off a good size of tobacco and yellow leaf it was wrapped in. He rolled it into a good size ball with his fingers. He stuck it on the left side of his mouth between the cheek and gum. He carefully folded up the plug tobacco plastic wrap back over his favorite plug tobacco and stuck it back in his lower right side tool pocket. He carefully flipped his banana knife closed with his right forefinger and slid it back in his right side bib overhaul pocket.

Bill who was watching Wilbur with the plug tobacco just shook is head in disgust and smiled at his old nicotine addicted country boy friend who needed a strong addictive fix.

They all got out of the truck and Wilbur took his hand saw he had brought for the occasion and started cutting down saplings and bushes to hide the truck which they did in about ten minutes and from time to time he spat his nicotine spit out onto the ground.

"The green beret would be proud of that camouflaged trick," said Bill who stood back and checked to see if he could see the truck which he didn't see any trace of it from the front holding the paint bucket and white chalk, Wilbur had given him to carry. "Yep—I say that about does it," responded Wilbur who stuck his saw in the milk crate that he picked up in his arms and he grabbed up his new pitch fork in his right hand.

"Well lets go—times a wasting,"said Clara Bell who walked off on her twisted root cane carrying her tied off lap top quilt under her left armpit.

They walked up the small hill and heard the rush of spillway water past the hill and they all saw the dam and river appear over the top of the small hill.

They walked toward the old dam and it was a solemn group of people who new in their hearts what they had come here to do.

"Well—here is where we make our ambush tonight and theirs no turning back now once we cross that line because we've reached the point of no return here unless you've changed your minds about risking all our lives tonight against overwhelming evil and turned chicken at the last second at the risk of death, but its not to late to turn back now and forget about it," spoke Clara Bell seriously who looked at her two partners in arms?

"I've always risked everything to save lives in my line of

law enforcement work and I ain't about to stop now with death and danger on the horizon. If I'm killed in the line of duty at least I tried to stop it and I can tell the man upstair's—I did just that," replied Bill bravely who winked at Clara Bell.

"I'm with Bill and for what ever fate that comes our way tonight doing the lords work to save lives," replied Wilbur who stood up taller on his tip toes beside of Bill to make his point.

"Then its agreed then. We will cross the line in the sand so to speak. We will move forward with our plan to save lives even at the risk of our own—no matter what comes our way out here this very night. Its life or death," said Clara Bell right proudly of the company she was in.

Clara Bell reached into her right front apron top pocket and pulled out a small potion bottle with a cork in the top of it.

"This is a sorceress magic potion bottle that I made myself and I concocted it from my glass medicine cabinet in the kitchen to aid in our fight. It has the hoof of a white bob tail deer for swift and fast reflexes. The hair of the wild black panther for keen smelling and cunning hunter of the jungle. The ferocious fighting heart and spirit of the great Greek warrior Achilles also the claw of a hawk for keen eyesight in the daytime or nighttime with a four leaf clover thrown in for good luck from my clover patch in my back yard where the fairy's play late at night and cast their magic spells with pixie dust which the clover is grown in and laced with to enchant the potion. Here each of you take a swig and the spell want wear off until day break," said Clara Bell who popped the cork and handed the bottle to Bill.

Bill took the bottle and turned it up and drank a taste of the magic potion bottle.

"Man that tasted like sassafras tea my mom use to make years ago when I was a little boy," said Bill who eyes bugged out and handed the bottle to Wilbur who took it and drank a big swig.

"Man that was good and I bet it will grow hair on your chest," said Wilbur who wiped his mouth with the back of his strong farm hand that looked younger beyond his old age in seconds.

Clara Bell took the potion bottle and drank the rest of it and she put the old cork back in the bottle and stuck it back in her apron pocket.

"There—that ought to do the trick for all of us—tonight," said Clara Bell who seemed to have an enchanted look about her pug nose looking face that seemed to radiate out over her wire rim spectacle's.

"You two go on to the gatehouse and create the trap inside and do it quick Wilbur while I stay here on watch," spoke Clara Bell with haste in her voice for they had little time to loose before dark settled over the whole area.

"Yes-Mam," said Wilbur who ushered Bill along with him. They made a fast pace toward the old gate house and were soon at the door and disappeared inside.

Sometime later Wilbur was humming to himself while he worked then he started to sing out loud good naturally like he always did working and plowing in the corn or tobacco fields of Stokes county on his old farm.

"Round that great white throne in heaven they'll be waiting for me. Round that great white throne they'll be praying for me. Round that great white throne they'll be singing for me. Round that great white throne where we will all meet on that glorious day," sang Wilbur as if he was in church on a hot summer Sunday evening old time revival meeting.

"Now for the chorus," spoke Wilbur out loud to his only audience who was Bill on lone lookout watching out the gatehouse door very nervously who wanted to get this part of their plan over with as soon as possible because he had a feeling of a cornered rat in a cage.

"Gimmie that old time religion—Gimmie that old time religion—Gimmine that old time religion its good enough for me," sang Wilbur while he painted the white pentagram on the ceiling out of the white paint can with the six inch brush.

"That's an old Holiness hymn song my daddy wrote for the Wholiness church some years ago when I was a little boy. You know its never too late to come to the lord to be saved Bill," said Wilbur to Bill who was still all eyes and ears watching out for any intruders or suspect's at the old gate house door who might mess up their surprise trap tonight for the wild pack of murderous wolves if they were discovered.

"Its too late for me Wilbur and I'm over the hill and well past religion. I'm a sinner and a big time hypocrite. I'd be the first to admit it and your born into sin and everybody does it for one reason or another lust, greed of money, sex to make a point of what I'm saying.

I'm basically a good moral person and in my line of work as a lawman who plays both sides and administer's judgment accordingly to the law of the land on the guilty and there's no room for religious beliefs or I couldn't do my job morally because I wouldn't have never become a lawman in the first place if I was raised very religious and I might have to take a life to uphold the law which I've done in my duties as a lawman before and broke one of the most sacred of ten commandments.

I doubt the bible belt can save my soul—Wilbur and I can't buy my way out of purgatory at any price now—old friend—I'm too far down the line and a lost warrior and I have to bear this earthly burden of sin. Lets just do what we came here to do quickly and quietly because time's a wasting with small talk," replied Bill softly who looked out the door across the big dam for any signs of danger and then he chuckled quietly to himself "hah, hah, hah" under his breath because he thought Wilbur was a crazy old codger with his gospel singing and religion.

Then he just shook his head in vain on second thought because he knew Wilbur was right on the other hand about God's saving grace thought Bill deep down in his own good heart and he wasn't ready for that kind of commitment just yet in his life, but he didn't say anything more.

Wilbur looked at Bill standing in the gatehouse door shadows who was in deep thought with disappointment in his eyes at what he had said, but kept on painting the ceiling with renewed religious energy to Finnish up his chore for Clara Bell his wife without another word spoken.

Bill had a flashback standing in the doorway to the early years of the 1980s when he was first promoted to detective after a few years of police officer patrol service in the city.

He had been given his first case to work on that week. It was to end in tragedy because he had gone out to Willow Creek Apartments off of University Parkway in Stanleyville on that Tuesday afternoon to serve his first warrant on a serial rapist who had also assaulted the female victim brutally too who had the courage to pick him out of a police line up of mug shots because the other female rape victims had been afraid to press charges for fear of their lives. Bill pulled into the driveway and drove down into the apartments slowly on the blacktop road.

He drove down the short hill past the pond on his left and first single bedroom apartment complex on his right and up into the main two bedroom apartments. Bill turned left and drove around the main pool and clubhouse that was filled with people swimming and having fun in the sun.

He drove past the basketball and tennis courts where people were playing until he came to the letter H set of apartments that was on the front side of the building. He parked his car in front of the apartment building and got out quickly locking his car door.

He went to number 101 apartment door with the warrant in his left coat pocket. The man was rumored to be living here with his girlfriend from time to time from his criminal connections out on the street. Bill knocked on the door and a young pretty blonde woman answered the door and opened it all the way.

Bill looked into the two bedroom apartment and saw his suspect sitting on the couch up against the back wall leisurely that matched the photo in his police line up that he carried in his right coat pocket for easy identification.

"Yes—what do you want," asked the young blonde woman who eyed Bill suspiciously?

"I'm detective Bill Christian with the Winston- Salem police department and I've come to serve an outstanding warrant on Ronnie White your boyfriend sitting there on the couch," replied Bill who showed her his detective badge on his belt buckle by pulling his side coat back for her to see.

The man jumped up off the couch and bolted out of the living room into the back left master bedroom to make his getaway. Bill pushed the young woman to the side of the doorway forcefully who tried in vain to block his way.

He ran into the living room pulling his snub nose 38 pistol from his holster in his right hand held with his elbow bent and arm straight up in the air beside his head at the ready with his finger straight out beside the trigger so he wouldn't accidently have a misfire in all the excitement.

Bill chased the man into the master bedroom and saw he had open the back door and ran out onto the cement patio behind the apartments to escape.

Bill took off in hot pursuit and ran out the back door with his mind and eyes on high alert. Bill heard the cars and trucks on the highway 52expressway behind the line of trees that blocked the highway and kept down the busy noise of highway traffic behind the apartment complex off to his right.

Bill spotted his suspect running and then falling on the slippery soft grass who moved his feet fast underneath him to get back up and jumped up trying to escape through the grass behind the apartments who was about twenty-five feet in front of him.

"Your under arrest—stop,"hollered Bill who had barely finished his sentence when the man slid to a stop in front of him and turned around reaching back behind him with his right hand.

Bill had only a instant to react and slid to a defensive front stance position with both hands on his 38 ready to fire and his feet wide apart. Bill aimed at the mans chest who had pulled a gun from his back side waste belt and fired off a quick shot "Bam," that passed between Bill's spread legs and kicked up dirt between them as he brought his weapon up to aim at Bill's body for a second shot at Bill who then squeezed the trigger twice in self defense "Bam, Bam."

The suspect was knocked backward into the air by the impact of the bullets and was dead before he hit the ground. Bill stood for a stunned second at what looked like slow motion in a blur and his mind regained its senses and he lowered his gun by his side.

Then he heard a scream behind him and turned and saw the girlfriend sobbing out on the patio deck holding onto the upper deck post that supported the top apartment patio.

"Get back inside there's nothing more you can do out here, its too late for your boyfriend," commanded Bill who watched the hysterical woman run crying into the apartment who then walked over to his suspect lying on the grassy ground and knelt down beside the dead man.

Bill checked his neck pulse and saw he was definitely dead. Bill felt incredible guilt well up in the back of his mind.

Bill reached down with his left hand fingers and dabbed them in the mans blood that oozed out of the two bullet holes in the mans front chest tee shirt. Bill slid his fingers back and forth rubbing the blood around just looking at it in disbelief at what he had done, then he came out of it and wiped the blood on the grass beside him.

He stood back up swaying a little bit from side to side and pulled out his police radio from his left side belt holder very shakily on his feet.

"This is detective Bill Christian I'm at Willow Creek apartments in Stanleyville to serve an arrest warrant—shots have been fired suspect is down need assistance and back up and an ambulance at apartment H," spoke Bill hoarsely who listen for a response.

"10-4 they are en route. Are you injured detective," asked the police dispatcher?

"No—I'm A-O. K.," replied Bill who only heard some words and static from his walkie talkie in his numb state of mind that took over his shocked nervous system in his body who now felt sick to his stomach and he freaked out at the last second.

Bill's head felt faint and his mouth was dry and he wished he could have a cold drink of water.

Bill's face turned a deathly shade of pale while he turned away from the dead suspect on the ground and stumbled over to the red brick apartment building and leaned up against it for support with his left hand that held the walkie talkie.

Bill retched several times in convulsions and then threw up nervous puke onto the ground that splattered onto his new wingtip shoes. Bill glassy eyes looked up and saw the people coming around the brick corner down below him between the apartment buildings to see what had happen. He new he had made a grave mistake by not having back up with him and the suspect had paid the ultimate price, but it was too late to worry about it now.

Then Bill heard the police sirens coming his way and he stood back up away from the building and mustered the last bit of inner strength from inside him to help him get a grip on his emotions and self control while he holstered his gun. He started walking past the crowd of curious gathered onlookers back to his unmarked police car to flag them down.

Bill standing in the gatehouse doorway shaking his head back and forth sadly from the flashback of his first kill and it had always haunted him in his nightmares with the mans dead face late at night, but he had learned to live with it. He had been labeled a hero by the police department and the local news media and he had even received a commendation for it which was the first of many in his long law enforcement career, but he felt he had never deserved it for taking a man's life even a guilty one of such bad crimes where many of his police friends had said he deserved it for dealing out justice at the end of a gun to the suspected serial rapist who was in fact guilty on all accounts and had tried to kill him that fateful day serving the warrant in his first felony case as he watched Wilbur busy at work painting the ceiling from his advantage point at the doorway.

Just before sundown Wilbur tossed the small empty paint can and paint brush into a oily old rag filled barrel in the corner and he stood back and admired his handy work in the dark light.

Bill had finished putting the stool bucket's back in place and was now ready to get out of there.

"Lets go —Wilbur we have done enough here the trap is set," said Bill who stuck the chalk stick in his left pocket after drawing a big pentagram on the floor under the one that Wilbur had painted on the ceiling in white paint that was quickly drying in the hot evening air by standing on the old stool bucket which he sat back in place hastily with the other ones.

They both walked outside and Wilbur carried his nice new

pitch fork in his right hand he had bought at the Rural Hall hardware store that very morning.

They crossed the Idols Dam in no time and walked up to Clara Bell who was waiting on look-out back at the access road side of the old dam.

"Lets hide in these bushes here and see what evil comes are way tonight when darkness falls across the land," spoke Clara Bell who ushered them into the bushes and she made a circle of sea salt around them with one of her mason jars.

"That's so they can't smell us hiding here, it creates a barrier from their senses,' said Clara Bell who looked at Bill with a smug look on her face and he didn't ask any questions, but he trusted her completely.

About an hour after sundown the woods came alive with the night sounds of nature all around them in the bushes and river.

Lady Victoria Basil shut her families mausoleum door behind her and took to the darkening skies above her and was soon flying high over the Hall of Justice building in Winston-Salem and then she flew past the new tall Wachovia building and gracefully flew out over I-40 and headed north to Clemmon's.

Later she flew across the Idol's Dam gate house side of the Yadkin river to watch the action she new was soon to take place and she safely landed on a big oak tree limb, that jutted out from a tall oak tree and tucked her skirt underneath her legs so it wouldn't flap in the breeze and give her hiding place away while she watched and waited to intercede and play her last ace up her sleeve if need be.

Bill saw the flash of car lights coming down the old river access road toward the dam where they lay in wait.

"Its game time," said Wilbur who also saw the cars lights coming toward them also who nudged his wife who had taken a cat nap beside him.

"Wake up honey the trap is almost sprung," said Wilbur and Clara Bell came wide awake very quickly as she always did. Clara Bell looked at Bill and winked and then she picked up her old twisted swamp root cane she had laid across her knees and prepared for battle with demonic forces.

The cars roared into the clearing and quickly parked below their old ford truck which was hidden from prying eyes.

The eight people they counted crossed there path and strolled across the dam toward the old gate house and vanished inside and they all saw the light come on dimly through the gate house windows and gate house door that was not completely shut.

At about that time the full moon had risen up in the night sky and came out overhead and shined it's bright light down on the Yadkin River which was reflected across the river water toward the old gatehouse and the whole river valley was lit up in a Erie glow.

They then all heard the terrible howling from across the water inside the old gate house as the transformation inside took place for the changeling humans transformation into werewolf's.

"Lets go—now's the time to do it," said Clara Bell who jumped up and left the hiding place in the bushes with Wilbur and Bill following behind her quick pace.

They crossed the dam and Wilbur set the crate down when they were halfway across the old dam.

Clara Bell pulled back the quilt from across her first mason jars full of firefly's and she stuck two of them in her front apron pockets and let the quilt fall back in place. Bill pulled out his snub nose 38 and cocked the hammer back ready to fire.

Then they heard a terrible howling from inside the old gate house of cussing and fighting going on inside.

Wilbur holding his new pitch fork took off toward the old gate house door and a werewolf came out of the old gate house door when he got almost to it and started to attack him while three others escaped out the back gate house door.

"Duck down Wilbur," screamed Bill which Wilbur did just that and Bill aimed his snub nose 38 and shot the werewolf through the heart "BAM," that fell in a heap on the dam from its leap toward Wilbur and rolled off the side of the dam dead while it started to change back to human form as it splashed into the water down below and off the dam side of the dam.

Wilbur got up and pushed inside the old gate house door with Bill and Clara Bell bringing up the rear. Once inside the old kerosene lantern on the old wire spool table lit up the area with dark shadows and within the pentigram was four trapped werewolf's that fought against the unseen force that held them spellbound inside the pentigram.

"You—your suppose to be dead by now—by our hired hit woman," said one low throaty werewolf voice that watched the heroic trio come into the gate house unopposed and unafraid.

"I wouldn't bet your life on it,' said Bill who aimed his snub nose 38 and squeezed the trigger and shot the werewolf dead "BAM," and it fell on the floor and started shaking as it changed back into human form.

"Save your silver bullets—Bill—your going to need them," said Clara Bell who walked past Bill and pulled out one of her quart mason jars from her apron pocket just outside of the pentigram. The other three werewolf's sounded the alarm to the pack out on the hunt as they howled out loud at the top of their demonic lungs "ooooOOOOOOHHHHHH,"!

"That mason jar can't hurt us," said the female werewolf who eyed Clara Bell with red disdained eyes who charged her and was repelled backward as it was thrown back from the invisible force field that had them trapped and it landed on its backside, but quickly got back up on its hind legs wanting to attack and kill its intended victim which was Clara Bell.

"Oh—it will do the trick—dear," said Clara Bell who threw the quart mason jar at the female werewolf and it crashed against the body on impact and exploded in a green fireball and consumed the young female werewolf in a green bluish explosion that incinerated in up into thin smoking air and it was gone in an instant.

Clara Bell pulled out her last mason jar and held it in her little hand. The other big werewolf that was obvious a male begged her to spare him.

"Please don't kill me. There has to be another way," said the male werewolf who ran to the other side of the pentigram to escape, but was thrown back by the invisible force field unto the old wire spool table and knocked over the old kerosene lantern which broke and caught the old wooden wire spool table on fire.

"Mercy is for the gullible weak or innocent if I let you live you will just keep your evil ways and keep on killing, only death releases you from your pact with Hell," said Clara Bell who threw the old mason jar at the male werewolf who howled a last howl "ooohhhhh"and the jar broke against its muscled harry body and was consumed by a greenish blue fire ball that burned it up into a puff of smoke and was gone in an instant. Bill came forward and shot the other male werewolf in the chest "BAM" that was fighting mad at being trapped by humans across the room on the other side of the pentigram and it fell on the floor dead and started to transform back into a human being again.

"Come we must leave here or we will be trapped here by the other werewolf's that heard the warning howl for the pack and are sure to come back here to join the ones that escaped outside and the fire is spreading inside the old gate house. We must make our final stand out on the dam where I sat my jars down in the milk crate in this final thriller of a battle against Hell's wolf hounds. We can fight and watch all sides out there and see them coming for us in the moonlight," said Clara Bell who turned and quickly walked toward the old gate house door with her twisted swamp root cane while the fire had spread to the old barrel trash's can off to the side, that had old paint cans and oily rags inside from years ago long gone by.

Wilbur looked outside quickly and the coast looked clear to him in the moonlight.

"Lets go," said Wilbur who locked arms with his wife and through the old gate house door they ran with his pitch fork in his right hand with the sharp forks sticking straight up just in case he need to fend off anything that might jump on them from above he didn't see with his tired old eyes.

Clara Bell also turned her old twisted swamp root cane straight up while she ran with Wilbur and they made a run for it!

The werewolf lurking on top of the old gate house saw the old elderly couple come running out the gate house door and saw his chance to spring his attack from above and tear them to pieces. The werewolf jumped out over top of the couple in mid air to strike a death blow with it outstretched claws.

Clara Bell 6th sense sensed the werewolf overtop of her and Wilbur while they ran together in locked arms.

"Unum—E—Plurisbus—Unium— Abner father of spiritual umbrella light come forth," commanded Clara Bell and her cane glowed with light on the end and a dome of light busted forth and shielded them from the air attack of the werewolf that was caught in its powerful magic beam of umbrella light.

The old silver and gray werewolf howled in pain "AHHH—oooOOOOHHHH" from the mystic magic spiritual light that had it trapped like it was encased in cement!

Clara Bell and Wilbur ran all the way to where her milk crate was in the middle of the old dam and stopped.

Bill who came out behind them watched in awe at the scene before him that was unbelievable as Clara Bell and Wilbur had a werewolf trapped in light from Clara Bells magic cane over top of their heads about ten feet off the ground.

Bill aimed his snub nose 38 at the werewolf that was trapped in the magic mystical light and fired off a quick shot "BAM,", but he missed at the long distance which the shot just sailed over to the left of the trapped werewolf at its position in the middle of the dam.

Clara Bell moved the canes magic light over to the side of the dam that held back the water.

"Hermon—Excelsior," commanded Clara Bell and the spiritual light shot upward over the water and the werewolf howled stark raving mad to be let loose.

"Wait till I get my claws on you two, you'll both be dead sorry," said the werewolf who looked with red fiendish eyes down on Clara Bell and Wilbur standing on the dam.

"You look all wet behind the ears," replied Clara Bell who winked confidently at her husband who stood tall beside her while she held onto her old twisted swamp root cane that had the werewolf trapped in its magic spiritual light. "Enchantment—Exodus," commanded Clara Bell and the light faded from the old twisted swamp root cane and the werewolf fell into the dams dark water with a big "splash" and it let out a surprised howl of "Yelp!"on impact of the chilly dark river water!

Lady Victoria Basil was watching the battle from her hiding place along the river bank big oak trees and saw the lone werewolf come charging down the dam toward Wilbur and Clara Bell's back who didn't see the threat and she sprang into action to save them from harm.

Clara Bell heard a flapping noise above and behind her and then she heard her dear old grandmother Anna call out her name.

"Clara Bell quick behind you," said Anna's voice from beyond the grave inside Clara Bell's clairvoyant mind who was always watching her granddaughter's back from the dark realm of seventh heaven above. Clara Bell spun around and then a blue blur flew by her just as she saw the gaping fangs of the werewolf that had leaped up high overhead and almost leaped upon her in mid strike.

Lady Victoria Basil had flew from her branch on the tall oak tree like lightening through the air and she flew past Clara Bell and met the charge of the werewolf head on and smacked him with the palms of her hands on his big hairy chest with the force of one hundred men and knocked him backward thirty feet down the dam and the werewolf rolled head over heels knocked silly for the first time in his long evil life.

Clara Bell's old limbs spun quickly around by the fast working potion that flowed through her good heart, that gave her strong will and the stength to fight another day. She raised her cane and clicked the side button and a long silver dagger shot out from the end and Lady Victoria Basil who had landed in front of Clara Bell to protect her reacted with shock that Clara Bell would attack her after she had just saved her.

Bill who had spotted his beloved fly out of her hiding place from among the trees tops along the river bank with hawk eyes out on the dam just down below them and saw her save his old friends from certain injury or death by one of the werewolf's they were fighting which she had knocked backwards down the dam by a surprise attack, that the werewolf hadn't seen coming. Quick as a bob tail deer he crossed the distance between them on the dam in no time at all and ran up to Clara Bell and Wilbur without a moment to lose fore fear of losing his beloved in the heat of battle by his friends mistaken for a foe. He instantly grabbed Clara Bell by her raised up arm before she could strike with her dagger cane.

"Hold up—Clara Bell—she's on our side," said Bill who quickly got in between Clara Bell and Lady Victoria Basil who looked somewhat stunned that Bill had now come to her aid.

"O.K.—Bill—I read you on this one—Bill—and this must be your little vampire girlfriend that you've been talking about and you look lovely tonight Lady Victoria and what a surprise entrance because you almost bought the farm from it by me, who's your seamstress dear and thanks for saving me and Wilbur. I'm sorry I took you for an adversary, but my heart medicine enriched by my magic potion, that I drank beforehand tonight is making me react faster than I can think, ?" replied Clara Bell in the heat of battle who clicked her secret button on her cane and the silver dagger disappeared back inside her old twisted root cane which she set back on the dam floor and leaned forward on it during a lull in the fighting!

"Yes—I'm here to assist you in anyway I can and I hope to be his woman someday and thank-you for the compliment and my clothes are made at Old Salem's Taylor shop and your welcome— anytime and don't worry about it, were in this together," said Lady Victoria Basil who then smiled at Clara Bell and Wilbur who both quickly beamed welcoming smiles back when they understood what was going on here at this very moment in time with no time for polite introductions.

Meanwhile the werewolf had climbed back up onto the dam behind the foursome and he howled in raged at them "AHHHH—OOOOOOOOH," for dumping him in the water!

Clara Bell turned around and looked at the dripping wet almost whipped dog in front of her with her hands on her hips holding her cane.

"I'll take care of him here hold my cane," said Clara Bell to Wilbur who took her cane.

Clara Bell reached down and picked up her red tied off lap quilt from the milk crate and unfolded it partially in front of her and to her surpirse Runt Runt her black cat with no tail pooped his head out from the old milk crate where he had been hiding under the red tie lap quilt and meowed "Meooow" cried Runt Runt the black cat with no tale who arched his back and stretched on top of the old quart mason jars filled with moonbeam charged fireflies that let off a glow in the jars!

"Well—do tell you must have come along for the ride," said Clara Bell who quickly looked at the werewolf down below her on the dam and back at her cat in the crate and Runt Runt looked down the dam and saw the big scary werewolf too and she hissed at it "SSSSsssss," and spit once or twice "Pissst, Pissst,"and dived under the rattling old mason jars in the crate to hide!

"Don't be afraid of that ole wolf Runt Runt I'll take care of it," said Clara Bell who reached down and stroked her cats back in the old milk crate who purred with its motor running and Runt Runt looked over the crate and watched its master go to work who had picked up the red tie lap quilt in her hands.

"Stand back everybody I'll handle this one," said Clara Bell fiercely with her lap quilt in her strong wrinkled old elderly hands.

Clara Bell walked toward the werewolf that was down below her and she unfolded the red tie lap quilt in front of her to its full length. Then she gave it a quick up and down shake with her hands and the red tied off lap quilt in front of her made a sharp whipping popping sound when it flapped and stretched straight out in the air to its full length "POP" while the werewolf charged straight at her down the dam running on all fours!

"I'm going to pull the wool over his eyes—so to speak," said Clara Bell who waited patiently for the charge in front of her while her friends and husband looked on with intense curiosity who then laughed gleefully to herself "hee, hee, hee" with a wicked looking smile on her face like a cat about to pounce on her prey that she had been stalking in the backyard.

'Invitro," commanded Clara Bell who then pulled the red tie lap quilt back by her side and then in one forward motion threw the red tie white magic lap quilt toward the charging werewolf and it twirled end over end and spread out in the air like she was hanging her weeks wash on her old clothes line to dry on a bright sunshiny day in her backyard down beside the old outhouse on the farm and the werewolf ran smack into the middle of the flying red tied white magic lap quilt which stretched stiffly outward and engulfed it and wrapped itself around the charging werewolf and it fell in a muffled bundle at Clara Bell's feet and it fought against the lap quilt which had it wrapped up tight as a bug in a rug with no way to escape.

"Now that's what I call a sleeper hold on somebody," said Bill who looked on in amazement at the red tie lap quilt that lay at their feet. Clara Bell walked over to her old milk crate and got out another quart mason jar.

Clara Bell walked back over to where the struggling werewolf was wrapped up in the lap quilt and pulled back a corner of the quilt and raised the old quart mason jar up beside her head and the firefly's glowed bright green as it lit up the night air around it.

The werewolf managed to get a clawed paw out from the quilt and it pawed at the air. Clara Bell threw the old mason jar inside the quilt and it smashed against the werewolf's body and broke into a million pieces inside the quilt and a bright green flame shot out of the quilt as Clara Bell let go of the corner of the lap quilt.

The werewolf howled in pain "oooOOOHHHH—ARF—ARF," as it was consumed by the fireball inside the quilt and it fell flat to the concrete dam empty of its burden!

"Uninvitro," commanded Clara Bell and the red tie lap quilt went soft and limp again.

Now that's the way you do it," said Clara Bell who rubbed her hands together as if she had just finished a household chore and picked up her red tie lap quilt and shook out the ashes, burnt molten glass and the melted can lid which fell onto the dam with a "clatter" onto the dam and folded it back up placing it on top of the old milk crate with Runt Runt who curled up quickly under the lap quilt for a nice warm cat nap in the near empty old milk crate.

"Another one bites the dust," shouted Wilbur with glee out loud to everybody standing on the dam beside them back to back in a defensive circle against attack who nodded their heads with approval.

"Stay warm my old cat and safe under the lap quilt in the milk crate and those darn cats always get into everything as you all well know and we will make our last final stand here now that were all together in arms," spoke Clara Bell apologetic for the cat in the bag to everybody who shook their heads in unison which meant "yes—its O.K." and Runt Runt gave a loud muffled "meow" to signal yes also to Clara Bell who looked back down at the milk crate and smiled at her old intelligent feline friend who had tagged along for the special nighttime ride and she winked at everybody that it was O.K. with him under the magic red tie lap quilt in the milk crate which kept him safe from the nightmares on the dam while Wilbur handed the old magic swamp root twisted cane back to Clara Bell who took it and set the point of the cane back on the dam and leaned on it for support with her right hand to rest a spell from all the excitement.

Meanwhile the werewolf that Lady Victoria Basil had knocked back down the dam rose to its feet and howled sorrowful "oooohhhhhhhh"!

It charge toward Lady Victoria Basil picking up speed into a blur and Lady Victoria Basil keen hearing picked up the charging wolf's padded running paws behind her. She turned and with a fast gun slinger draw she drew and fired her old 45 pistol "BAM," and shot the werewolf between the eyes which knocked it backward.

It rolled head over heals back down the dam a few feet from lady Victoria until it fell half off the dam and it started its transformation back into a human being again where it lay dead on top of the old dam.

Off in the distance the leader of the pack heard the alarm howl that echoed over the rolling country side and surrounding woods and the werewolf pack leader new that it's lair was in danger and it took off changing course from hunting its nightly prey at the local Clemmon's shopping center to running at break neck speed toward the dam to save its wolf's lair that was in some kind of danger.

The werewolf tore back threw the woods in a deadly bluring run of motion through dodging trees among the forest and jumping bushes and fallen trees unto it came out along the river bank and it took the deer trail that ran along side the Yadkin river.

The beast tore along the trail until it came up to the back of the old gate house which it then stopped abruptly and took in its surroundings by sniffing the air and looking around the scene it saw the old gate house was on fire inside with smoke rolling out the gate house back door and windows.

It smelled the humans on the other side and it bared its razor sharp fangs in anger and crouching down on all fours it jumped in one bounding leap to the roof top of the old gate house.

The werewolf flashed across the old tar and tin roof until it was at the edge of the roof. The werewolf saw most of its pack laying dead strewn about on the old dam and then it saw the humans standing in the middle of the old dam with the vampire woman of the night who seeing him flashed her mad red eyes at him, that had changed from golden blue and showed her pearly white fang teeth in a threatening stance of attack at him with gun in hand ready to shoot and had played her last Ace card to the very end from up her sleeve.

"What in Hades have you done to my changeling pups and your all suppose to be dead by now and I see the hit woman has betrayed us and joined forces with you and she's a vampire who cleverly hid that from us," said the werewolf pack leader in a loud angry throaty ruff voice to the group of people standing on the dam.

Bill turned swiftly around at the sound of the voice and for a moment he felt his heighten senses working from the magic potion he had drank earlier and he smelled the disgusting beast, he also thought he recognized it—the dark voice from up top and the others in his war party gazed up where the huge werewolf stood on top of the old gate house roof above the front gate house door that belched out black smoke and flames from the inside.

"This one's mine, he must be the pack leader," shouted Bill who took off across the old dam to close the distance for a better shot because the smoke from the flames was hiding the werewolf in a cloud of smoke on top of the gate house at times. The werewolf sensed a threat against its being and pawed the tar roof in anger and its red demon eyes raged in hatred and anger and its fur stood on end enraged by the fury of Hell deep within its black soulless being. Then it leaped down to the dam through the pitch black thick smoke to attack its new found threat and save it's lair.

Bill took a kneeling position and aimed his gun and shot at the wolf "BAM", but he missed as the werewolf darted in a sig sag line across the smoke filled dam toward him and he stood up quickly for a better shot while peering through the thick smoke in front of him trying to spot his target!

The others who had a better advantage point at seeing through the thick black swirling smoke on the dam way back behind Bill who was blinded by the stinging smoke in his teary eyes who rubbed his eyes quickly with the back of his left hand and they saw the werewolf who was headed right for him and about to strike a fateful blow. "WATCH OUT BILL," they all cried in unison when the wcrewolf charging leaped on top of Bill who took an awkward but heighten instinct lucky step backward being pulled by his Guardian Angel over his right shoulder with Heaven sent hands from out of the smoke just in time that might have just saved his life and they both fell tumbling backward off the dam into the spillway water below them with "splash, splash," was all his friends heard from up top and Bill had kicked at the werewolf with both legs knocking it off him into the air out away from him as they fell into the water and he heard the ripping of his new suit from the werewolf's clutching claws that tore lose in mid air!

Bill's 38 snub nose gun was knocked out of his hand and hit on the open dam gate "clang, clang," and fell into the water "splash,"!

Bill stood up in the knee deep spillway water and on the hard river rocks beneath his feet and clutched at his silver cross necklace and to his amazement it was gone as the silver chain pulled from around his neck broken and it dangled in his hand.

Bill wrapped it around his right hand with the intent to punch the werewolf in the mouth with jaw breaker strength while the huge werewolf pack leader reared up on its hind legs all wet to the fur that seemed to bristle outward in fury and the steam rose up off the wet fur coat into the cold night time air.

The red eyes flamed up in anger at Bill and his companions who had destroyed its wolfs lair who looked puny beside this monstrosity of death before him and its face was a mask of pure Evil that raged with Hell's eternal fires that burned within its mind that radiated its red flame outward through the Demonic red raging eyes and razor sharp drooling fangs whose lips quivered in a mad rage.

Bill new the silver cross necklace wouldn't save him this time and his eyes darted back and forth looking in the water for his gun it was his only chance, because he sensed he was standing at death's door and he wasn't about to go down on his knees like a coward, but die if need be standing on his on two feet.

He also new his friends couldn't get here in time to save him from being bitten to death or tore apart in time, because they were fighting for their very own lives up top on the dam against the other attacking werewolf's who were trying defend their lair and his own mortality flashed through his own mind in vivid detail.

Then Bill eyes darted back and forth quickly looking around the river water at the base of the old dam for his lost gun and his Guardian Angel flew down from the dam and hovered over his gun lying in the water and it directed the moon light through its spirit body to shine a moon beam on the gun in the water. Then Bill spotted an object lying in the water not a few feet from him that sparkled on the bottom of rocks from the moons light shining across the dam spillway water redirected by his Guardian Angel and a glimmer of hope leaped into his eye's.

"You will meet your doom here tonight and I'll have my revenge on your friends above for what you have all done to my pack and the hit woman will get an awful last taste of death for betraying all of us with a wooden steak through her black vampire heart," said the werewolf pack leader in a low throaty angry voice who got ready to attack a defenseless Man in its sights thought the werewolf to himself.

"I'd say Death is all way's on our on our backside and some gets it sooner than others and there's two will's here tonight both want to live, but one has to die unfortunately," replied Bill who kept the conversation going while he bought some extra time for a fighting chance to live.

"Death comes to all in time and it's merely a stepping stone into the dark afterlife and its your turn tonight," said the werewolf leader who looked skyward and howled at the moon "ooooOOOOOHHHHH," and barred its teeth and claws ready to tear Bill from limb to limb.

He would fight the others to the death if need be after he was through with this pitiful man who had interfered with his pack and this would be revenge enough even if he failed with the others thought the werewolf to it's evil self.

Bill saw his chance and dove to the exact spot where he saw the sparkling object and felt around in the water and his heart was pounding and to his joy he touched his gun handle which he quickly grabbed it and stood back up facing the huge werewolf with seconds to spare who crouched to strike.

"Every dog has it day," replied Bill fast who aimed his gun at the werewolf's chest and then it hit him in all the excitement had he fired five or six shots already and the gun barrel felt suddenly very heavy in Bill's right hand while he slightly lowered the revolver downward with a trembling hand and the werewolf started forward to pounce on Bill.

"You will be at deaths door in just a second, because your gun is wet and empty—you fool," replied the werewolf who charged through the river water toward Bill in a mindless leap of deadly rage.

Bill reacted with fear while his body became rigid to brace for the attack and quickly swallowed hard "Gulp"and hoped it was his enduring lucky night. He pointed his gun lightening fast at the charging beast in the moonlight and squeezed the trigger "BAM" came the surprised blast that took a second to register in his shocked mind. He saw the werewolf clutch its right chest with its massive right paw through squinted eyes and fall back against the dam floodgate mortally wounded in the chest!

Bill smiled quickly with relief and the fear he had felt quickly melted away.

He quickly wiped his wet and sweating forehead with his shaking gun backhand.

"Whew' said Bill nervously relieved that he was out of that pinch he was in and he quickly pushed the barrel release because he new that had to be his last shot. Bill pointed the gun barrel straight up and pushed the spent cartridge release and the spent shell casing's fell into the river "ploosh, ploosh, ploosh,"!

Bill reached into his right trench coat pocket and felt the wet cartridge box and he tore it apart with his hand and pulled out some silver bullets.

He quickly inserted them into the barrel chamber and snapped the barrel shut and stuck the few remaining bullets in his hand back into his wet trench coat pocket.

Bill gathered his wits about him and walked and splashed through the river water to get over to the wolf he had shot for a better look. He watched the transformation to see who this pack leader was and when the old gray wolfs head and snout transformed back into a man's clear face Bill "gasped" in shock!

It was father Marion from back at the catholic church back in town thought Bill to himself with a smug I new it look on his face.

"I had a hunch it was you after finding that priest outfit in the old gate house Father and your black wolfs head tattoo on your right back hand which was painted on top of your round table in your wolf's lair and on the hands of other member's of your pack which all added up with the clues I've found and gave you away, its time for your confession—Father," spoke Bill who had waded over to a very much naked man of the cloth who was lying on the dam floodgate with blood flowing from his gaping left chest wound.

"Yes—it was me that started all this mess and its been a long night mare fore I was bitten in Kazakhstan, Russia by a werewolf when I was training to be a apprentice priest over a decade ago and I have the mark of the beast on my left shoulder as you can now see and I moved around in the service of the church all over the world and this country until I came here some years ago to the catholic church in Winston-Salem and it was a good cover for my raging bloodlust as a werewolf. No one ever suspected anything unto you and your meddling friends came along. I never thought that a dumb old country boy city slicker detective would ever catch me in the act or let alone figure it out and expose me and my pack to vigilante justice," said Father Marion who now looked old beyond his years while he lay dying in the cold river water.

"Well father—confession its good for the soul and I had a little help from my good old country friends who are no bodies fool about the darkening side of Hell for they have been trained in the ways of white magic and the knowledge of good and evil forces that has been handed down from generation to generation in their family and I do see the bite mark on your left shoulder breast in the moonlight from your past encounter from the werewolf that got you some time ago in a foreign land,' replied Bill intrigued who heard the fighting above him and stood back up to look at the action going on somewhere above him for a moment.

"Yes—I had to try and kill you and your old friends in my evil mind too protect my pack, but I know now that you can't win against the righteous trained at Heavens Gates of the Alter Realm as your friends are by what I found out about them and you who were a viable threat to our evil existence. I've felt Hell's eternal fires lapping at my feet every night of the full moon and I've fallen far from glory. I want it to be finely over with and justice served, there's been a battle raging between good and evil in my tormented soul and evil won the battle as you can now see for your self and I've destroyed so many lives along my twisted dark path," moaned Father Marion who looked at Bill with pleading eyes to end it for him tonight and Bill understood what must be done.

"As you wish Father—to Hell—I'll gladly send you back

which won your soul and good will win the day here and the powers of darkness shall not prevail against Heaven—this very night—say your prayers Father, your dark path ends here—this righteous night," replied Bill with grim conviction in his voice.

"I'm ready to meet my maker and pay for my sins," replied Father Marion with a soft hoarse sounding voice of all hope was lost for him.

"Their's no resurrection for you either on judgement day because of the evil things you've done along your life's path is my guess," said Bill who aimed his 38 snub nose at the mans heart while the Father started to pray under his last breath and Bill pulled the trigger "BAM" knowing he'd never get a conviction against the priest with his tall tale of a pack of killer werewolf's on the prowl in the big city by a jury!

Father Marion's body jerked from the impact "plunk"of the 38 silver slug and he died instant laying in the river baptism water that had flowed over countless people who came to the Yadkin river from churches all over the Triad to be baptized by the pure river water down stream that now flowed over his lifeless and bloody body on the dam gate and washed his sins away.

Bill's 38 snub nose gun barrel felt hot to his touch and was still smoking and he thought justice had been handed down from the end of his gun with extreme conviction while he stood over his dead cornered suspect in the dam spillway water.

He new he had been to the dark side of the moon and had killed in the name of the law which he had done before when his limit had been pushed and his killer instinct had kicked in to protect his self in the performance of his duties when he was a big city detective for the police department trying to arrest murderers or rapist who pulled guns on him to resist arrest and prosecution in a court of law out on the cities mean unforgiven streets and dark back alleyway's to close the tough cases he had be given and to protect the general public from felonious fugitives who might otherwise commit other crimes again such as rape or murder and robbery to evade capture who were on a crime spree thought Bill to himself confidently with authority of the law behind him and ice water flowed coldly through his vein's from a tough life dealing out justice as a lawman.

He would kill again if need be to protect innocent lives legally within the law and he hated to put a man six feet in the ground like he had just done if he had a choice otherwise, but not tonight thought Bill who just shrugged his shoulders to shake the thought off without any guilt what so ever in his conscious mind and he new he was right.

He looked for a foothold on the old dam to start his climb back up and get back in the on going battle up top.

At that very moment in time Wilbur checked over his right shoulder and saw the werewolf come running out of the flames of the old gate house as its roof fell in a burning heap inside the burning building with its fur smoking and zinged from the fire and heat while a bunch of big wolf rats vacated the building also.

"Look at those big old wolf rats run in all directions from the fire in the old gate house. Man look yonder at that one, its as big as a cat with a foot long tail and a long snout full of big mean looking rotten teeth. They must have had big nests in that old gate house walls and I've had them take up root in my barn back home and they are nothing, but nasty vermin that carry disease," exclaimed Wilbur who jumped in his shoes with sickening fright when one big gray wolf rat ran underneath his feet across the dam to safety and disappeared over the side of the old dam into the river water.

"Those rats can't hurt us and besides were after bigger vermin," replied Clara Bell who watched the wolf rats scurry past her to safety from the fire across the old dam.

"Watch out everybody there's another monster," cried out Wilbur who had turned back around lightening fast from the potion running through his veins and forgot about the pack of wolf rats and stuck his pitch fork out in a fighting stance as he faced the werewolf who growled a low throaty warning of imminent death "GRRR, GRRR," in front of him!

The werewolf took off and ran the distance between them in a flash and leaped up over top of Wilbur to attack from above. "Yaaa—Hooo," shouted Wilbur who was in a fighting right prone stance braced for the attack who then fiercely jabbed his pitch fork straight up and stuck his pitch fork into the beast's stomach and it screamed out in rage "GRRRRR" overhead and then instantly in pain "ARF—ARF," while Wilbur spit "Piissss—splat," a big stream of plug nicotine tobacco into the werewolf's eyes to blind it while over his head and at the same time flipped the werewolf over him and Clara Bell who was standing just behind him on the dam. The beast tumbled and rolled down the old dam in a state of shock from the violent encounter with Wilbur who was protecting his wife Clara Bell behind him valiantly.

Lady Victoria had flew off the dam to check out the area for the other werewolf's and saw one come from the access road side of the dam from where it had been hiding in the bushes to attack Wilbur and Clara Bell standing on the middle of the dam when it had a fighting chance to strike which it did if its mate failed.

The werewolf ran down the dam at break neck speed past his tumbling and bleeding companion and leaped up in the air with its claws barred to strike a fatal Blow on Clara Bell who threw up her arms in defense before Wilbur could react in time to save his wife who was now in front of him!

Lady Victoria Basil flew like lightening back to the dam and flew under the beast and in front of Clara Bell who beamed with thankfulness at seeing lady Victoria Basil come to her rescue once again and with 45 pistol in hand she shot the werewolf out of the air in mid strike aiming at its chest "BAM" at point blank range!

The force of the impact of the shot carried the werewolf over the backside of the dam where it fell into the water with a big "splash" dead and the current lodged the body into one of the flood gates in the dam as the transformation started from supernatural beast back to human being.

Lady Victoria flew down onto the dam beside Clara bell and Wilbur who hugged her for saving them again and Lady Victoria looked over Wilbur's shoulder and saw the other werewolf get back up on its feet down below them on the dam after the pitch fork wounds had healed back up supernaturally and it tried to rub the nicotine spit tobacco out of its madding stinging eyes with its paws and prepared to charge them once again.

"Look out," screamed Lady Victoria Basil who started to aim her gun and Clara Bell smashed the end of her cane down on the old dam with a solid loud "bang" "Coram–Lupus–Infobala-swamp witch Latasha come forth," spoke Clara Bell with authority.

The old magic cane glowed brightly and the magic hand carved symbols in the cane changed into different shape's along the shaft. Then a blue mist rose out of the bottom of the cane and rose up over top of them in a big blue sparkling cloud and it exploded with a bright blue sparkling light and old swamp witch Latasha appeared in the bright blue light with a cackling laugh "hee, hee, hee" that resembled a fortune teller's giant magic crystal ball which was from the Alter Realm at Heaven's Gate.

"Take care of that dark demon of a Lycan in front of us," commanded Clara Bell who held her cane stoutly on the old dam in front of her and Lady Victoria was stunned to see this phantom appear in front of her and Clara Bell while she let her gun fall to her wayside in awe.

"Mrs. Parker—where in heavens name does your power come from within that cane," asked Lady Victoria who was stunned at the power of the magic cane in front of her?

"It comes deep from within my very good soul and from my inner life force kinda like a trained Jedi Knight so to speak, but from the Alter Realm where I was trained as a young school girl by my dear departed grandmother and my master teacher swamp witch Latasha who was a good and powerful sorceress and Latasha made this old magic cane over a century ago who trained all of us in my family who transcends time we are God's Centurion's—keeper of King Solomon's magic seals of sorcery and a secret society that is blessed and empowered by God," replied Clara Bell with a confidently smile on her pug nose face with powerful lit eyes through her wire rimmed glasses.

"Oh—yes I saw all the blockbuster movies at the local late night theater in Winston over the years when they came out and I've never met a sorceress, before but I've heard of them and I understand now how you acquired your magic power—cool," replied Lady Victoria with admiring glee in her red eyes.

"Do what I command—Latasha," spoke Clara Bell who turned her attention back to the task at hand.

"My pleasure dear," replied swamp witch Latasha who stuck out her old wrinkled hands toward the werewolf which had long ragged and broken nails on them and fore an instant she looked beautiful and young again just like she had found the fountain of youth and drank from it. Then she looked old beyond her age again and the youthfulness was gone before their very enchanted eyes. "Bestia—Malum—Daemon—Necator—Habra," Chanted swamp witch Latasha. Then blue and reddish silver thunder bolts of lightening flew from her fingertips and engulfed the werewolf on the old dam still rubbing its eyeballs with its paws.

The beast didn't see it coming but howled in pain "AAAHHHHHHH" at being shocked on contact and it shook back and forth electrified by the bolts of blue and reddish silver lighting that struck it and shook it with awesome force over and over again.

Its fur was smoking from the intense heat and then it went limp and fell dead on the dam in a heap of smoke.

Latasha saw the beast fall and she spoke "factum est"-meaning-it is done," said Latasha who with drew her hands back briefly to herself in the bright blue cloud.

"Call me anytime Clara Bell dear if you need any help and its good to be back among the living on God's good green earth," said Latasha who bowed toward Clara Bell from the bright blue cloud. Bestia—Malum—Daemon—Necator—Habra" cackled swamp witch Latasha who gave the werewolf another jolt of blue and reddish silver lightening from her fingertips to make sure it was dead for good measure which shook the beast once again laying on the old dam.

"Factum est"-meaning-it is done, said Latasha and the blue and reddish silver lightening disappeared from her old wrinkled hands.

"Thank-you Latasha," replied Clara Bell quickly who smiled at her old master teacher of black and white magic arts.

"Neplusultra—Back to Adinfinitum," commanded Clara Bell and swamp witch Latasha who was floating inside her blue cloud sparkling crystal ball was quickly pulled down inside the magic swamp cane bottom. It disappeared inside it and then the cane quit glowing and was silent in Clara Bell's strong old hand.

Bill stood at the side of the dam where he had climbed back up on from down below the spillway water and was glad to be standing back on solid ground.

"Bill—I heard the shot down below the dam did you get

him. Did you kill the pack leader," asked Wilbur looking all around standing nervously on the dam beside his wife?

"Yeah–I got him, he was the preacher at a local church back in town of all things out here tonight—he's toast and he's getting baptized lying in the river spillway water beside the dam's floodgate for his sins," replied Bill sternly, but with a tired voice.

"Well—I'll be a son of a gun— good for you Bill," replied Wilbur somewhat relieved that the battle might be over now.

"Bill had watched the magic show in front of him in awe at the swamp witch who appeared out of Clara Bell's cane and killed the last werewolf or so he had thought.

"Clara Bell you keep amazing me with those tricks up your sleeve or cane in this case," said Bill who shuffled his feet in nervous anticipation of what happens next out here this very night.

"Bill—God shines his ever loving light on the good and evil. If you do good things then good is returned to you, but if you do evil things, then to all things of that nature must come to a tragic end, sooner or later, its just up to us how we use his guidance to do good things instead of bad things like these werewolf's have done and they got their poetic justice tonight I'd say," replied Clara Bell who clutched her cane firmly with both hands.

"I think that's just about does it," said Bill who walked down the dam away's and nudged the huge male dead werewolf's smoking head with his right foot to make sure it was dead which it was and the transformation was beginning from beast to man.

He turned back to walk toward his companions when out of nowhere the last werewolf who was smart and deceptive struck from the underside of the dam where it had been hiding in wait among the ruins of the old power station looking for the right time to strike at Bill's blind side in retaliation for killing its pack leader and mates which it saw happen from its hiding spot.

The werewolf charged over the dam in a flash knocking Bill down on the dam as it landed on top of him from the ambush and dug in its huge claws into Bill's body and Bill dropped his gun in pain. Bill quenched his fist to withstand the pain from the claws that had latched on to his body and his street tough never give up and never surrender mind quickly regained it's senses.

Lady Victoria and Clara Bell with Wilbur screamed in fear for Bill all at once " OOOHH—NOOOO,"!

"Shoot, shoot —do it now," screamed Bill in anguish who looked wildly back at them with fear in his eyes.

Lady Victoria had only one shot before the werewolf either bit Bill or killed him while it toyed with him like a cat with its prey in hand.

Bill grabbed the werewolf by its massive head and pushed it up with all his strength and Lady Victoria instantly spread her legs and aimed her gun with both hands for a steady and better shot and quickly squeezed off a round from the old 45 colt pistol "BAM,"! The werewolf's head was knocked back out of Bill's hand on impact from the velocity of the bullet which struck it dead between the eyes and blood spurted out from the wound onto Bill's neck and suit.

The body went limp and fell on top of Bill who was surprised he was still alive and kicking.

Bill wiggled out from under the dead wolf's changing corpse while Clara Bell and Wilbur came running up to him with Lady Victoria Basil flying over head.

She landed beside Bill who looked up in gratitude at seeing this most beautiful sight for sore eyes and he looked like death warmed over by his close call. He was sitting up staring at her in stark disbelief at his good fortune that the werewolf had lost the battle by the best shot he had ever seen any woman shoot.

"Are you alright Bill," asked a smiling Lady Victoria Basil who offered Bill a helping hand while she took her handkerchief from her left sleeve and wiped the blood away from Bill's neck and suit with it?

"I—I—I guess so—lady luck was on my side tonight," replied Bill who looked dazed and confused at seeing his life flash before his very eyes once more when he had looked into the werewolf's flaming red eyes overtop of him with horror of an awful death.

"Yes—I was," said Lady Victoria who hugged Bill quickly around the neck to reassure him everything was alright and she stood back up with a out stretched hand.

Bill grabbed her strong hand and rose shakily to his feet and Wilbur steady Bill by grabbing his other arm who swayed for a moment and then his life force kicked into high gear and he felt better at cheating death tonight while he regained his strength back. "That was the last one I was looking for including the one killed at your house a few night's ago—for a total of 12 dark Knights in Satan's Service and I say good riddance to them all and you lived to tell the tale—again Bill," said Clara Bell who had kept up with the number of werewolf's in the pack and she was always right.

"Well—I hope your right Clara Bell, but we need to call the police and get them out here and clean up this crime scene," said Bill who felt for his cell phone in his left wet coat pocket and new it was ruined by his night time dip.

"My-my-my cell phone took a dip in the river," mumbled Bill who was still very shakily and weak in the knees who looked for help from his friends there on the old dam.

"Here's your gun back Bill that I picked up off the dam for you from where you was knocked down by that wolf of a devil," spoke Wilbur softly who was glad his old friend was alright and handed the loaded gun over to his old pal.

"Thanks a million," replied Bill who took the gun and pulled back his wringing wet right side coat jacket. He put it back in his soaked right side holster and secured it by the leather snap.

"You can use my new cell phone," said Lady Victoria Basil who pulled it out from her left vest pocket and handed it over to Bill cheerfully while she tucked her handkerchief back in her left sleeve.

"Well—you managed to save all of us here tonight dear and by no small means. No good deed goes unrewarded and I was right about you being a good person deep down in your spiritual soul," said Clara Bell who kindly rubbed Lady Victoria Basil on her arm when Bill took the cell phone to make the call.

"I'm here to be of service and I had to protect my man which is reward enough," replied Lady Victoria Basil who smiled coldly warm at Clara Bell with Wilbur who looked on in earnest standing on the dam at what she had said. Then they both thought about it and they looked at each other and they began to laugh at each other from some unseen joke at what she had said about protecting her man while Lady Victoria raised her eyebrows in wonder at what was funny.

"Oh –I'm sure we can do something tomorrow night at my farmhouse out on Payne Road where we are going to have a victory party," said Clara Bell who got out a note pad and pencil from her milk crate and started writing on the note pad.

"I don't think you can help my situation with any little rewards," replied Lady Victoria Basil who folded her arms across her chest in defiance at the suggestion of help which she new was always a dead end for her in the past.

"Come and will see," said Clara Bell who handed her the paper she tore out of the note pad.

"Well—anything's worth a try and I've haven't been to a

real party in a long time," replied Lady Victoria Basil who took the paper and stuck it in her right vest pocket.

Bill had dialed Dickies home phone number from memory and waited why it rang.

"Hello," answered a sleepy voice and Dicky rubbed his sleep filled eyes with his free hand.

"Dicky—wake up—it's Bill calling and I've got good news about our case," replied Bill who waited to hear that the man had woke up wide awake.

Dicky sat up in bed and thought about what Bill had just said. "O.K.—it had better be good news at this late hour," said Dicky who was now wide awake.

"I've found the killers hideout and we had to kill them to defend ourselves," replied Bill who listen for a response.

"You—found them—well—its about time where are you," asked Dicky who was now all ears now on the phone?

"I'm out at the Old Idol's Dam out in Clemmon's and we need local police and the ambulances out here to clean up this mess," replied Bill who smiled at his friends who were listening to his conversation.

"I'll personally come out there and make sure this is done by the book," said Dicky who hung up the phone.

"See—ya—then," replied Bill who pushed the button cutting off the cell phone and he handed it back to Lady Victoria Basil who took it and stuck back in her left vest pocket.

"I have to go before they get here and they wouldn't understand me and it would cause big trouble for me," said lady Victoria Basil who kissed Bill on his cheek.

"Don't forget about tomorrow night at my place," said Clara Bell who grinned at this brave supernatural woman of the night who had impressed her this very night. "Till then," said Lady Victoria Basil who flew off from the dam and over the tree tops who then vanished among the stars in the night time sky while they watched from the dam in awe.

Police chief Dicky cut on his lamp on the beside night stand and made another call after hanging up from Bill's late night call. He dialed 9-11 and waited patently while the phone ringed on the other end with his mind racing into action.

"This is 9-11 what is your emergency," asked the female emergency police dispatcher who looked at the address on her computer screen and new instantly it was the police chief?

"This is police chief Dicky Poser talking—please scramble all available units out to the old Clemmons idol's dam access road where there's been a shooting by an undercover office who's on scene there with suspects down and needs assistance there," spoke Chief Dicky with authority in his sleepy voice.

"Yes-sir I'm making the call now chief Dicky anything else I can do for you," asked the dispatcher who got back on the line?

"Call the Forsyth County Sheriff's office and tell them to call and wake up Sheriff David Holiday and have him meet me on scene out their A-S-A-P," said Chief Dicky who was fumbling with his clothes on the chair beside his night table where he always put them incase he had to get dressed fast and tonight was one of those nights.

"Will do," responded the emergency police dispatcher who started alerting all available Sheriff's units too and called the night squad on duty at the Sheriff's office downtown to alert them.

"Thank-you I'm on my way right now," replied police Chief Dicky who hung the phone up back in its cradle on the night stand while he put on his pants quickly.

"Man this is the call. I've been hoping for after all these years of dead ends on these triad murder case's and I hope it's finely over and Bill solved the case," said Chief Dicky with a long felt heart ache relief.

He accidently fell back on the bed excited with one leg in his pants while he fought to put them on and he leaned over the bed. He grabbed his socks and shoes to quickly put them on almost over joyed with happiness that was long overdue, but with a concerned mind about what fate might be now in his hands at the crime scene.   Some time later that night the Winston-Salem police and Forsyth County Sheriff's Department were all over the crime scene and Bill was telling police chief Dicky an incredible story who listen beside the smoldering ruins of the old gate house while his men checked the bodies they had found on the dam and in the river water from which they had pulled them from and laid them under the five white blood stained sheets on the old dam to hide the evil sight of death and the Clemmon's Volunteer Fire Department Firemen sprayed the remaining small fires in and around the burnt out old gate house with their fire hoses from their fire truck parked back on the river road access side of the river which lay in partial destruction while they started their search for two more bodies among the burning rubble that Bill said where still somewhere trapped inside the burnt out shell of a building.

"Bill—that's one incredible story about a pack of wild werewolf's killing the public at large, but no one would believe it, I don't even believe it. Those are dead human bodies under those white sheets not dead animals. It sounds like a bunch of mystic jumbo mumbo if you ask me or at the very least one cock-and-bull story," said Dicky who watched Bill intently while he shook his head with the High Sheriff of Forsyth County David Holiday by his side who was taking all this in with conviction.

"You can lead a stubborn horse to water, but you can't make him drink it—it's the God's honest truth if you asked me," spoke Wilbur who shuffled his clod knocker feet nervously on the dam beside Bill fearing the outcome for them all tonight might be jail time and their good names ruined.

"It's hard for nonbelievers to believe the truth who don't understand the supernatural world we exist in among our mortal world," said Clara Bell who backed up Bill's story with Wilbur nodding his head yes by her side.

Dicky thought about that one and he thought for a long moment before responding.

"Bill me and you go way back and I've never known you to lie about anything and we started out in the Winston- Salem police department as rookies over some twenty years ago. We moved up through the ranks by doing good honest police work and saving peoples lives was our motto and you was as good a lawman as there is up until you retired some years ago and became a private eye detective. Alright—Bill—I'll cover for you on this one and I know you are telling the truth as y'all see it and I wasn't here to witness anything, but I can't change fate—if that's what happen here tonight, but I can change the outcome of circumstances," replied Dicky who looked at them all with a concerned face.

"My report will read that a wild gang of criminal killers on crystal meth and other drugs were robbing the public at large and killing them like wild animals had done it to cover their tracks so to speak as to leave no witnesses behind fore "Dead men tell no tales" as you well know and that you and your friends tracked them to Idol's Dam by clues you had uncovered in your investigation which was their hide out and they discovered you all messing around the old dam looking for clues and attacked you all and in defending yourselves while being undercover cops by my appointment on a murder case, you had a wild shoot out with them and killed them all in a firefight," said police chief Dicky who stood up on tip toes to make his point.

"Well—part of the story is true and the rest of it is mixed in with a white lie which will make it sound convincing to the public who just might buy it," replied Bill who nodded his head in agreement knowing it was the right thing to do.

"You all can leave now, your free to go home and we will clean up the mess here, if we need any further information we will be in touch and Bill y'all did a good job out here tonight and I hope it ends our killer crime wave problem which is a sign of the times in these parts here lately," said Dicky who gestured them off the dam toward their beat up old pick up truck with his right thumb that the police had discovered and uncovered in the cut bushes and saplings between the trees.

Wilbur who was a little disgusted like his wife and Bill about their incredible story that no one would believe out here picked up the old milk crate from the dam beside his feet and put it under his left arm with the black cat with no tail tucked safely inside under the lap quilt.

Then the quiet trio walked across the dam without another word spoken among law enforcement officers standing around in small groups whispering among themselves about what they thought had taken place out here in this Erie place and they all got in the old beat up truck after Wilbur put the old milk crate in the back truck bed behind the drivers rear window along with his blood stained pitch fork.

Wilbur spit his plug tobacco chew out the window he had rolled down and grabbed a bottle of spring water from his dashboard and unscrewed the lid and took a swig.

He sloshed it around in his mouth and spit out any excess tobacco out the truck window. He put the cap back on the bottle of spring water and put it back on the dash in front of him.

Bill who was watching him just shook his head and looked out the window in deep thought about how he admired these old country folk even with their old backwoods ways.

Wilbur then started it up and pulled out from among the trees and turned on his truck headlights moving past the fire truck while he drove down the old grown up dirt and gravel river dam access road moving among the parked police cruisers, Sheriff's deputy patrol cars, parked Crime Scene vans and ambulances to pick up the bodies for transportation to the city morgue on the side of the old river dam access road.

In the morning hours of that same night Lady Victoria Basil was flying back from the Idol's Dam in Clemmon's and had followed I-40 expressway on into Winston-Salem and she flew over the tall buildings.

She turned north over liberty street and soon flew over the Patterson Avenue street corner intersection looking for her homeless friend Richard Clearly whom she saw standing down on the corner with her vampire night vision with some other homeless street people keeping warm over a nice fire in a trash can.

Her and Richard would walk the streets late at night talking about their lives and current events around the world and she had grown to love him like a brother and he loved her as a sister that he said he never had.

He never asked any questions about her past life, but she could see the questions and suspicious in his eyes, but he never asked them when she had shared his liquor bottle with him out of respect for her as his friend.

He new she wanted to keep her secrets to herself, just as he did his own too and was always thankful when she slipped him some money to eat on in his ragged front shirt pocket when they parted ways late at night before dawn. She new those homeless men must be good honest folk just down on their luck due to a job loss or something else of that nature and she new they were good men if they were hanging out with Richard down on the street corner just minding their own business trying to survive another day out on these mean city streets late at night not bothering no body, but just enjoying the evening night air as law abiding good citizens.

She hoped that someday good Christian people would help them get their lives back on track.

She was just checking on him to be sure he was safe and she was glad he was O.K. and then she smiled to herself happily satisfied. Then she flew on over the intersection of Patterson Avenue and on down Liberty Street where she saw the car jacking taking place down below her just in the nick of time at the corner of Liberty Street and 25 Street.

"Give me all your money," spoke the young man in the hooded sweat shirt who pulled out a gun from his pants.

"I—I—I don't have any money on me—honest. Here take my purse," replied the frighten young mother who was scared for her two young children in her backseat!

"All right lady say your prayers and I'll take your car instead," said the young man in the hooded sweat shirt whose face was hidden by the hood and sunglasses while he pointer the 9 millimeter hand gun at the young mother in the Tan SUV and he cocked the hammer back on the pistol while her two small boys in car seats in the backseat got scared at seeing this spooky man run to the car from the curb and they started two cry from fright.

Lady Victoria Basil looked for the police up and down the road and the streets were deserted this time of night.

Where's a cop when you need one thought Lady Victoria Basil who new she had to act quickly to save them from certain harm. Lady Victoria Basil flew down supersonic to Liberty Street and she stuck her right hand in front of the muzzle of the gun just as it went off "BAM" and jerked it out of the surprised car jacker's hand who turned around in shock as Lady Victoria Basil put a death hold around the car jacker's shoulders and it knocked his sunglasses off his head that went flying from the sudden impact!

She lifted him up off the street powerfully knocking the socks off of him and leaving a tennis shoe laying in the street beside the curb with the young mother staring up out of her car window in a surprise smile while she watched them both leave her on the street in her Tan SUV and disappear up into the night sky.

"Momma did you see that woman save us from that bad man, she picked him up and flew off with him locked in her arms with the gun just like superman," asked the little boy in the back seat of the Tan SUV who looked at his smiling little brother who looked back at him with wide bright eyes?

"The lord works in mysterious ways and that was a superwoman of the eternal night which the old folks told me about from when I was a small child like ya'll growing up here and they haunt the night," said the young mother to her son that she looked back at over her shoulder from the drivers seat who then gave up a silent prayer of thanks and she floored the Tan SUV and ran the red light while she got the blazes out of there with her children headed safely home.

Lady Victoria Basil landed in a back alleyway and dropped the car jacker on the street who had a white shocked look on his face from his brief encounter with the vampire vixen and was speechless.

"I'm feeling like a good savior tonight and I haven't seen you around here before and I'm going to spare your life, but if I ever see you out here again trying to rob and kill innocent people, I'm going to eat you alive. I'm a man eater and I'll chew you up and spit you out in the gutter where you belong you little rat of a man," said Lady Victoria Basil whose eyes glowed red with fire and she showed the young car jacker her fanged pearly white teeth and his fired bullet in her hand and she let it fall to the pavement "ding" from her hand and to make a point she bent his gun into a U and handed it back to the young man whose shaking hand tried to grab the broken gun and his fear got the best of him and he let it slip through his hand and fall to the pavement with a metal "Clang" beside him!

"Just remember there are things that go bump in the night and were always watching in the shadows when night falls," said Lady Victoria Basil who lifted up into the air and flew off back to the family Mausoleum at Gods Acker in Old Salem for the first rays of dawn was breaking.

"Yyyyes—mame. I believe—it—now—I just got scared straight," said the young car jacker who was still dumb stuck at his good fortune while he sat on the pavement and his wide eyes watched a superwoman fly off into the night air and then it registered first in his mind, then it hit him.

The young car jacker got up and screamed "A-A-A-H-H-H-H," and ran off down the alleyway street a changed man who now believed in creatures of the night and that crime didn't pay at least not around here no more and he disappeared down the road at a fast pace.

Near daybreak Lady Victoria Basil opened her dorm size refrigerator beside her vault that she had installed herself and got out a pint of O type blood in a donor plastic bag which she bought on the black market late at night.

She bit the corner of it with her teeth and tore open a small drinkable hole in the plastic bag and she took a big gulp of cold blood and swallowed thirstily to quench her blood lust and the silky color returned to her cheeks and deep dark red eyes turned golden blue again while she relaxed leaning back on her vault and used her handkerchief to wipe her mouth which had been tucked into her left long sleeve dress and she felt rejuvenated.

She looked at her long beautiful vested Victorian style dresses that had been hand made for her in Old Salem in moveable metal racks across the mausoleum floor beside her mother and fathers sealed vaults sitting on the floor and she longed for their embrace which she new would never come in this life or the next.

She finished her meal and tossed the pint bag of empty

blood in her small garbage can and she cried out loud at her solemn empty life.

"oooHHHH—what a world to be in all alone and shunned by society," cried Lady Victoria and she wanted to live again which she thought was impossible and her soul ached in torment for a human touch again.

She would have shed real human tears, but it was impossible as a vampire vixen who only cried blood tears not real tears and she was dying to get out of here permanently at any cost for the new moon of each month always's reminded her of this stark raving mad lunatic dark life she had led for centuries because she was a woman wrapped in satanic chains by the dark lord from Hell. Sometimes late at night sitting outside her Mausoleum she had screamed at the big glowing moon with a raving madness of why her and she had only heard the silence of the big dark graveyard in return.

Crying big red tears which she wiped with her handkerchief from her left sleeve. She open the centuries old wooden coffin and crawled inside and shut the lid on another dark night and coming day with only a sobbing sound "boo, hoo, hoo,"coming from the inner darkness of the tomb.

The very next night sometime after the setting sun had long gone down at Clara Bell's and Wilbur farm out on Payne Road and the crescent moon had risen high over head in the night sky and late evening had set in.

Bill was eating his celebration supper in the barn on the picnic table Clara Bell had fixed which consisted of fried chicken and mash potato's with collard greens and cornbread baked fresh from the old antic 1901 cast iron stove in Clara Bell's kitchen which could heat hot water from a tank on the side for a hot bath in a old porcelain clawed tub or you could bake pies in the heated pie safe from burning kindling wood or cook fried chicken in a old cast iron skillet on the top of hot round burner lids or bake bread in the oven which at that time was a modern wonder of the age and nothing tasted better than food cooked on a old wood cast iron cook stove. Wilbur was devouling his second helping of fried chicken and Clara Bell was looking at the night time stars through the barn doors.

"I guess she's not coming tonight," said Clara Bell who took a sip of her percolated coffee in her white farm mug.

"She'll be here—give her time," replied Wilbur who took a bite of his chicken leg and chewed happily fore he loved to eat setting across from Bill at the picnic table that set just inside the dirt floor of the big red barn doors.

"Well—I had hoped she shows up tonight—I was wanting to see her again," said Bill who sat down his fork on his plate and wiped his mouth with his cloth napkin and looked at Runt Runt the black cat with no tail laying under the picnic table. Then Bill saw a black panther laying there for just a second.

He quickly blinked his eyes and looked again and all he saw was the old black cat yawing with its mouth wide open showing it's pointed teeth and long pink tongue. Then it laid its head back down on its front paws and went back to sleep.

He new better then to say anything after all he had seen with these good people of another realm and he went back to eating his food feeling very humbled at what he thought he had seen or had his eyes been playing tricks on him again and he just shook his head feeling a bit out of place.

"Oh— you will see me again—and its right now," said a soft female voice from outside the barn and Lady Victoria Basil flew in through the barn doors and gently landed on her feet in front of her new friends sitting at the picnic table.

"Want you join us for some food and refreshments," asked Clara Bell who waved her hand over the bounty of food on the picnic table? "I'll have some red wine," replied Lady Victoria Basil who sat down beside Bill and looked dreamy eyed at him and Bill blushed with embarrassment in front of Wilbur and Clara Bell who pretended not to notice.

"I'll have to go for that back at the house," said Wilbur very politely.

Wilbur left and went to the farm house and came back some minutes later with a open bottle of Merlot wine and a lead crystal wine glass.

Wilbur set the wine glass down beside Lady Victoria Basil and poured her glass full and set the wine bottle down on the picnic table within easy reach of Lady Victoria Basil who lifted her glass and smell the wine then tastes it and then she smile at everybody with approval.

Wilbur set down beside his wife and resumed eating his second helping of food.

"Lady Victoria I have a real treat in store for you tonight and I hope you participate with us," spoke Clara Bell who got up and walked across the barn floor to a cement floor on the other side of the barn which was used to wash down the cows or horses on cleaning day at the barn for the county fair.

Lady Victoria Basil got up walked over and saw the star of David drawn in blue chalk on the cement floor with tall candles at each corner of the star.

"What's this," asked Lady Victoria Basil who was some what taken a back at the sight of a Christian symbol?

"This is hope for you from God—but you have to want to give it a try—too—you have to ask in order to receive his blessing and remember what I told you the other night about no good deed goes unrewarded," replied Clara Bell who gestured for Lady Victoria to get into the middle of the star of David.

Lady Victoria Basil looked around at the old red barn while she pondered what Clara Bell had said to her. "I'm game—anything is better than this old dark and evil life and I had hoped that somehow you would help me here tonight. That's why I had come," said Lady Victoria Basil who stepped into the middle of the star and Clara Bell smiled confidently watching this lovely vision of a woman who after all these years still had hope deep inside her to become a whole human again which Clara Bell had realized from the moment she had met her back at the old dam and she had wanted to help free her soul from the dark side of satanic evil.

"Wilbur quit eating your food and get over here and light the candles—the Holiness ceremony is about to start and that means you too Bill," said Clara Bell who watched Wilbur drop his food onto his plate and wipe his mouth off with the cloth napkin from around his shirt front and he got up from the picnic table quickly and walk hastily over to where they were at in the Barn who was then followed by Bill who set his coffee cup down on the picnic table and got up from his seat on the bench and followed behind Wilbur.

Wilbur reached into his bib overhaul pocket and pulled out a Bic lighter and started lighting the candles one by one while Clara Bell waited with patience.

"Bill you stand over there behind your woman at the back of the star of David and Wilbur you stand there beside Bill and I'm in front and everybody hold hands in a circle," said Clara Bell who got ready for prayer at that very moment in time and reached out and grabbed Wilbur's hand and then she grabbed Bill's hand.

"We are the Father and the Son and the Holly ghost represented in the outside of the star of David by us—everyone bow our heads," said Clara Bell who began to pray out loud.

"Our heavenly father we ask for your grace and mercy and that your ever loving light shine down on this lost soul who is here tonight to ask forgiveness of her earthly sins who has the heart of repentance and wants your divine love and blessing and too be saved on Jesus name your divine son who gave his life so that others might live again and defeat the dark forces of Satan here tonight," said Clara Bell who looked up when the barns hayloft doors suddenly busted open and the moons light shined down through the barn and bathed them all in a glowing white light that surrounding the star of David from which they all stood.

Clara Bell new the gateway to heaven was through the moon and she looked in awe at seeing five angels with great mighty white wings suddenly appear and start swirling down the moonbeam from Heavens Gate high in the moonlit sky above them.

Bill and Wilbur came to attention at the sound of the hayloft doors opening up too and followed Clara Bells gaze and they too saw the angels descending down upon them in the old big red barn.

Lady Victoria Basil was glowing a brilliant white with her head bowed and then she looked skyward through the barn doors and she too saw the angels floating down on big white wings wearing white shining togas with swords in their belts and she smiled at the sight of Gods mighty hand before her eyes.

The four angels landed in front of the barn and in walked the fifth angel who walked over to the star of David.

"You may release your grip around the star of David for God has heard your mighty prayer and has sent us his messengers," said the angel who was bathed in white and glowed. Bill and Wilbur and Clara Bell released their hands and they stepped back in awe at the sight before them in wide eye wonder.

"My name is Arc Angel Gabriel and I am the keeper of the seven seals of heaven," said Arc Angel Gabriel who drew his sword with his right hand.

"Knee down Lady Victoria," commanded Arc Angel Gabriel who approached the lovely vision in white inside the star of David who kneeled down as commanded on bended knee and bowed her lovely dark haired head.

"I bestow upon you the coveted seal of Noctu which it means by night and the Arc Angel Gabriel took his sword and touched the tip of his blade on her shoulders one at a time and then she was bathed in a blinding white light once again from Heaven above and Bill with Wilbur and Clara Bell standing off to one side grimaced from the blinding white light. Then they shielded their eyes with their hands over their faces, because the light was so powerful to look at with mere mortal eyes.

During the day you will be human, but when night falls your vampire powers will return fore God has commanded it be done so shall it be written in the book of life and do good deeds with your powers of Noctu and your reward will be great in Heaven when your humanly body dies," said Arc Angel Gabriel and he resheathed his sword back in his belt who then bowed to Lady Victoria and the satanic look about her disappeared who's skin now turned a beautiful satin white as life returned to her body and her hungry vampire red black pupil eyes turned a natural human blue again and her lungs breath life that flowed vibrantly threw her human body again being pumped by a real beating live heart while she stood in God's power of healing brilliant white light from heaven above and then it was gone and all that was left was the moon beam shining in the old red barn through the hayloft doors above them.

Lady Victoria exhaled her breath in jubilation time after time and she danced around on the barn floor with a happy beating red heart again that she felt with her on hand over her breathing chest and she was filled with the wonderment of rapture.

Arch Angel Gabriel turned and ran on his feet and his mighty wings beat a strong wind that blew dust and straw back on the people standing in the barn and lifted him out of the barn door into the night and the other angels waiting on guard outside beat their mighty white wings and flew up into the night sky with him and flew up along the moon beam which retreated back to the moon which was the gate way to

Heaven and they soon vanished into the face of the moon while everybody in the barn watched in wide eyed wonderment.

"I'm hungry for real food," said Lady Victoria Basil who beamed with natural beauty from her lovely face and natural blue eyes.

"Come dear— there's plenty left on the picnic table," said Clara Bell who walked her over and gave her a plate.

They all sat and watched Lady Victoria Basil eat her fill of food until she could eat no more and pushed her plate away.

"That's the best meal I've had in over a hundred years or so and I'm darn lucky to have it," said Lady Victoria Basil who wiped her mouth on her linen cloth napkin and sipped her wine glass with joy in her heart.

"Come lets take a walk," asked Bill seeing she had finished up her meal who then helped her up from the picnic table and they walked out of the barn hand in hand together?

"Those two young lovers deserve some privacy—Wilbur lets clean up and head back to the farmhouse," said Clara Bell who started racking the scraps for the pigs off the plates with a fork while Wilbur stuck the dirty plates in Clara Bells picnic basket on the picnic table.

Later in the evening Bill and Lady Victoria were watching the horses graze in Wilbur's pasture beside the big red barn and Bill waved at Clara Bell and Wilbur who walked by after feeding the pigs the table scraps in their pig pen on the other side of the big red barn who headed for their farmhouse.

"What are those twelve dozen or so big round green rings doing in your backyard grass in front of the child's swing set. I've never seen anything like that before," asked Lady Victoria looking at Clara Bell with questioning eyes?

"Those are fairy rings my dear. They come out to play and dance around after late midnight and they leave their essence on the four leaf clover ground after doing magic tricks with their pixie dust and magic wands which makes the green grass grow into a big ring circle where they were floating over top of on tip toe casting their magic spells by flying around on their wings playing and dancing around in the moon beams outer light.

Then they go back to the Alter Realm where they come from before dawn breaks, but no one's ever really seen them at play before but if you do see one or catch one.

They have to grant you one magical wish of your hearts desire and then you must let them go free or they will melt in dawn's early light and your wish want come true.

I sometimes use the four leaf clover in my magic potions because pixie dust has magical qualities that can't be duplicated by a mere magic good sorceress spell, it multiplies it ten fold when used properly," replied Clara Bell with a smug wink who swung her pail back and forth slowly while she walked quickly after her husband Wilbur who was up ahead.

They slowly ascended the back porch steps and disappeared inside the backdoor kitchen and the lights went out in the old tin roof farmhouse kitchen and in a few seconds later lights came on upstairs in the back master bedroom then winked off after a few minutes later.

Bill and Lady Victoria new that the old folks had gone to bed early so they would rise early to do the farm chores tomorrow because it was just another day on the farm for them. The old farmhouse was then lit up only in the glow from the big full moon's majestic light shining down from high overhead that illuminated the farm and surrounding hills.

Bill had heard the back door shut off in the distance on the quiet serene farm out on Payne Road and them being all alone was what he had been waiting for. He saw his chance to pop the question if he mustered up the nerve tonight which he had been thinking about for some time now.

"The stars never looked so bright tonight and I can never thank your friends enough for what they did for me here tonight and this place on the farm is just magical too me now and beyond my wildest imagination or expectations," said Lady Victoria Basil who looked lovely tonight with the moons glow on her radiate face thought Bill to himself while he listen to her wonderful voice and leaned on the fence post with her.

"Yes—this is a magical time for both of us here in this eternal night of bliss and i have something to ask of you and I hope I get the answer of my dreams," said Bill who got down on one knee in the bright starlit night and he took Lady Victoria hand in his.

"Lady Victoria Basil you have charmed me from the moment my eyes laid on your beautiful body and I ask for your hand in marriage tonight—please say yes," asked Bill keeling on the ground who pulled out a one carat princess cut 14 karat gold diamond ring from his coat pocket that was his mothers and held it up to her and it caught the moon's rays and sparkled in the nighttime air?

Lady Victoria Basil was taken by the mans charms and love for her and she stood looking down at him for a spell.

"Yes—I'd love too and please take me home to your real house tonight and not back to a graveyard," came the reply from Lady Victoria Basil deep husky shocked voice who slipped on the ring over her left trembling ring finger which was a perfect fit.

"Your wish is my command," said a Bill overjoyed with emotion.

Bill got up and danced a old time jig on the grass and then he picked up Lady Victoria Basil high up into the air under her arm pits and twirled around and her blue Victorian full length vested dress flowed through the air like a parasol and he brought her back down to the ground and he kissed her sweet smiling warm lips that never tasted so good and delicious to him.

They headed back happily toward the big old red barn and once inside they climbed the hayloft ladder and disappeared behind the bales of hay and then sweet laughter came down from the hayloft of young lovers madly in love.

The cows in there stalls eating their cud and the horses in there stalls perked up their ears and listen to the joy's of fresh and blood human beings making love sweet sounds somewhere above them in the hayloft and the night which was still young went marching on in the moonlight toward the coming dawn.

Months later Bill stood at the alter in his white tux with his beloved bride to be who looked absolutely stunning in her long white bridal gown and veil that covered her beautiful radiate face. The small church that was painted white with a small steeple cross on top of the front roof of the old Pentecostal Holiness church out on Payne Road was packed with family members and friends also elected official's in the old time oak church pews.

It was an hot Indian summer's day outside during winter and such a gorgeous day to have a wedding in the bright sunshine of matrimony.

"Do you Bill take this woman as your lawful wedded wife to have and to hold as long as you both shall live and in sickness and in health,' asked the Holiness preacher?

"Yes—I do," replied Bill who looked through the white veil into Lady Victorias pretty blue eyes with love in his eyes.

The Holiness preacher turned to Lady Victoria standing at the alter with Bill who held her hand in his.

"Do you take this man to be your lawful wedded husband to have and to hold as long as you both shall live and in sickness and health," asked the Holiness preacher to Lady Victoria who smiled at Clara bell and Wilbur sitting in the front church pew in their Sunday best clothes and then back at Bill.

"Yes—I do," replied Lady Victoria with a smile toward the crowd in the church pews who listen to every breath that was spoken inside the old house of faith.

"Now the rings," said the Holiness preacher and Bill and Lady Victoria took the rings from her bridesmaid and best man who coughed them quickly up to the couple from deep in their pockets. "With this ring I thee wed you Lady Victoria," said Bill who repeated what the Holiness preacher had spoken to him while he slipped his mothers old 18 karat gold wedding ring on his brides left ring finger next to the diamond engagement ring he had given her that wonderful night.

"With this ring I thee wed you Bill," said Lady Victoria who repeated what the Holiness preacher had said to her moments before and she slipped her fathers 18 karat gold wedding ring on Bill's left ring finger which had been left in a locked trust box at BB&T for so many years ago by her long departed family and had it resized to fit Bill's ring finger at Camel Pawn shop in downtown Winston-Salem just for this occasion. "If anyone objects to this union let him speak now or forever hold his peace," said the Holiness preacher who looked out from the pulpit toward the crowd of onlookers. For a few minuets it was all quiet in the old house of faith and you could have heard a pin drop, but no one spoke up!

"Well—with that said and done I now pronounce you man and wife—you may kiss the bride and let no man put asunder," said the Holiness preacher to lady Victoria and Bill who lifted up the white veil and gave Lady Victoria's ruby red lips a passionate quick kiss of love which she returned in kind holding her white bridal bouquet in her lovely white satin hands.

"Please turn toward the crowd of loved ones and friends," asked the Holiness preacher to Bill and his new Bride who turned in kind? "Ladies and Gentleman I present to you Bill and Victoria Christian a newly married couple this very day," said the Holiness preacher to the crowed who stood up in the old house of faith and applauded the new married couple while the wedding photographer took wedding pictures of their big day.

Later Bill and Victoria were dancing the waltz on their first dance in the basement of the old house of faith at the reception while the crowd of onlookers watched and then they cut the six layer wedding cake together after the dance and they posed for a funny picture of cake in Bill and Victoria's mouth for the camera man who had been hired to photograph there wedding day.

They had all kinds of food for the crowd which ranged from southern fried foods to Italian food and also Mexican food with delicious finger dips which was a big hit at the reception party at the long table along the back church wall.

Bill and Victoria open their wedding gifts which was pots and pans and a new toaster. They had a gift of bath towels from Wilbur and Clara Bell which they just loved.

"May I have the next dance," asked Wilbur who held out his hand to Victoria sitting in her seat with gifts all around her and Bill? "Yes–you may," replied Victoria Christian who sat down one of her gifts and grabbed Wilbur's hand and off they went to the center of the floor and the music boom box tape started to play which was Wilbur's favorite country music tune " The closer you get the further I fall" by the country group Alabama and the place was starting to rock by then and they took off cutting a rug out on the dance floor to everybody's amazement.

Toward the end Bill finely got up the nerve to ask his good friend Clara Bell for a dance.

"May– I have this last dance with you Clara Bell," asked Bill who had got up from his seat and walked over to where she had been sitting with Wilbur. "I thought you'd never ask," replied Clara Bell modestly who got up and put her empty paper plate and fork in her seat and she grabbed Bill's out stretched hand and they strode to the dance floor to dance with everybody else.

Later Bill was drinking rum punch with his old police pal chief Dicky at the catered food table and talking small talk with him.

"Bill—I'm going to break the news story about our solved murder case to the public tomorrow on Monday while your on your honeymoon," said Dicky nonchalantly while he took a sip of cold rum punch.

"That's good news for the public who has been wondering what happen out in Clemmon's that night from all the gossip around town—lately and the reporters can't run me down for a story and bother me with out end which I don't need and mum's the word on any of my cases anyhow and I'll let you handle it anyway because that's what you get paid to do on your job as police chief anyhow because you make your living off the people's tax's," replied Bill who smiled at his wife across the basement floor who was with Clara Bell sitting at a crowed table drinking their own cold rum punch.

"Yes—your right, that's my job and I think, I'll have my dance with the new bride now," said Chief Dicky who handed Bill his empty cup and took off across the basement room toward Lady Victoria before Bill could say another word.

Bill moved around the throng of people at the catered table and got him another cup of cold rum punch from the big bowel. He watched his lovely new wife dance with his old friend the police chief around the basement floor to the old time music and Bill had the proudest grin you ever saw on his old tan rugged face.

After the reception was over they lined the doorway from the old house of faith out to the waiting white limousine and when Bill and Lady Victoria walked the gauntlet they showered them with rice for good luck! At the limousine Clara Bell and Wilbur waited and Wilbur kissed the new bride and shook Bill's hand. "You are both a match made in Heaven. We will take care of the gifts and the clean up here. Have a good time dear," said Clara Bell who kissed Bill on the cheek and gave him a envelope.

"Thanks for always being there for me when I needed you the most Clara Bell," replied Bill modestly with gratitude in his good heart.

"Your welcome and I'd do it anytime for a old friend and good neighbor,' said Clara Bell who warmheartedly smiled back at Bill while she adjusted he wire rim spectacles in the bright sunlight and she took out her handkerchief from her dress pocket and wiped away a tear in her corner eye.

"Good by and have a great time," said Wilbur who held the door open for them to get into the limousine.

"Thanks for everything," replied Bill who shook Wilbur's hand at the limousine door.

The bride then threw her bridal bouquet to the young girls who jumped for it in the crowd of well wishers and one lucky young female girl screamed when she caught it and showed it to her friends and they went running off wildly screaming and hollering happily around the old house of faith foolishly like young girls do to show their boyfriends who were in back of the old church on a cigarette break at their parked cars while they got in the limousine out front.

Dicky Poser and his top police officers lined the old church driveway waiting for them to leave and gave a snappy honorable salute. "Attention," snapped Dicky and they all saluted at the new bride and groom with a rousing send off as the limousine left the driveway of the old Holiness church.

Bill waved at his old police friend's and opened the envelope that Clara Bell gave him and saw the old twenty dollar bills mixed in with the new twenty dollar bills.

Something old and something new for good luck—that was nice of Clara Bell and Wilbur Parker to do that thought Bill who kissed his new bride and settled back for the ride to the Smith Reynolds airport to catch a plane ride to start their honey moon trip and stuck the money envelope inside his tux jacket while his new bride opened a bottle of champaign.

After a month long honeymoon on the sunny Bahama beaches the young newlywed lovers Bill and Victoria his new wife had arrived back at home late at night from their long tiring trip so they went straight to bed totally exhausted.

Bill woke up later around 10:00 o-clock P:M and noticed his wife had left the bed and was gone. He called out to her in the dark "Victoria where are you" and he listen for her wonderful voice but the house was only silent?

Bill laid his head back on his pillow to try and go back asleep. She must be out on her new night time patrol to watch over the public thought Bill who smiled to himself and gently fell back asleep in his nice warm bed.

Lady Victoria Basil Christian had left her new home by the back door and had flown over the neighborhood's of Winston-Salem looking for any criminal activity and had found none and all was quiet.

She flew past the tall lighted buildings that was the night skyline of Winston -Salem in the Piedmont Triad and was soon over the neighborhood of Buna Vista and her keen hearing picked up a little girl down below on the street crying and she flew low to investigate what was going on in the city street.

"Boo—hoo—hoo—my cat climbed the light pole, because a mean dog ran it up the pole that had been chasing it," cried the little blonde girl who sat on the curb with her head in her hands crying her little eyes out and lady Victoria floated down out of the night sky with hardly a sound and she landed feet first beside the crying child sitting on the curb of the road.

She felt a warm gentile hand on her shoulder and she looked up at the nice lady standing beside her in a beautiful blue long flowing Victorian style dress wearing a blue vest with jet black hair and radiate deep blue eyes on a smiling pretty face with ruby red lips. "Don't worry I'll get your cat for you, but you must not tell," said. Lady Victoria who flew up into the trees beside the light pole to grab the frisky feline cat that was meowing its head off at its predicament on top of the light pole "meow, meow, meow,"!

"Here kitty—kitty—kitty," said Lady Victoria who gently picked the scared cat off the top of the creosote wooden light pole and she stroked it and the cats motor started running and it purred all the way back down to the ground in her warm satin white hands.

"Here you go—your cats safe and sound—now," said Lady Victoria who handed the purring ball of fur back to the little girl and she patted the little girls head with her loving hand who jumped up and took the cat tightly in her arms and ran to tell her mommy anyway at what she had saw the pretty lady in the long blue dress do.

"Thanks for getting fluffy down," cried the little blonde girl to Lady Victoria who ran inside her front door and started telling her momma what had happen sitting in the living room.

"A lady came down out of the sky and said she'd get my cat and she flew up threw the air and got my cat off the light pole and then she flew back down with fuffy and gave her to me," said the little blonde girl who's mother stared at her with an open mouth in the living room.

"Land sakes girl where do you get these wild tall tales from. Its time for bed—right now," said the Momma who smacked the little blonde girls behind "smack"!

The little girl made a silly wrinkled pug nose face at her mom. "Hmph,' she said and stuck out her tongue and she ran toward the stairs with her cat and off to her upstairs bedroom she madly marched.

Lady Victoria had floated up to the front window and watched all the excitement in the child's living room.

Well—I told her not to tell thought Lady Victoria who smiled and flew straight up the face of the house and over it and she disappeared into the dark night air without a trace or sound.

Sometime later that morning Bill had come to his office that had been closed fo a month while he was on his honey moon that started in Hawaii then on to Paris France then on to Rome Italy and ending up in the Bahamas and finely coming back home to good old Winston-Salem, North Carolina.

He was glad he had put a stop on his Dailey newspaper delivery over a month ago until he got his affairs in order and was glad there wasn't a backlog of old newspaper on his office step he thought while he organized his desk files and checked his mail he had picked up that had been slipped through his mail slot in his office door.

Then later Bill was going over his case file about The Yadkin River Werewolf Case at his desk and he closed the file shut.

He was in deep thought for a while when there was a loud knock on his office door "KNOCK, KNOCK," which made him come back to reality.

The door opened up and in came Winston-Salem's top police chief Dicky Poser with his escort of top police commanders at his beck and call.

"Hey Bill—I came buy to settle up with you after I heard you was back from your honeymoon and how's you new bride," asked Dicky who took a seat in a chair by his desk?

"Well—I've ready for a big payday after the money, I spent for my vacation honeymoon has left me a little in debt and the wife is still charming and a night owl," replied Bill who looked humbled in his seat.

Dicky took in Bill's small office and looked at the file cabinet's along the back wall and pictures and public awards hanging in the frames on the back wall and the other decorated pictures on the opposite walls behind him. He was impressed with the little office.

"Lets—get right down to business," said Dicky who adjusted his big red striped black tie with his right hand under his white shirt collar and stretched out his neck making himself look important and in control of his surroundings while he did it.

Dicky then leaned over toward the desk and pulled out a business envelope from his inside jacket pocket and flipped it onto Bill's desk along with an old Winston-Salem Journal newspaper he had carried in under his left arm.

"Here's your payment and reward all in one check and I'm glad the mayor is finely off my back and things have returned to normal in this big Triad city and I'm glad your new wife is doing well for you and here's your headline you missed which you earned it by doing excellent detective work," said Dicky who looked very pleased at Bill's good investigative work that had closed the triad murder case's for good.

"Well it must be Friday payday and it's good to know the city is back to law and order," replied Bill who was somewhat poised and at ease among old police buddies.

"Everybody's happy with the way you tracked them killers down at their hideout and dealt out swift justice. The mayor couldn't be more happy with the way the public well wisher's who have called into his office congratulating him on a job well done by his police department and people. He has their vote next election which is a done deal for him and like I said the city has gone back to normal with no more murders to speak of anymore and the mayor said if you ever need anything he's just a phone call away," replied Dicky who looked pleased to be the bearer of good news for once.

"Well—I need a favor once in awhile and my old friends should get some credit too. We were just lucky that our plan came together and everything worked out to our advantage. It was a tough case, but we came out smelling like a rose," replied Bill who smiled confidently on a job well done.

Like—I said you get all the reward money and then some, you earned every penny of it and your friends will be in our good grace too for a couple of favors if need be," said Dicky who beamed with a joyous mood on his tanned leather face.

"Oh—you owe them big time. I couldn't have done it without their help," replied Bill who was being modest about his old friends.   Bill picked up the business envelope off his desk and peered inside by opening the envelope with his right hand finger and thumb and he saw the high six figure check with his name on it inside which made him smile.

He stuck the envelope with the big check in his inside left jacket pocket for safe keeping until he got to the bank and he unfolded the month old Winston-Salem Journal newspaper and read the big front page headline in big black bold letters

"Triad Murders Solved by Ex-police Detective and Private Investigator Bill Christian"

"Crazy Crystal Meth Cocaine Drug Addicted Killers and Robbers Killed in a Wild Shootout at their Hideout by Local Police and Undercover Officers at the Old Abandon Idols Dam in Clemmon's."

"Five year Winston-Salem Police Department Veteran Officer Mike Darker Killed In The Ensuing Gun Battle"!

"Thanks—Dicky it couldn't have come at a better time and it's a pleasure doing business with you and I've been too busy with matters of the heart to keep up with the news and I'd say that headline satisfies your public about the serial killings around these parts and it looks like your cover story worked for the public and they got served their own brand of justice with no one left to dispute it and you saved the department from any embarrassment by Officer Darker's ill fated involvement and you never know I might need a favor one day from the mayor," replied Bill who looked quiet happy and at peace on his sincere face after reading the big story cover headline that was influenced by the police chief's final report to the media at that time.

He laid the month old Winston-Salem Journal newspaper on his desk and leaned back in his chair with a smug confidence on his face.

"Bill—the city has hired a demolition crew to tear down the old Idol's Dam. It was unsafe for the public who trespassed on it and we don't want anybody else using it for criminal activity. It will be demolished starting next week," spoke Dicky who folded his arms in self satisfaction.

"I'd say that was a good ideal," replied Bill who smiled at Dicky with conservation in mind.

"Bill I owe you one and you have a good day. I've got matters to attend to back at the precinct and the bodies we finely identified from Idol's Dam have been let loose to the families for burial and the murder case's is closed as far as I'm concern and you can keep the newspaper as a souvenir—until we meet again," said Dicky who left quickly with his police commanders and the door was softly shut with respect behind them after they left.

Bill sat there in deep thought about the events of the last few months and was glad it was finely over and it was now time to move on with other new exciting cases to investigate.

Then he pulled out his rubber ink pad and stamp from his right desk drawer that were on top of a big box of Churchill Maduro cigars which he sat on the desk in front of him.

Bill moved the ink pad and stamp off the cigar box onto the desk top and rubbed his palm hands back and forth quickly in anticipation.

Then he open the cigar box and got out one of the fine cigars and he reached back in his right drawer and pulled out a double blade cigar cutter. He clipped the end off the cigar into his ashtray on the desk and stuck the fresh cut cigar into his mouth.

Bill reached into his right pants side pocket and pulled out a nice new shiny Zippo lighter and he flipped open the small metal lid. He clicked the flint wheel with his right thumb and lit the lighter with sparks flying from the flint wheel in his right hand.

The blue flame on the lighter seemed almost magical to Bill for just a moment while he stared at it just like the night out on the old Idol's dam when Clara Bell his old friend was working her white magic light show to save them all from the shadows of death and his new wife had helped save them also then he smiled to himself with that thought, then he lit his cigar in celebration of sorts.

Bill flipped the Zippo shut then laid the lighter on his desk top while he took a deep inhale of smoke and then blew it out into the air above his desk where it hung lazily in the air with a satisfied look on his face while he enjoyed a really good delicious cigar.

Bill stuck the cigar into the right side of his mouth and bit down on it real smugly with his side teeth while he enjoyed the taste of the Maduor wrapper on the cigar in his mouth. He then grabbed the ink stamp and opened the top lid on the ink pad. He stamped his ink stamp real hard "BAM" with his right hand down into the dark ink pad ! He then stamped a big "X" on the case file named The Yadkin River Werewolf Case!

Detective Christian stood up and shut the ink pad putting the ink stamp on top of it, pushing his desk chair back and grabbed the case file and walked over to his last file cabinet along the back wall of his small office.

He pulled open the bottom "X" drawer and put the file in it with his other weird cases and slammed it shut!

As far as he was concerned, the case was... Closed.

The End